Beggars in Spain

BEGGARS in SPAIN

NANCY KRESS

An Imprint of HarperCollins*Publishers*

A portion of this book appeared in slightly altered form in both *Isaac Asimov's Science Fiction Magazine,* April 1991, and as a novella published by Axolotl Press, also entitled *Beggars in Spain.*

This book was originally published in 1993 by Avon Books and reprinted in mass market editions in 1994 by Avon Books and in 1999 by Avon Eos, an imprint of HarperCollins Publishers.

HarperCollins books may be purchased for educational, business, or sales promotional use. For information, please e-mail the Special Markets Department at SPsales@harpercollins.com.

First Eos trade paperback published 2004.

Eos is a federally registered trademark of HarperCollins Publishers Inc.

Designed by Nicola Ferguson

The Library of Congress has cataloged the hardcover edition as follows:

Kress, Nancy.
    Beggars in Spain / Nancy Kress.
      p. cm.
    ISBN 0-688-12189-6
    1. Women lawyers—Fiction. 2. Genetic engineering—Fiction. I. Title.
PS3561.R46 B4 1993
813'.54—dc20   92025070

ISBN 0-06-073348-9 (pbk.)

HB 12.30.2022

FOR MY SISTER KATE

contents

PREFACE

Beggars in Spain was first published in 1993, but its history began long before that. It began in my childhood, somewhere back in the Dark Ages of the 1950s.

Different writers write for very different reasons, including but not limited to the classic Hemingway quartet of "fame, glory, money, and the love of women" (or of whomever). Hemingway missed a few motivations, however, including "envy." Being a person who needs a lot of sleep, I have always envied those who do not. In childhood, I missed all the best parts of sleepovers. In adolescence, I was asleep for those slumber-party phone calls to cute boys. As an adult, I could not stay up till 2:00 A.M. balancing work, toddlers, laundry, and social life. By needing so much sleep, I figure I have lived about two hours less per day than my peers, for about fifty years. That adds up to about four lost years and a lot of envy.

So I created people who never need to sleep at all. Take that, metabolism! Vicarious triumph through the power of imagination!

The first time I created the Sleepless was in a dreadful short story written in 1977. Sleeplessness was a spontaneous genetic mutation, and the characters were isolated mountaineers. The story was rejected by every editor in the business (Robert Silverberg, who changed editorial positions while I was cycling through the available markets, rejected it twice). Even I, fledgling writer with no ability to objectively evaluate my own stuff, could see that this story was not going to sell. I retired the manuscript.

Five years later I tried again. This time sleeplessness was a deliberate genetic mutation, created by a rogue mad scientist–type who eventually kills himself. Melodrama and nihilism. Again everybody rejected the story.

By 1990 I was ready to try a third time; envy was still operating strongly. But this time, my circumstances had changed. I had just become a full-time writer. My children were adolescents, and adolescent characters were much on my mind. And I was finally interested in exploring how science actually works (no more rogue mad scientists working in their basements).

The result was the novella version of *Beggars in Spain*, which won both the Nebula and the Hugo Awards. But I was nagged by the feeling that Leisha's story had only begun. I wanted to explore the long-range economic effects of creating a favored class of people in a United States becoming increasingly polarized between rich and poor. I also wanted to work out my reactions to other writers' philosophies: to Ayn Rand's belief that no human being owes anything to any other except what is agreed to in a voluntary contract. To Ursula Le Guin's belief, expressed in the wonderful novel *The Dispossessed*, that humankind could live without government if it lived without personal property. I didn't believe Rand or Le Guin, but what *did* I believe? Like many greater authors, I wrote to find out.

In *Beggars*, sleeplessness is the result of altering a few genes in vitro. We still cannot do this reliably, but since 1990 we have moved a lot closer. Genetic engineering is becoming a reality, one that many people are not ready to acknowledge, let alone allow. But you cannot put the genie back in the bottle. We know how to manipulate the human genome and so, inevitably, we will. The two sequels to *Beggars in Spain*, *Beggars and Choosers* and *Beggars Ride*, explore that issue in as much detail as I could invent. Even so, I didn't come close to covering the excitement, the changes, the shock, and the controversy that genetic engineering will bring in the coming decades. I just wish that I could stick around for a hundred years or so to see it—and to write about it.

Another cause for envy. Some things just never change.

Nancy Kress
February 15, 2004

BOOK
ONE

LEISHA

2008

> "With energy and sleepless
> vigilance go forward and
> give us victories."
>
> —ABRAHAM LINCOLN,
> TO MAJOR GENERAL
> JOSEPH HOOKER, 1863

I

They sat stiffly on his antique Eames chairs, two people who didn't want to be here, or one person who didn't want to and one who resented the other's reluctance. Dr. Ong had seen this before. Within two minutes he was sure: the woman was the silently furious resister. She would lose. The man would pay for it later, in little ways, for a long time.

"I presume you've performed the necessary credit checks already," Roger Camden said pleasantly, "so let's get right on to details, shall we, Doctor?"

"Certainly," Ong said. "Why don't we start by your telling me all the genetic modifications you're interested in for the baby."

The woman shifted suddenly on her chair. She was in her late twenties—clearly a second wife—but already had a faded look, as if keeping up with Roger Camden was wearing her out. Ong could easily believe that. Mrs. Camden's hair was brown, her eyes were brown, her skin had a brown tinge that might have been pretty if her cheeks had had any color. She wore a brown coat, neither fashionable nor cheap, and shoes that looked vaguely orthopedic. Ong glanced at his records for her name: Elizabeth. He would bet people forgot it often.

Next to her, Roger Camden radiated nervous vitality, a man in late middle age whose bullet-shaped head did not match his careful haircut and Italian-silk business suit. Ong did not need to consult his file to recall anything about Camden. A caricature of the bullet-shaped head had been the leading graphic for yesterday's online edition of the *Wall Street Journal:* Camden had led a major coup in cross-border data-atoll investment. Ong was not sure what cross-border data-atoll investment was.

"A girl," Elizabeth Camden said. Ong hadn't expected her to speak first. Her voice was another surprise: upper-class British. "Blonde. Green eyes. Tall. Slender."

Ong smiled. "Appearance factors are the easiest to achieve, as I'm sure you already know. But all we can do about slenderness is give her a genetic disposition in that direction. How you feed the child will naturally—"

"Yes, yes," Roger Camden said, "that's obvious. Now: intelligence. *High* intelligence. And a sense of daring."

"I'm sorry, Mr. Camden, personality factors are not yet understood well enough to allow genet—"

"Just testing," Camden said, with a smile that Ong thought was probably supposed to be lighthearted.

Elizabeth Camden said, "Musical ability."

"Again, Mrs. Camden, a disposition to be musical is all we can guarantee."

"Good enough," Camden said. "The full array of corrections for any potential gene-linked health problem, of course."

"Of course," Dr. Ong said. Neither client spoke. So far theirs was a fairly modest list, given Camden's money; most clients had to be argued out of contradictory genetic tendencies, alteration overload, or unrealistic expectations. Ong waited. Tension prickled in the room like heat.

"And," Camden said, "no need to sleep."

Elizabeth Camden jerked her head sideways to look out the window.

Ong picked up a paper magnet from his desk. He made his voice pleasant. "May I ask how you learned whether that genetic-modification program exists?"

Camden grinned. "You're not denying it exists. I give you full credit for that, Doctor."

Ong held his temper. "May I ask how you learned whether the program exists?"

Camden reached into an inner pocket of his suit. The silk crinkled and pulled; body and suit came from different classes. Camden was, Ong remembered, a Yagaiist, a personal friend of Kenzo Yagai himself. Camden handed Ong hard copy: program specifications.

"Don't bother hunting down the security leak in your data banks, Doctor. You won't find it. But if it's any consolation, neither will anybody else. Now." He leaned forward suddenly. His tone changed. "I know that you've created twenty children who don't need to sleep at all, that so far nineteen are healthy, intelligent, and psychologically normal. In fact, they're better than normal; they're all unusually precocious. The oldest is already four years old and can read in two languages. I know you're thinking of offering this genetic modification on the open market in a few years. All I want is a chance to buy it for my daughter *now*. At whatever price you name."

Ong stood. "I can't possibly discuss this with you unilaterally, Mr. Camden. Neither the theft of our data—"

"Which wasn't a theft—your system developed a spontaneous bubble regurgitation into a public gate. You'd have a hell of a time proving otherwise—"

"—*nor* the offer to purchase this particular genetic modification lie in my sole area of authority. Both have to be discussed with the Institute's board of directors."

"By all means, by all means. When can I talk to them, too?"

"You?"

Camden, still seated, looked up at him. It occurred to Ong that there were few men who could look so confident eighteen inches below eye level. "Certainly. I'd like the chance to present my offer to whoever has the actual authority to accept it. That's only good business."

"This isn't solely a business transaction, Mr. Camden."

"It isn't solely pure scientific research, either," Camden retorted.

"You're a for-profit corporation here. *With* certain tax breaks available only to firms meeting certain fair-practice laws."

For a minute Ong couldn't think what Camden meant. "Fair-practice laws . . ."

". . . are designed to protect minorities who are suppliers. I know it hasn't ever been tested in the case of customers, except for redlining in Y-energy installations. But it could be tested, Dr. Ong. Minorities are entitled to the same product offerings as nonminorities. I know the Institute would not welcome a court case, Doctor. None of your twenty genetic beta-test families is either Black or Jewish."

"A court . . . but you're not Black *or* Jewish!"

"I'm a different minority. Polish-American. The name was Kaminsky." Camden finally stood. And smiled warmly. "Look, it is preposterous. You know that, and I know that, and we both know what a grand time journalists would have with it anyway. And you know that I don't want to sue you with a preposterous case just to use the threat of premature and adverse publicity to get what I want. I don't want to make threats at all, believe me I don't. I just want this marvelous advancement you've come up with for my daughter." His face changed, to an expression Ong wouldn't have believed possible on those particular features: wistfulness. "Doctor, do you know how much more I could have accomplished if I hadn't had to *sleep* all my life?"

Elizabeth Camden said harshly, "You hardly sleep now."

Camden looked down at her as if he had forgotten she was there. "Well, no, my dear, not now. But when I was young . . . college, I might have been able to finish college and still support . . . Well. None of that matters now. What matters, Doctor, is that you and I and your board come to an agreement."

"Mr. Camden, please leave my office now."

"You mean before you lose your temper at my presumptuousness? You wouldn't be the first. I'll expect to have a meeting set up by the end of next week, whenever and wherever you say, of course. Just let my personal secretary, Diane Clavers, know the details. Anytime that's best for you."

Ong did not accompany them to the door. Pressure throbbed behind his temples. In the doorway Elizabeth Camden turned. "What happened to the twentieth one?"

"What?"

"The twentieth baby. My husband said nineteen of them are healthy and normal. What happened to the twentieth?"

The pressure grew stronger, hotter. Ong knew that he should not answer; that Camden probably already knew the answer even if his wife didn't; that he, Ong, was going to answer anyway; that he would regret the lack of self-control, bitterly, later.

"The twentieth baby is dead. His parents turned out to be unstable. They separated during the pregnancy, and his mother could not bear the twenty-four-hour crying of a baby who never sleeps."

Elizabeth Camden's eyes widened. "She killed it?"

"By mistake," Camden said shortly. "Shook the little thing too hard." He frowned at Ong. "Nurses, Doctor. In shifts. You should have picked only parents wealthy enough to afford nurses in shifts."

"That's horrible!" Mrs. Camden burst out, and Ong could not tell if she meant the child's death, the lack of nurses, or the Institute's carelessness. Ong closed his eyes.

When they had gone, he took ten milligrams of cyclobenzaprine-III. For his back—it was solely for his back. The old injury was hurting again. Afterward he stood for a long time at the window, still holding the paper magnet, feeling the pressure recede from his temples, feeling himself calm down. Below him Lake Michigan lapped peacefully at the shore; the police had driven away the homeless in another raid just last night, and they hadn't yet had time to return. Only their debris remained, thrown into the bushes of the lakeshore park: tattered blankets, newspapers, plastic bags like pathetic trampled standards. It was illegal to sleep in the park, illegal to enter it without a resident's permit, illegal to be homeless and without a residence. As Ong watched, uniformed park attendants began methodically spearing newspapers and shoving them into clean self-propelled receptacles.

Ong picked up the phone to call the chairman of Biotech Institute's board of directors.

Four men and three women sat around the polished mahogany table of the conference room. *Doctor, lawyer, Indian chief,* thought Susan Melling, looking from Ong to Sullivan to Camden. She smiled. Ong caught the smile and looked frosty. Pompous ass. Judy Sullivan, the Institute lawyer, turned to speak in a low voice to Camden's lawyer, a thin nervous man with the look of being owned. The owner, Roger Camden, the Indian chief himself, was the happiest-looking person in the room. The lethal little man—what did it take to become that rich, starting from nothing? She, Susan, would certainly never know— radiated excitement. He beamed, he glowed, so unlike the usual parents-to-be that Susan was intrigued. Usually the prospective daddies and mommies—especially the daddies—sat there looking as if they were at a corporate merger. Camden looked as if he were at a birthday party.

Which, of course, he was. Susan grinned at him, and was pleased when he grinned back. Wolfish, but with a sort of delight that could only be called innocent—what would he be like in bed? Ong frowned majestically and rose to speak.

"Ladies and gentlemen, I think we're ready to start. Perhaps introductions are in order. Mr. Roger Camden, Mrs. Camden, are of course our clients. Mr. John Jaworski, Mr. Camden's lawyer. Mr. Camden, this is Judith Sullivan, the Institute's head of Legal; Samuel Krenshaw, representing Institute Director Dr. Brad Marsteiner, who unfortunately couldn't be here today; and Dr. Susan Melling, who developed the genetic modification affecting sleep. A few legal points of interest to both parties—"

"Forget the contracts for a minute," Camden interrupted. "Let's talk about the sleep thing. I'd like to ask a few questions."

Susan said, "What would you like to know?" Camden's eyes were very blue in his blunt-featured face; he wasn't what she had expected. Mrs. Camden, who apparently lacked both a first name and a lawyer, since Jaworski had been introduced as her husband's but not hers, looked either sullen or scared, it was difficult to tell which.

Ong said sourly, "Then perhaps we should start with a short presentation by Dr. Melling."

Susan would have preferred a Q&A, to see what Camden would ask. But she had annoyed Ong enough for one session. Obediently she rose.

"Let me start with a brief description of sleep. Researchers have known for a long time that there are actually three kinds of sleep. One is 'slow-wave sleep,' characterized on an EEG by delta waves. One is 'rapid-eye-movement sleep,' or REM sleep, which is much lighter sleep and contains most dreaming. Together these two make up 'core sleep.' The third type of sleep is 'optional sleep,' so-called because people seem to get along without it with no ill effects, and some short sleepers don't do it at all, sleeping naturally only three or four hours a night."

"That's me," Camden said. "I trained myself into it. Couldn't everybody do that?"

Apparently they were going to have a Q&A after all. "No. The actual sleep mechanism has some flexibility, but not the same amount for every person. The raphe nuclei on the brain stem—"

Ong said, "I don't think we need that level of detail, Susan. Let's stick to basics."

Camden said, "The raphe nuclei regulate the balance among neurotransmitters and peptides that leads to a pressure to sleep, don't they?"

Susan couldn't help it; she grinned. Camden, the laser-sharp ruthless financier, sat trying to look solemn, a third-grader waiting to have his homework praised. Ong looked sour. Mrs. Camden looked away, out the window.

"Yes, that's correct, Mr. Camden. You've done your research."

Camden said, "This is my *daughter*," and Susan caught her breath. When was the last time she had heard that note of reverence in anyone's voice? But no one in the room seemed to notice.

"Well, then," Susan said, "you already know that the reason people sleep is because a pressure to sleep builds up in the brain. Over the past twenty years, research has determined that's the *only* reason. Neither slow-wave sleep nor REM sleep serve functions that can't be carried on while the body and brain are awake. A lot goes on during sleep, but it can go on during wakefulness just as well, if other hormonal adjustments are made.

"Sleep served an important evolutionary function. Once Clem Pre-Mammal was done filling his stomach and squirting his sperm around, sleep kept him immobile and away from predators. Sleep was an aid to survival. But now it's a left-over mechanism, a vestige like the appendix. It switches on every night, but the need is gone. So we turn off the switch at its source, in the genes."

Ong winced. He hated it when she oversimplified like that. Or maybe it was the lightheartedness he hated. If Marsteiner were making this presentation, there'd be no Clem Pre-Mammal.

Camden said, "What about the need to dream?"

"Not necessary. A left-over bombardment of the cortex to keep it on semialert in case a predator attacked during sleep. Wakefulness does that better."

"Why not have wakefulness instead then? From the start of the evolution?"

He was testing her. Susan gave him a full, lavish smile, enjoying his brass. "I told you. Safety from predators. But when a modern predator attacks—say, a cross-border data-atoll investor—it's safer to be awake."

Camden shot at her, "What about the high percentage of REM sleep in fetuses and babies?"

"Still an evolutionary hangover. Cerebrum develops perfectly well without it."

"What about neural repair during slow-wave sleep?"

"That does go on. But it can go on during wakefulness, if the DNA is programmed to do so. No loss of neural efficiency, as far as we know."

"What about the release of human growth enzyme in such large concentrations during slow-wave sleep?"

Susan looked at him admiringly. "Goes on without the sleep. Genetic adjustments tie it to other changes in the pineal gland."

"What about the—"

"The *side effects*?" Mrs. Camden said. Her mouth turned down. "What about the bloody side effects?"

Susan turned to Elizabeth Camden. She had forgotten she was there. The younger woman stared at Susan, mouth turned down at the corners.

"I'm glad you asked that, Mrs. Camden. Because there are side effects." Susan paused; she was enjoying herself. "Compared to their age mates, the nonsleep children—who have *not* had IQ genetic manipulation—are more intelligent, better at problem-solving, and more joyous."

Camden took out a cigarette. The archaic, filthy habit surprised Susan. Then she saw that it was deliberate: Roger Camden was drawing attention to an ostentatious display to draw attention away from what he was feeling. His cigarette lighter was gold, monogrammed, innocently gaudy.

"Let me explain," Susan said. "REM sleep bombards the cerebral cortex with random neural firings from the brain stem; dreaming occurs because the poor besieged cortex tries so hard to make sense of the activated images and memories. It spends a lot of energy doing that. Without that energy expenditure, nonsleep cerebrums save the wear-and-tear and do better at coordinating real-life input. Thus, greater intelligence and problem-solving.

"Also, doctors have known for sixty years that antidepressants, which lift the mood of depressed patients, also suppress REM sleep entirely. What they have proved in the past ten years is that the reverse is equally true: suppress REM sleep and people don't *get* depressed. The nonsleep kids are cheerful, outgoing . . . *joyous*. There's no other word for it."

"At what cost?" Mrs. Camden said. She held her neck rigid, but the corners of her jaw worked.

"No cost. No negative side effects at all."

"So far," Mrs. Camden shot back.

Susan shrugged. "So far."

"They're only four years old! At the most!"

Ong and Krenshaw were studying her closely. Susan saw the moment the Camden woman realized it; she sank back into her chair, drawing her fur coat around her, her face blank.

Camden did not look at his wife. He blew a cloud of cigarette smoke. "Everything has costs, Dr. Melling."

She liked the way he said her name. "Ordinarily, yes. Especially in genetic modification. But we honestly have not been able to find any here, despite looking." She smiled directly into Camden's eyes. "Is it too much to believe that just once the universe has given us something wholly good, wholly a step forward, wholly beneficial? Without hidden penalties?"

"Not the universe. The intelligence of people like you," Camden said, surprising Susan more than anything else that had gone before. His eyes held hers. She felt her chest tighten.

"I think," Dr. Ong said dryly, "that the philosophy of the universe may be beyond our concerns here. Mr. Camden, if you have no further medical questions, perhaps we can return to the legal points Ms. Sullivan and Mr. Jaworski have raised. Thank you, Dr. Melling."

Susan nodded. She didn't look again at Camden. But she knew what he said, how he looked, that he was there.

The house was about what she had expected, a huge mock Tudor on Lake Michigan north of Chicago. The land was heavily wooded between the gate and the house, open between the house and the surging water. Patches of snow dotted the dormant grass. Biotech had been working with the Camdens for four months, but this was the first time Susan had driven to their home.

As she walked toward the house another car drove up behind her.

No, a truck, continuing around the curved driveway to a service entry at the side of the house. One man rang the service bell; a second began to unload a plastic-wrapped playpen from the back of the truck. White, with pink and yellow bunnies. Susan briefly closed her eyes.

Camden opened the door himself. She could see his effort not to look worried. "You didn't have to drive out, Susan; I'd have come into the city!"

"No, I didn't want you to do that, Roger. Mrs. Camden is here?"

"In the living room." Camden led her into a large room with a stone fireplace. English country-house furniture, and prints of dogs or boats, all hung eighteen inches too high; Elizabeth Camden must have done the decorating. She did not rise from her wing chair as Susan entered.

"Let me be concise and fast," Susan said, "I don't want to make this any more drawn-out for you than I have to. We have all the amniocentesis, ultrasound, and Langston test results. The fetus is fine, developing normally for two weeks, no problems with the implant on the uterine wall. But a complication has developed."

"What?" Camden said. He took out a cigarette, looked at his wife, and put it back unlit.

Susan said quietly, "Mrs. Camden, by sheer chance both your ovaries released eggs last month. We removed one for the gene surgery. By more sheer chance the second was fertilized and implanted. You're carrying two fetuses."

Elizabeth Camden grew still. "Twins?"

"No," Susan said. Then she realized what she had said. "I mean, yes. They're twins, but nonidentical. Only one has been genetically altered. The other will be no more similar to her than any two siblings. It's a so-called normal baby. And I know you didn't want a so-called normal baby."

Camden said, "No. I didn't."

Elizabeth Camden said, "I did."

Camden shot her a fierce look that Susan couldn't read. He took out the cigarette again, and lit it. His face was in profile to Susan, and he was thinking intently; she doubted he knew the cigarette was there, or that he was lighting it. "Is the baby being affected by the other one's being there?"

"No," Susan said. "No, of course not. They're just . . . coexisting."

"Can you abort it?"

"Not without aborting both of them. Removing the unaltered fetus would cause changes in the uterine lining that would probably lead to a spontaneous miscarriage of the other." She drew a deep breath. "There's that option, of course. We can start the whole process over again. But as I told you at the time, you were very lucky to have the *in vitro* fertilization take on only the second try. Some couples take eight or ten tries. If we started all over, the process could be a lengthy one."

Camden said, "Is the presence of this second fetus harming my daughter? Taking away nutrients or anything? Or will it change anything for her later on in the pregnancy?"

"No. Except that there is a chance of premature birth. Two fetuses take up a lot more room in the womb, and if it gets too crowded, birth can be premature. But the—"

"How premature? Enough to threaten survival?"

"Most probably not."

Camden went on smoking. A man appeared at the door. "Sir, London calling. James Kendall for Mr. Yagai."

"I'll take it." Camden rose. Susan watched him study his wife's face. When he spoke, it was to her. "All right, Elizabeth. All right." He left the room.

For a long moment the two women sat in silence. Susan was aware of disappointment; this was not the Camden she had expected to see. She became aware of Elizabeth Camden watching her with amusement.

"Oh, yes, Doctor. He's like that."

Susan said nothing.

"Completely overbearing. But not this time." She laughed softly, with excitement. "Two. Do you . . . do you know what sex the other one is?"

"Both fetuses are female."

"I wanted a girl, you know. And now I'll have one."

"Then you'll go ahead with the pregnancy."

"Oh, yes. Thank you for coming, Doctor."

She was dismissed. No one saw her out. But as she was getting into her car, Camden rushed out of the house, coatless. "Susan! I wanted to thank you. For coming all the way out here to tell us yourself."

"You already thanked me."

"Yes. Well. You're sure the second fetus is no threat to my daughter?"

Susan said deliberately, "Nor is the genetically altered fetus a threat to the naturally conceived one."

He smiled. His voice was low and wistful. "And you think that should matter to me just as much. But it doesn't. And why should I fake what I feel? Especially to you?"

Susan opened her car door. She wasn't ready for this, or she had changed her mind, or something. But then Camden leaned over to close the door, and his manner held no trace of flirtatiousness, no smarmy ingratiation. "I better order a second playpen."

"Yes."

"And a second car seat."

"Yes."

"But not a second night-shift nurse."

"That's up to you."

"And you." Abruptly he leaned over and kissed her, a kiss so polite and respectful that Susan was shocked. Neither lust nor conquest would have shocked her; this did. Camden didn't give her a chance to react; he closed the car door and turned back toward the house. Susan drove toward the gate, her hands shaky on the wheel until amusement replaced shock: It *had* been a deliberately distant, respectful kiss, an engineered enigma. And nothing else could have guaranteed so well that there would have to be another.

She wondered what the Camdens would name their daughters.

*   *   *

Dr. Ong strode the hospital corridor, which had been dimmed to half-light. From the nurse's station in Maternity a nurse stepped forward as if to stop him—it was the middle of the night, long past visiting hours—got a good look at his face, and faded back into her station. Around a corner was the viewing glass to the nursery. To Ong's annoyance, Susan Melling stood pressed against the glass. To his further annoyance, she was crying.

Ong realized that he had never liked the woman. Maybe not any women. Even those with superior minds could not seem to refrain from being made damn fools by their emotions.

"Look," Susan said, laughing a little, swiping at her face. "Doctor—*look.*"

Behind the glass Roger Camden, gowned and masked, was holding up a baby in a white undershirt and pink blanket. Camden's blue eyes—theatrically blue—a man really should not have such garish eyes—glowed. The baby's head was covered with blond fuzz; it had wide eyes and pink skin. Camden's eyes above the mask said that no other child had ever had these attributes.

Ong said, "An uncomplicated birth?"

"Yes," Susan Melling sobbed. "Perfectly straightforward. Elizabeth is fine. She's asleep. Isn't she beautiful? He has the most adventurous spirit I've ever known." She wiped her nose on her sleeve; Ong realized that she was drunk. "Did I ever tell you that I was engaged once? Fifteen years ago, in med school? I broke it off because he grew to seem so ordinary, so boring. Oh, God, I shouldn't be telling you all this, I'm sorry. I'm sorry."

Ong moved away from her. Behind the glass Roger Camden laid the baby in a small wheeled crib. The nameplate said BABY GIRL CAMDEN #1. 5.9 POUNDS. A night nurse watched indulgently.

Ong did not wait to see Camden emerge from the nursery or to hear Susan Melling say to him whatever she was going to say. Ong went to have the OB paged. Melling's report was not, under the circumstances, to be trusted. A perfect, unprecedented chance to record every detail of gene alteration with a nonaltered control, and Melling was more interested in her own sloppy emotions. Ong would obviously have to do the report himself, after talking to the OB. He was hungry for every detail. And not just about the pink-cheeked baby in Camden's arms. He wanted to know everything about the birth of the child in the other glass-sided crib: BABY GIRL CAMDEN #2. 5.1 POUNDS. The dark-haired baby with the mottled red features, lying scrunched down in her pink blanket, asleep.

2

L eisha's earliest memory was flowing lines that were not there.
She knew they were not there because when she reached out her
fist to touch them, her fist was empty. Later she realized that the
flowing lines were light: sunshine slanting in bars between curtains in
her room, between the wooden blinds in the dining room, between the
crisscross lattices in the conservatory. The day she realized the golden
flow was light she laughed out loud with the sheer joy of discovery, and
Daddy turned from putting flowers in pots and smiled at her.

The whole house was full of light. Light bounded off the lake,
streamed across the high white ceilings, puddled on the shining
wooden floors. She and Alice moved continually through light, and
sometimes Leisha would stop and tip back her head and let it flow over
her face. She could feel it, like water.

The best light, of course, was in the conservatory. That's where
Daddy liked to be when he was home from making money. Daddy potted plants and watered trees, humming, and Leisha and Alice ran between the wooden tables of flowers with their wonderful earthy smells,
running from the dark side of the conservatory where the big purple
flowers grew to the sunshine side with sprays of yellow flowers, running back and forth, in and out of the light. "Growth," Daddy said to
her, "flowers all fulfilling their promise. Alice, be careful! You almost

knocked over that orchid!" Alice, obedient, would stop running for a while. Daddy never told Leisha to stop running.

After a while the light would go away. Alice and Leisha would have their baths, and then Alice would get quiet, or cranky. She wouldn't play nice with Leisha, even when Leisha let her choose the game or even have all the best dolls. Then Nanny would take Alice to bed, and Leisha would talk with Daddy some more until Daddy said he had to work in his study with the papers that made money. Leisha always felt a moment of regret that he had to go do that, but the moment never lasted very long because Mamselle would arrive and start Leisha's lessons, which she liked. Learning things was so interesting! She could already sing twenty songs and write all the letters in the alphabet and count to fifty. And by the time lessons were done, the light had come back, and it was time for breakfast.

Breakfast was the only time Leisha didn't like. Daddy had gone to the office, and Leisha and Alice had breakfast with Mommy in the big dining room. Mommy sat in a red robe, which Leisha liked, and she didn't smell funny or talk funny the way she would later in the day, but still breakfast wasn't fun. Mommy always started with The Question.

"Alice, sweetheart, how did you sleep?"

"Fine, Mommy."

"Did you have any nice dreams?"

For a long time Alice said no. Then one day she said, "I dreamed about a horse. I was riding him." Mommy clapped her hands and kissed Alice and gave her an extra sticky bun. After that Alice always had a dream to tell Mommy.

Once Leisha said, "I had a dream, too. I dreamed light was coming in the window and it wrapped all around me like a blanket and then it kissed me on my eyes."

Mommy put down her coffee cup so hard that coffee sloshed out of it. "Don't lie to me, Leisha. You did not have a dream."

"Yes, I did," Leisha said.

"Only children who sleep can have dreams. Don't lie to me. You did not have a dream."

"Yes I did! I did!" Leisha shouted. She could see it, almost: the light streaming in the window and wrapping around her like a golden blanket.

"I will not tolerate a child who is a liar! Do you hear me, Leisha—I won't tolerate it!"

"You're a liar!" Leisha shouted, knowing the words weren't true, hating herself because they weren't true but hating Mommy more and that was wrong, too, and there sat Alice stiff and frozen with her eyes wide, Alice was scared and it was Leisha's fault.

Mommy called sharply, "Nanny! Nanny! Take Leisha to her room at once. She can't sit with civilized people if she can't refrain from telling lies!"

Leisha started to cry. Nanny carried her out of the room. Leisha hadn't even had her breakfast. But she didn't care about that; all she could see while she cried was Alice's eyes, scared like that, reflecting broken bits of light.

But Leisha didn't cry long. Nanny read her a story, and then played Data Jump with her, and then Alice came up and Nanny drove them both into Chicago to the zoo where there were wonderful animals to see, animals Leisha could not have dreamed—nor Alice *either*. And by the time they came back Mommy had gone to her room and Leisha knew that she would stay there with the glasses of funny-smelling stuff the rest of the day and Leisha would not have to see her.

But that night, she went to her mother's room.

"I have to go to the bathroom," she told Mamselle. Mamselle said, "Do you need any help?" maybe because Alice still needed help in the bathroom. But Leisha didn't, and she thanked Mamselle. Then she sat on the toilet for a minute even though nothing came, so that what she had told Mamselle wouldn't be a lie.

Leisha tiptoed down the hall. She went first into Alice's room. A little light in a wall socket burned near the crib. There was no crib in Leisha's room. Leisha looked at her sister through the bars. Alice lay on her side with her eyes closed. The lids of the eyes fluttered quickly, like curtains blowing in the wind. Alice's chin and neck looked loose.

Leisha closed the door very carefully and went to her parents' room.

They didn't sleep in a crib but in a huge enormous bed, with enough room between them for more people. Mommy's eyelids weren't fluttering; she lay on her back making a hrrr–hrrr sound through her nose. The funny smell was strong on her. Leisha backed away and tiptoed over to Daddy. He looked like Alice, except that his neck and chin looked even looser, folds of skin collapsed like the tent that had fallen down in the back yard. It scared Leisha to see him like that. Then Daddy's eyes flew open so suddenly that Leisha screamed.

Daddy rolled out of bed and picked her up, looking quickly at Mommy. But she didn't move. Daddy was wearing only his underpants. He carried Leisha out into the hall, where Mamselle came rushing up saying, "Oh, Sir, I'm sorry, she just said she was going to the bathroom—"

"It's all right," Daddy said. "I'll take her with me."

"No!" Leisha screamed, because Daddy was only in his underpants and his neck had looked all funny and the room smelled bad because of Mommy. But Daddy carried her into the conservatory, set her down on a bench, wrapped himself in a piece of green plastic that was supposed to cover up plants, and sat down next to her.

"Now, what happened, Leisha? What were you doing?"

Leisha didn't answer.

"You were looking at people sleeping, weren't you?" Daddy said, and because his voice was softer Leisha mumbled, "Yes." She immediately felt better; it felt good not to lie.

"You were looking at people sleeping because you don't sleep and you were curious, weren't you? Like Curious George in your book?"

"Yes," Leisha said. "I thought you said you made money in your study all night!"

Daddy smiled. "Not all night. Some of it. But then I sleep, although not very much." He took Leisha on his lap. "I don't need much sleep, so I get a lot more done at night than most people. Different people need different amounts of sleep. And a few, a very few, are like you. You don't need any."

"Why not?"

"Because you're special. Better than other people. Before you were born, I had some doctors help make you that way."

"Why?"

"So you could do anything you want to and make manifest your own individuality."

Leisha twisted in his arms to stare at him; the words meant nothing. Daddy reached over and touched a single flower growing on a tall potted tree. The flower had thick white petals like the cream he put in coffee, and the center was a light pink.

"See, Leisha—this tree made this flower. Because it *can*. Only this tree can make this kind of wonderful flower. That plant hanging up there can't, and those can't either. Only this tree. Therefore the most important thing in the world for this tree to do is grow this flower. The flower is the tree's individuality—that means just *it*, and nothing else— made manifest. Nothing else matters."

"I don't understand, Daddy."

"You will. Someday."

"But I want to understand *now*," Leisha said, and Daddy laughed with pure delight and hugged her. The hug felt good, but Leisha still wanted to understand.

"When you make money, is that your indiv . . . that thing?"

"Yes," Daddy said happily.

"Then nobody else can make money? Like only that tree can make that flower?"

"Nobody else can make it just the way I do."

"What do you do with the money?"

"I buy things for you. This house, your dresses, Mamselle to teach you, the car to ride in."

"What does the tree do with the flower?"

"Glories in it," Daddy said, which made no sense. "Excellence is what counts, Leisha. Excellence supported by individual effort. And that's *all* that counts."

"I'm cold, Daddy."

"Then I better bring you back to Mamselle."

Leisha didn't move. She touched the flower with one finger. "I want to sleep, Daddy."

"No, you don't, sweetheart. Sleep is just lost time, wasted life. It's a little death."

"Alice sleeps."

"Alice isn't like you."

"Alice isn't special?"

"No. You are."

"Why didn't you make Alice special, too?"

"Alice made herself. I didn't have a chance to make her special."

The whole thing was too hard. Leisha stopped stroking the flower and slipped off Daddy's lap. He smiled at her. "My little questioner. When you grow up, you'll find your own excellence, and it will be a new order, a specialness the world hasn't ever seen before. You might even be like Kenzo Yagai. He made the Yagai generator that powers the world."

"Daddy, you look funny wrapped in the flower plastic." Leisha laughed. Daddy did, too. But then she said, "When I grow up, I'll make my specialness find a way to make Alice special, too," and Daddy stopped laughing.

He took her back to Mamselle, who taught her to write her name, which was so exciting she forgot about the puzzling talk with Daddy. There were six letters, all different, and together they were *her name*. Leisha wrote it over and over, laughing, and Mamselle laughed too. But later, in the morning, Leisha thought again about the talk with Daddy. She thought of it often, turning the unfamiliar words over and over in her mind like small hard stones, but the part she thought about most wasn't a word. It was the frown on Daddy's face when she told him she would use her specialness to make Alice special, too.

Every week Dr. Melling came to see Leisha and Alice, sometimes alone, sometimes with other people. Leisha and Alice both liked Dr. Melling, who laughed a lot and whose eyes were bright and warm. Often Daddy

was there, too. Dr. Melling played games with them, first with Alice and
Leisha separately and then together. She took their pictures and
weighed them. She made them lie down on a table and stuck little metal
things to their temples, which sounded scary but wasn't because there
were so many machines to watch, all making interesting noises, while
they were lying there. Dr. Melling was as good at answering questions
as Daddy. Once Leisha said, "Is Dr. Melling a special person? Like
Kenzo Yagai?" And Daddy laughed and glanced at Dr. Melling and
said, "Oh, yes, indeed."

When Leisha was five she and Alice started school. Daddy's driver
took them every day into Chicago. They were in different rooms, which
disappointed Leisha. The kids in Leisha's room were all older. But from
the first day she adored school, with its fascinating science equipment
and electronic drawers full of math puzzlers and other children to find
countries on the map with. In half a year she had been moved to yet a
different room, where the kids were still older, but they were nonetheless nice to her. Leisha started to learn Japanese. She loved drawing the
beautiful characters on thick white paper. "The Sauley School was a
good choice," Daddy said.

But Alice didn't like the Sauley School. She wanted to go to school
on the same yellow bus as Cook's daughter. She cried and threw her
paints on the floor at the Sauley School. Then Mommy came out of her
room—Leisha hadn't seen her for a few weeks, although she knew Alice
had—and threw some candlesticks from the mantelpiece on the floor.
The candlesticks, which were china, broke. Leisha ran to pick up the
pieces while Mommy and Daddy screamed at each other in the hall by
the big staircase.

"She's my daughter, too! And I say she can go!"

"You don't have the right to say anything about it! A weepy drunk,
the most rotten role model possible for both of them . . . and I thought
I was getting a fine English aristocrat!"

"You got what you paid for! Nothing! Not that you ever needed
anything from me or anybody else!"

"Stop it!" Leisha cried. "Stop it!" There was silence in the hall.

Leisha cut her fingers on the china; blood streamed onto the rug. Daddy rushed in and picked her up. "Stop it," Leisha sobbed, and didn't understand when Daddy said quietly, "*You* stop it, Leisha. Nothing *they* do should touch you at all. You have to be at least that strong."

Leisha buried her head in Daddy's shoulder. Alice transferred to Carl Sandburg Elementary School, riding there on the yellow school bus with Cook's daughter.

A few weeks later Daddy told them that Mommy was going away to a hospital, to stop drinking so much. When Mommy came out, he said, she was going to live somewhere else for a while. She and Daddy were not happy. Leisha and Alice would stay with Daddy and they would visit Mommy sometimes. He told them this very carefully, finding the right words for truth. Truth was very important, Leisha already knew. Truth was being true to yourself, your specialness. Your individuality. An individual respected facts, and so always told the truth.

Mommy—Daddy did not say but Leisha knew—did not respect facts.

"I don't want Mommy to go away," Alice said. She started to cry. Leisha thought Daddy would pick Alice up, but he didn't. He just stood there looking at them both.

Leisha put her arms around Alice. "It's all right, Alice. It's all right! We'll make it all right! I'll play with you all the time we're not in school so you don't miss Mommy!"

Alice clung to Leisha. Leisha turned her head so she didn't have to see Daddy's face.

3

Kenzo Yagai was coming to the United States to lecture. The title of his talk, which he would give in New York, Los Angeles, and Chicago, with a repeat in Washington as a special address to Congress, was "The Further Political Implications of Inexpensive Power." Leisha Camden, eleven years old, was going to have a private introduction after the Chicago talk, arranged by her father.

She had studied the theory of cold fusion at school, and her global studies teacher had traced the changes in the world resulting from Yagai's patented, low-cost applications of what had, until him, been unworkable theory: the rising prosperity of the Third World; the death throes of the old communistic systems; the decline of the oil states; the renewed economic power of the United States. Her study group had written a news script, filmed with the school's professional-quality equipment, about how a 1985 American family lived with expensive energy costs and a belief in tax-supported help, while a 2019 family lived with cheap energy and a belief in the contract as the basis of civilization. Parts of her own research puzzled Leisha.

"Japan thinks Kenzo Yagai was a traitor to his own country," she said to Daddy at supper.

"No," Camden said, "*some* Japanese think that. Watch out for generalizations, Leisha. Yagai patented and licensed Y-energy in the United States because here there were at least the dying embers of individual enterprise. Because of his invention, our entire country has slowly swung back toward an individual meritocracy, and Japan has slowly been forced to follow."

"Your father held that belief all along," Susan said. "Eat your peas, Leisha." Leisha ate her peas. Susan and Daddy had only been married less than a year; it still felt a little strange to have her there. But nice. Daddy said Susan was a valuable addition to their household: intelligent, motivated, and cheerful. Like Leisha herself.

"Remember, Leisha," Camden said, "a man's worth to society and to himself doesn't rest on what he thinks other people should do or be or feel, but on himself. On what he can actually do, and do well. People trade what they do well, and everyone benefits. The basic tool of civilization is the contract. Contracts are voluntary and mutually beneficial. As opposed to coercion, which is wrong."

"The strong have no right to take anything from the weak by force," Susan said. "Alice, eat your peas, too, honey."

"Nor the weak to take anything by force from the strong," Camden said. "That's the basis of what you'll hear Kenzo Yagai discuss tonight, Leisha."

Alice said, "I don't like peas."

Camden said, "Your body does. They're good for you."

Alice smiled. Leisha felt her heart lift; Alice didn't smile much at dinner any more. "My body doesn't have a contract with the peas."

Camden said, a little impatiently, "Yes, it does. Your body benefits from them. Now eat."

Alice's smile vanished. Leisha looked down at her plate. Suddenly she saw a way out. "No, Daddy, look—Alice's body benefits, but the peas don't! It's not a mutually beneficial consideration, so there's no contract! Alice is right!"

Camden let out a shout of laughter. To Susan he said, "Eleven years old . . . *eleven*." Even Alice smiled, and Leisha waved her spoon triumphantly, light glinting off the bowl and dancing silver on the opposite wall.

But even so, Alice did not want to go hear Kenzo Yagai. She was going to sleep over at her friend Julie's house; they were going to curl their hair together. More surprisingly, Susan wasn't coming either. She and Daddy looked at each other a little funny at the front door, Leisha thought, but Leisha was too excited to think about this. She was going to hear *Kenzo Yagai*.

Yagai was a small man, dark and slim. Leisha liked his accent. She liked, too, something about him that took her a while to name. "Daddy," she whispered in the half-darkness of the auditorium, "he's a joyful man."

Daddy hugged her in the darkness.

Yagai spoke about spirituality and economics. "A man's spirituality, which is only his dignity as a man, rests on his own efforts. Dignity and worth are not automatically conferred by aristocratic birth; we have only to look at history to see that. Dignity and worth are not automatically conferred by inherited wealth. A great heir may be a thief, a wastrel, cruel, an exploiter, a person who leaves the world much poorer than he found it. Nor are dignity and worth automatically conferred by existence itself. A mass murderer exists, but is of negative worth to his society and possesses no dignity in his lust to kill.

"No, the only dignity, the only spirituality, rests on what a man can achieve with his own efforts. To rob a man of the chance to achieve, and to trade what he achieves with others, is to rob him of his spiritual dignity as a man. This is why communism has failed in our time. *All* coercion—all force to take from a man his own efforts to achieve—causes spiritual damage and weakens a society. Conscription, theft, fraud, violence, welfare, lack of legislative representation—*all* rob a man of his chance to choose, to achieve on his own, to trade the results of his achievement with others. Coercion is a cheat. It produces nothing new. Only freedom—the freedom to achieve, the freedom to trade freely the results of achievement—creates the environment proper to the dignity and spirituality of man."

Leisha applauded so hard her hands hurt. Going backstage with Daddy, she thought she could hardly breathe. Kenzo Yagai!

But backstage was more crowded than she had expected. There

were cameras everywhere. Daddy said, "Mr. Yagai, may I present my daughter Leisha," and the cameras moved in close and fast—on *her*. A Japanese man whispered something in Kenzo Yagai's ear, and he looked more closely at Leisha. "Ah, yes."

"Look over here, Leisha," someone called, and she did. A robot camera zoomed so close to her face that Leisha stepped back, startled. Daddy spoke very sharply to someone, then to someone else. The cameras didn't move. A woman suddenly knelt in front of Leisha and thrust a microphone at her. "What does it feel like to never sleep, Leisha?"

"What?"

Someone laughed. The laugh was not kind. "Breeding geniuses . . ."

Leisha felt a hand on her shoulder. Kenzo Yagai gripped her very firmly, and pulled her away from the cameras. Immediately, as if by magic, a line of Japanese men formed behind Yagai, parting only to let Daddy through. Behind the line, the three of them moved into a dressing room, and Kenzo Yagai shut the door.

"You must not let them bother you, Leisha," he said in his wonderful accent. "Not ever. There is an old Asian proverb: 'The dogs bark but the caravan moves on.' You must never let your individual caravan be slowed by the barking of rude or envious dogs."

"I won't," Leisha breathed, not sure yet what the words really meant, knowing there was time later to sort them out, to talk about them with Daddy. For now she was dazzled by Kenzo Yagai, the actual man himself who was changing the world without force, without guns, by trading his special individual efforts. "We study your philosophy at my school, Mr. Yagai."

Kenzo Yagai looked at Daddy. Daddy said, "A private school. But Leisha's sister also studies it, although cursorily, in the public system. Slowly, Kenzo, but it comes. It comes." Leisha noticed that he did not say why Alice was not here tonight with them.

Back home, Leisha sat in her room for hours, thinking over everything that had happened. When Alice came home from Julie's the next morning, Leisha rushed toward her. But Alice seemed angry about something.

"Alice—what is it?"

"Don't you think I have enough to put up with at school already?" Alice shouted. "Everybody knows, but at least when you stayed quiet it didn't matter too much! They'd stopped teasing me! Why did you have to do it?"

"Do what?" Leisha said, bewildered.

Alice threw something at her: a hard-copy morning paper, on newsprint flimsier than the Camden systems used. The paper dropped open at Leisha's feet. She stared at her own picture, three columns wide, with Kenzo Yagai. The headline said, "Yagai and the Future: Room for the Rest of Us? Y-Energy Inventor Confers With 'Sleep-Free' Daughter of Mega-Financier Roger Camden."

Alice kicked the paper. "It was on TV last night too—on *TV*. I work hard not to look stuck-up or creepy, and you go and do this! Now Julie probably won't even invite me to her slumber party next week!" She rushed up the broad curving stairs to her room.

Leisha looked down at the paper. She heard Kenzo Yagai's voice in her head: *The dogs bark but the caravan moves on.* She looked at the empty stairs. Aloud she said, "Alice—your hair looks really pretty curled like that."

4

I want to meet the rest of them," Leisha said. "Why have you kept them from me this long?"

"I haven't kept them from you at all," Camden said. "Not offering is not the same as denial. Why shouldn't you be the one to do the asking? You're the one who now wants it."

Leisha looked at him. She was fifteen, in her last year at the Sauley School. "Why didn't you offer?"

"Why should I?"

"I don't know," Leisha said. "But you gave me everything else."

"Including the freedom to ask for what you want."

Leisha looked for the contradiction, and found it. "Most things that you provided for my education I didn't ask for, because I didn't know enough to ask and you as the adult did. But you've never offered the opportunity for me to meet any of the other sleepless mutants—"

"Don't use that word," Camden said sharply.

"—so you must either think it was not essential to my education or else you had another motive for not wanting me to meet them."

"Wrong," Camden said. "There's a third possibility. That I think meeting them is essential to your education, that I do want you to, but this issue provided a chance to further the education of your self-initiative by waiting for *you* to ask."

"All right," Leisha said, a little defiantly; there seemed to be a lot of defiance between them lately, for no good reason. She squared her shoulders. Her new breasts thrust forward. "I'm asking. How many of the Sleepless are there, who are they, and where are they?"

Camden said, "If you're using that term—'the Sleepless'—you've already done some reading on your own. So you probably know that there are 1,082 of you so far in the United States, more in foreign countries, most of them in major metropolitan areas. Seventy-nine are in Chicago, most of them still small children. Only nineteen anywhere are older than you."

Leisha didn't deny reading any of this. Camden leaned forward in his study chair to peer at her. Leisha wondered if he needed glasses. His hair was completely gray now, sparse and stiff, like lonely broom straws. The *Wall Street Journal* listed him among the hundred richest men in America; *Women's Wear Daily* pointed out that he was the only billionaire in the country who did not move in the society of international parties, charity balls, and social secretaries. Camden's jet ferried him to business meetings around the world, to the chairmanship of the Yagai Economics Institute, and to very little else. Over the years he had grown richer, more reclusive, and more cerebral. Leisha felt a rush of her old affection.

She threw herself sideways into a leather chair, her long slim legs dangling over the arm. Absently she scratched a mosquito bite on her thigh. "Well, then, I'd like to meet Richard Keller." He lived in Chicago and was the beta-test Sleepless closest to her own age. He was seventeen.

"Why ask me? Why not just go?"

Leisha thought there was a note of impatience in his voice. He liked her to explore things first, then report on them to him later. Both parts were important.

Leisha laughed. "You know what, Daddy? You're predictable."

Camden laughed, too. In the middle of the laugh Susan came in. "He certainly is not. Roger, what about that meeting in Buenos Aires on Thursday? Is it on or off?" When he didn't answer, her voice grew shriller. "Roger? I'm talking to you!"

Leisha averted her eyes. Two years ago Susan had finally left genetic research to run Camden's house and schedule; before that she had tried hard to do both. Since she had left Biotech, it seemed to Leisha, Susan had changed. Her voice was tighter. She was more insistent that Cook and the gardener follow her directions exactly, without deviation. Her blond braids had become stiff sculptured waves of platinum.

"It's on," Roger said.

"Well, thanks for at least answering. Am I going?"

"If you like."

"I like."

Susan left the room. Leisha rose and stretched. Her long legs rose on tiptoe. It felt good to reach, to stretch, to feel sunlight from the wide windows wash over her face. She smiled at her father, and found him watching her with an unexpected expression.

"Leisha—"

"What?"

"See Keller. But be careful."

"Of what?"

But Camden wouldn't answer.

The voice on the phone had been noncommittal. "Leisha Camden? Yes, I know who you are. Three o'clock on Thursday?" The house was modest, a thirty-year-old colonial on a quiet suburban street where small children on bicycles could be watched from the front window. Few roofs had more than one Y-energy cell. The trees, huge old sugar maples, were beautiful.

"Come in," Richard Keller said.

He was no taller than she, stocky, with a bad case of acne. Probably no genetic alterations except sleep, Leisha guessed. He had thick dark hair, a low forehead, and bushy black brows. Before he closed the door Leisha saw him stare at her car and driver, parked in the driveway next to a rusty ten-speed bike.

"I can't drive yet," she said. "I'm still fifteen."

"It's easy to learn," Richard said. "So, you want to tell me why you're here?"

Leisha liked his directness. "To meet some other Sleepless."

"You mean you never have? Not any of us?"

"You mean the rest of you know each other?" She hadn't expected that.

"Come to my room, Leisha."

She followed him to the back of the house. No one else seemed to be home. His room was large and airy, filled with computers and filing cabinets. A rowing machine sat in one corner. It looked like a shabbier version of the room of any bright classmate at the Sauley School, except there was more space without a bed. She walked over to the computer screen.

"Hey—you working on Boesc equations?"

"On an application of them."

"To what?"

"Fish migration patterns."

Leisha smiled. "Yeah, that would work. I never thought of that."

Richard seemed not to know what to do with her smile. He looked at the wall, then at her chin. "You interested in Gaea patterns? In the environment?"

"Well, no," Leisha confessed. "Not particularly. I'm going to study politics at Harvard. Pre-law. But of course we had Gaea patterns at school."

Richard's gaze finally came unstuck from her face. He ran a hand through his dark hair. "Sit down, if you want."

Leisha sat, looking appreciatively at the wall posters, shifting green on blue, like ocean currents. "I like those. Did you program them yourself?"

"You're not at all what I pictured," Richard said.

"How did you picture me?"

He didn't hesitate. "Stuck-up. Superior. Shallow, despite your IQ."

She was more hurt than she had expected to be.

Richard blurted, "You're one of only two Sleepless who're really rich. You and Jennifer Sharifi. But you already know that."

"No, I don't. I've never checked."

He took the chair beside her, stretching his stocky legs straight in front of him, in a slouch that had nothing to do with relaxation. "It makes sense, really. Rich people don't have their children genetically modified to be superior—they think any offspring of theirs is already superior. By their values. And poor people can't afford it. We Sleepless are upper-middle class, no more. Children of professors, scientists, people who value brains and time."

"My father values brains and time," Leisha said. "He's the biggest supporter of Kenzo Yagai."

"Oh, Leisha, do you think I don't already know that? Are you flashing me or what?"

Leisha said with great deliberateness, "I'm *talking* to you." But the next minute she could feel the hurt break through on her face.

"I'm sorry," Richard muttered. He shot off his chair and paced to the computer and back. "I *am* sorry. But I don't . . . I don't understand what you're doing here."

"I'm lonely," Leisha said, astonished at herself. She looked up at him. "It's true. I'm lonely. I am. I have friends and Daddy and Alice. But no one really knows, really understands—what? I don't know what I'm saying."

Richard smiled. The smile changed his whole face, opened up its dark planes to the light. "I do. Oh, do I. What do you do when they say, 'I had such a dream last night'?"

"Yes!" Leisha said. "But that's even really minor. It's when *I* say, 'I'll look that up for you tonight' and they get that funny look on their face that means, 'She'll do it while I'm asleep.'"

"But that's even really minor," Richard said. "It's when you're playing basketball in the gym after supper and then you go to the diner for food and then you say, 'Let's have a walk by the lake,' and they say, 'I'm really tired. I'm going home to bed now.'"

"But that's really minor," Leisha said, jumping up. "It's when you really are absorbed by the movie and then you get the point and it's so goddamn beautiful you leap up and say, 'Yes! Yes!' and Susan says, 'Leisha, really, you'd think nobody but you ever enjoyed anything before.'"

"Who's Susan?" Richard said.

The mood was broken. But not really; Leisha could say, "My stepmother," without much discomfort over what Susan had promised to be and what she had become. Richard stood inches from her, smiling that joyous smile, understanding, and suddenly relief washed over Leisha so strong that she walked straight over to him and put her arms around his neck, only tightening them when she felt his startled jerk. She started to sob—she, Leisha, who never cried.

"Hey," Richard said. "Hey."

"Brilliant," Leisha said, laughing. "Brilliant remark."

She could feel his embarrassed smile. "Wanta see my fish migration curves instead?"

"No," Leisha sobbed, and he went on holding her, patting her back awkwardly, telling her without words that she was home.

Camden waited up for her, although it was past midnight. He had been smoking heavily. Through the blue air he said quietly, "Did you have a good time, Leisha?"

"Yes."

"I'm glad," he said, and put out his last cigarette, and climbed the stairs—slowly, stiffly, he was nearly seventy now—to bed.

They went everywhere together for nearly a year: swimming, dancing, the museums, the theater, the library. Richard introduced her to the others, a group of twelve kids between fourteen and nineteen, all of them intelligent and eager. All Sleepless.

Leisha learned.

Tony Indivino's parents, like her own, had divorced. But Tony, fourteen, lived with his mother, who had not particularly wanted a Sleepless child, while his father, who had, acquired a red sports car and a young girlfriend who designed ergonomic chairs in Paris. Tony was not allowed to tell anyone—relatives, schoolmates—that he was Sleep-less. "They'll think you're a freak," his mother said, eyes averted from her son's face. The one time Tony disobeyed her and told a friend that he never slept, his mother beat him. Then she moved the family to a new neighborhood. He was nine years old.

Jeanine Carter, almost as long-legged and slim as Leisha, was training for the Olympics in ice skating. She practiced twelve hours a day, hours no Sleeper still in high school could ever have. So far the newspapers had not picked up the story. Jeanine was afraid that if they did, they would somehow not let her compete.

Jack Bellingham, like Leisha, would start college in September. Unlike Leisha, he had already started his career. The practice of law had to wait for law school; the practice of investing required only money. Jack didn't have much, but his precise financial analyses par-layed $600 saved from summer jobs to $3,000 through stock-market investing, then to $10,000, and then he had enough to qualify for information-fund speculation. Jack was fifteen, not old enough to make legal investments; the transactions were all in the name of Kevin Baker, the oldest of the Sleepless, who lived in Austin. Jack told Leisha, "When I hit 84 percent profit over two consecutive quarters, the data analysts logged onto me. Just sniffing. Well, that's their job, even when the overall amounts are actually small. It's the patterns they care about. If they take the trouble to cross-reference data banks and come up with the fact that Kevin is a Sleepless, will they try to stop us from in-vesting somehow?"

"That's paranoid," Leisha said.

"No, it's not," Jeanine said. "Leisha, you don't *know*."

"You mean because I've been protected by my father's money and caring," Leisha said. No one grimaced; all of them confronted ideas openly, without shadowy allusions. Without dreams.

"Yes," Jeanine said. "Your father sounds terrific. And he raised you to think that achievement should not be fettered—Jesus Christ, he's a Yagaiist. Well, good. We're glad for you." She said it without sarcasm. Leisha nodded. "But the world isn't always like that. They hate us."

"That's too strong," Carol said. "Not hate."

"Well, maybe," Jeanine said. "But they're different from us. We're better, and they naturally resent that."

"I don't see what's natural about it," Tony said. "Why shouldn't it be just as natural to admire what's better? We do. Does any one of us resent Kenzo Yagai for his genius? Or Nelson Wade, the physicist? Or Catherine Raduski?"

"We don't resent them because we *are* better," Richard said. "*Q.E.D.*"

"What we should do is have our own society," Tony said. "Why should we allow their regulations to restrict our natural, honest achievements? Why should Jeanine be barred from skating against them and Jack from investing on their same terms just because we're Sleepless? Some of them are brighter than others of them. Some have greater persistence. Well, we have greater concentration, more biochemical stability, and more time. All men are not created equal."

"Be fair, Jack—no one has been barred from anything yet," Jeanine said.

"But we will be."

"*Wait,*" Leisha said. She was deeply troubled by the conversation. "I mean, yes, in many ways we're better. But you quoted out of context, Tony. The Declaration of Independence doesn't say all men are created equal in ability. It's talking about rights and power; it means that all are created equal *under the law*. We have no more right to a separate society or to being free of society's restrictions than anyone else does. There's no other way to freely trade one's efforts, unless the same contractual rules apply to all."

"Spoken like a true Yagaiist," Richard said, squeezing her hand.

"That's enough intellectual discussion for me," Carol said, laughing. "We've been at this for hours. We're at the beach, for Chrissake. Who wants to swim with me?"

"I do," Jeanine said. "Come on, Jack."

All of them rose, brushing sand off their suits, discarding sunglasses.

Richard pulled Leisha to her feet. But just before they ran into the water, Tony put his skinny hand on her arm. "One more question, Leisha. Just to think about. If we achieve better than most other people, and if we trade with the Sleepers when it's mutually beneficial, making no distinction there between the strong and the weak—what obligation do we have to those so weak they don't have anything to trade with us? We're already going to give more than we get; do we have to do it when we get nothing at all? Do we have to take care of their deformed and handicapped and sick and lazy and shiftless with the products of our work?"

"Do the Sleepers have to?" Leisha countered.

"Kenzo Yagai would say no. He's a Sleeper."

"He would say they would receive the benefits of contractual trade even if they aren't direct parties to the contract. The whole world is better-fed and healthier because of Y-energy."

"Come on!" Jeanine yelled. "Leisha, they're ducking me! Jack, you stop that! Leisha, help me!"

Leisha laughed. Just before she grabbed for Jeanine, she caught the look on Richard's face, and on Tony's: Richard frankly lustful, Tony angry. At her. But why? What had she done, except argue in favor of dignity and trade?

Then Jack threw water on her, and Carol pushed Jack into the warm spray, and Richard was there with his arms around her, laughing.

When she got the water out of her eyes, Tony was gone.

Midnight. "Okay," Carol said. "Who's first?"

The six teenagers in the brambly clearing looked at each other. A Y-lamp, kept on low for atmosphere, cast weird shadows across their faces and over their bare legs. Around the clearing Roger Camden's trees stood thick and dark, a wall between them and the closest of the estate's outbuildings. It was very hot. August air hung heavy, sullen. They had voted against bringing an air-conditioned Y-field because this was a return to the primitive, the dangerous; let it be primitive.

Six pairs of eyes stared at the glass in Carol's hand.

"Come *on*," she said. "Who wants to drink up?" Her voice was jaunty, theatrically hard. "It was difficult enough to get this."

"How *did* you get it?" said Richard, the group member—except for Tony—with the least influential family contacts, the least money. "In a drinkable form like that?"

"Jennifer got it," Carol said, and five sets of eyes shifted to Jennifer Sharifi, who two weeks into her visit with Carol's family was confusing them all. She was the American-born daughter of a Hollywood movie star and an Arab prince who had wanted to found a Sleepless dynasty. The movie star was an aging drug addict; the prince, who had taken his fortune out of oil and put it into Y-energy when Kenzo Yagai was still licensing his first patents, was dead. Jennifer Sharifi was richer than Leisha would someday be, and infinitely more sophisticated about procuring things. The glass held interleukin-1, an immune-system booster, one of many substances which as a side effect induced the brain to swift and deep sleep.

Leisha stared at the glass. A warm feeling crept through her lower belly, not unlike the feeling when she and Richard made love. She caught Jennifer watching her, and flushed.

Jennifer disturbed her. Not for the obvious reasons she disturbed Tony and Richard and Jack: the long black hair, the tall, slim body in shorts and halter. Jennifer didn't laugh. Leisha had never met a Sleepless who didn't laugh, nor one who said so little, with such deliberate casualness. Leisha found herself speculating on what Jennifer Sharifi wasn't saying. It was an odd sensation to feel toward another Sleepless.

Tony said to Carol, "Give it to me!"

Carol handed him the glass. "Remember, you only need a little sip."

Tony raised the glass to his mouth, stopped, and looked at them over the rim from his fierce eyes. He drank.

Carol took back the glass. They all watched Tony. Within a minute he lay on the rough ground; within two, his eyes closed in sleep.

It wasn't like seeing parents sleep, siblings, friends. It was Tony. They looked away, avoided each other's eyes. Leisha felt the warmth between her legs tug and tingle, faintly obscene. She didn't look at Jennifer.

When it was Leisha's turn, she drank slowly, then passed the glass to Richard. Her head turned heavy, as if it were being stuffed with damp rags. The trees at the edge of the clearing blurred. The portable lamp blurred, too. It wasn't bright and clean anymore but squishy, blobby; if she touched it, it would smear. Then darkness swooped over her brain, taking it away: *taking away her mind.* "Daddy!" She tried to call, to clutch for him, but then the darkness obliterated her.

Afterward, they all had headaches. Dragging themselves back through the woods in the thin morning light was torture, compounded by an odd shame. They didn't touch each other. Leisha walked as far away from Richard as she could.

Jennifer was the only one who spoke. "So now we know," she said, and her voice held a strange satisfaction.

It was a whole day before the throbbing left the base of Leisha's skull, or the nausea her stomach. She sat alone in her room, waiting for the misery to pass, and despite the heat, her whole body shivered.

There had not even been any dreams.

"I want you to come with me tonight," Leisha said, for the tenth or twelfth time. "We both leave for college in just two days; this is the last chance. I really want you to meet Richard."

Alice lay on her stomach across her bed. Her hair, brown and lusterless, fell around her face. She wore an expensive yellow jumpsuit, silk by Ann Patterson, which rucked up around her knees.

"Why? What do you care if I meet Richard or not?"

"Because you're my sister," Leisha said. She knew better than to say "my twin." Nothing got Alice angry faster.

"I don't want to." The next moment Alice's face changed. "Oh, I'm sorry, Leisha—I didn't mean to sound so snotty. But . . . but I don't want to."

"It won't be all of them. Just Richard. And just for an hour or so. Then you can come back here and pack for Northwestern."

"I'm not going to Northwestern."

Leisha stared at her.

Alice said, "I'm pregnant."

Leisha sat on the bed. Alice rolled onto her back, brushed the hair out of her eyes, and laughed. Leisha's ears closed against the sound. "Look at you," Alice said. "You'd think it was *you* who was pregnant. But you never would be, would you, Leisha? Not until it was the proper time. Not you."

"How?" Leisha said. "We both had our caps put in. . . ."

"I had the cap removed," Alice said.

"You wanted to get pregnant?"

"Damn flash I did. And there's not a thing Daddy can do about it. Except, of course, cut off all credit completely, but I don't think he'll do that, do you?" She laughed again. "Even to me?"

"But Alice . . . why? Not just to anger Daddy!"

"No," Alice said. "Although you would think of that, wouldn't you? Because I want something to love. Something of my *own*. Something that has nothing to do with this house."

Leisha thought of herself and Alice running through the conservatory, years ago, her and Alice, darting in and out of the sunlight. "It hasn't been so bad growing up in this house."

"Leisha, you're stupid. I don't know how anyone so smart can be so stupid. Get out of my room! Get out!"

"But Alice—a *baby*—"

"Get out!" Alice shrieked. "Go to Harvard! Go be successful! Just get out!"

Leisha jerked off the bed. "Gladly! You're irrational, Alice. You don't think ahead, you don't plan, a *baby*—" But she could never sustain anger. It dribbled away, leaving her mind empty. She looked at Alice, who suddenly put out her arms. Leisha went into them.

"You're the baby," Alice said wonderingly. "You *are*. You're so . . . I don't know what. You're a *baby*."

Leisha said nothing. Alice's arms felt warm, felt whole, felt like two children running in and out of sunlight. "I'll help you, Alice. If Daddy won't."

Alice abruptly pushed her away. "I don't need your help."

Alice stood. Leisha rubbed her empty arms, fingertips scraping across opposite elbows. Alice kicked the empty, open trunk in which she was supposed to pack for Northwestern, and then abruptly smiled a smile that made Leisha look away. She braced herself for more abuse. But what Alice said, very softly, was, "Have a good time at Harvard."

5

She loved it.

From the first sight of Massachusetts Hall, older than the United States by a half century, Leisha felt something that had been missing in Chicago: Age. Roots. Tradition. She touched the bricks of Widener Library, the glass cases in the Peabody Museum, as if they were the grail. She had never been particularly sensitive to myth or drama; the anguish of Juliet seemed to her artificial, that of Willy Loman merely wasteful. Only King Arthur, struggling to create a better social order, had interested her. But now, walking under the huge autumn trees, she suddenly caught a glimpse of a force that could span generations, fortunes left to endow learning and achievement the benefactors would never see, individual effort spanning and shaping centuries to come. She stopped, and looked at the sky through the leaves, at the buildings solid with purpose. At such moments she thought of Camden, bending the will of an entire genetic research institute to create her in the image he wanted.

Within a month, she had forgotten all such mega-musings.

The work load was incredible, even for her. The Sauley School had encouraged individual exploration at her own pace; Harvard knew what it wanted from her, at its pace. In the past twenty years, under the academic leadership of a man who in his youth had watched Japanese economic domination with dismay, Harvard had become the controversial leader of a return to hard-edged learning of facts, theories, applications, problem-solving, and intellectual efficiency. The school accepted one of every 200 applicants from around the world. The daughter of England's prime minister had flunked out her first year and been sent home.

Leisha had a single room in a new dormitory, the dorm because she had spent so many years isolated in Chicago and was hungry for people, the single so she would not disturb anyone else when she worked all night. Her second day a boy from down the hall sauntered in and perched on the edge of her desk.

"So you're Leisha Camden."

"Yes."

"Sixteen years old."

"Almost seventeen."

"Going to out-perform us all, I understand, without even trying."

Leisha's smile faded. The boy stared at her from under lowered downy brows. He was smiling, his eyes sharp. From Richard and Tony and the others Leisha had learned to recognize the anger that presents itself as contempt.

"Yes," Leisha said coolly, "I am."

"Are you sure? With your pretty little-girl hair and your mutant little-girl brain?"

"Oh, leave her alone, Hannaway," said another voice. A tall blond boy, so thin his ribs looked like ripples in brown sand, stood in jeans and bare feet, drying his wet hair. "Don't you ever get tired of walking around being an asshole?"

"Do you?" Hannaway said. He heaved himself off the desk and started toward the door. The blond moved out of his way. Leisha moved into it.

"The reason I'm going to do better than you," she said evenly, "is because I have certain advantages you don't. Including sleeplessness. And then after I out-perform you, I'll be glad to help you study for your tests so that you can pass, too."

The blond, drying his ears, laughed. But Hannaway stood still, and into his eyes came an expression that made Leisha back away. He pushed past her and stormed out.

"Nice going, Camden," the blond said. "He deserved that."

"But I meant it," Leisha said. "I will help him study."

The blond lowered his towel and stared. "You did, didn't you? You meant it."

"Yes! Why does everybody keep questioning that?"

"Well," the boy said, "*I* don't. You can help me if I get into trouble." Suddenly he smiled. "But I won't."

"Why not?"

"Because I'm just as good at anything as you are, Leisha Camden."

She studied him. "You're not one of us. Not Sleepless."

"Don't have to be. I know what I can do. Do, be, create, trade."

She said, delighted, "You're a Yagaiist!"

"Of course." He held out his hand. "Stewart Sutter. How about a fishburger in the Yard?"

"Great," Leisha said. They walked out together, talking excitedly. When people stared at her, she tried not to notice. She was here. At Harvard. With space ahead of her, time, to learn, and with people like Stewart Sutter who accepted and challenged her.

All the hours he was awake.

She became totally absorbed in her class work. Roger Camden drove up once, walking the campus with her, listening, smiling. He was more at home than Leisha would have expected: he knew Stewart Sutter's father and Kate Addams's grandfather. They talked about Harvard, business, Harvard, the Yagai Economics Institute, Harvard. "How's Alice?" Leisha asked once, but Camden said he didn't know; she had moved out and did not want to see him. He made her an allowance through his attorney. While he said this, his face remained serene.

Leisha went to the Homecoming Ball with Stewart, who was also majoring in pre-law but was two years ahead of Leisha. She took a weekend trip to Paris with Kate Addams and two other girlfriends, taking the Concorde III. She had a fight with Stewart over whether the metaphor of superconductivity could apply to Yagaiism, a stupid fight they both knew was stupid but had anyway, and afterward they became lovers. After the fumbling sexual explorations with Richard, Stewart was deft, experienced, smiling faintly as he taught her how to have an orgasm both by herself and with him. Leisha was dazzled. "It's so *joyful*," she said, and Stewart looked at her with a tenderness she knew was part disturbance but didn't know why.

At midsemester she had the highest grades in the freshman class. She got every answer right on every single question on her midterms. She and Stewart went out for a beer to celebrate, and when they came back Leisha's room had been destroyed. The computer was smashed, the data banks wiped, hard-copies and books smoldered in a metal wastebasket. Her clothes were ripped to pieces, her desk and bureau hacked apart. The only thing untouched, pristine, was the bed.

Stewart said, "There's no way this could have been done in silence. Everyone on the floor—hell, on the floor *below*—had to know. Someone will talk to the police." No one did. Leisha sat on the edge of the bed, dazed, and looked at the remnants of her Homecoming gown. The next day Dave Hannaway gave her a long, wide smile.

Camden flew east, taut with rage. He rented her an apartment in Cambridge with E-lock security and a bodyguard named Toshio. After he left, Leisha fired the bodyguard but kept the apartment. It gave her and Stewart more privacy, which they used to endlessly discuss the situation. It was Leisha who argued that it was an aberration, an immaturity.

"There have always been haters, Stewart. Hate Jews, hate Blacks, hate immigrants, hate Yagaiists who have more initiative and dignity than you do. I'm just the latest object of hatred. It's not new, it's not remarkable. It doesn't mean any basic kind of schism between the Sleepless and Sleepers."

Stewart sat up in bed and reached for the sandwiches on the night stand. "Doesn't it? Leisha, you're a different kind of person entirely. More evolutionarily fit, not only to survive but to prevail. Those other objects of hatred you cite—they were all powerless in their societies. They occupied *inferior* positions. You on the other hand—all three

Sleepless in Harvard Law are on the *Law Review*. All of them. Kevin Baker, your oldest, has already founded a successful bio-interface software firm and is making money, a lot of it. Every Sleepless is making superb grades, none have psychological problems, all are healthy, and most of you aren't even adults yet. How much hatred do you think you're going to encounter once you hit the high-stakes world of finance and business and scarce endowed chairs and national politics?"

"Give me a sandwich," Leisha said. "Here's my evidence you're wrong: you yourself. Kenzo Yagai. Kate Addams. Professor Lane. My father. Every Sleeper who inhabits the world of fair trade and mutually beneficial contracts. And that's most of you, or at least most of you who are worth considering. You believe that competition among the most capable leads to the most beneficial trades for everyone, strong and weak. Sleepless are making real and concrete contributions to society, in a lot of fields. That has to outweigh the discomfort we cause. We're *valuable* to you. You know that."

Stewart brushed crumbs off the sheets. "Yes. I do. Yagaiists do."

"Yagaiists run the business and financial and academic worlds. Or they will. In a meritocracy, they *should*. You underestimate the majority of people, Stew. Ethics aren't confined to the ones out front."

"I hope you're right," Stewart said. "Because, you know, I'm in love with you."

Leisha put down her sandwich.

"Joy," Stewart mumbled into her breasts, "you are joy."

When Leisha went home for Thanksgiving, she told Richard about Stewart. He listened tight-lipped.

"A Sleeper."

"A *person*," Leisha said. "A good, intelligent, achieving person!"

"Do you know what your good intelligent achieving Sleepers have done, Leisha? Jeanine has been barred from Olympic skating. 'Genetic alteration, analogous to steroid abuse to create an unsportsmanlike advantage.' Chris Devereaux has left Stanford. They trashed his laboratory, destroyed two years' work in memory-formation proteins. Kevin Baker's software company is fighting a nasty advertising campaign, all underground of course, about kids using software designed by nonhuman minds. Corruption, mental slavery, satanic influences: the whole bag of witch-hunt tricks. Wake up, Leisha!"

They both heard his words. Minutes dragged by. Richard stood like a boxer, forward on the balls of his feet, teeth clenched. Finally he said, very quietly, "Do you love him?"

"Yes," Leisha said. "I'm sorry."

"Your choice," Richard said coldly. "What do you do while he's asleep? Watch?"

"You make it sound like a perversion!"

Richard said nothing. Leisha drew a deep breath. She spoke rapidly but calmly, a controlled rush: "While Stewart is asleep I work. The same as you do. Richard—don't do this. I didn't mean to hurt you. And I don't want to lose the group. I believe the Sleepers are the same species as we are. Are you going to punish me for that? Are you going to *add* to the hatred? Are you going to tell me that I can't belong to a wider world that includes all honest, worthwhile people whether they sleep or not? Are you going to tell me that the most important division is by genetics and not by economic spirituality? Are you going to force me into an artificial choice, us or them?"

Richard picked up a bracelet. Leisha recognized it; she had given it to him in the summer. His voice was quiet. "No. It's not a choice." He played with the gold links a minute, then looked at her. "Not yet."

By spring break, Camden walked more slowly. He took medicine for his blood pressure, his heart. He and Susan, he told Leisha, were getting a divorce. "She changed, Leisha, after I married her. You saw that. She was independent and productive and happy, and then after a few years she stopped all that and became a shrew. A whining shrew." He shook his head in genuine bewilderment. "You saw the change."

Leisha had. A memory came to her: Susan leading her and Alice in "games" that were actually controlled cerebral-performance tests, Susan's braids dancing around her sparkling eyes. Alice had loved Susan then, as much as Leisha had.

"Dad, I want Alice's address."

"I told you up at Harvard, I don't have it," Camden said. He shifted in his chair, the impatient gesture of a body that never expected to wear out. In January Kenzo Yagai had died of pancreatic cancer; Camden had taken the news hard. "I make her allowance through an attorney. By her choice."

"Then I want the address of the attorney."

The attorney, a quenched-looking man named John Jaworski, refused to tell Leisha where Alice was. "She doesn't want to be found, Ms. Camden. She wanted a complete break."

"Not from me," Leisha said.

"Yes," Jaworski said, and something flickered in his eyes, something she had last seen in Dave Hannaway's face.

She flew to Austin before returning to Boston, making her a day late for classes. Kevin Baker saw her instantly, canceling a meeting with IBM. She told him what she needed, and he set his best datanet people on it, without telling them why. Within two hours she had Alice's address from Jaworski's electronic files. It was the first time, she realized, that she had ever turned to one of the Sleepless for help, and it had been given instantly. Without trade.

Alice was in Pennsylvania. The next weekend Leisha rented a hovercar and driver—she had learned to drive, but only groundcars as yet—and went to High Ridge, in the Appalachian Mountains.

It was an isolated hamlet, twenty-five miles from the nearest hospital. Alice lived with a man named Ed, a silent carpenter twenty years older than she, in a cabin in the woods. The cabin had water and electricity but no news net. In the early spring light the earth was raw and bare, slashed with icy gullies. Alice and Ed apparently worked at nothing. Alice was eight months pregnant.

"I didn't want you here," she said to Leisha. "So why are you?"

"Because you're my sister."

"God, look at you. Is that what they're wearing at Harvard? Boots like that? When did you become fashionable, Leisha? You were always too busy being intellectual to care."

"What's this all about, Alice? Why here? What are you doing?"

"Living," Alice said. "Away from dear Daddy, away from Chicago, away from drunken, broken Susan—did you know she drinks? Just like Mom. He does that to people. But not to me. I got out. I wonder if you ever will."

"Got out? To *this*?"

"I'm happy," Alice said angrily. "Isn't that what it's supposed to be about? Isn't that the aim of your great Kenzo Yagai—happiness through individual effort?"

Leisha thought of saying that Alice was making no efforts that she could see. She didn't say it. A chicken ran through the yard of the cabin. Behind, the mountains rose in layer upon layer of blue haze. Leisha thought what this place must have been like in winter, cut off from the world where people strived toward goals, learned, changed.

"I'm glad you're happy, Alice."

"Are you?"

"Yes."

"Then I'm glad, too," Alice said, almost defiantly. The next moment she abruptly hugged Leisha, fiercely, the huge, hard mound of her belly crushed between them. Alice's hair smelled sweet, like fresh grass in sunlight.

"I'll come see you again, Alice."

"Don't," Alice said.

6

S leepless Mutie Begs for Reversal of Gene Tampering," screamed the headline in the Food Mart. " 'Please Let Me Sleep Like Real People!' Child Pleads."

Leisha typed in her credit number and pressed the news kiosk for a printout, although ordinarily she ignored the electronic tabloids. The headline went on circling the kiosk. A Food Mart employee stopped stacking boxes on shelves and watched her. Bruce, Leisha's bodyguard, watched the employee.

She was twenty-two, in her final year at Harvard Law, editor of the *Law Review*, clearly first in her graduating class. The closest three contenders were Jonathan Cocchiara, Len Carter, and Martha Wentz. All Sleepless.

In her apartment she skimmed the printout. Then she accessed the Groupnet run from Austin. The files had more news stories about the child, with comments from other Sleepless, but before she could call them up Kevin Baker came on-line himself, on voice.

"Leisha. I'm glad you called. I was going to call you."

"What's the situation with this Stella Bevington, Kev? Has anybody checked it out?"

"Randy Davies. He's from Chicago but I don't think you've met him; he's still in high school. He's in Park Ridge, Stella's in Skokie. Her parents wouldn't talk to him—they were pretty abusive, in fact—but he got to see Stella face-to-face anyway. It doesn't look like an abuse case, just the usual stupidity: parents wanted a genius child, scrimped and saved, and now they can't handle that she *is* one. They scream at her to sleep, get emotionally abusive when she contradicts them, but so far no violence."

"Is the emotional abuse actionable?"

"I don't think we want to move on it yet. Two of us will keep in close touch with Stella—she does have a modem, and she hasn't told her parents about the net—and Randy will drive out weekly."

Leisha bit her lip. "A tabloid shitpiece said she's seven years old."

"Yes."

"Maybe she shouldn't be left there. I'm an Illinois resident, I can file an abuse grievance from here if Candy's got too much in her brief-case. . . ." *Seven years old.*

"No. Let it sit a while. Stella will probably be all right. You know that."

She did. Nearly all of the Sleepless stayed all right, no matter how much opposition came from the stupid segment of society. And it was only the stupid segment, Leisha argued, a small if vocal minority. Most people could, and would, adjust to the growing presence of the Sleep-less, when it became clear that that presence included not only growing power but growing benefits to the country as a whole.

Kevin Baker, now twenty-six, had made a fortune in microchips so revolutionary that Artificial Intelligence, once a debated dream, was yearly closer to reality. Carolyn Rizzolo had won the Pulitzer Prize in drama for her play *Morning Light*. She was twenty-four. Jeremy Robin-son had done significant work in superconductivity applications while still a graduate student at Stanford. William Thaine, *Law Review* editor when Leisha first came to Harvard, was now in private practice. He had never lost a case. He was twenty-six, and the cases were becoming im-portant. His clients valued his ability more than his age.

But not everyone reacted that way.

Kevin Baker and Richard Keller had started the datanet that bound the Sleepless into a tight group, constantly aware of each other's personal fights. Leisha Camden financed the legal battles, the educational costs of Sleepless whose parents were unable to meet them, the support of children in emotionally bad situations. Rhonda Lavelier got herself licensed as a foster mother in California, and whenever possible the Group maneuvered to have young Sleepless who were removed from their homes assigned to Rhonda. The Group now had three licensed lawyers; within the next year it would gain four more, licensed to practice in five different states.

The one time they had not been able to remove an abused Sleepless child legally, they kidnapped him.

Timmy DeMarzo, four years old. Leisha had been opposed to the action. She had argued the case morally and pragmatically—to her they were the same thing—thus: If they believed in their society, in its fundamental laws and in their ability to belong to it as free-trading productive individuals, they must remain bound by the society's contractual laws. The Sleepless were, for the most part, Yagaiists. They should already know this. And if the FBI caught them, the courts and press would crucify them.

They were not caught.

Timmy DeMarzo—not even old enough to call for help on the datanet, they had learned of the situation through the automatic police-record scan Kevin maintained through his company—was stolen from his own back yard in Wichita. He had lived the last year in an isolated trailer in North Dakota; no place was too isolated for a modem. He was cared for by a legally irreproachable foster mother who had lived there all her life. The foster mother was second cousin to a Sleepless, a broad cheerful woman with a much better brain than her appearance indicated. She was a Yagaiist. No record of the child's existence appeared in any data bank: not the IRS, not any school's, not even the local grocery store's computerized checkout slips. Food specifically for the child was shipped in monthly on a truck owned by a Sleepless in State College, Pennsylvania. Ten of the Group knew about the kidnapping, out of the total 3,428 sleepless born in the United States. Of those, 2,691 were part of the Group via the net. An additional

701 were as yet too young to use a modem. Only 36 Sleepless, for whatever reason, were not part of the Group.

The kidnapping had been arranged by Tony Indivino.

"It's Tony I wanted to talk to you about," Kevin said to Leisha. "He's started again. This time he means it. He's buying land."

She folded the tabloid very small and laid it carefully on the table. "Where?"

"Allegheny Mountains. In southern New York State. A lot of land. He's putting in the roads now. In the spring, the first buildings."

"Jennifer Sharifi still financing it?" It had been six years since the interleukin-drinking in the woods, but the evening remained vivid to Leisha. So did Jennifer Sharifi.

"Yes. She's got the money to do it. Tony's starting to get a following, Leisha."

"I know."

"Call him."

"I will. Keep me informed about Stella."

She worked until midnight at the *Law Review*, then until 4:00 A.M. preparing her classes. From four to five she handled legal matters for the Group. At 5:00 A.M. she called Tony, still in Chicago. He had finished high school, done one semester at Northwestern, and at Christmas vacation had finally exploded at his mother for forcing him to live as a Sleeper. The explosion, it seemed to Leisha, had never ended.

"Tony? Leisha."

"The answer is yes, yes, no, and go to hell."

Leisha gritted her teeth. "Fine. Now tell me the questions."

"Are you really serious about the Sleepless withdrawing into their own self-sufficient society? Is Jennifer Sharifi willing to finance a project the size of building a small city? Don't you think that's a cheat of all that can be accomplished by patient integration of the Group into the mainstream? And what about the contradictions of living in an armed restricted city and still trading with the Outside?"

"I would never tell *you* to go to hell."

"Hooray for you," Tony said. After a moment he added, "I'm sorry. That sounds like one of *them*."

"It's wrong for us, Tony."

"Thanks for not saying I couldn't pull it off."

She wondered if he could. "We're not a separate species, Tony."

"Tell that to the Sleepers."

"You exaggerate. There are haters out there, there are *always* haters, but to give up . . ."

"We're not giving up. Whatever we create can be freely traded: software, hardware, novels, information, theories, legal counsel. We can travel in and out. But we'll have a safe place to return *to*. Without the leeches who think we owe them blood because we're better than they are."

"It isn't a matter of owing."

"Really?" Tony said. "Let's have this out, Leisha. All the way. You're a Yagaiist—what do you believe in?"

"Tony . . ."

"*Do it*," Tony said, and in his voice she heard the fourteen-year-old she had been introduced to by Richard. Simultaneously, she saw her father's face: not as he was now, since the bypass, but as he had been when she was a little girl, holding her on his lap to explain that she was special.

"I believe in voluntary trade that is mutually beneficial. That spiritual dignity comes from supporting one's life through one's own efforts, and from trading the results of those efforts in mutual cooperation throughout the society. That the symbol of this is the contract. And that we need each other for the fullest, most beneficial trade."

"Fine," Tony bit off. "Now what about the beggars in Spain?"

"The what?"

"You walk down a street in a poor country like Spain and you see a beggar. Do you give him a dollar?"

"Probably."

"Why? He's trading nothing with you. He has nothing to trade."

"I know. Out of kindness. Compassion."

"You see six beggars. Do you give them all a dollar?"

"Probably," Leisha said.

"You would. You see a hundred beggars and you haven't got Leisha Camden's money. Do you give them each a dollar?"

"No."

"Why not?"

Leisha reached for patience. Few people could make her want to cut off a comlink; Tony was one of them. "Too draining on my own resources. My life has first claim on the resources I earn."

"All right. Now consider this. At Biotech Institute—where you and I began, dear pseudo-sister—Dr. Melling has just yesterday—"

"*Who?*"

"Dr. Susan Melling. Oh, God, I completely forgot—she used to be married to your father!"

"I lost track of her," Leisha said. "I didn't realize she'd gone back to research. Alice once said . . . never mind. What's going on at Biotech?"

"Two crucial items, just released. Carla Dutcher has had first-month fetal genetic analysis. Sleeplessness is a dominant gene. The next generation of the Group won't sleep either."

"We all knew that," Leisha said. Carla Dutcher was the world's first pregnant Sleepless. Her husband was a Sleeper. "The whole world expected that."

"But the press will have a field day with it anyway. Just watch. Muties Breed! New Race Set to Dominate Next Generation of Children!"

Leisha didn't deny it. "And the second item?"

"It's sad, Leisha. We've just had our first death."

Her stomach tightened. "Who?"

"Bernie Kuhn. Seattle." She didn't know him. "A car accident. It looks pretty straightforward; he lost control on a steep curve when his brakes failed. He had only been driving a few months. He was seventeen. But the significance here is that his parents have donated his brain and body to Biotech, in conjunction with the pathology department at the Chicago Medical School. They're going to take him apart to get the first good look at what prolonged sleeplessness does to the body and brain."

"They should," Leisha said. "That poor kid. But what are you so afraid they'll find?"

"I don't know. I'm not a doctor. But whatever it is, if the haters can use it against us, they will."

"You're paranoid, Tony."

"Impossible. The Sleepless have personalities calmer and more reality-oriented than the norm. Don't you read the literature?"

"Tony—"

"What if you walk down that street in Spain and a hundred beggars each want a dollar and you say no and they have nothing to trade you but they're so rotten with anger about what you have that they knock you down and grab it and then beat you out of sheer envy and despair?"

Leisha didn't answer.

"Are you going to say that's not a human scenario, Leisha? That it never happens?"

"It happens," Leisha said evenly. "But not all that often."

"Bullshit. Read more history. Read more *newspapers*. But the point is: What do you owe the beggars then? What does good Yagaiist who believes in mutually beneficial contracts do with people who have nothing to trade and can only take?"

"You're not—"

"*What*, Leisha? In the most objective terms you can manage, what do we owe the grasping and nonproductive needy?"

"What I said originally. Kindness. Compassion."

"Even if they don't trade it back? Why?"

"Because . . ." She stopped.

"Why? Why do law-abiding and productive human beings owe anything to those who neither produce very much nor abide by just laws? What philosophical or economic or spiritual justification is there for owing them anything? Be as honest as I know you are."

Leisha put her head between her knees. The question gaped

beneath her, but she didn't try to evade it. "I don't know. I just know we do."

"*Why?*"

She didn't answer. After a moment, Tony did. The intellectual challenge was gone from his voice. He said, almost tenderly, "Come down in the spring and see the site for Sanctuary. The buildings will be going up then."

"No," Leisha said.

"I'd like you to."

"No. Armed retreat is not the way."

Tony said, "The beggars are getting nastier, Leisha. As the Sleepless grow richer. And I don't mean in money."

"Tony—" she said, and stopped. She couldn't think what to say.

"Don't walk down too many streets armed with just the memory of Kenzo Yagai."

In March, a bitterly cold March with wind whipping down the Charles River, Richard Keller came to Cambridge. Leisha had not seen him for three years. He didn't send her word on the Groupnet that he was coming. She hurried up the walk to her townhouse, muffled to the eyes in a red wool scarf against the snowy cold, and he stood there blocking the doorway. Behind Leisha, her bodyguard tensed.

"Richard! Bruce, it's all right, this is an old friend."

"Hello, Leisha."

He was heavier, sturdier-looking, with a breadth of shoulder she didn't recognize. But the face was Richard's, older but unchanged: dark low brows, unruly dark hair. He had grown a beard.

"You look beautiful," he said.

Inside, she handed him a cup of coffee. "Are you here on business?" From the Groupnet she knew that he had finished his master's and had done outstanding work in marine biology in the Caribbean but had left that a year ago and disappeared from the net.

"No. Pleasure." He smiled suddenly, the old smile that opened up his dark face. "I almost forgot about that for a long time. Contentment, yes. We're all good at the contentment that comes from sustained work. But pleasure? Whim? Caprice? When was the last time you did something silly, Leisha?"

She smiled. "I ate cotton candy in the shower."

"Really? Why?"

"To see if it would dissolve in gooey pink patterns."

"Did it?"

"Yes. Lovely ones."

"And that was your last silly thing? When was it?"

"Last summer," Leisha said, and laughed.

"Well, mine is sooner than that. It's now. I'm in Boston for no other reason than the spontaneous pleasure of seeing you."

Leisha stopped laughing. "That's an intense tone for a spontaneous pleasure, Richard."

"Yup," he said, intensely. She laughed again. He didn't.

"I've been in India, Leisha. And China and Africa. Thinking, mostly. Watching. First I traveled like a Sleeper, attracting no attention. Then I set out to meet the Sleepless in India and China. There are a few, you know, whose parents were willing to come here for the operation. They pretty much are accepted and left alone. I tried to figure out why desperately poor countries—by our standards anyway; over there Y-energy is mostly available only in big cities—don't have any trouble accepting the superiority of Sleepless, whereas Americans, with more prosperity than any time in history, build in resentment more and more."

Leisha said, "Did you figure it out?"

"No. But I figured out something else, watching all those communes and villages and *kampongs*. We are too individualistic."

Disappointment swept Leisha. She saw her father's face: *Excellence is what counts, Leisha. Excellence supported by individual effort. . . .* She reached for Richard's cup. "More coffee?"

He caught her wrist and looked up into her face. "Don't misunderstand me, Leisha. I'm not talking about work. We are too much individuals in the rest of our lives. Too emotionally rational. Too much alone. Isolation kills more than the free flow of ideas. It kills joy."

He didn't let go of her wrist. She looked down into his eyes, into depths she hadn't seen before. It was the feeling of looking into a mine shaft, both giddy and frightening, knowing that at the bottom might be gold or darkness. Or both.

Richard said softly, "Stewart?"

"Over long ago. An undergraduate thing." Her voice didn't sound like her own.

"Kevin?"

"No, never—we're just friends."

"I wasn't sure. Anyone?"

"No."

He let go of her wrist. Leisha peered at him timidly. He suddenly laughed. "Joy, Leisha." An echo sounded in her mind, but she couldn't place it, and then it was gone and she laughed too, a laugh airy and frothy and pink cotton candy in summer.

"Come home, Leisha. He's had another heart attack."

Susan Melling's voice on the phone was tired. Leisha said, "How bad?"

"The doctors aren't sure. Or say they're not sure. He wants to see you. Can you leave your studies?"

It was May, the last push toward her finals. The *Law Review* proofs were behind schedule. Richard had started a new business, marine consulting to Boston fishermen plagued with sudden inexplicable shifts in ocean currents, and was working twenty hours a day. "I'll come," Leisha said.

Chicago was colder than Boston. The trees were half-budded. On Lake Michigan, filling the huge east windows of her father's house, whitecaps tossed up cold spray. Leisha saw that Susan was living in the house; her brushes were on Camden's dresser, her journals on the cre-denza in the foyer.

"Leisha," Camden said. He looked old. Gray skin, sunken cheeks, the fretful and bewildered look of men who accepted potency like air, indivisible from their lives. In the corner of the room, on a small eighteenth-century slipper chair, sat a short, stocky woman with brown braids.

"*Alice.*"

"Hello, Leisha."

"*Alice.* I've looked for you. . . ." The wrong thing to say. Leisha had looked, but not very hard, deterred by the knowledge that Alice had not wanted to be found. "How are you?"

"I'm fine," Alice said. She seemed remote, gentle, unlike the angry Alice of six years ago in the raw Pennsylvania hills. Camden moved painfully on the bed. He looked at Leisha with eyes which, she saw, were undimmed in their blue brightness.

"I asked Alice to come. And Susan. Susan came a while ago. I'm dying, Leisha."

No one contradicted him. Leisha, knowing his respect for facts, remained silent. Love hurt her chest.

"John Jaworski has my will. None of you can break it. But I wanted to tell you myself what's in it. The past few years I've been selling, liquidating. Most of my holdings are accessible now. I've left a tenth to Alice, a tenth to Susan, a tenth to Elizabeth, and the rest to you, Leisha, because you're the only one with the individual ability to use the money to its full potential for achievement."

Leisha looked wildly at Alice, who gazed back with her strange remote calm. "Elizabeth? My . . . mother? Is alive?"

"Yes," Camden said.

"You told me she was dead! Years and years ago!"

"Yes. I thought it was better for you that way. She didn't like what you were, was jealous of what you could become. And she had nothing to give you. She would only have caused you emotional harm."

Beggars in Spain . . .

"That was wrong, Daddy. You were *wrong*. She's my mother . . ." She couldn't finish the sentence.

Camden didn't flinch. "I don't think I was. But you're an adult now. You can see her if you wish."

He went on looking at her with his bright, sunken eyes, while around Leisha the air heaved and snapped. Her father had lied to her. Susan watched her closely, a small smile on her lips. Was she glad to see Camden fall in his daughter's estimation? Had she all along been that jealous of their relationship, of Leisha. . . .

She was thinking like Tony.

The thought steadied her a little. But she went on staring at Camden, who went on staring back implacably, unbudged, a man positive even on his deathbed that he was right.

Alice's hand was on her elbow, Alice's voice so soft that no one but Leisha could hear. "He's done talking now, Leisha. And after a while you'll be all right."

Alice had left her son in California with her husband of two years, Beck Watrous, a building contractor she had met while waiting on tables in a resort on the Artificial Islands. Beck had adopted Jordan, Alice's son.

"Before Beck there was a real bad time," Alice said in her remote voice. "You know, when I was carrying Jordan I actually used to dream that he would be Sleepless? Like you. Every night I'd dream that, and every morning I'd wake up and have morning sickness with a baby that was only going to be a stupid nothing like me. I stayed with Ed—in the Appalachian Mountains, remember? You came to see me there once— for two more years. When he beat me, I was glad. I wished Daddy could see. At least Ed was touching me."

Leisha made a sound in her throat.

"I finally left because I was afraid for Jordan. I went to California, did nothing but eat for a year. I got up to 190 pounds." Alice was, Leisha estimated, five-foot-four. "Then I came home to see Mother."

"You didn't tell me," Leisha said. "You knew she was alive and you didn't tell me."

"She's in a drying-out tank half the time," Alice said, with brutal simplicity. "She wouldn't see you if you wanted to. But she saw me, and she fell slobbering all over me as her 'real' daughter, and she threw up on my dress. And I backed away from her and looked at the dress and knew it *should* be thrown up on, it was so ugly. Deliberately ugly. She

started screaming how Dad had ruined her life, ruined mine, all for
you. And do you know what I did?"

"What?" Leisha said. Her voice was shaky.

"I flew home, burned all my clothes, got a job, started college, lost
fifty pounds, and put Jordan in play therapy."

The sisters sat silent. Beyond the window the lake was dark, unlit by
moon or stars. It was Leisha who suddenly shook, and Alice who patted
her shoulder.

"Tell me . . ." Leisha couldn't think what she wanted to be told, except that she wanted to hear Alice's voice in the gloom, Alice's voice as
it was now, gentle and remote, without damage any more from the
damaging fact of Leisha's existence. Her very existence as damage.
"Tell me about Jordan. He's five now? What's he like?"

Alice turned her head to look levelly into Leisha's eyes. "He's a
happy, ordinary little boy. Completely ordinary."

Camden died a week later. After the funeral, Leisha tried to see her
mother at the Brookfield Drug and Alcohol Abuse Center. Elizabeth
Camden, she was told, saw no one except her only child, Alice Camden
Watrous.

Susan Melling, dressed in black, drove Leisha to the airport. Susan
talked deftly, determinedly, about Leisha's studies, about Harvard,
about the *Law Review*. Leisha answered in monosyllables, but Susan
persisted, asking questions, quietly insisting on answers: When would
Leisha take her bar exams? Where was she interviewing for jobs?
Gradually Leisha began to lose the numbness she had felt since her father's casket was lowered into the ground. She realized that Susan's
persistent questioning was a kindness.

"He sacrificed a lot of people," Leisha said suddenly.

"Not me," Susan said. "Only for a while there, when I gave up my
work to do his. Roger didn't respect sacrifice much."

"Was he wrong?" Leisha said. The question came out with a kind of
desperation she hadn't intended.

Susan smiled sadly. "No. He wasn't wrong. I should never have left my research. It took me a long time to come back to myself after that."

He does that to people, Leisha heard inside her head. Susan? Or Alice? She couldn't, for once, remember clearly. She saw her father in the old conservatory, now empty, potting and repotting the exotic flowers he had loved.

She was tired. It was muscle fatigue from stress, she knew; twenty minutes of rest would restore her. Her eyes burned from unaccustomed tears. She leaned her head back against the car seat and closed her eyes.

Susan pulled the car into the airport parking lot and turned off the ignition. "There's something I want to tell you, Leisha."

Leisha opened her eyes. "About the will?"

Susan smiled tightly. "No. You really don't have any problems with how he divided the estate, do you? It seems reasonable to you. But that's not it. The research team from Biotech and Chicago Medical has finished its analysis of Bernie Kuhn's brain."

Leisha turned to face Susan. She was startled by the complexity of Susan's expression. It held determination, and satisfaction, and anger, and something else Leisha could not name.

Susan said, "We're going to publish next week, in the *New England Journal of Medicine.* Security has been unbelievably restricted—no leaks to the popular press. But I want to tell you now, myself, what we found. So you'll be prepared."

"Go on," Leisha said. Her chest felt tight.

"Do you remember when you and the other Sleepless kids took interleukin-1 to see what sleep was like? When you were sixteen?"

"How did you know about that?"

"You kids were watched a lot more closely than you think. Remember the headache you got?"

"Yes." She and Richard and Tony and Carol and Brad and Jeanine . . . after her rejection by the Olympic Committee, Jeanine had never skated again. She was a kindergarten teacher in Butte, Montana.

"Interleukin-1 is what I want to talk about. At least partly. It's one of a whole group of substances that boost the immune system. They stimulate the production of antibodies, the activity of white blood cells, and a host of other immunoenhancements. Normal people have surges of IL-1 released during the slow-wave phases of sleep. That means that they—we—are getting boosts to the immune system during sleep. One of the questions we researchers asked ourselves twenty-eight years ago was: will Sleepless kids who don't get those surges of IL-1 get sick more often?"

"I've never been sick," Leisha said.

"Yes, you have. Chicken pox and three minor colds by the end of your fourth year," Susan said precisely. "But in general you were all a very healthy lot. So we researchers were left with the alternate theory of sleep-driven immunoenhancement: that the burst of immune activity existed as a counterpart to a greater vulnerability of the body in sleep to disease, probably in some way connected to the fluctuations in body temperature during REM sleep. In other words, sleep *caused* the immune vulnerability that endogenous pyrogens like IL-1 counteracted. Sleep was the problem, immune-system enhancements were the solution. Without sleep, there would be no problem. Are you following this?"

"Yes."

"Of course you are. Stupid question." Susan brushed her hair off her face. It was going gray at the temples. There was a tiny brown age spot beneath her right ear.

"Over the years we collected thousands, maybe hundreds of thousands, of Single Photon Emission Tomography scans of you kids' brains, plus endless EEG's, samples of cerebrospinal fluid, and all the rest of it. But we couldn't really see inside your brains, really know what's going on in there. Until Bernie Kuhn hit that embankment."

"Susan," Leisha said, "give it to me straight. Without more buildup."

"You're not going to age."

"What?"

"Oh, cosmetically, a little—sagging due to gravity, maybe. But the absence of sleep peptides and all the rest of it affects the immune and tissue-restoration systems in ways we don't understand. Bernie Kuhn had a perfect liver. Perfect lungs, perfect heart, perfect lymph nodes, perfect pancreas, perfect medulla oblongata. Not just healthy, or young—*perfect*. There's a tissue regeneration enhancement that clearly derives from the operation of the immune system but is radically different from anything we ever suspected. Organs show no wear and tear, not even the minimal amount expected in a seventeen-year-old. They just repair themselves, perfectly, on and on . . . and on."

"For how long?" Leisha whispered.

"Who the hell knows? Bernie Kuhn was young. Maybe there's some compensatory mechanism that cuts in at some point and you'll all just collapse, like an entire fucking gallery of Dorian Grays. But I don't think so. Neither do I think it can go on forever; no tissue regeneration can do that. But a long, long time."

Leisha stared at the blurred reflections in the car windshield. She saw her father's face against the blue satin of his casket, banked with white roses. His heart, unregenerated, had given out.

Susan said, "The future is all speculative at this point. We know that the peptide structures that build up the pressure to sleep in normal people resemble the components of bacterial cell walls. Maybe there's a connection between sleep and pathogen receptivity. We don't know. But ignorance never stopped the tabloids. I wanted to prepare you because you're going to get called supermen, *homo perfectus*, who-all-knows what. Immortal."

The two women sat in silence. Finally Leisha said, "I'm going to tell the others. On our datanet. Don't worry about the security. Kevin Baker designed Groupnet; nobody knows anything we don't want them to."

"You're that well organized already?"

"Yes."

Susan's mouth worked. She looked away from Leisha. "We better go in. You'll miss your flight."

"Susan . . ."

"What?"

"Thank you."

"You're welcome," Susan said, and in her voice Leisha heard the thing she had seen before in Susan's expression and had not been able to name: it was longing.

Tissue regeneration. A long, long time, sang the blood in Leisha's ears on the flight to Boston. *Tissue regeneration*. And, eventually: *immortal*. No, not that, she told herself severely. Not that. The blood didn't listen.

"You sure smile a lot," said the man next to her in first class, a business traveler who had not recognized Leisha. "You coming from a big party in Chicago?"

"No. From a funeral."

The man looked shocked, then disgusted. Leisha looked out the window at the ground far below. Rivers like micro-circuits, fields like neat index cards. And on the horizon, fluffy white clouds like masses of exotic flowers, blooms in a conservatory filled with light.

The letter was no thicker than any hard-copy mail, but hard-copy mail addressed by hand to either of them was so rare that Richard was nervous. "It might be explosive." Leisha looked at the letter on their hall credenza. MS. LIESHA CAMDEN. Block letters, misspelled.

"It looks like a child's writing," she said.

Richard stood with head lowered, legs braced apart. But his expression was only weary. "Perhaps deliberately like a child's. You'd be more open to a child's writing, they might have figured."

" 'They'? Richard, are we getting that paranoid?"

He didn't flinch from the question. "Yes. For the time being."

A week earlier the *New England Journal of Medicine* had published Susan's careful, sober article. An hour later the broadcast and datanet news had exploded in speculation, drama, outrage, and fear. Leisha and Richard, along with all the Sleepless on the Groupnet, had tracked and charted each of four components, looking for a dominant reaction: speculation ("The Sleepless may live for centuries, and this might lead to the following events. . . ."); drama ("If a Sleepless marries only Sleepers, he may have lifetime enough for a dozen brides, and several dozen children, a bewildering blended family. . . ."); outrage ("Tampering with the law of nature has only brought among us unnatural so-called people who will live with the unfair advantage of time: time to accumulate more kin, more power, more property than the rest of us could ever know. . . ."); and fear ("How soon before the Super-race takes over?").

"They're all fear, of one kind or another," Carolyn Rizzolo finally said, and the Groupnet stopped its differentiated tracking.

Leisha was taking the final exams of her last year of law school. Each day comments followed her to the campus, along the corridors and in the classroom; each day she forgot them in the grueling exam sessions, in which all students were reduced to the same status of petitioner to the great university. Afterward, temporarily drained, she walked silently back home to Richard and the Groupnet, aware of the looks of people on the street, aware of her bodyguard Bruce striding between her and them.

"It will calm down," Leisha said. Richard didn't answer.

The town of Salt Springs, Texas, passed a local ordinance that no Sleepless could obtain a liquor license, on the grounds that civil rights statutes were built on the "all men were created equal" clause of the Declaration of Independence, and Sleepless clearly were not covered. There were no Sleepless within a hundred miles of Salt Springs and no one had applied for a new liquor license there for the past ten years, but the story was picked up by United Press and by Datanet News, and within 24 hours heated editorials appeared, on both sides of the issue, across the nation.

More local ordinances were passed. In Pollux, Pennsylvania, the Sleepless could be denied an apartment rental on the grounds that their prolonged wakefulness would increase both wear-and-tear on the landlord's property and utility bills. In Cranston Estates, California, Sleepless were barred from operating 24-hour businesses: "unfair competition." Iroquois County, New York, barred them from serving on county juries, arguing that a jury containing Sleepless, with their skewed idea of time, did not constitute "a jury of one's peers."

"All those statutes will be thrown out in superior courts," Leisha said. "But God! The waste of money and docket time to do it!" A part of her mind noticed that her tone as she said this was Roger Camden's.

The state of Georgia, in which some sex acts between consenting adults were still a crime, made sex between a Sleepless and a Sleeper a third-degree felony, classing it with bestiality.

Kevin Baker had designed software that scanned the newsnets at high speed, flagged all stories involving discrimination or attacks on Sleepless, and categorized them by type. The files were available on Groupnet. Leisha read through them, then called Kevin. "Can't you create a parallel program to flag defenses of us? We're getting a skewed picture."

"You're right," Kevin said, a little startled. "I didn't think of it."

"Think of it," Leisha said, grimly. Richard, watching her, said nothing.

She was most upset by the stories about Sleepless children. Shunning at school, verbal abuse by siblings, attacks by neighborhood bullies, confused resentment from parents who had wanted an exceptional child but had not bargained for one who might live centuries. The school board of Cold River, Iowa, voted to bar Sleepless children from conventional classrooms because their rapid learning "created feelings of inadequacy in others, interfering with their education." The board made funds available for Sleepless to have tutors at home. There were no volunteers among the teaching staff. Leisha started spending as much time on Groupnet with the kids, talking to them all night long, as she did studying for her bar exams, scheduled for July.

Stella Bevington stopped using her modem.

Kevin's second program cataloged editorials urging fairness toward Sleepless. The school board of Denver set aside funds for a program in which gifted children, including the Sleepless, could use their talents and build teamwork through tutoring even younger children. Rive Beau, Louisiana, elected Sleepless Danielle du Cherney to the City Council, although Danielle was twenty-two and technically too young to qualify. The prestigious medical research firm of Halley-Hall gave much publicity to their hiring of Christopher Amren, a Sleepless with a Ph.D. in cellular physics.

Dora Clarq, a Sleepless in Dallas, opened a letter addressed to her and a plastic explosive blew off her arm.

Leisha and Richard stared at the envelope on the hall credenza. The paper was thick, cream-colored, but not expensive, the kind of paper made of bulky newsprint dyed the shades of vellum. There was no return address. Richard called Liz Bishop, a Sleepless who was majoring in criminal justice in Michigan. He had never spoken with her before—neither had Leisha—but she came on the Groupnet immediately and told them how to open it. Or, she could fly up and do it if they preferred. Richard and Leisha followed her directions for remote detonation in the basement of the townhouse. Nothing blew up. When the letter was open, they took it out and read it:

Dear Ms. Camden,

You been pretty good to me and I'm sorry to do this but I quit. They are making it pretty hot for me at the union not officially but you know how it is. If I was you I wouldn't go to the union for another bodyguard I'd try to find one privately. But be careful. Again I'm sorry but I have to live too.

Bruce

"I don't know whether to laugh or cry," Leisha said. "The two of us getting all this equipment, spending hours on this setup so an explosive won't detonate . . ."

"It's not as if I at least had a whole lot else to do," Richard said. Since the wave of antiSleepless sentiment, all but two of his marine-consulting clients, vulnerable to the marketplace and thus to public opinion, had canceled their accounts.

Groupnet, still up on Leisha's terminal, shrilled in emergency override. Leisha got there first. It was Tony Indivino.

"Leisha. I need your legal help, if you'll give it. They're trying to fight me on Sanctuary. Please fly down here."

*   *   *

Sanctuary was raw brown gashes in the late-spring earth. It was situated in the Allegheny Mountains of southern New York State, old hills rounded by age and covered with pine and hickory. A superb road led from the closest town, Conewango, to Sanctuary. Low, maintenance-free buildings, whose design was plain but graceful, stood in various stages of completion. Jennifer Sharifi, unsmiling, met Leisha and Richard. She hadn't changed much in six years but her long black hair was uncombed and her dark eyes enormous with strain. "Tony wants to talk to you, but first he asked me to show you both around."

"What's wrong?" Leisha asked quietly.

Jennifer didn't try to evade the question. "Later. First look at Sanctuary. Tony respects your opinion enormously, Leisha; he wants you to see everything."

The dormitories each held fifty, with communal rooms for cooking, dining, relaxing, and bathing, and a warren of separate offices and studios and labs for work. "We're calling them 'dorms' anyway, despite the etymology," Jennifer said, and even in this remark, which from anybody else would have been playful, Leisha heard the peculiar combination of Jennifer's habitual deliberate calm with her present strain.

She was impressed, despite herself, with the completeness of Tony's plans for lives that would be both communal and intensely private. There was a gym, a small hospital—"By the end of next year, we'll have eighteen AMA-certified doctors, you know, and four of them are thinking of coming here"—a daycare facility, a school, and an intensive-crop farm. "Most of the food will come in from the outside, of course. So will most people's jobs, although they'll do as much of them as possible from here, over datanets. We're not cutting ourselves off from the world, only creating a safe place from which to trade with it." Leisha didn't answer.

Apart from the power facilities, self-supported Y-energy, she was most impressed with the human planning. Tony had interested

Sleepless from virtually every field they would need both to care for themselves and to deal with the outside world. "Lawyers and accountants come first," Jennifer said. "That's our first line of defense in safeguarding ourselves. Tony recognizes that most modern battles for power are fought in the courtroom and boardroom."

But not all. Last, Jennifer showed them the plans for physical defense. For the first time, her taut body seemed to relax slightly.

Every effort had been made to stop attackers without hurting them. Electronic surveillance completely circled the 150 square miles Jennifer had purchased. Some *counties* were smaller than that, Leisha thought, dazed. When breached, a force field a half-mile within the E-gate activated, delivering electric shocks to anyone on foot—"but only on the *outside* of the field. We don't want any of our kids hurt," Jennifer said. Unmanned penetration by vehicles or robots was identified by a system that located all moving metal above a certain mass within Sanctuary. Any moving metal that did not carry a special signaling device designed by Donald Pospula, a Sleepless who had patented important electronic components, was suspect.

"Of course, we're not set up for an air attack or an outright army assault," Jennifer said. "But we don't expect that. Only the haters in self-motivated hate."

Leisha touched the hard-copy of the security plans with one finger. They troubled her. "If we can't integrate ourselves into the world . . . Free trade should imply free movement."

Jennifer said swiftly, "Only if free movement implies free minds," and at her tone Leisha looked up. "I have something to tell you, Leisha."

"What?"

"Tony isn't here."

"Where is he?"

"In Cattaraugus County jail in Conewango. It's true we're having zoning battles about Sanctuary—zoning! In this isolated spot! But this is something else, something that just happened this morning. Tony's been arrested for the kidnapping of Timmy DeMarzo."

The room wavered. "FBI?"

"Yes."

"How . . . how did they find out?"

"Some agent eventually cracked the case. They didn't tell us how. Tony needs a lawyer, Leisha. Bill Thaine has already agreed, but Tony wants you."

"Jennifer—I don't even take the bar exams until July!"

"He says he'll wait. Bill will act as his lawyer in the meantime. Will you pass the bar?"

"Of course. But I already have a job lined up with Morehouse, Kennedy & Anderson in New York . . ." She stopped. Richard was looking at her hard, Jennifer inscrutably. Leisha said quietly, "What will he plead?"

"Guilty," Jennifer said, "with—what is it called legally? Extenuating circumstances."

Leisha nodded. She had been afraid Tony would want to plead not guilty: more lies, subterfuge, ugly politics. Her mind ran swiftly over extenuating circumstances, precedents, tests to precedents. . . . They could use *Clements* v. *Voy.* . . .

"Bill is at the jail now," Jennifer said. "Will you drive in with me?" She made the question a challenge.

"Yes," Leisha said.

In Conewango, the county seat, they were not allowed to see Tony. William Thaine, as his attorney, could go in and out freely. Leisha, not officially an attorney at all, could go nowhere. This was told to them by a man in the D.A.'s office whose face stayed immobile while he spoke to them, and who spat on the ground behind their shoes when they turned to leave, even though this left him with a smear of spittle on his court-house floor.

Richard and Leisha drove their rental car to the airport for the flight back to Boston. On the way Richard told Leisha he was leaving. He was moving to Sanctuary, now, even before it was functional, to help with the planning and building.

*   *   *

She stayed most of the time in her townhouse, studying ferociously for the bar exams or checking on the Sleepless children through Groupnet. She had not hired another bodyguard to replace Bruce, which made her reluctant to go outside very much; the reluctance in turn made her angry with herself. Once or twice a day she scanned Kevin's electronic news clippings.

There were signs of hope. The *New York Times* ran an editorial, widely reprinted on the electronic news services:

PROSPERITY AND HATRED:
A LOGIC CURVE WE'D RATHER NOT SEE

The United States has never been a country that much values calm, logic, and rationality. We have, as a people, tended to label these things "cold." We have, as a people, tended to admire feeling and action. We exalt in our stories and our memorials—not the creation of the Constitution but its defense at Iwo Jima; not the intellectual achievements of a Linus Pauling but the heroic passion of a Charles Lindbergh; not the inventors of the monorails and computers that unite us but the composers of the angry songs of rebellion that divide us.

A peculiar aspect of this phenomenon is that it grows stronger in times of prosperity. The better off our citizenry, the greater their contempt for the calm reasoning that got them there, and the more passionate their indulgence in emotion. Consider, in the past century, the gaudy excesses of the roaring twenties and the antiestablishment contempt of the sixties. Consider, in our own century, the unprecedented prosperity brought about by Y-energy—and then consider that Kenzo Yagai, except to his followers, was seen as a greedy and bloodless logician, while our national adulation goes to neo-nihilist writer Stephen Castelli, to "feelie" actress Brenda Foss, and to daredevil gravity-well diver Jim Morse Luter.

But most of all, as you ponder this phenomenon in your Y-energy houses, consider the current outpouring of irrational feeling directed at the "Sleepless" since the publication of the joint findings of the Biotech Institute and the Chicago Medical School concerning Sleepless tissue regeneration.

Most of the Sleepless are intelligent. Most of them are calm, if you define that much-maligned word to mean directing one's energies into solving problems rather than to emoting about them. (Even Pulitzer Prize winner Carolyn Rizzolo gave us a stunning play of ideas, not of passions run amuck.) All of them show a natural bent toward achievement, a bent given a decided boost by the one-third more time in their days to achieve. Their achievements lie, for the most part, in logical fields rather than emotional ones: Computers. Law. Finance. Physics. Medical research. They are rational, orderly, calm, intelligent, cheerful, young, and possibly very long-lived.

And, in our United States of unprecedented prosperity, they are increasingly hated.

Does the hatred that we have seen flower so fully over the past few months really grow, as many claim, from the "unfair advantage" the Sleepless have over the rest of us in securing jobs, promotions, money, and success? Is it really envy over the Sleepless' good fortune? Or does it come from something more pernicious, rooted in our tradition of shoot-from-the-hip American action: hatred of the logical, the calm, the considered? Hatred in fact of the superior mind?

If so, perhaps we should think deeply about the founders of this country: Jefferson, Washington, Paine, Adams—inhabitants of the Age of Reason, all. These men created our orderly and balanced system of laws precisely to protect the property and achievements created by the individual efforts of balanced and rational minds. The Sleepless may be our severest internal test yet of our own sober belief in law and order. No, the Sleepless were not "created equal," but our attitudes toward them should be examined with a care equal to our soberest jurisprudence. We may not like what we learn about our own motives, but our credibility as a people may depend on the rationality and intelligence of the examination.

Both have been in short supply in the public reaction to last month's research findings.

Law is not theater. Before we write laws reflecting gaudy and dramatic feelings, we must be very sure we understand the difference.

Leisha hugged herself, gazing in delight at the screen, smiling. She called the *New York Times* and asked who had written the editorial. The receptionist, cordial when she answered the phone, grew brusque. The *Times* was not releasing that information, "prior to internal investigation."

It could not dampen her mood. She whirled around the apartment, after days of sitting at her desk or screen: Delight demanded physical action. She washed dishes, picked up books. There were gaps in the furniture patterns where Richard had taken pieces that belonged to him; a little quieter now, she moved the furniture to close the gaps.

Susan Melling called to tell her about the *Times* editorial; they talked warmly for a few minutes. When Susan hung up, the phone rang again.

"Leisha? Your voice still sounds the same. This is Stewart Sutter."

"Stewart." She had not seen him for four years. Their romance had lasted two years and then dissolved, not from any painful issue so much as from the press of both their studies. Standing by the comm terminal, hearing his voice, Leisha suddenly felt again his hands on her breasts in the cramped dormitory bed: All those years before she had found a good use for a bed. The phantom hands became Richard's hands, and a sudden pain pierced her.

"Listen," Stewart said, "I'm calling because there's some information I think you should know. You take your bar exams next week, right? And then you have a tentative job with Morehouse, Kennedy & Anderson."

"How do you know all that, Stewart?"

"Men's room gossip. Well, not as bad as that. But the New York legal community—that part of it, anyway—is smaller than you think. And you're a pretty visible figure."

"Yes," Leisha said neutrally.

"Nobody has the slightest doubt you'll be called to the bar. But there is some doubt about the job with Morehouse, Kennedy. You've got two senior partners, Alan Morehouse and Seth Brown, who have changed their minds since this . . . flap. 'Adverse publicity for the firm,' 'turning law into a circus,' blah blah blah. You know the drill. But you've also got two powerful champions, Ann Carlyle and Michael Kennedy, the old man himself. He's quite a mind. Anyway, I wanted you to know all this so you can recognize exactly what the situation is and know whom to count on in the infighting."

"Thank you," Leisha said. "Stew . . . why do you care if I get it or not? Why should it matter to you?"

There was a silence on the other end of the phone. Then Stewart said, very low, "We're not all noodleheads out here, Leisha. Justice does still matter to some of us. So does achievement."

Light rose in her, a bubble of buoyant light.

Stewart said, "You have a lot of support here for that stupid zoning fight over Sanctuary, too. You might not realize that, but you do. What the Parks Commission crowd is trying to pull is . . . but they're just being used as fronts. You know that. Anyway, when it gets as far as the courts, you'll have all the help you need."

"Sanctuary isn't my doing. At all."

"No? Well, I meant the plural you."

"Thank you. I mean that. How are you doing?"

"Fine. I'm a daddy now."

"Really! Boy or girl?"

"Girl. A beautiful little bitch named Justine, drives me crazy. I'd like you to meet my wife sometime, Leisha."

"I'd like that," Leisha said.

She spent the rest of the night studying for her bar exams. The bubble stayed with her. She recognized exactly what it was: joy.

It was going to be all right. The contract, unwritten, between her and her society—Kenzo Yagai's society, Roger Camden's society—would hold. With dissent and strife and yes, some hatred. She suddenly thought of Tony's beggars in Spain, furious at the strong because the beggars were not. Yes. But it would hold.

She believed that.

She did.

7

L eisha took her bar exams in July. They did not seem hard to her. Afterward three classmates, two men and a woman, made a fakely casual point of talking to Leisha until she had climbed safely into a taxi whose driver obviously did not recognize her, or stop signs. The three were all Sleepers. A pair of undergraduates, cleanshaven blond men with the long faces and pointless arrogance of rich stupidity, eyed Leisha and sneered. Leisha's female classmate sneered back.

Leisha had a flight to Chicago the next morning. Alice was going to join her there. They had to clean out the big house on the lake, dispose of Roger's personal property, put the house on the market. Leisha had had no time to do it earlier.

She remembered her father in the conservatory, wearing an ancient flat-topped hat he had picked up somewhere, potting orchids and jasmine and passion flowers.

When the doorbell rang she was startled; she almost never had visitors. Eagerly, she turned on the outside camera—maybe it was Jonathan or Martha, back in Boston to surprise her, to celebrate—why hadn't she thought before about some sort of celebration?

Richard stood gazing up at the camera. He had been crying.

She tore open the door. Richard made no move to come in. Leisha saw that what the camera had registered as grief was actually something else: tears of rage.

"Tony's dead."

Leisha put out her hand, blindly. Richard didn't take it.

"They killed him in prison. Not the authorities—the other prisoners. In the recreation yard. Murderers, rapists, looters, scum of the earth— and they thought they had the right to kill *him* because he was different."

Now Richard did grab her arm, so hard that something, some bone, shifted beneath the flesh and pressed on a nerve. "Not just different— *better*. Because he was better, because we all are, we goddamn just don't stand up and shout it out of some misplaced feeling for *their* feelings . . . God!"

Leisha pulled her arm free and rubbed it, numb, staring at Richard's contorted face.

"They beat him to death with a lead pipe. No one even knows how they got a lead pipe. They beat him on the back of the head and then they rolled him over and—"

"Don't!" Leisha said. It came out a whimper.

Richard looked at her. Despite his shouting, his violent grip on her arm, Leisha had the confused impression that this was the first time he had actually seen her. She went on rubbing her arm, staring at him in terror.

He said quietly, "I've come to take you to Sanctuary, Leisha. Dan Jenkins and Vernon Bulriss are in the car outside. The three of us will carry you out, if necessary. But you're coming. You see that, don't you? You're not safe here, with your high profile and your spectacular looks. You're a natural target if anyone is. Do we have to force you? Or do you finally see for yourself that we have no choice—the bastards have left us no choice—except Sanctuary?"

Leisha closed her eyes. Tony, at fourteen, at the beach. Tony, his eyes ferocious and shining, the first to reach out his hand for the glass of interleukin-1. Beggars in Spain.

"I'll come."

*   *   *

She had never known such anger. It scared her, coming in bouts throughout the long night, receding but always returning again. Richard held her in his arms, sitting with their backs against the wall of her library, and his holding made no difference at all. In the living room Dan and Vernon talked in low voices.

Sometimes the anger erupted in shouting, and Leisha heard herself and thought, *I don't know you.* Sometimes it became crying, sometimes talking about Tony, about all of them. Neither the shouting nor the crying nor the talking eased her at all.

Planning did, a little. In a cold, dry voice she didn't recognize, Leisha told Richard about the trip to close the house in Chicago. She had to go; Alice was already there. If Richard and Dan and Vernon put Leisha on the plane, and Alice met her at the other end with union bodyguards, she should be safe enough. Then she would change her return ticket from Boston to Conewango and drive with Richard to Sanctuary.

"People are already arriving," Richard said. "Jennifer Sharifi is organizing it, greasing the Sleeper suppliers with so much money they can't resist. What about this townhouse here, Leisha? Your furniture and terminal and clothes?"

Leisha looked around her familiar office. Law books, red and green and brown, lined the walls although most of the same information was on-line. A coffee cup rested on a printout on the desk. Beside it was the receipt she had requested from the taxi driver this afternoon, a giddy souvenir of the day she had passed her bar exams; she had thought of having it framed. Above the desk was a holographic portrait of Kenzo Yagai.

"Let it rot," Leisha said.

Richard's arm tightened around her.

"I've never seen you like this," Alice said, subdued. "It's more than just clearing out the house, isn't it?"

"Let's get on with it," Leisha said. She yanked a suit from her father's closet. "Do you want any of this stuff for your husband?"

"It wouldn't fit."

"The hats?"

"No," Alice said. "Leisha—what is it?"

"Let's just *do* it!" She yanked all the clothes from Camden's closet, piled them on the floor, scrawled, FOR VOLUNTEER AGENCY on a piece of paper and dropped it on top of the pile. Silently, Alice started adding clothes from the dresser, which already bore a taped paper scrawled, ESTATE AUCTION.

The curtains were already down throughout the house; Alice had done that yesterday. She had also rolled up the rugs. Sunset glared red on the bare wooden floors.

"What about your old room?" Leisha said. "What do you want there?"

"I've already tagged it," Alice said. "A mover will come Thursday."

"Fine. What else?"

"The conservatory. Sanderson has been watering everything, but he didn't really know what needed how much, so some of the plants are—"

"Fire Sanderson," Leisha said curtly. "The exotics can die. Or have them sent to a hospital, if you'd rather. Just watch out for the ones that are poisonous. Come on, let's do the library."

Alice sat slowly on a rolled-up rug in the middle of Camden's bedroom. She had cut her hair; Leisha thought it looked ugly, like jagged brown spikes around her broad face. She had also gained more weight. She was starting to look like their mother.

Alice said, "Do you remember the night I told you I was pregnant? Just before you left for Harvard?"

"Let's do the library!"

"Do you?" Alice said. "For God's sake, can't you just once listen to someone else, Leisha? Do you have to be so much like Daddy every single minute?"

"I'm not Daddy!"

"The hell you're not. You're exactly what he made you. But that's not the point. Do you remember that night?"

Leisha walked over the rug and out the door. Alice simply sat. After a minute Leisha walked back in. "I remember."

"You were near tears," Alice said implacably. Her voice was quiet. "I don't even remember exactly why. Maybe because I wasn't going to college after all. But I put my arms around you, and for the first time in years—years, Leisha—I felt you really were my sister. Despite all of it—the roaming the halls all night and the showoff arguments with Daddy and the special school and the artificially long legs and golden hair—all that crap. You seemed to need me to hold you. You seemed to need me. You seemed to *need*."

"What are you saying?" Leisha demanded. "That you can only be close to someone if they're in trouble and need you? That you can only be a sister if I was in some kind of pain, open sores running? Is that the bond between you Sleepers? 'Protect me while I'm unconscious, I'm just as crippled as you are'?"

"No," Alice said. "I'm saying that *you* could be a sister only if you were in some kind of pain."

Leisha stared at her. "You're stupid, Alice."

Alice said calmly, "I know that. Compared to you, I am. I know that."

Leisha jerked her head angrily. She felt ashamed of what she had just said, and yet it was true, and they both knew it was true, and anger still lay in her like a dark void, formless and hot. It was the formless part that was the worst. Without shape, there could be no action; without action, the anger went on burning her, choking her.

Alice said, "When I was twelve Susan gave me a dress for our birthday. You were away somewhere, on one of those overnight field trips your fancy progressive school did all the time. The dress was silk, pale blue, with antique lace—very beautiful. I was thrilled, not only because it was beautiful but because Susan had gotten it for me and gotten software for you. The dress was mine. Was, I thought, *me.*" In the gathering gloom

Leisha could barely make out her broad, plain features. "The first time I wore it a boy said, 'Stole your sister's dress, Alice? Snitched it while she was *sleeping*?' Then he laughed like crazy, the way they always did.

"I threw the dress away. I didn't even explain to Susan, although I think she would have understood. Whatever was yours was yours, and whatever wasn't yours was yours, too. That's the way Daddy set it up. The way he hard-wired it into our genes."

"You, too?" Leisha said. "You're no different from the other envious beggars?"

Alice stood up from the rug. She did it slowly, leisurely, brushing dust off the back of her wrinkled skirt, smoothing the print fabric. Then she walked over and hit Leisha in the mouth.

"Now do you see me as real?" Alice asked quietly.

Leisha put her hand to her mouth. She felt blood. The phone rang, Camden's unlisted personal line. Alice walked over, picked it up, listened, and held it calmly out to Leisha. "It's for you."

Numb, Leisha took it.

"Leisha? This is Kevin. Listen, something's happened. Stella Bevington called me, on the phone, not Groupnet; I think her parents took away her modem. I picked up the phone and she screamed, 'This is Stella! They're hitting me, he's drunk—' and then the line went dead. Randy's gone to Sanctuary—hell, they've *all* gone. You're closest to her, she's still in Skokie. You better get there fast. Have you got bodyguards you trust?"

"Yes," Leisha said, although she hadn't. The anger, finally, took form. "I can handle it."

"I don't know how you'll get her out of there," Kevin said. "They'll recognize you, they know she called somebody, they might even have knocked her out. . . ."

"I'll handle it," Leisha said.

"Handle what?" Alice said.

Leisha faced her. Even though she knew she shouldn't, she said, "What your people do. To one of ours. A seven-year-old kid who's getting beaten by her parents because she's Sleepless—because she's *better* than you are—" She ran down the stairs and out to the rental car she had driven from the airport.

Alice ran right down with her. "Not your car, Leisha. They can trace a rental car just like that. My car."

Leisha screamed, "If you think you're—"

Alice yanked open the door of her battered Toyota, a model so old the Y-energy cones weren't even concealed but hung like drooping jowls on either side. She shoved Leisha into the passenger seat, slammed the door, and rammed herself behind the wheel. Her hands were steady. "Where?"

Blackness swooped over Leisha. She put her head down, as far between her knees as the cramped Toyota would allow. It had been two—no, three—days since she had eaten. Not since the night before the bar exams. The faintness receded, swept over her again as soon as she raised her head.

She told Alice the address in Skokie.

"Stay way in the back," Alice said. "And there's a scarf in the glove compartment—put it on. Low, to hide as much of your face as possible."

Alice had stopped the car along Highway 42. Leisha said, "This isn't—"

"It's a quick-guard place. We have to look like we have some protection, Leisha. We don't need to tell him anything. I'll hurry."

She was out in three minutes with a huge man in a cheap dark suit. He squeezed into the front seat beside Alice and said nothing at all. Alice did not introduce him.

The house was small, a little shabby, with lights on downstairs, none upstairs. The first stars shone in the north, away from Chicago. Alice said to the guard, "Get out of the car and stand here by the car door—no, more in the light—and don't do anything unless I'm attacked in some way." The man nodded. Alice started up the walk. Leisha scrambled out of the back seat and caught her sister two-thirds of the way to the plastic front door.

"Alice, what the hell are you doing? *I* have to—"

"Keep your voice down," Alice said, glancing at the guard. "Leisha, *think*. You'll be recognized. Here, near Chicago, with a Sleepless daughter—these people have looked at your picture in magazines for years. They've watched long-range holovids of you. They know you. They know you're going to be a lawyer. Me they've never seen. I'm nobody."

"Alice—"

"For Chrissake, get back in the car!" Alice hissed, and pounded on the front door.

Leisha drew off the walk, into the shadow of a willow tree. A man opened the door. His face was completely blank.

Alice said, "Child Protection Agency. We got a call from a little girl, this number. Let me in."

"There's no little girl here."

"This is an emergency, priority one," Alice said. "Child Protection Act 186. Let me in!"

The man, still blank-faced, glanced at the huge figure by the car. "You got a search warrant?"

"I don't need one in a priority-one child emergency. If you don't let me in, you're going to have legal snarls like you never bargained for."

Leisha clamped her lips together. No one would believe that, it was legal gobbledygook. . . . Her lip throbbed where Alice had hit it.

The man stood aside to let Alice enter.

The guard started forward. Leisha hesitated, then let him. He entered with Alice.

Leisha waited, alone, in the dark.

In three minutes they were out, the guard carrying a child. Alice's broad face gleamed pale in the porch light. Leisha sprang forward, opened the car door, and helped the guard ease the child inside. The guard was frowning, a slow puzzled frown shot with wariness.

Alice said, "Here. This is an extra hundred dollars. To get back to the city by yourself."

"Hey . . ." the guard said, but he took the money. He stood looking after them as Alice pulled away.

"He'll go straight to the police," Leisha said despairingly. "He has to, or risk his union membership."

"I know," Alice said. "But by that time we'll be out of the car."

"Where?"

"At the hospital," Alice said.

"Alice, we can't—" Leisha didn't finish. She turned to the back seat. "Stella? Are you conscious?"

"Yes," said the small voice.

Leisha groped until her fingers found the rear-seat illuminator. Stella lay stretched out on the seat, her face distorted with pain. She cradled her left arm in her right. A single bruise colored her face, above the left eye. Her red hair was tangled and dirty.

"You're Leisha Camden," the child said, and started to cry.

"Her arm's broken," Alice said.

"Honey, can you . . ." Leisha's throat felt thick, she had trouble getting the words out ". . . can you hold on till we get you to a doctor?"

"Yes," Stella said. "Just don't take me back there!"

"We won't," Leisha said. "Ever." She glanced at Alice and saw Tony's face.

Alice said, "There's a community hospital about ten miles south of here."

"How do you know that?"

"I was there once. Drug overdose," Alice said briefly. She drove hunched over the wheel, with the face of someone thinking furiously. Leisha thought, too, trying to see a way around the legal charge of kidnapping. They probably couldn't say the child came willingly. Stella would undoubtedly cooperate but at her age and in her condition she was probably *non sui juris,* her word would have no legal weight . . .

"Alice, we can't even get her into the hospital without insurance information. Verifiable on-line."

"Listen," Alice said, not to Leisha but over her shoulder, toward the back seat, "here's what we're going to do, Stella. I'm going to tell them you're my daughter and you fell off a big rock you were climbing while we stopped for a snack at a roadside picnic area. We're driving from California to Philadelphia to see your grandmother. Your name is Jordan Watrous and you're five years old. Got that, honey?"

"I'm seven," Stella said. "Almost eight."

"You're a very large five. Your birthday is March 23. Can you do this, Stella?"

"Yes," the little girl said. Her voice was stronger.

Leisha stared at Alice. "Can *you* do this?"

"Of course I can," Alice said. "I'm Roger Camden's daughter."

Alice half-carried, half-supported Stella into the Emergency Room of a small community hospital. Leisha watched from the car: the short stocky woman, the child's thin body with the twisted arm. Then she drove Alice's car to the farthest corner of the parking lot, under the dubious cover of a skimpy maple, and locked it. She tied the scarf more securely around her face.

Alice's license plate number, and her name, would be in every police and rental-car databank by now. The medical banks were slower; often they uploaded from local precincts only once a day, resenting the governmental interference in what was still, despite a half-century of battle, a private-sector enterprise. Alice and Stella would probably be all right in the hospital. Probably. But Alice could not rent another car.

Leisha could.

But the data file that would flash to rental agencies on Alice Camden Watrous might or might not include that she was Leisha Camden's twin.

Leisha looked at the rows of cars in the lot. A flashy luxury Chrysler, an Ikeda van, a row of middle-class Toyotas and Mercedes, a vintage '99 Cadillac—she could imagine the owner's face if that were missing—ten or twelve cheap runabouts, a hovercar with the uniformed driver asleep at the wheel. And a battered farm truck.

Leisha walked over to the truck. A man sat at the wheel, smoking. She thought of her father.

"Hello," Leisha said.

The man rolled down his window but didn't answer. He had greasy brown hair.

"See that hovercar over there?" Leisha said. She made her voice sound young, high. The man glanced at it indifferently; from this angle you couldn't see that the driver was asleep. "That's my bodyguard. He thinks I'm inside, the way my father told me to, getting this lip looked at." She could feel her mouth swollen from Alice's blow.

"So?"

Leisha stamped her foot. "So I don't want to be inside. He's a shit and so's Daddy. I want *out*. I'll give you 4,000 bank credits for your truck. Cash."

The man's eyes widened. He tossed away his cigarette and looked again at the hovercar. The driver's shoulders were broad, and the car was within easy screaming distance.

"All nice and legal," Leisha said, trying to smirk. Her knees felt watery.

"Let me see the cash."

Leisha backed away from the truck, to where he could not reach her. She took the money from her arm clip. She was used to carrying a lot of cash; there had always been Bruce, or someone like Bruce. There had always been safety.

"Get out of the truck on the other side," Leisha said, "and lock the door behind you. Leave the keys on the seat, where I can see them from here. Then I'll put the money on the roof where you can see it."

The man laughed, a sound like gravel pouring. "Regular little Dabney Engh, aren't you? Is that what they teach you society debs at your fancy schools?"

Leisha had no idea who Dabney Engh was. She waited, watching the man try to think of a way to cheat her, and tried to hide her contempt. She thought of Tony.

"All right," he said, and slid out of the truck.

"Lock the door!"

He grinned, opened the door again, and locked it. Leisha put the money on the roof, yanked open the driver's door, clambered in, locked the door, and powered up the window. The man laughed. She put the key into the ignition, started the truck, and drove toward the street. Her hands trembled.

She drove slowly around the block twice. When she came back, the man was gone, and the driver of the hovercar was still asleep. She had wondered if the man would wake him, out of sheer malice, but he had not. She parked the truck and waited.

An hour and a half later Alice and a nurse wheeled Stella out of the Emergency entrance. Leisha leaped out of the truck and yelled, "Coming, Alice!" waving both her arms. It was too dark to see Alice's expression; Leisha could only hope that Alice showed no dismay at the battered truck, that she had not told the nurse to expect a red car.

Alice said, "This is Julie Bergadon, a friend that I called while you were setting Jordan's arm." The nurse nodded, uninterested. The two women helped Stella into the high truck cab; there was no back seat. Stella had a cast on her arm and looked drugged.

"How?" Alice said as they drove off.

Leisha didn't answer. She was watching a police hovercar land at the other end of the parking lot. Two officers got out and strode purposefully toward Alice's locked car under the skimpy maple.

"My God," Alice said. For the first time, she sounded frightened.

"They won't trace us," Leisha said. "Not to this truck. Count on it."

"Leisha." Alice's voice spiked with fear. "Stella's *asleep*."

Leisha glanced at the child, slumped against Alice's shoulder. "No, she's not. She's unconscious from painkillers."

"Is that all right? Normal? For . . . her?"

"We can black out. We can even experience substance-induced sleep." Tony and she and Richard and Jeanine in the midnight woods. . . . "Didn't you know that, Alice?"

"No."

"We don't know very much about each other, do we?"

They drove south in silence. Finally Alice said, "Where are we going to take her, Leisha?"

"I don't know. Any one of the Sleepless would be the first place the police would check—"

"You can't risk it. Not the way things are," Alice said. She sounded weary. "But all my friends are in California. I don't think we could drive this rust bucket that far before getting stopped."

"It wouldn't make it anyway."

"What should we do?"

"Let me think."

At an expressway exit was a pay phone. It wouldn't be data-shielded, as Groupnet was. Would Kevin's open line be tapped? Probably.

There was no doubt the Sanctuary line would be.

Sanctuary. All of them were going there or already there, Kevin had said. Holed up, trying to pull the worn Allegheny Mountains around them like a safe little den. Except for the children like Stella, who could not.

Where? With whom?

Leisha closed her eyes. The Sleepless were out; the police would find Stella within hours. Susan Melling? But she had been Alice's all-too-visible stepmother, and was a cobeneficiary of Camden's will; they would question her almost immediately. It couldn't be anyone traceable to Alice. It could only be a Sleeper that Leisha knew, and trusted, and why should anyone at all fit that description? Why should she risk so much on anyone who did?

She stood a long time in the dark phone kiosk. Then she walked to the truck. Alice was asleep, her head thrown back against the seat. A tiny line of drool ran down her chin. Her face was white and drained in the bad light from the kiosk. Leisha walked back to the phone.

"Stewart? Stewart Sutter?"

"Yes?"

"This is Leisha Camden. Something has happened." She told the story tersely, in bald sentences. Stewart did not interrupt.

"Leisha—" Stewart said, and stopped.

"I need help, Stewart." *'I'll help you, Alice.' 'I don't need your help.'*

A wind whistled over the dark field beside the kiosk and Leisha shivered. She heard in the wind the thin keen of a beggar. In the wind, in her own voice.

"All right," Stewart said, "this is what we'll do. I have a cousin in Ripley, New York, just over the state line from Pennsylvania, the route you'll be driving east. It has to be in New York; I'm licensed in New York. Take the little girl there. I'll call my cousin and tell her you're coming. She's an elderly woman, was quite an activist in her youth. Her name is Janet Patterson. The town is—"

"What makes you so sure she'll get involved? She could go to jail. And so could you."

"She's been in jail so many times you wouldn't believe it. Political protests going all the way back to Vietnam. But no one's going to jail. I'm now your attorney of record, I'm privileged. I'm going to get Stella declared a ward of the state. That shouldn't be too hard with the hospital records you established in Skokie. Then she can be transferred to a foster home in New York. I know just the place, people who are fair and kind. Then Alice—"

"Stella's resident in Illinois. You can't—"

"Yes, I can. Since those research findings about the Sleepless life span have come out, legislators have been railroaded by stupid constituents scared or jealous or just plain angry. The result is a body of so-called law riddled with contradictions, absurdities, and loopholes. None of it will stand in the long run—or at least I hope not—but in the meantime it can all be exploited. I can use it to create the most god-damn convoluted case for Stella that anybody ever saw, and in the meantime she won't be returned home. But that won't work for Alice. She'll need an attorney licensed in Illinois."

"We have one," Leisha said. "Candace Holt."

"No, not a Sleepless. Trust me on this, Leisha. I'll find somebody good. There's a guy in—are you crying?"

"No," Leisha said, crying.

"Ah, God," Stewart said. "Bastards. I'm sorry all this happened, Leisha."

"Don't be," Leisha said.

When she had directions to Stewart's cousin, she walked back to the truck. Alice was still asleep, Stella still unconscious. Leisha closed the truck door as quietly as possible. The engine balked and roared, but Alice didn't wake.

There was a crowd of people with them in the narrow and darkened cab: Stewart Sutter, Tony Indivino, Susan Melling, Kenzo Yagai, Roger Camden.

To Stewart Sutter she said, You called to inform me about the situation at Morehouse, Kennedy. You are risking your career and your cousin for Stella. And you stand to gain nothing. Like Susan telling me in advance about Bernie Kuhn's brain. Susan, who lost her life to Daddy's dream and regained it by her own strength. A contract without consideration for each side is not a contract: Every first-year student knows that.

To Kenzo Yagai she said, Trade isn't always linear. You missed that. If Stewart gives me something, and I give Stella something, and ten years from now Stella is a different person because of that and gives something to someone else as yet unknown—it's an ecology. An ecology of trade, yes, each niche needed, even if they're not contractually bound. Does a horse need a fish? Yes.

To Tony she said, Yes, there are beggars in Spain who trade nothing, give nothing, do nothing. But there are *more* than beggars in Spain. Withdraw from the beggars, you withdraw from the whole damn country. And you withdraw from the possibility of the ecology of help. That's what Alice wanted, all those years ago in her bedroom. Pregnant, scared, angry, jealous, she wanted to help *me*, and I wouldn't let her because I didn't need it. But I do now. And she did then. Beggars need to help as well as be helped.

And finally, there was only Daddy left. She could *see* him, bright-eyed, holding thick-leaved exotic flowers in his strong hands. To Camden she said, You were wrong. Alice *is* special. Oh, Daddy—the specialness of Alice! You were wrong.

As soon as she thought this, lightness filled her. Not the buoyant bubble of joy, not the hard clarity of examination, but something else: sunshine, soft through the conservatory glass, where two children ran in and out. She suddenly felt light herself, not buoyant but translucent, a medium for the sunshine to pass clear through, on its way to somewhere else.

She drove the sleeping woman and the wounded child through the night, east, toward the state line.

BOOK two

SANCTUARY

2051

"A nation may be said to consist of its territories, its people, and its laws. The territory is the only part which is of certain durability."

—ABRAHAM LINCOLN,
MESSAGE TO CONGRESS,
DECEMBER 1, 1862

8

ordan Watrous stood just outside the front gate of the We-Sleep scooter factory, facing the dusty Mississippi road. Electrified fence eight feet high stretched away on either side. Not a Y-energy field, not sophisticated technology, but it would do. For now, anyway, while attacks on the factory were minor, unorganized, and verbal. Later on, they would need a Y-field. Hawke said so.

Across the river, in Arkansas, the Y-energy cones of the Samsung-Chrysler plant glinted in the early morning sun.

Jordan squinted down the road. Sweat matted his hair and trickled down his neck. The guard, a stringy, tow-headed woman in faded jeans, stuck her head out of her kiosk and called, "Hot enough for you, Jordan?"

Over his shoulder he said, "Always is, Mayleen."

She laughed. "You California boys just wilt up in God's natural heat."

"I guess we're not as tough as you river rats."

"Boy, ain't *nobody* as tough as us. You just look at Mr. Hawke."

As if were possible for anyone at a We-Sleep factory to do otherwise! Not that Hawke hadn't earned the reverence in Mayleen's voice. When Mayleen had been hired last winter, Jordan, only four weeks into his own job as Hawke's personal assistant, had gone with Hawke to her shack for the interview. Although adequately heated and provisioned through the cheap Y-energy that was every citizen's right under the Dole, the shack had no indoor plumbing, little furniture, and few toys for the skinny tow-headed kids that had stared at Jordan's leather jacket and lapel comlink. Last week, Mayleen had announced with pride that she'd just bought a toilet and a lace pillow set. The pride, Jordan now knew, was as practical as the toilet. He knew because Calvin Hawke had taught him.

Jordan returned to studying the road. Mayleen said, "Expecting someone?"

Slowly Jordan turned around. "Didn't Hawke call it in?"

"Call what in? He didn't tell me nothing."

"Jesus *Christ*," Jordan said. The terminal in the kiosk shrilled and Mayleen pulled her head back in. Jordan watched her through the plastiglass. As she listened, her face hardened as only these Mississippi faces could. Instantaneous ice in the steaming heat. He had never seen that in California.

Obviously, Hawke was telling her not only to admit a visitor, but who the visitor was.

"Yes, sir," she mouthed at the terminal, and Jordan winced. Nobody at the plant called Hawke "sir" unless they were furious. And nobody got furious at Hawke. They displaced it. Always.

Mayleen stepped away from her kiosk. "This your doing, Jordan?"

"Yes."

"Why?" She spat the word, and Jordan finally, *finally*—Hawke said it always took him too long to get angry—felt his own face harden.

"Is that your business, Mayleen?"

"Anything goes on in this here plant's my business," Mayleen said, which was only the truth. Hawke had made it the truth, for all 800 employees. "We don't want her kind here."

"Hawke apparently does."

"I asked you why."

"Why don't you ask *him* why?"

"I'm asking *you*. Why, dammit?"

Along the road, a dust cloud advanced. A groundcar. Jordan felt a sudden stab of dread: had anyone told her not to come in a Samsung-Chrysler? But she could be trusted to already know something like that. She always did.

Mayleen snarled, "I done asked you a question, Jordan! What's Mr. Hawke doing letting one of *them* in our plant?"

"You made a demand, not asked a question." The anger felt good now, sweeping away his nervousness. "But I'll answer it anyway, Mayleen. Just for you. Leisha Camden is here because she asked to come and Hawke gave her permission."

"I can see that! What I can't see is why!"

The car pulled up at the gate. It was heavily armored, and packed with bodyguards. The driver got out to open the doors. The car was not a Samsung-Chrysler.

"Why?" Mayleen repeated, with such hatred that even Jordan was startled. He turned. Her thin mouth twisted in a snarl, but in her eyes was a fear that Jordan recognized—Hawke had taught him to recognize it—a fear not of bone-and-blood people but of the degrading choices those people had indirectly caused: two dollars for a half pack of cigarettes, or two dollars for a pair of warm socks? Extra milk for the kids above the Dole allotment, or a haircut? The fear was not of starving, not in a country of prosperity built on cheap energy, but of being shut out from that prosperity. Second class. Not good enough for that basic badge of adult dignity, work. A parasite. The anger oozed out of Jordan; sadly he felt it go. Anger was so much easier.

As gently as he could, he said to Mayleen, "Leisha Camden's here because she's my mother's sister. My aunt."

He wondered how long it would take Hawke this time to redeem him.

"And each scooter takes sixteen assembly-line operations?" Leisha asked.

"Yes," Jordan said. They stood with Leisha's bodyguards, everybody in hard hats and goggles, watching Station 8-E. Two dozen scooters were swarmed over by three workers, who in their zeal completely ignored the visitors. The zeal was more notable than the results. But of course Leisha would already know that.

Six months ago, at his little sister's eighteenth birthday party in California, Leisha had questioned Jordan about the factory so closely that he had known, like cold water around his bones, that eventually she would ask to visit. What he hadn't expected was that Hawke would let her.

She said, "I thought Mr. Hawke might join us. I came to meet him, after all."

"He said to bring you to the office after the tour."

Beneath the heavy safety glasses, Leisha's mouth smiled. "Showing me my place?"

"I guess so," Jordan said heavily. He hated it when Hawke, always unpredictable, descended to playing one-upmanship.

To Jordan's surprise, Leisha laid a hand on his arm. "Don't mind on my behalf, Jordan. It's not as if he's not entitled."

And what could Jordan say to that? Entitlement, after all, was the entire issue. Who got what, and how, and why.

Somehow Jordan didn't feel like the proper person to comment on that. He wasn't even certain who within his own family was entitled to what, or why.

His mother and his aunt had such a strange relationship. Or maybe "strained" was a better word. And yet it wasn't. Leisha visited the Watrous family in California only on ceremonial occasions; Alice never visited Leisha in Chicago at all. Yet Alice, who loved gardening, had a fresh bouquet from her garden flown to Leisha's apartment every single day, at a cost Jordan considered insane. And the flowers were ordinary, hardy garden blooms: phlox and sunflowers and day lilies and lemon-drop marigolds, which Leisha could have bought on the streets of Chicago for a few dollars. "Doesn't Aunt Leisha prefer those indoor exotics?" Jordan asked once. "Yes," his mother said, smiling.

Leisha always brought Jordan and his sister Moira wonderful presents: junior electronics kits, telescopes, two shares of a stock to follow on the datanets. Alice always seemed as pleased by the gifts as the kids were. Yet when Leisha showed Jordan and Moira how to use each one—how to adjust the telescope to azimuth and altitude, how to do Japanese calligraphy on rice paper—Alice always left the room. After the first few years, Jordan sometimes wished Leisha would leave, too, and let him and Moira just read the instructions themselves. Leisha explained too fast, and too hard, and too long, and got upset that Jordan and Moira didn't remember everything the first time. It didn't even help that Aunt Leisha's upset seemed to be with herself, not with them. It made Jordan feel stupid. "Leisha has her own ways," was all that Alice would say. "And we have ours."

Strangest of all was Alice's Twin Group. Leisha had looked first shocked, then sad, then angry when she heard about the Twin Group. Alice volunteered there three days a week. The Group kept datafiles about twins who could communicate with each other across vast distances, who knew what each other was thinking, who felt pain when the other was in trouble. They also studied pairs of twins in preschool to see how they learned to differentiate themselves as separate people. This jumble of ESP, parapsychology, and scientific method bewildered Jordan, then seventeen. "Aunt Leisha says the statistics of coincidence can account for most of your 'ESP.' And I thought you and her weren't even monozygotic twins!" "We're not," Alice said.

In the last two years Jordan had seen a lot of his aunt, without telling his mother. Leisha was a Sleepless, the economic enemy. She was also fair, generous, and idealistic. It troubled him.

So many things troubled him.

Touring the plant took over an hour. Jordan tried to see the place through Leisha's eyes: people instead of cost-efficient robots, shouted arguments on the line, rock music blaring. Rejected parts from Receiving Inspection half-repacked in dirty cartons. Somebody's gnawed-on sandwich kicked into a corner.

When Jordan finally led Leisha into Hawke's office, Hawke rose from behind his massive, rough-hewn desk of Georgia pine. "Ms. Camden. An honor."

"Mr. Hawke."

She held out her hand. Hawke took it, and Jordan watched her slight recoil. People meeting Calvin Hawke for the first time usually recoiled; not until that second had Jordan realized how intently he'd wondered if Leisha would. It wasn't Hawke's huge size as much as his disconcerting physical sharpness: beaked nose, cheekbones like chisels, piercing black eyes, even the necklace of sharpened wolf's teeth which had belonged to his great-great-great-grandfather, a mountain man who had married three Indian women and killed three hundred braves. Or so Hawke said. Would wolf's teeth nearly two hundred years old, Jordan wondered, still be so sharp?

Hawke's would.

Leisha smiled up at Hawke, nearly a foot taller despite her own height, and said, "Thank you for letting me come." When Hawke said nothing, she added directly, "Why did you?"

He pretended she'd asked a different question. "You're safe enough here. Even without your goons. There is no baseless hatred in my plants."

Jordan thought of Mayleen, but said nothing. You didn't contradict Hawke in public.

Leisha said coolly, "An interesting use of 'baseless,' Mr. Hawke. In the law we call a usage like that insinuating. But now that I *am* here, I'd like to ask some questions, if I may."

"Of course," Hawke said. He folded his enormous arms across his chest and leaned back against his desk, apparently all agreeable helpfulness. On the desk sat a comlink, a coffee mug with the Harvard logo, and a Cherokee ceremonial doll. None of them had been there this morning. Hawke, Jordan saw, had been assembling his stage set. The back of Jordan's neck prickled.

Leisha said, "Your scooters are stripped-down models, with the simplest possible Y-cones and fewer options than any other model on the market."

"That's right," Hawke said pleasantly.

"And their reliability is less than any other model. They need more replacement parts, sooner. In fact, nothing but the Y-cone deflector shield carries any kind of warranty, and of course the deflectors are under patent and aren't subcontracted here."

"You've done your homework," Hawke said.

"The scooters can reach a maximum of only thirty miles per hour."

"True."

"They sell for 10 percent more than a comparable Schwinn or Ford or Sony."

"Also true."

"Yet you've captured 32 percent of the domestic market, you've opened three new plants in the last year, and you've filed a corporate return on assets of 28 percent when the industry average is barely 11 percent."

Hawke smiled.

Leisha took a step toward him. She said intently, "Don't go on doing it, Mr. Hawke. It's a terrible mistake. Not for us—for *you*."

Hawke said genially, "Are you threatening my plant, Ms. Camden?"

Jordan's stomach tightened. Hawke was deliberately misinterpreting what Leisha had said, turning it from a plea into a threat so he could have a fight instead of a discussion. So this was why he'd let her visit a We-Sleep plant: he wanted the cheap thrill of a face-to-face confrontation. The dirt-poor leader of a national political movement going to the mat with the big-time Sleepless lawyer. Disappointment swept through Jordan; Hawke was bigger than that.

He needed Hawke to be bigger than that.

Leisha said, "Of course I'm not threatening you, Mr. Hawke, and you know it. I'm merely trying to point out that your We-Sleep Movement is dangerous to the country, and to yourselves. Don't be so hypocritical as to pretend not to understand."

Hawke went on smiling genially, but Jordan saw a tiny muscle in his neck, just above a yellowed wolf tooth, begin to beat rhythmically.

"I could hardly help understand, Ms. Camden. You've hammered on this one stone in the press for years now."

"And I'll go on hammering. Whatever drives Sleepers and Sleepless

farther apart is ultimately no good for either of us. You have people buying your scooters not because they're good, not because they're cheap,
not because they're beautiful, but solely because they're made by
Sleepers, with profits going only to Sleepers. You—and all your followers in other industries—are splitting the country in two economically,
Mr. Hawke, creating a dual economy based on hate. That's dangerous
for everyone!"

"But especially for the economic interests of Sleepless?" Hawke
asked, apparently all disinterested interest. Jordan saw that he thought
he'd gained ground by Leisha's sudden emotion.

"No," Leisha said wearily. "Come on, Mr. Hawke, you know better.
Sleepless economic interests are based in the global economy, especially in finance and high-tech skills. You could manufacture every ve-
hicle, building, and widget in America and not touch them."

Them, Jordan thought. Not *us.* He tried to see if Hawke had noticed.

Hawke said silkily, "Then why are you here, Ms. Camden?"

"For the same reason I go to Sanctuary. To rail against stupidity."

The tiny muscle in Hawke's neck beat faster; Jordan saw that he
hadn't expected Leisha to bracket him with Sanctuary, the enemy.
Hawke reached across his desk and pressed a buzzer. Leisha's bodyguards tensed. Hawke tossed them a look of contempt: traitors to their
own biological side. The office door opened and a young black woman
entered, looking puzzled.

"Hawke? Coltrane say you'all want to see me?"

"Yes, Tina. Thank you. This lady is interested in our plant. Would
you mind telling her a little about your job here?"

Tina turned obediently, and without recognition, to Leisha. "I work
Station Nine," she said. "Before that, I don't have nothing. My family
don't have nothing. We walk to Dole, pick up the food, walk home, eat
it. We wait to die." She went on, telling a story familiar by now to Jordan, different only in Tina's melodramatic approach to telling it. Which
was undoubtedly why Hawke had had her waiting. Fed, sheltered,
clothed cheaply by the Dole—and completely unable to compete beyond that economic level. Until Calvin Hawke and the We-Sleep

Movement provided a job that paid wages, because the market for it had been wrested out of the national market on wholly uneconomic terms. "I buy only We-Sleep products, I get to sell my We-Sleep products," Tina chanted fervently. "The only way we get any of the pie!"

Hawke said, "And if somebody in your community buys a different product because it's cheaper or better . . ."

"That somebody ain't *in* my community very long," Tina said darkly. "We take care of our own."

"Thank you, Tina," Hawke said. Tina seemed to know this was dismissal; she left, but not before throwing Hawke the same look they all did. Jordan hoped that Leisha recognized the look from legal clients she had kept from a different sort of prison. His stomach relaxed slightly.

Leisha said wryly to Hawke, "Quite a performance."

"More than just a performance. The dignity of individual effort— an old Yagaiist tenet, isn't it? Or can't you allow yourself to recognize economic facts?"

"I recognize all the limitations of a free-market economy, Mr. Hawke. Supply and demand puts workers on the exact same footing as widgets, and people are not widgets. But you cannot create economic health by unionizing consumers the way you would unionize workers."

"That's just how I *am* creating economic health, Ms. Camden."

"Only temporarily," Leisha said. Abruptly she leaned forward. "Do you expect your consumers to stay away from better products forever on the basis of class hatred? Class hatred diminishes when prosperity lets people rise in class."

"My people will never rise in class to equal Sleepless. And you know it. Yours is the Darwinian edge. So we capitalize on what we *do* have: sheer numbers."

"But it doesn't have to be a Darwinian struggle!"

Hawke stood. The muscle in his neck was still now; Jordan could see that Hawke felt he'd won. "Doesn't it, Ms. Camden? Who made it so? The Sleepless control 28 percent of the economy now, despite the fact that you're a tiny minority. The percentage is growing. You yourself are a stockholder, through the Aurora Holding Company, in the Samsung–Chrysler plant across the river."

Jordan was jolted. He had not known that. For a second, suspicion flooded him, corrosive as acid. His aunt had asked to come here, asked to talk to Hawke. . . . He looked again at Leisha. She was smiling. No, that wasn't her motive. What was wrong with him? Would he spend his whole life uncertain about everything?

Leisha said, "There is nothing illegal in owning stock, Mr. Hawke. I do it for the most obvious of reasons: to turn a profit. A profit on the best possible goods and services that can be produced in fair competition, offered to anyone who wishes to buy. *Anyone.*"

"Very commendable," Hawke said bitingly. "But of course, not everyone *can* buy."

"Just so."

"Then we agree on at least one thing: Some people are shut out of your wonderful Darwinian economy. Do you want them to take that meekly?"

Leisha said, "I want to open the doors and bring them in."

"How, Ms. Camden? How do we compete on equal grounds with the Sleepless, or with mainstream companies funded in whole or in part by Sleepless financial genius?"

"Not with hatred creating two economies."

"Then with what? Tell me."

Before Leisha could answer, the door suddenly swung open and three men leaped into the room.

Leisha's bodyguards immediately blocked her, guns drawn. But the men must have expected this: They brandished cameras, not guns, and began filming. Since all they could see was the phalanx of bodyguards, they filmed that. This bewildered the guards, who looked at one another sideways. Meanwhile Jordan, backed into a corner, was the only one who saw the sudden, slight, telltale brightening of an optic panel high on the wall, in a room widely touted as being without surveillance of any kind.

"Out," the head bodyguard, or whatever he was called, said between

his teeth. The film crew obligingly left. And no one but Jordan had seen Hawke's camera.

Why? What did Hawke want with a clandestine still he could claim was taken by a legitimate film crew? And should Jordan tell his aunt that Hawke had it? Could it harm her?

Hawke was watching Jordan. Hawke nodded once, with such warmth in his eyes, such tender understanding of Jordan's dilemma that Jordan was immediately reassured. Hawke meant no personal harm to Leisha. He didn't operate that way. His goals were large ones, sweeping ones, *right* ones, but they took note of individuals, as no Sleepless except Leisha ever seemed to do. No matter what the history books said was necessary, Hawke did not break individual eggs to create his revolution.

Jordan relaxed.

Hawke said, "I'm sorry, Ms. Camden."

Leisha looked at him bleakly. "No harm done, Mr. Hawke." After a moment she added deliberately, "Is there?"

"No. Let me give you a memento of your visit."

"A . . ."

"A memento." From a closet—the bodyguards tensed all over again—Hawke wheeled a We-Sleep scooter. "Of course, it probably won't go as fast, or far, or reliably as the one you already have. If you ever deign to use a scooter instead of a ground- or aircar, as over 50 percent of the population has to do."

Leisha, Jordan saw, had finally lost her patience. She let her breath out between her teeth; it whistled fitfully. "No thank you, Mr. Hawke. I ride a Kessler-Eagle. A high-quality scooter made, I believe, at a factory owned by Native American Sleepers in New Mexico. They are trying very hard to market a superior product at a fair price, but of course they represent a minority without a built-in protected market. Hopi, I believe."

Jordan didn't dare look at Hawke's face.

As she climbed into her car, Leisha said to Jordan, "I'm sorry for that last jab."

"Don't be," Jordan said.

"Well, for your sake. I know you believe in what you're doing here, Jordan—"

"Yes," Jordan said quietly. "I do. Despite."

"When you say that, you look like your mother."

The same couldn't be said for Leisha, Jordan thought, and he felt immediately disloyal. But it was true. Alice looked older than forty-three, Leisha much younger. The aging caused by gravity was in the fine-boned face; the aging caused by tissue decay was not. Shouldn't she, then, look 21.5? Half the aging. She didn't; she looked about thirty and, apparently, always would. A beautiful and tense thirty, the faint lines around her eyes more like delicate micro-circuitry than soft gullies.

Leisha said, "How is your mother?"

Jordan heard all the complexities in the question. He didn't feel up to grappling with them. "Fine," he said. And then, "Are you going from here to Sanctuary?"

Leisha, half in and half out of her car, lifted her face to his. "How did you know?"

"You have the look you get when you're going to or coming from."

She looked down; he shouldn't have mentioned Sanctuary. She said, "Tell Hawke I won't make a legal fuss over the wall camera. And don't you agonize about not telling me, either. You've got enough contradictions to reconcile already, Jordy. But you know, I get tired of these overwhelming physical presences like your Mr. Hawke. All charisma and outsized ego, using the intensity of their beliefs to hit you like a fist. It's wearing."

She swung her long legs into the car. Jordan laughed, a sound that made Leisha glance at him, a slight question in her green eyes, but he just shook his head, kissed her, and closed the car door. As the car pulled away he straightened, not laughing. *Charisma. Outsized egos. Overwhelming physical presences.*

How was it possible, after all this time, that Leisha didn't know she was one, too?

* * *

Leisha leaned her head against the leather seat of the Baker Enterprises corporate plane. She was the only passenger. Below her the Mississippi plain began to climb into the foothills of the Appalachian Mountains. Leisha's hand brushed the book on the seat beside her and she picked it up. It was a diversion from Calvin Hawke.

They had made the cover too garish. Abraham Lincoln, beardless, stood in black frock coat and top hat against the background of a burning city—Atlanta? Richmond?—grimacing horribly. Crimson and marigold flames licked at a purple sky. Crimson and marigold and *fuchsia*. On-line, the colors would be even more lurid. In three-dimensional hologram, they would be practically fluorescent.

Leisha sighed. Lincoln had never stood in a burning city. At the time of her book's events, he had been bearded. And the book itself was a careful scholarly study of Lincoln's speeches in the light of Constitutional law, not the light of battle. Nothing in it grimaced. Nothing burned.

She ran her finger over the embossed name on the cover: Elizabeth Kaminsky.

"Why?" Alice had asked in her blunt way.

"Isn't it obvious?" Leisha had said. "My law cases get too much notoriety as it is. I want the book to earn whatever scholarly attention it's really worth rather than a—"

"I see *that*," Alice retorted. "But why that pseudonym, of all choices?" Leisha hadn't had an answer. A week later she thought of one, but by that time the stiff little visit was over and Leisha wasn't in California to deliver it. Leisha almost phoned her, but it was 4:00 A.M. in Chicago, 2:00 A.M. in Morro Bay, and of course Alice and Beck would be asleep. And she and Alice seldom phoned each other anyway.

Because of something Lincoln said in 1864, Alice. Combined with the facts that I'm 43 years old, the same age our father was when we were born, and that no one, not even you, believes that I get tired of it all.

But the truth was, she probably wouldn't have said that to Alice, not in Chicago nor in California. Somehow whatever she said to Alice turned faintly pompous. And whatever Alice said to her—like that mystic nonsense of the Twin Group—seemed to Leisha riddled with holes in both logic and evidence. They were like two people trying to communicate in a language foreign to both of them, reduced to nodding and smiling, the initial good will not quite enough to offset the strain.

Twenty years ago, for one moment, it had seemed as if it might be different between them. But now . . .

Twenty-two thousand Sleepless on Earth, 95 percent of them in the United States. Eighty percent of those within Sanctuary. And since nearly all Sleepless babies were now born, not created *in vitro,* most Sleepless were now born inside Sanctuary. Parents across the country continued to purchase other genetic alterations: enhanced IQ, sharpened sight, a strong immune system, high cheekbones—anything at all, it sometimes seemed to Leisha, within the legal parameters, no matter how trivial. But not Sleeplessness. Genetic alterations were expensive; why purchase for your beloved baby a lifetime of bigotry, prejudice, and physical danger? Better to choose an assimilated genemod. Beautiful or brainy children might encounter natural envy, but usually not virulent hatred. They were not viewed as a different race, one endlessly conspiring at power, endlessly controlling behind the scenes, endlessly feared and scorned. The Sleepless, Leisha had written for a national magazine, were to the twenty-first century what Jews had been to the fourteenth.

Twenty years of legal fighting to change that perception, and nothing had changed.

"I am tired," Leisha said experimentally, aloud. The pilot didn't turn around; he wasn't much for conversation. The foothills, unchanging, continued to slide away 20,000 feet below.

Leisha unfolded her work station. It accomplished no good to be tired: not of the troubling gulf between her and Alice, not of Calvin Hawke in the fight behind her, not of Sanctuary in the fight ahead. They would all still be there. And meanwhile, she could at least get some work done. Three more hours to upstate New York, two back to Chicago, enough time to finish the brief for *Calder* v. *Hansen Metallurgy.*

She had a client meeting in Chicago at 4:00 P.M., a deposition at 5:30 P.M., another client meeting at 8:00 P.M., and then the rest of the night to prepare for trial tomorrow. She might just fit everything in.

The law was the one thing she never tired of. The one thing—despite twenty years of the inevitable crap that went with its practice—she still believed in. A society with a functioning, reasonably uncorrupted (say, 80 percent) judicial system was a society that still believed in itself.

More cheerful now, Leisha settled into a knotty question of *prima facie* assumption. But the book still lay on the seat, distracting her, along with Alice's question, and her unspoken answer.

In April 1864 Lincoln had written to Kentuckian A. G. Hodges. The northern states were enraged over the racial massacre of black soldiers at Fort Pillow, the federal treasury was nearly empty, the war was costing the Union two million dollars a day. Daily Lincoln was reviled in the press; weekly he was locked in combat with Congress. In the next month Grant would lose 10,000 men at Cold Harbor, more at Spotsylvania Courthouse. Lincoln wrote to Hodges, "I claim not to have controlled events, but confess plainly that events have controlled me."

Leisha shoved her book under the seat of the plane and bent over her workstation, leaning into the law.

Jennifer Sharifi raised her forehead from the ground, rose gracefully, and bent to roll up her prayer rug. The rough mountain grass was slightly wet; blades clung crookedly to the underside of the rug. Holding it away from the white folds of her *abbaya*, Jennifer walked across the small clearing in the woods to her aircar. Her long, unbound black hair stirred in the faint wind.

A light plane streaked overhead. Jennifer frowned: Leisha Camden, already. Jennifer was late.

Let Leisha wait. Or let Richard deal with her. Jennifer had not wanted Leisha here in the first place. Why should Sanctuary welcome a woman who worked against it at every turn? Even the Quran, in its quaint pre-globalnet simplicity, was explicit about traitors: *"Whosoever commits aggression against you, you commit/ him like as he has committed against you."*

The small plane with the Baker Enterprises logo disappeared into the trees.

Jennifer slipped into her car, her mind busy with the rest of the day ahead. Were it not for the solace and quiet of morning and afternoon prayer, she didn't think she could face some of her days. "But you have no religious faith," Richard had said, smiling, "you're not even a believer." Jennifer hadn't tried to explain to him that religious belief was not the point. The will to believe created its own power, its own faith, and, ultimately, its own will. Through the practice of faith, whatever its specific rituals, one brought into existence the object of that faith. The believer became the Creator.

I believe, Jennifer said each dawn and each noon, kneeling on the grass or the leaves or the snow, *in Sanctuary.*

She shaded her eyes, trying to see exactly where Leisha's plane had disappeared. It was being tracked, Jennifer assumed, by both the Langdon sensors and the antiaircraft lasers. She lifted her aircar, flying well under the Y-field dome.

What would her paternal great-grandmother, Najla Fatima Noor el-Dahar, have said about a faith such as hers? On the other hand, her maternal great-grandmother, whose granddaughter became an American movie star, had herself survived as an Irish immigrant turned Brooklyn cleaning lady and thus probably understood something about power and will.

Not that great-grandmothers, anybody's great-grandmothers, mattered any longer. Nor grandfathers nor fathers. A new race had always been required to sacrifice its roots to its own survival. Zeus, Jennifer would guess, had mourned neither Cronus nor Rhea.

Sanctuary spread below her in the morning sun. In twenty-two years it had grown to nearly 300 square miles, occupying a fifth of Cattaraugus County, New York. Jennifer had acquired the Allegany Indian Reservation, immediately after the repeal of Congressional trust restrictions. She had paid a sum that made the Seneca tribe that sold it comfortable in Manhattan, Paris, and Dallas. There hadn't actually been very many Senecas left to sell; not all threatened groups, Jennifer well knew, had the adaptable skills of the Sleepless—skills such as buying land when the owners were initially reluctant to sell. Or acquiring antiaircraft lasers on the international arms market. Or, if those other groups did have these skills, they lacked the cause to make them focused and clean and holy. To call survival itself what it actually was: a holy war. *Jihad.*

Allegany had been unique among Native American reservations in containing an entire non-Indian city, Salamanca, leased from the Senecas by city residents since 1892. Salamanca had been included in Jennifer's purchase. The lessees all had received eviction notices, and after multiple court fights for which Salamanca residents had little money and Sanctuary had the donated services of the best Sleepless lawyers in the country, the city's outdated buildings, gutted, had become the shells of Sanctuary's high-tech city—research hospital, college, securities exchange, power and maintenance centers, and the most sophisticated telecommunications in existence, all surrounded by ecologically maintained woodland.

In the distance, beyond Sanctuary's gates, Jennifer could see the daily line of trucks toiling up the mountain road, bringing in food, building materials, low-tech supplies—everything Sanctuary would rather import than produce, which included everything nonchallenging, nonprofitable, or nonessential. Not that Sanctuary was dependent on the daily trucks. It had enough of everything to run self-sufficiently for a year, if necessary. It wouldn't be necessary. Sleepless controlled too many factories, distribution channels, agricultural research projects, commodity exchanges, and law offices on the Outside. Sanctuary had not ever been planned as a survivalist retreat; it was a fortified command center.

The airfield groundcar was already parked in front of the house Jennifer shared with her husband and two children at the edge of Argus City. The house was a geodesic dome, graceful and efficient, but not opulent. Build the security facilities first, Tony Indivino had argued twenty-two years ago. Then build the technical and educational facilities, then the storage warehouses, and the individual dwellings last. Only now was Sanctuary getting around to new individual dwellings.

Jennifer adjusted the folds of her *abbaya,* took a deep breath, and entered her house.

Leisha stood by the southern glass wall of the living room, staring at the gold-framed holo portrait of Tony, who stared back from smiling, youthful eyes. Sunlight caught in Leisha's blonde hair and blazed. When she heard Jennifer and turned, Leisha was backlit by the windows and Jennifer couldn't see her expression.

The two women stared at each other.

"Jennifer."

"Hello, Leisha."

"You're looking well."

"As are you."

"And Richard? How are he and the kids?"

"Fine, thank you," Jennifer said.

There was a silence, prickly as heat.

Leisha said, "I think you know why I'm here."

"Why, no, I don't," Jennifer said, although of course she did. Sanctuary monitored the movements of all Sleepless who remained outside, but none more than Leisha Camden and Kevin Baker.

Leisha made a brief, impatient noise. "Don't be evasive with me, Jennifer. If we can't agree on anything else, let's at least agree to be honest."

She never changed, Jennifer thought. All that intelligence, all that experience, and yet she did not change. A triumph of naive idealism over both intelligence and experience.

The deliberately blind deserved not to see.

"All right, Leisha. We'll be honest. You're here to find out if yesterday's attack on the We-Sleep textile factory in Atlanta originated in Sanctuary."

Leisha stared before she exploded. "Good God, Jennifer, of course I'm not! Don't you think I know you don't fight that way? Especially not against a low-tech operation grossing less than half a million annual?"

Jennifer muffled a smile; the pairing of objections, moral and economic, was pure Leisha. And of course Sanctuary hadn't directed the attack. The We-Sleep people were insignificant. She said, "I'm relieved to hear your opinion of us has improved."

Leisha waved her arm. Inadvertently, her hand brushed Tony's holo; the image turned its head in her direction. "My opinion is irrelevant, as you've made clear enough. I'm here because Kevin gave me this." She pulled hard-copy from her pocket and thrust it at Jennifer, who realized with a nasty jolt what it was.

She made her face impassive, realizing too late that impassivity would tell Leisha just as much as emotion. How had Leisha and Kevin gotten the hard-copy? Her mind ran over the possibilities, but she wasn't a datanet expert. She would have to pull Will Rinaldi and Cassie Blumenthal off their other projects immediately to go over the entire net for gates and bubbles and geysers. . . .

"Don't bother," Leisha said. "Kevin's wizards didn't get it off the Sanctuary net. This was mailed to me—to me directly—by one of your own."

That was even worse. Someone inside Sanctuary, someone who secretly sided with the Sleeper-lovers, someone who was without the ability to recognize a war of survival. . . . Unless of course Leisha was lying. But Jennifer had never caught Leisha in a lie. It was part of Leisha's pathetic, dangerous naivete to prefer unadjusted truth.

Leisha crumpled the paper in her hand and threw it across the living room. "How could you divide us further like this, Jennifer? Set up a separate Sleepless Council in secret, with membership limited to those who take this so-called oath of solidarity; 'I vow to hold the interests of Sanctuary above all other loyalties, personal, political, and economic, and to pledge, to its survival and so to my own, my life, fortune, and sacred honor.' Good God—what an unholy alliance of religious fanaticism and the Declaration of Independence! But you always did have a tin ear!"

Jennifer gazed at her impassively. "You are being stupid." It was the

worst epithet either of them had. "Only you and Kevin and your handful of soft-minded doves don't see that this is a war of survival. War
demands clearly drawn lines, especially for strategic information. We
can't afford voting privileges for the fifth column."

Leisha's eyes narrowed. "This is *not* a war. A war is attack and response. If we don't counterattack, if we go on being productive and
law-abiding citizens, eventually we'll win assimilation by sheer economic power—like every other newly-franchised group. But not if we
split into factions like this! You used to know that, Jenny!"

She said sharply, "Don't call me that!" Just barely did she stop herself from glancing at Tony's picture.

Leisha didn't apologize.

More calmly, Jennifer added, "Assimilation doesn't come with
economic power alone. It's won by political power, which we don't
have, and in a democracy never will have. There aren't enough of us to
form a significant voting bloc. *You* used to know *that.*"

"You've already set up the strongest covert lobby in Washington.
You *buy* the votes you need. Political power flows from money, it always
has; the concept of society is *about* money. Any values we want to change
or advocate, we have to change or advocate within the framework of
money. And we *are*. But how can we advocate a single trade ecology for
Sleeper and Sleepless if you split us into warring factions?"

"We wouldn't be split if you and yours could recognize a war when
you saw one."

"I recognize hatred when I see it. It's in your stupid oath."

They had reached an impasse, the same old impasse. Jennifer
crossed the room to the bar. Her black hair floated behind her. "Would
you like a drink, Leisha?"

"Jennifer . . ." Leisha said, and stopped. After a moment, with a
visible effort, she went on. "If your Sanctuary Council becomes a reality . . . you'll shut us out. Me and Kevin and Jean-Claude and Stella
and the others. We won't have a voting voice in statements to the media, we won't be included in governance decisions, we won't even be
able to help with the new Sleepless kids because nobody who takes the

oath will be allowed to use Groupnet, only the Sanctuary net. . . . What's next? A boycott on doing business with any of us?"

Jennifer didn't answer, and Leisha said slowly, "Oh my God. You are. You are thinking of an economic boycott. . . ."

"That would not be my decision. It would take the whole Sanctuary Council. I doubt they would vote such a boycott."

"But you would."

"I was never a Yagaiist, Leisha. I don't believe in the predominance of individual excellence over the welfare of the community. Both are important."

"This isn't about Yagaiism and you know it. This is about control, Jennifer. You hate everything you can't control—just like the worst of the Sleepers do. But you go farther than they do. You make control into something holy because *you* need holiness as well. This is all about what you, Jennifer Sharifi, need. Not what the community needs."

Jennifer walked from the room, gripping her hands together to keep them from shaking. It was her own fault, of course, that any other person had enough power over her to cause them to shake. A fault, a weakness, that she had failed to root out. Her failure. In the hall her children barreled into her from their playroom.

"Mom! Come see what we built!"

Jennifer put one hand on each of their heads. There was a knot somewhere in Najla's coarse hair. Ricky's, darker than his older sister's but finer, felt like cool silk. Jennifer's hands steadied.

The children caught sight of the living room. "Aunt Leisha! Aunt Leisha's here!" Their hair left Jennifer's fingers. "Aunt Leisha, come see what we built on CAD!"

"Of course," Jennifer heard Leisha's voice say. "I want to. But let me just ask your mother one more thing."

Jennifer didn't turn around. If the traitor Inside had mailed Leisha notice of the oath of solidarity, what else had she been mailed?

But all Leisha said was, "Did Richard receive the subpoena for *Simpson* v. *Offshore Fishing?*"

"Yes. He did. He's preparing his expert testimony now, in fact."

"Good," Leisha said bleakly.

Ricky looked from Leisha to his mother. His voice had lost some of its exuberance. "Mom . . . should I go get Dad? Aunt Leisha will want to see Dad . . . won't she?"

Jennifer smiled at her son. She could feel the lavishness of her own smile, lush with relief. Offshore fishing rights: Almost she could pity Leisha. Her days were given to such triviality. "Yes, of course, Ricky," she said, turning the lavish smile on Leisha, "go get your father. Your Aunt Leisha will want to visit with him. Of course she will."

9

L eisha," said the receptionist in her law office, "This gentleman
has been waiting to see you for three hours. He doesn't have an
appointment. I told him you might not even be back today, but he
stayed anyway."

The man stood, lurching a little with the stiffness of someone who
has held muscles too long in one tense position. He was short and thin,
oddly wispy, dressed in a rumpled brown suit that was neither cheap
nor expensive. In one hand he held a folded kiosk tabloid. *Sleeper*,
Leisha thought. She always knew.

"Leisha Camden?"

"I'm sorry, but I'm not seeing any new clients. If you need a lawyer,
you'll need to ask elsewhere."

"I think you'll take this case," the man said, surprising her. His voice
was considerably less wispy than his appearance. "At any rate, you'll
want to know about it. Please give me ten minutes." He opened the
tabloid and held it out to her. On the front page was her picture with
Calvin Hawke, over the headline, "Sleepless Worried Enough to Inves-
tigate We-Sleep Movement. . . . Have We Got Them on the Run?"

Now she knew why Hawke had permitted her to visit the scooter
factory.

"It says this picture was taken this *morning*," the man said. "My, my,
my," and Leisha knew he did not work in telecommunications.

"Come into my office, Mr. . . ."

"Adam Walcott. Dr. Adam Walcott."

"A medical doctor?"

He looked directly at her. His eyes were a pale, milky blue, like frosted glass. "Genetic researcher."

The sun was setting over Lake Michigan. Leisha transluced the glass wall, sat down opposite Dr. Walcott, and waited.

Walcott twisted his legs, which were remarkably spindly, into pretzels around the legs of his chair. "I work for a private research firm, Ms. Camden. Samplice Biotechnical. We develop refinements on genetic modeling and alteration and offer these products to the bigger houses that do *in vitro* gene altering. We developed the Pastan procedure for preternaturally sharp hearing."

Leisha nodded neutrally; preternaturally sharp hearing had always struck her as a terrible idea. The benefits of hearing a whisper six rooms away were outweighed by the pain of hearing shatter-rock three rooms away. P-hearing kids were fitted for sound-control implants at two months of age.

"Samplice gives its researchers a lot of leeway." Walcott stopped to cough, a sound so thin and tentative that Leisha thought of ghosts coughing. "They say they hope we'll stumble on something wonderful, but the truth is that the company is in a terrible state of disorganization and they just don't know how to supervise scientists. About two years ago I asked for permission to work on some of the peptides associated with Sleeplessness."

Leisha said wryly, "I wouldn't think there was anything associated with Sleeplessness that hadn't been researched already."

Walcott seemed to find this funny; he gave a gasping chuckle, untwisted his skinny legs from around the chair, and twisted them around each other. "Most people think not. But I was working with the peptides in adult Sleepless, and I was using some new approaches pioneered at L'Institut Technique de Lyons. By Gaspard-Thiereux. Do you know his work?"

"I've heard of him."

"You probably don't know this new approach. It's very new itself."
Walcott wound a hand through his hair and tugged; both hand and hair
were insubstantial. "I should have started by asking how secure this
office was."

"Completely," Leisha said. "Or you wouldn't be in it." But Walcott
only nodded; apparently he was not one of those Sleepers offended by
Sleepless security. Her estimation of him rose a little.

"To shorten this recital, what I think I've found is a way to create
sleeplessness in adults who were born Sleepers."

Leisha's hands moved to pick up . . . what? Something. The hands
stopped. She stared at them. "To . . ."

"Not all the problems are worked out yet." Walcott launched into a
complicated thesis of altered peptide manufacture, neuron synapses,
and redundant information coding in DNA, none of which Leisha
could follow. She sat quietly, while the universe took a different shape.

"Dr. Walcott . . . you're sure?"

"About lysine transference redundancy?"

"*No*. About creating sleeplessness in Sleepers—"

Walcott ran his other hand through his hair. "No, of course we're
not sure. How could we be? We need controlled experiments, additional replications, not to mention funding for—"

"But in theory you can do it."

"Oh, *theory*," Walcott said, and even in her shock this seemed an
odd dismissal for a scientist to make. Evidently Walcott was a pragma-
tist. "Yes, we can do it in theory."

"With all the side effects? Including . . . longevity?"

"Well, that's one of the things we don't know. This is all very rough
yet. But before we go any further, we need a lawyer."

The sentence centered Leisha. Something was not right here. She
found it. "Why are you here alone, Dr. Walcott? Surely any legal situation connected with this research is the responsibility of Samplice, and
surely the firm has its own counsel."

"Director Lee doesn't know I'm here. I'm acting on my own. I need
a lawyer in a personal capacity."

Leisha picked up a paper magnet—that must have been what her fingers had been searching for, yes, why not—turned it on, turned it off, stroked it with her fingers. The transluced window glowed behind Walcott's head. "Go on."

"When I first realized where this line of research was heading, my assistant and I took it off-line. Completely. We kept no records in the company datanet, ran no simulations on anything except free-standing computers, wiped all programs each night, and took hard-copies— the only copies—of all progress home with us each night in portable safes, in duplicate. We told no one what we were doing, not even the director."

"Why did you do that, Doctor?"

"Because Samplice is a public company, and 62 percent of the stock is divided between two mutual funds controlled by Sleepless."

When he turned his head, the pale milky eyes seemed to absorb light.

"One of the mutual funds is offered by Canniston Fidelity; the other is traded from Sanctuary. Forgive me, Ms. Camden, for being so blunt, and even more for the reasoning behind the bluntness. But Director Lee is not a particularly admirable man. He has been indicted before— although not convicted—of misuse of funds. My assistant and I were afraid that if he was approached by anyone from Sanctuary to discontinue the research . . . or anything . . . in the beginning my assistant and I had only a glimmer. A wild enough glimmer that we weren't sure we could interest any other reputable research company. To tell the truth, we're still not. It's still just theory. And Sanctuary could have offered so very much money to just cut the whole thing off. . . ."

Leisha was careful to not answer.

"Well. Two months ago, something odd happened. We knew, of course, that the Samplice net probably wasn't secure—what net is, realistically? That's why we weren't on it. But Timmy and I—Timmy is my assistant, Dr. Timothy Herlinger—didn't realize that people scanned the nets not only for what was on it, but for what *wasn't*. Apparently they do. Somebody outside the company must have been routinely matching lists of employees with net files, because Timmy and I came into our lab one morning and there was a message on our terminal: 'What the hell have you two guys been working on for two months?' "

Leisha said, "How do you know the message was from outside the company and not a snide hint of discovery from your director?"

"Because our director couldn't discover a boil on his ass," Walcott said, surprising her again. "Although that's not the real reason. The message was signed 'stockholder.' But what really scared us, Timmy and me, was that it was on a free-standing computer. No telelinks of any kind. Not even electricity. It's an IBM-Y, running directly off Y-energy cones. And the lab was locked."

Something prickled in Leisha's stomach. "Other keys?"

"Only Director Lee. Who was at a conference in Barbados."

"He gave his key to someone. Or a duplicate of it. Or lost it. Or Dr. Herlinger did."

Walcott shrugged. "Not Timmy. But let me go on with my story. We ignored the message. But we decided to put the work we had—by this time we were almost there—somewhere safe. So we destroyed all but a single copy, rented a safe-deposit box in the downtown branch of the First National Bank, and took just one key. At night we buried the key in my back yard, under a rose bush. An Endicott Perfection—triple roses blooming consecutively throughout your spring and fall garden."

Leisha looked at Walcott as if he had lost his mind. He smiled faintly. "Didn't you read pirate books as a child, Ms. Camden?"

"I never read much fiction."

"Well. I suppose it sounds melodramatic, but we couldn't think what else to do." He ran his left hand again through the thinning hair, which had begun to look like tangled fringe. All at once his voice lost its confident strength, turning wispy and tired. "The key is still there, under the rose bush. I dug it up this morning. But the research papers are gone from the safe-deposit box. It's empty."

Leisha got up and walked to the window. Unthinking, she cleared the glass. Blood-red light low over Lake Michigan stained the water. In the east a crescent moon rode high.

"When did you discover this theft?"

"This morning. I dug up the key to go get the papers so Timmy and I could add something, and then we went to the bank. I told the bank officials the box was empty. They said there was nothing registered as in it. I told them I had personally put nine sheets of paper into the box."

"You verified that on-line at the time of rental."

"Yes, of course."

"Did you get a hard-copy receipt?"

"Yes." He passed it to her. Leisha examined it. "But then when the bank manager called up the electronic record, it showed that Dr. Adam Walcott had come back the next day and removed all the papers, and that Dr. Adam Walcott had signed a receipt to that effect. And Ms. Camden—they *had* that receipt."

"With your signature."

"Yes. But I never signed it! It's a forgery!"

"No, it'll be your handwriting," Leisha said. "How many documents a month do you sign at Samplice, Doctor?"

"Dozens, I suppose."

"Supplies requests, fund disbursements, routing slips. Do you read them all?"

"No, but—"

"Have any secretaries left recently?"

"Why . . . I suppose so. Director Lee has great trouble keeping support staff." The wispy brows rushed together. "But the director had no idea what we were working on!"

"No, I'm sure he didn't." Leisha put both hands across her stomach. Long ago clients had stopped making her queasy. Any lawyer who practiced for twenty years got used to misfits, criminals, manipulators, heroes, charlatans, nut cases, victims, and shitballs. You put your belief in the law, not in the client.

But no lawyer had ever before had a client who could turn Sleepers into Sleepless.

She willed the queasiness away. "Go on, Doctor."

"It's not that anyone could duplicate our work," Walcott said, still in that faint, die-away voice. "For one thing, we didn't get to put on the last, very critical equations, which Timmy and I are still working out. But all of the work is *ours*, and we want it back. Timmy gave up several chamber-music rehearsals to our efforts. And, of course, there will be medical prizes someday."

Leisha gazed at Walcott's face. An alteration in body chemistry that could transform the human race, and this wispy man seemed to see it primarily in terms of rose bushes, pirate games, prizes, and chamber music. She said, "You wanted a lawyer to tell you where you stood legally. Personally."

"Yes. And to represent Timmy and me against the bank, or Samplice, if it comes to that." Suddenly he looked at her with that disconcerting directness that he seemed able to summon but not maintain. "We came to you because you're a Sleepless. And because you're Leisha Camden. Everyone knows you don't believe in separating the human race into two so-called species, and of course our work would end that sort of . . . this sort of . . ." He waved the tabloid picture of her and Calvin Hawke. "And, of course, theft is theft, even within a company."

"Samplice didn't steal your research, Dr. Walcott. Neither did the bank."

"Then who . . ."

"I have no evidence. But I'd like to see both you and Dr. Herlinger here tomorrow at 8:00 A.M. And in the meantime—this is important—don't write anything down. Anywhere."

"I understand."

She said, not knowing she was going to speak until the words were out, "*Making Sleepers into Sleepless . . .*"

"Yes," he said, "well." And he turned away from her face to stare across her otherwise utilitarian office at the exotic flowers, riotous with color or pale as moonlight, planted under artificial light in their specially-built corner bed.

"They're all legitimate," Kevin said. He came into Leisha's study from his own, hard-copy in hand. She looked up from her brief for *Simpson*

v. *Offshore Fishing*. The flowers that Alice insisted on sending daily sat on her desk: sunflowers and daisies and genemod alumbines. The things never wilted before the next shipment arrived. Even in winter the apartment was filled with California blooms Leisha didn't really like but couldn't bring herself to throw away.

Lamplight glowed on Kevin's glossy brown hair, strong smooth face. He looked younger than 47, younger in fact than Leisha, although he was four years older. *Blanker*, Alice had said to Leisha, but she had only said it once.

"All legitimate?"

"The whole file drawer," he said. "Walcott was State University of New York at Potsdam and Deflores University, not distinguished but acceptable. Middling student. Two minor publications, clean police record, sits square with the IRS. Two teaching posts, two research, no official acrimony when he left either of them, so maybe he's just a restless type. Herlinger is different. He's only twenty-five, this is his first job. Berkeley and U.C. Irvine in biochemistry, graduated in the top five percent of his class, promising future. But just before his Ph.D. was granted he was arrested, tried, and convicted for gene-altering controlled substances. He got a suspended sentence, but that's enough to make problematical a job anywhere better than Samplice. At least for a while. No tax problems, but then no income yet either to speak of."

"Which controlled substance?"

"Luna snow, altered for electrical storms in the limbic. Makes you think you're a religious prophet. Trial records show Herlinger saying he had no other way to make med school tuition. He appears very bitter; maybe you want to call up the records for yourself."

Leisha said, "I will. Does it feel to you like a young man's temporary bitterness over a bad break? Or a part of his character?"

Kevin shrugged. She should have known better; that was not the kind of determination Kevin would make. Consequences interested him; motivations didn't. Leisha said, "Only two minor publications for Walcott, and mediocre school performance, yet he's capable of a breakthrough like this?"

Kevin smiled. "You always were an intellectual snob, my darling."

"As are we all. All right, researchers get lucky. Or maybe Herlinger did the real DNA work, not Walcott; maybe Herlinger's very capable intellectually but either is an exploitable innocent or just can't follow rules. What about Samplice?"

"Legitimate, struggling company, mediocre earnings profile, ROA less than 3 percent last year, which is low for a high-tech organization that made no major capital investments. I give them another year, two at the most. It's badly managed; the director, Lawrence Lee, has the job solely because of his name. His father was Stanton Lee."

"Nobel Prize in physics?"

"Yes. And Director Lee claims descent from General Robert E. as well, although that claim's bogus. But it looks good in publicity releases. Walcott told you the truth; record-keeping at Samplice is a mess. I doubt they can find things in their own electronic files. There's no leadership. And Lee has a board of directors' reprimand for mismanagement of funds."

"And First National Bank?"

"Absolutely square. All the records for that safe-deposit box are complete and accurate. Of course, that doesn't mean that they weren't tampered with from the outside, both electronically and in hard-copy. But I'd be really surprised if the bank is involved."

"I never thought it was," Leisha said grimly. "It's got strong security?"

"The best. We designed it."

She hadn't known that. "Then there are only two groups that can manage that kind of electronic wizardry, and your company's one of them."

Kevin said gently, "That may not be true. There are Sleepers who are good deck rats. . . ."

"Not that good."

Kevin didn't repeat his statement about her intellectual snobbery. Instead he said quietly, "If Walcott's research is accurate, this could change the world, Leisha. Again."

"I know." She found herself staring at him, and wondered what emotions had been on her face. "Want a glass of wine, Kevin?"

"I can't, Leisha. I've got all this work to finish."

"Actually, so do I. You're right."

He went back to his study. Leisha picked up her notes for *Simpson* v. *Offshore Fishing*. She had trouble concentrating. How long had it been since she and Kevin had made love? Three weeks? Four?

There was so much work to do. Events were happening so fast. Maybe she could see him before she left again in the morning. No—he was taking the other plane to Bonn. Well then, later in the week. If they were in the same city, if they both had time. She felt no sense of urgency about sex with Kevin. But, then, she never had.

A memory twisted in her: Richard's hands on her breasts.

She leaned closer to the terminal, widening her search for legal precedents in marine law.

Leisha said levelly, "You stole Adam Walcott's research papers from a safe-deposit box in the First National Bank in Chicago."

Jennifer Sharifi raised her eyes to Leisha's. The two women stood at opposite ends of Jennifer's living room in Sanctuary. Behind the glossy mound of Jennifer's bound hair, the portrait of Tony Indivino blinked and smiled.

"Yes," Jennifer said. "I did."

"Jennifer!" Richard cried, in anguish.

Leisha turned slowly toward him. It seemed to her that the anguish was not for the deed, but for the admitting of it. Richard knew.

He stood on the balls of his feet, his head with the bushy eyebrows lowered. He looked just the same as he had at seventeen, the day she'd gone to meet him in the small suburban house in Evanston. Almost thirty years ago. Richard had found something in Sanctuary, something he needed, some sense of community—maybe he had always needed it. And Sanctuary was, always had been, Jennifer. Jennifer and Tony. Nonetheless, to be part of this criminal theft, Richard must have changed. To be a part of this, he must have changed beyond her knowing.

He said thickly, "Jennifer will say nothing without her lawyer present."

Leisha said acidly, "Well, that shouldn't be too difficult. How many lawyers has Sanctuary captured by now? Candace Holt. Will Sandaleros. Jonathan Cocchiara. How many others?"

Jennifer sat down on the sofa, drawing the folds of her *abbaya* around her. Today the glass wall was opaqued; soft blue-green patterns played over it. Jennifer, Leisha remembered suddenly, had never liked cloudy days.

Jennifer said, "If you're bringing legal charges, Leisha, deliver the warrant."

"You know I'm not a prosecutor. I represent Dr. Walcott."

"Then you plan on handing this alleged theft over to the D.A.?"

Leisha hesitated. She knew, and probably Jennifer knew, there was insufficient evidence for even a grand jury session. The papers were gone, but the bank record showed that Dr. Walcott had been the one to remove them. The best she could possibly do was establish that some new employee or other at First National also had access to the receipts—if it had even been a new employee. How thorough was Sanctuary's advance planning? Their covert information net was extensive enough to cover minor researchers working in third-rate biotechs, if the minor research concerned Sleepless. And Leisha would bet her eyes that no new employee at First National had ever been an old employee at Samplice. She had nothing but hearsay—and, of course, her knowledge of what Jennifer, a Sleepless, would do. But the law was not interested in her inner knowledge. That, too, was only hearsay.

Hopelessness swamped her, frightening because it was so rare, followed by memory: Richard at seventeen, running in and out of the surf with her and Tony and Carol and Jeanine, all of them laughing, sand and water and sky opening up all around in infinite receding light. . . . She sought Richard's eyes.

He turned his back.

Jennifer said composedly, "Why exactly are you here, Leisha? If you have no legal business to transact with me or Richard or Sanctuary, and if your client has nothing to do with us—"

"You just told me you took the papers."

"Did I?" Jennifer smiled. "No, you're mistaken. I would not do or say that."

"I see. You just wanted me to know. And now you just want me to leave."

"I do," Jennifer said, and for a bizarre moment Leisha heard echoes of the marriage ceremony. Jennifer's mind was opaque to her. Standing in her living room, watching the green swirls form and break and re-form on the window, watching Richard's hunched shoulders, Leisha suddenly knew she would never stand anywhere in Sanctuary again.

To Richard—not Jennifer—she said, "The research is still in Walcott's and Herlinger's heads. You can't stop this from coming, if it's real. When I go back to Chicago, I'm going to have my client write it all out and put multiple copies in very safe places. I want you to know this, Richard."

He did not turn around. She watched the bent curve of his spine.

Jennifer said, "Have a nice flight."

Adam Walcott did not take disappointment well. "You mean there's nothing we can do? *Nothing?*"

"There's insufficient evidence." Leisha got up from her desk and walked around it to sit in a chair opposite Walcott's. "You have to understand, Doctor, that the courts are still struggling with the limitations of electronic documents as evidence. They've been struggling with it longer than I've been alive. At first computer-generated documents were treated as hearsay because they weren't originals. Then they were barred because there were just too many people who could break systems security. Now since *Sabino* v. *Lansing* they're treated as a separate, inherently weaker category of evidence. Signed hard-copies are what count, which means burglars and thieves who can manipulate the tangible are kings of even electronic crime. Right back where we started."

Walcott did not look interested in this informal judicial history. "But, Ms. Camden—"

"Dr. Walcott, you don't seem to be focused on the main point here. You have all the research in your head, research that could change the world. And whoever took your documents has only nine-tenths of it because the final piece is *only* in your head. That's what you told me, correct?"

"Correct."

"So write it down again. Now. Here."

"Now?" The wispy little man seemed taken aback by this idea. "Why?"

And Jennifer thought that Leisha was an innocent. Leisha spoke very carefully, choosing her words. "Dr. Walcott, this research is potentially a very valuable property. Worth billions, over time, to you or to Samplice or, more likely, to you both in some percentage deal. I'm prepared to represent you with that, if you so choose—"

"Oh, goody," Walcott said. Leisha looked at him hard, but he truly did not seem sarcastic. His left hand wrapped absently around the back of his head to scratch his right ear.

She said patiently, "But you must realize that whenever billions are involved, thieves are involved. You've already seen that. And you've told me you haven't yet filed for any patents because you didn't want Director Lee to know what you were working on." After a moment she added, "Correct?" There was no point in assuming anything with this man.

"Correct."

"Fine. Then what you must also realize is that people who will thieve for millions might also—I don't say this would happen, only that it could—might also—"

She couldn't finish the sentence. The pains in her stomach were back, and she folded her arms across her abdomen. *Richard, holding her in his shabby bedroom in Evanston, she fifteen years old, meeting a fellow Sleepless for the first time and filled with exhilaration like light. . . .*

Walcott said, "You mean the thieves might try to kill me. Me and Timmy. Even without the final part of the research."

Leisha said, "Write it all down. Now. Here."

She gave him a free-standing computer and a private office. He was only in it twenty-five minutes, which surprised her. But, then, how long could formulas and assumptions take to write down? It wasn't like a legal brief.

She realized that she'd been expecting him to fumble over the task because he was a Sleeper.

She made eight hard-copies of the papers on the small free-standing copier she used for privileged client-attorney information, resisting the desire to read them. She probably wouldn't have understood them anyway. She gave him one copy, plus the free-standing deck. "Just so there's no misunderstanding, Doctor. These seven copies will go into various vaults. One in the safe here, one at Baker Enterprises, Kevin Baker's firm, which I assure you is impregnable." Walcott gave no sign of knowing who Kevin Baker was; it wasn't possible for any genetic researcher to not know who Kevin Baker was.

"Tell as many people as you like that there are multiple copies of your current unnamed research project with different people. I'll do the same. The more people who know, the less of a target you are. Also, I urge you as counsel to tell Director Lee what you've been doing and to file patents on this work, in your own name. I should be with you when you approach Lee, if we're going to establish personal ownership of part of this work apart from Samplice."

"Fine," Walcott said. He combed his hand through his negligible hair. "You've been so frank . . . I feel I have to be frank, too."

Something in his tone made Leisha glance up sharply.

"The fact is, I . . . the research I just wrote out for you . . ." He ran the other hand through his hair and stood on one foot, an embarrassed diminutive crane.

"Yes?"

"It's not all there. I left off the last piece. The piece the thieves don't have either."

He was more cautious, then, than she had suspected. On the whole, Leisha approved; reckless clients were worse than untrusting ones. Even when the person untrusted was the client's own attorney.

Walcott looked past her, out the window. He still stood on one foot. The weirdly intermittent forcefulness returned to his voice. "You said yourself you don't know who stole the first copy. But it's potentially very valuable to replicate. Or not replicate. And you're a Sleepless, Ms. Camden."

"I understand. But it's important that you write down that last piece as well, Doctor, for your own protection. If not here, then somewhere else completely secure." And where, she wondered, was that? "You should also—this is an important point—tell as many people as possible that all the research exists somewhere else besides your head."

Walcott finally lowered his raised foot to the floor. He nodded. "I'll think about that. Do you really think I could be in actual physical danger, Ms. Camden?"

Leisha thought of Sanctuary. The queasiness returned to her stomach; it had nothing to do with what did or did not happen to Walcott. She folded her arms across her belly.

"Yes," she said. "I do."

10

Jordan Watrous poured himself another drink at the Hepplewhite secretary set up as a bar in his mother's living room. His third? Fourth? Maybe no one was counting. From the deck cantilevered over the ocean floated the sound of laughter. To Jordan's ears the laughter sounded nervous, as well it might. What the hell was Hawke saying now? And to whom?

He hadn't wanted to bring Hawke. This was his stepfather's fiftieth birthday; Beck had wanted a small family party. But Jordan's mother had just finished decorating her new house and she wanted to show it off. For twenty years Alice Camden Watrous had lived as if she had no money, not touching the inheritance from her father except, Jordan later learned, to pay for his and Moira's schooling and computers and sports. She had treated her money as if it were a large, dangerous dog she had custody of but would not approach. Then, on her fortieth birthday, something apparently happened inside his mother, something Jordan didn't understand. That didn't surprise him. Much of people's behavior baffled him.

His mother had suddenly built this big house on the ocean at Morro Bay, where a few miles out gray whales lifted their flukes and spouted past. She had furnished it with expensive, understated British antiques bought in Los Angeles, New York, and London. Beck, easily the sweetest-tempered man Jordan had ever met, smiled indulgently, even though his wife had hired a different contractor, not Beck, to build the house. Some days Jordan, driving out to the site with his mother, had found Beck working alongside the union carpenters and their robots, nailing boards and aligning joists. When the house was finished, Jordan had waited apprehensively for what new sides of his mother might emerge. Social climbing? Plastic surgery? Lovers? But Alice had ignored their fashionable neighbors, let her stocky figure stay stocky, and hummed contentedly about her British antiques and her beloved garden.

"Why British?" Jordan had said once, fingering the back of a Sheraton chair. "Why antiques?"

"My mother was British," Alice said, the first and last time Jordan had ever heard her mention her mother.

The birthday party for Beck was also a housewarming. Alice had invited all of her and Beck's friends, her colleagues from the Twin Group, Moira's graduate-school friends and professors, Leisha Camden and Kevin Baker, and a Sleepless whom Jordan had never laid eyes on before, a pretty young redhead named Stella Bevington whom Alice had hugged and kissed as if she were another Moira. Calvin Hawke had invited himself.

"I don't think so, Hawke," Jordan had said in the factory office in Mississippi, and with anyone else that would have ended it.

"I'd like to meet your mother, Jordy. Most men don't speak as well of their mothers as you do. Or as often."

Jordan couldn't help it; he felt himself flush. Since he was in grade school he had been open to the charges of being a mama's boy. Hawke hadn't meant anything . . . or had he? Lately everything Hawke said stung. Was that Jordan's fault or Hawke's? Jordan couldn't tell.

"It's really a family celebration, Hawke."

"I certainly wouldn't want to intrude on family," Hawke said smoothly. "But didn't you say it was a big housewarming, too? I have a gift I'd like your mother to have for her house. Something that belonged to my mother."

"That's very generous of you," Jordan said, and Hawke grinned.

The manners Alice had drilled into her son amused Hawke. Jordan was astute enough to see this, but not astute enough to know what to do about it. He steeled himself to frankness. "But I don't want you there. My aunt will be there. And some other Sleepless."

"I perfectly understand," Hawke said, and Jordan thought the matter was closed. But somehow it kept coming up. And somehow the stings got worse in Hawke's innocent-sounding phrases, and because they were innocent Jordan felt guilty at snapping back at Hawke. And somehow now Hawke stood out on his mother's deck talking to Beck and Moira and an admiring crowd of Moira's college friends while Leisha, completely silent, watched Hawke with a blank expression, and Jordan slipped away to splash his third—fourth?—whiskey into his glass so fast it spilled on his mother's new pale-blue rug.

"It's not your fault," said a voice behind him. Leisha. He hadn't heard her footsteps.

He said, "What do you do for whiskey spills? Carbo-eaters? Or would they hurt the rug?"

"Forget the rug. I mean it's not your fault that Hawke is here. I'm sure you didn't want him to be, and I'm sure he steamrolled right over you. Don't blame yourself, Jordan."

"No one can ever tell him no," Jordan said miserably.

"Oh, Alice could have, if she'd wanted to. Don't doubt that. He's here because she said it was all right, not because he maneuvered you into an invitation."

The question had bothered him for a long time. "Leisha, does Mom approve of what I do? Of the whole We-Sleep Movement?"

Leisha was silent for a long time. Finally she said, "She wouldn't tell me, Jordan," which was of course true. It had been a stupid question, stupidly blurted out. He mopped ineffectively at the rug with a napkin.

Leisha said, "Why don't you ask her?"

"We don't talk about . . . Sleepers and Sleeplessness."

"No, I can believe that," Leisha said. "There's a lot this family doesn't talk about, isn't there?"

He said, "Where's Kevin?"

Leisha looked at him with genuine surprise. "That wasn't a non sequitur, was it?"

Embarrassment flooded him. "I didn't mean to imply—"

"It's all right, Jordan. Stop apologizing all the time. Kevin had to see a client on an orbital."

Jordan whistled. "I didn't know there were Sleepless on any of the orbitals."

Leisha frowned. "There aren't. But most of Kevin's work is for international clients who aren't necessarily, or even usually, Sleepless but who—"

"—are rich enough to afford him," Hawke said, coming up behind them. "Ms. Camden, you haven't spoken to me all night."

"Was I supposed to?"

He laughed. "Certainly not. Why would Leisha Camden have anything to say to a union organizer of underclass morons who waste a third of their life in zombie nonproductivity?"

She said evenly, "I have never thought of Sleepers that way."

"Really? Do you think of them as equals? Do you know what Abraham Lincoln said about equality, Ms. Camden? You published a book about Lincoln's view of the Constitution, didn't you, under the pseudonym Elizabeth Kaminsky?"

She didn't answer. Jordan said, "That's enough, Hawke."

Hawke said, "Lincoln said about the man who is denied economic equality: 'When you have put him down and made it impossible for him to be but as the beasts of the field; when you have extinguished his soul in this world and placed him where the ray of hope is blown out as in the darkness of the damned, are you quite sure that the demon you have roused will not turn and rend you?'"

Leisha said, "Do you know what Aristotle said about equality? 'Equals revolt that they may become superior. Such is one state of mind that creates revolutions.'"

Hawke's face sharpened. To Jordan it actually seemed the bones grew even more pointed; something moved behind Hawke's eyes. He started to say something, evidently thought better of it, and smiled enigmatically. Then he turned and walked away.

After a moment Leisha said, "I'm sorry, Jordan. That was unforgivable at a party. I'm too used to courtrooms, I guess."

"You look terrible," Jordan said abruptly, surprising himself. "You've lost too much weight. Your neck is all scrunched up, and your face is drawn."

"Looking my age," Leisha said, suddenly amused. Now why should that amuse her? Maybe it wasn't the Sleepless he didn't understand; maybe it was women. He turned his head toward the deck for a glimpse of the tiny flashing lights Stella Bevington wore in her red hair.

Leisha leaned forward and gripped his wrist. "Jordan—do you ever wish you could become a Sleepless?"

He stared into her green eyes, so different from Hawke's: her eyes reflected all light back at you. Like a parcel refused. All of a sudden his uncertainty left him. "Yes, Leisha. I do wish it. We all do. But we can't. That's why I work with Hawke in unionizing underclass morons who waste a third of their life asleep. Because we can't be you."

His mother came up behind them. "Is everything all right in here?" Alice asked, looking from her son to her sister. She wore, Jordan suddenly noticed, her usual warm expression and a truly hideous dress, an expensive green silk that did nothing to flatter her stoutness. Around her neck was the antique pendant Beck had given her. It had once belonged to some British duchess.

"Fine," Jordan said, and couldn't think of anything else to say. Twins—they were *twins*. The three of them smiled at each other, silent, until Alice spoke. Jordan was startled to see that his mother was a little drunk.

"Leisha, did I tell you about the new case registered with our Twin Group? Twins raised apart from birth, but when one broke his arm, the other felt pain for weeks in the same arm and couldn't figure out why?"

"Or thought he felt the pain," Leisha said, "in retrospect."

"Ah," Alice said, as if Leisha had answered some other question entirely, and Jordan saw that his mother's eyes were more knowing than he had ever seen them, and fully as dark as Calvin Hawke's own.

In the early morning the New Mexico desert was incandescent with pearly light. Sharp-edged shadows, blue and pink and colors Leisha had never imagined shadows could be, crept like living things across the vast emptiness. On the distant horizon the Sangre de Cristo Mountains rose clear and precise.

"Beautiful, isn't it?" Susan Melling said.

Leisha said, "I never knew light could look like that."

"Not everybody likes the desert. Too desolate, too empty, too hostile to human life."

"You like it."

"Yes," Susan said. "I do. What do you want, Leisha? This isn't just a social visit; your crisis air is at gale force. A civilized gale. Solemn urgent sweeps of very cold air."

Despite herself, Leisha smiled. Susan, now seventy-eight, had left medical research when her arthritis worsened. She had moved to a tiny town fifty miles from Santa Fe, a move inexplicable to Leisha. There was no hospital, no colleagues, few people to talk to. Susan lived in a thick-walled adobe house with sparse furniture and a sweeping view from the roof, which she used as a terrace. On the deep, whitewashed window sills and few tables she set out rocks, polished to a high gloss by the wind, or vases of tough-stemmed wildflowers, or even animal bones, bleached by the sun to the same incandescent whiteness as the snow on the distant mountains. Walking uneasily through the house for the first time, Leisha had felt a palpable relief, like a small pop in her chest, when she saw the terminal and medical journals in Susan's study. All Susan would say about her retirement was, "I worked with my mind for a long time. Now I'm groping for the rest of it," a statement that Leisha understood intellectually—she had doggedly read the standard mystics—but no other way. The 'rest' of what, exactly? She had been reluctant to question Susan further, in case this was like Alice's

Twin Group: pseudopsychology tricked out as scientific fact. Leisha didn't think she could bear to see Susan's fine mind seduced by the deceptive comforts of hokum. Not Susan.

Susan said now, "Let's go inside, Leisha. The desert is wasted on you. You're not old enough for it yet. I'll make tea."

The tea was good. Sitting beside Susan on her sofa, Leisha said, "Have you kept up with your field, Susan? With, for instance, the genetic-alteration research Gaspard-Thiereux published last year?"

"Yes," Susan said. A gleam of amusement came and went in her eyes, sunken now but still bright. She had stopped dying her hair; it hung in white braids only slightly less thick than Leisha remembered from childhood. But Susan's skin had the veined transparency of eggshells. "I haven't renounced the world like some flagellant monk, Leisha. I access the journals regularly, although I have to say it's been a long time since there was anything really worth studying, except the work of Gaspard-Thiereux."

"There is now." Leisha told her about Walcott, Samplice, the research and its theft. She didn't mention Jennifer, or Sanctuary. Susan sipped her tea, listening quietly. When Leisha finished, Susan said nothing.

"Susan?"

"Let me see the research notes." She put down her tea cup; it rattled hard on the glass table.

Susan studied the papers for a long time. Then she disappeared into her study to run some equations. "Use only a free-standing deck," Leisha said, "and wipe the program afterward. Completely." After a moment Susan nodded slowly.

Leisha wandered around the living room, gazing at rocks with holes bored through them by freak winds, rocks so smooth they might have lain for a million years at the bottom of an ocean, rocks with sudden protuberances like malignant growths. She picked up an animal skull and ran her fingers across the clean bone.

When Susan returned, she was calmer, all critical faculties at full RAM. "Well, it looks like a genuine line of research, as far as it goes. That's what you wanted to know, isn't it?"

"Does it go far enough?"

"Depends on what's in that missing piece. What he has here is new, but it's new more in the way of not having been explored before because it's a semibizarre byway, rather than being new because it's an inevitable but difficult extension of existing knowledge, if you see the difference."

"I do see it. But what *is* there that could logically support a final piece that could actually alter Sleepers into Sleepless?"

"It's possible," Susan said. "He's made some unorthodox departures on Gaspard-Thiereux's work, but as far as I can tell from this . . . yes. Yes. It's possible."

Susan sank onto the sofa and covered her face with her hands.

Leisha said, "How many of the side effects might be . . . is it possible that . . ."

"Are you asking me whether Sleepers who become Sleepless beyond *in vitro* might still have the non-aging organs of the rest of you? God, *I* don't know. The biochemistry of that is still so murky." Susan lowered her hands and smiled, without humor. "You Sleepless don't provide us with enough research specimens. You don't die often enough."

"Sorry," Leisha said dryly. "We all have such full calendars."

"Leisha," Susan said, her voice not quite steady, "what happens now?"

"Apart from the infighting at Samplice? We file for patents in Walcott's name. Actually, I've already started that, before anybody else can. Then, after Walcott and Herlinger—and that's another problem."

"What's another problem?"

"Walcott-and-Herlinger. I suspect that Herlinger might have done much of this work, and that Walcott is not going to want to share credit with him if he can avoid it. Walcott's a sort of meek belligerent. Walks absently through the world, oblivious of how it actually functions, until someone crosses him, and then he howls and hangs on with all his incisors."

"I know the type," Susan said. "Nothing like your father."

Leisha looked at her; Susan rarely spoke of Roger Camden. Susan picked up the same animal skull Leisha bad been fingering. "What do you know about Georgia O'Keeffe?"

"An artist, wasn't she? Nineteenth century?"

"Twentieth. She painted these skulls. And this desert. Many times." Susan suddenly dropped the skull; it shattered on the stone floor. "Leisha, have that baby you and Kevin are always talking about. There's no guarantee that just because no female Sleepless has gone into menopause yet, you never will. Even Fallopian tubes that don't them-selves seem to age can't manufacture new gametes. Your eggs are forty-three years old."

Leisha moved toward her. "Susan—are you saying you regret . . . that you wish . . ."

"No, I'm not," Susan said crisply. "I had you, and Alice, and I still do. Biological daughters couldn't be more important to me than you two. But who do you have, Leisha? Kevin—"

Leisha said quickly, "Kevin and I are fine."

Susan looked at her with a tender, skeptical expression that made Leisha repeat, "We're *fine*, Susan. We work together really well. That's what really matters, after all."

But Susan only went on looking at her with the same tender doubt, Adam Wolcott's research papers in her arthritic hands.

Simpson v. *Offshore Fishing* was a complicated case. Leisha's client, James Simpson, was a Sleepless fisherman alleging deliberate disrup-tions of Lake Michigan fish-migration patterns through the illegal use of retroviruses, themselves legal, by a competing firm. The competitor, Offshore Fishing, Limited, was owned by Sleepers. The case would turn on judicial interpretation of the Canton-Fenwick Act governing uses of biotechnology in restraint of trade. Leisha had to be in court by 10:00 A.M., so she had asked for a seven o'clock meeting at Samplice.

"Well, nobody's likely to *be* there at seven o'clock," Walcott had grumbled, "including me." Leisha had stared hard at his wispy face on her comlink, amazed all over again at the petty obtuseness of the mind that was going to remake the biological and social world. Had Newton been like this? Einstein? Callingwood? Actually, they had. Einstein could not remember his stops on trains; Callingwood, the genius of Y-energy applications, regularly lost the shoes off his feet and refused to allow anyone to change his bedsheets for months at a time. Walcott wasn't unique, he was a type, although not a common one. Sometimes it seemed to Leisha that the process of intellectual maturity was merely discovering that exotics and uniques were only members of rarer sets. She called Samplice herself and insisted on the 7:00 A.M. meeting.

Director Lawrence Lee, a tanned, handsome man who wore Italian silk headbands a little too young for him, turned out to be as difficult as Walcott said he was. "We *own* this research, whatever the hell it is, even if it turns out to be valuable, and believe you me, I have my doubts. These two . . . *researchers* work for me, and don't any of you fancy lawyers forget it!"

Leisha was the only fancy lawyer in sight. Samplice legal counsel was Arnold Seeley, a hard-eyed man with an aggressively shaved head who nonetheless fumbled questions on which he should have been pressing Leisha hard. She leaned across the table. "I forget very little, Mr. Lee. There are legal precedents about scientific work, especially scientific work with commercial applications. Dr. Walcott is not in the same labor category as a carpenter fixing your front porch. There are also ambiguities in the contract Dr. Walcott signed with Samplice at the beginning of his employment. I presume you have a copy with you, Mr. Seeley?"

"Uh, no . . . wait . . ."

"Why don't you?" Lee snapped. "Where is it? What's it say?"

"I'd need to check. . . ."

Impatience filled Leisha, the same impatience she always felt in the presence of incompetence. She pushed the impatience down; this was too important to jeopardize with inept shows of bad feeling. Or additional shows of it. Lee and Seeley and Walcott, who in their ineptly warring hands held eight hours a day for hundreds of thousands of people, all searched electronic notebooks for the employment contract.

"Got it?" Leisha said crisply. "All right, second paragraph, third line . . ." She took them through the poorly-phrased language, the legal precedents for shared scientific copyrights, the landmark *Boeing* v. *Fain* "auteur" ruling. Seeley shifted his hard eyes over his screen and drummed his fingers on the table. Lee blustered. Walcott sat with a small smug smile. Only Herlinger, the twenty-five-year-old assistant, listened with comprehension. He had surprised Leisha: heavyset and already balding at twenty-five, Herlinger would have looked like a thug except for a kind of bitter dignity, a stoic disillusionment that didn't seem to belong either with his youth or with Walcott's spiky, eccentric presumed-genius. They were an unlikely team.

". . . and so I'd like to suggest an out-of-court settlement about the patents."

Lee started to bluster again. Seeley said quickly, "What type of settlement? A percentage or an up-front sum?"

Leisha kept her face impassive. She had him. "We would have to work that out, Mr. Seeley."

Lee almost shouted, "If you think you can get away with taking from me what belongs to this firm—"

Seeley turned coolly to him. "I think the shareholders might disagree about whose firm it was."

The "shareholders" included Sanctuary, although Lee would not necessarily know that Leisha knew that. Leisha and Seeley both waited for Lee to come to this realization. As he did, his small button mouth pursed, and he looked at Leisha with a fearful sneer. She thought that it had been a long time since she had disliked someone so much.

"Maybe," Lee said, "we could *talk* about a settlement. On my terms."

Leisha said, "Fine. Let's talk terms."

She had him.

Afterward, Walcott accompanied her and her bodyguard to the car. "Will they settle?"

"Yes," Leisha said. "I think so. You have an interesting set of colleagues, Doctor."

He eyed her warily.

"Your director forgets he runs a publicly-traded company, your firm's lawyer can't put together a decent class-six employee contract, and your assistant in Sleepless genetic research is riding away on a We-Sleep scooter."

Walcott airily waved his hand. "He's young. Can't afford a car. And of course, if this research goes through, there won't be any We-Sleep Movement. Nobody will have to sleep."

"Except those who can't afford the operation. Or a car."

Walcott regarded her with amusement. "Shouldn't you be arguing the other side, Ms. Camden? In favor of the economic elite? After all, very few people can afford to genetically alter their *in vitro* embryos for sleeplessness."

"I was not arguing, Dr. Walcott. Merely correcting your false statement." In a subtler way, he was just as unlikable as Lee.

Walcott waved his hand. "Ah, well, I suppose you can't help it. Once a lawyer . . ."

She slammed the car door hard enough that her bodyguard jumped.

She was late for court. The judge was looking around irritably. "Ms. Camden?"

"I'm sorry, Your Honor. I was unavoidably detained."

"Avoid it, Counselor."

"Yes, Your Honor." The courtroom was nearly empty, despite the importance of the case to Constitutional law. Fish-migration patterns did not rivet the newsgrids. In addition to the opposing parties and their counsel, she saw one reporter, state and federal environmental officials, three youngsters she guessed to be either law or ecology students, one ex-judge, and three witnesses.

And Richard Keller, who was not due to testify as her expert witness until tomorrow.

He sat in the back of the room, as upright as if on brainies, a thick-set man surrounded by four bodyguards. That must be what happened when you lived year in and year out in Sanctuary; the rest of the world looked even more dangerous than it was. Richard caught her eye. He didn't smile. Something in Leisha's chest turned cold.

"If you're finally ready to start, Counselor . . ."

"Yes, Your Honor. We are. I call Carl Tremolia to the stand."

Tremolia, a burly fisherman who was a hostile witness, stalked up the aisle. Leisha's client's eyes narrowed. Tremolia wore a We-Sleep electronic pin on his lapel. There was a disturbance by the door; someone was talking to the bailiff in an insistent undertone.

"Your Honor, I petition the court to order the witness to remove his lapel pin," Leisha said. "Given the circumstances of the case, political opinions of the witness, whether expressed by words or jewelry, are prejudicial."

The judge said, "Remove the pin."

The fisherman tore if off his jacket. "You can make me take off the pin but you can't make me buy Sleepless!"

"Strike that," the judge said. "Mr. Tremolia, if you do not answer only when spoken to I will charge you with contempt . . . What *is* it, Bailiff?"

"Sorry, Your Honor. Message for Ms. Camden. Personal and urgent."

He handed Leisha a slip of hard-copy. *Call Kevin Baker at office immediately. Urgent and personal.* "Your Honor . . ."

The judge sighed. "Go, go."

In the corridor she pulled a comlink from her briefcase. Kevin's face appeared on the miniature screen.

"Leisha. About Walcott—"

"This is an unshielded link, Kevin—"

"I know. It doesn't matter, this is in the public record. Hell, in a few hours the whole fucking world will know. Walcott can't file for those patents."

"Why not? Samplice—"

"Forget Samplice. The patents were filed two months ago. Neat, clean, unbreakable. In the name of Sanctuary, Incorporated . . . Leisha?"

"I'm here," she said numbly. Kevin had always told her that nobody could falsify the government's patent files. There were too many backups, electronic and hard-copy and free-standing off-line. Nobody.

Kevin said, "There's more. Leisha . . . Timothy Herlinger is dead."

"Dead! I saw him not a half-hour ago! Riding away on a scooter!"

"He was hit by a car. The deflection shields on his scooter failed. A cop happened to come by a few minutes later, put it right on the Med-Net, and of course I have all nets monitored to flag key names."

She said unsteadily, "Who hit him?"

"A woman named Stacy Hillman, gave her address as Barrington. I have wizards checking her now. But it looks like an accident."

"Scooter deflector shields are Y-energy cones. They don't fail; it's one of their main marketing points. They just don't. Not even on a shoddy We-Sleep scooter."

Kevin whistled. "He was riding a We-Sleep scooter?"

Leisha closed her eyes. "Kevin, send two bodyguards to find Walcott. The best bodyguards you can hire. No—your own. He was at Samplice a half-hour ago. Have him escorted to our apartment. Or would your office be safer?"

"My office."

"I can't leave court until two at the earliest. And I can't ask for a recess. Not again." She had already used recesses in this case to go to Mississippi and to Sanctuary. To Sanctuary twice.

Kevin said, "Just go ahead with your case. I'll keep Walcott safe."

Leisha opened her eyes. From the courtroom door the bailiff watched her. She had always liked that bailiff, a gentle old man who liked to show her too-expensive holos of his grandchildren. At the other end of the corridor stood Richard Keller, back preternaturally straight, waiting. For her. He knew what Kevin's call was about, and now he stood waiting. She knew it, as certainly as she knew her own name.

How had he known what Kevin was about to tell her?

She went back to court to ask the judge for a recess.

* * *

Leisha led Richard to her office a block away, not touching him as they walked, not looking at him. Inside, she opaqued the window all the way to black. The exotics, passion flowers and ginger and flame orchids, began to close.

She said quietly, "Tell me."

Richard gazed at the closing flowers. "Your father grew those."

She knew that tone of voice; she had heard it in police interrogation rooms, in jails, in court: the voice of a man who will say anything that comes into his head, anything at all, because he has already lost everything. The tone carried a certain amount of freedom, of a kind that always made Leisha want to look away.

She didn't look away now. "Tell me, Richard."

"Sanctuary stole Walcott's research papers. There's a network, Inside wizards and Outside Sleeper underworld, very complex. Jennifer's been building it for years. They did it all: Samplice, First National Bank."

This was nothing new. Richard had told her as much in Sanctuary, in Jennifer's presence. "I have to say something, Richard. Listen carefully. You're talking to Walcott's counsel, and nothing you say here is off the record. Nothing. Marital privilege of confidentiality won't apply to anything Jennifer said to you in front of a third party or parties, such as the Sanctuary Council—Article 861 of United States Code. You can be required to repeat what you say here under oath. Do you understand?"

He smiled, almost whimsically. The tone was still in his voice. "Of course. That's why I'm here. Record it if you like."

"Recording on." To Richard she said, "Go on."

"Sanctuary altered the file patents. Again, both electronically and hard-copy. The dates were chosen carefully—all the hard-copy applications in Washington are stamped 'Received,' but none have reached the review stage of significant official signatures or fingerprints. That's what Kevin was telling you, wasn't he?"

"He told me he didn't think anybody could get into the federal system, not even his people."

"Ah, but he would be trying from the Outside alone."

"Do you have specifics? Names, dates, said in front of third parties as part of conversations that would have taken place even if you and Jennifer weren't husband and wife?"

"Yes."

"Do you have written proof?"

Richard smiled slightly. "No. All hearsay."

Leisha burst out, "*Why*, Richard? Not Jennifer—but you? Why did you?"

"Could anybody give a simple answer to a question like that? It's a whole lifetime of decisions. To go to Sanctuary, to marry Jennifer, to have the kids—" He got up and walked over to the flowers. The way he fingered their hairy leaves made Leisha rise and follow him.

"Then why tell me this now?"

"Because this is the only way I have left to stop Jennifer." He raised his eyes to Leisha, but she knew he didn't see her. "For *her* sake. There's no one in Sanctuary who can stop her anymore—hell, they encourage her, especially Cassie Blumenthal and Will Sandaleros. My kids . . . Criminal charges over the patents will at least scare off some of her Outside contacts. They're scary people, Leisha, and I don't want her dealing with them. I know that even with my testimony, unsupported hearsay, you don't have much of a case, and probably the whole thing will get thrown out of court—do you think I'd be here if I thought she could be indicted for anything? I studied *Wade* v. *Tremont* and *Jastrow* v. *United States* very carefully and I want it on the record that I did. I just want Jenny stopped. My kids—the hatred for Sleepers they're learning, the sense of entitlement to do anything—anything, Leisha—in the name of self-protection; it scares me. This isn't what Tony intended!"

Leisha and Richard had never, after the first time, been able to discuss what Tony Indivino had intended.

Richard said, outwardly more calm, "Tony was wrong. I was wrong. You become different, walled away with only other Sleepless for decades. My kids—"

"Different how?"

But Richard only shook his head. "What happens now, Leisha? You turn this over to the U.S. Attorney and he brings charges? For theft and tampering with government records?"

"No. For murder."

She watched him closely. His eyes widened and flared, and she would have bet her life, then, that he knew nothing about Timothy Herlinger's death. But a week ago she would have bet her life that Richard knew nothing about stealing, either.

"Murder?"

"Timothy Herlinger died an hour ago. Under suspicious circumstances."

"And you think—"

Her mind was ahead of his. She saw him catch up, and she took a step backward.

He said slowly, "You're going to charge Jennifer with murder. And make me testify against her. Because of what I've said here."

Somehow she got the word out. "Yes."

"Nobody at Sanctuary planned a murder!" When she didn't answer he seized her wrist hard. "Leisha—nobody at Sanctuary . . . not even Jennifer . . . nobody . . ."

His faltering was the worst thing yet. Richard was unsure that his wife was incapable of political murder. Leisha looked at him levelly. She had to hear it, all of it, because . . . because why? Because she did. Because she had to know.

But there was no more of it to hear. Richard's fist closed on the flower he held and he started to laugh. "Don't!" she begged, but he went on laughing anyway, a braying heaving sound that went on and on, until Leisha opened the office door and told her secretary to call the District Attorney.

The foamstone cell was five paces by six. It held a built-in bed platform, two recyclable blankets, one pillow, a sink, a chair, and a toilet, but no window or terminal. Will Sandaleros, prisoner's counsel, had protested the lack of a terminal; all but isolation cells had some sort of simple read-only terminal of unbreakable alloy, welded to the wall. His client was allowed access to newsgrids, to approved library items, and to the United States E-postal system. The county jailer ignored the protest; he wasn't trusting any Sleepless with a terminal. Nor would he allow the prisoner communal exercise or dining, or visitors in the cell, even Sandaleros. Twenty years ago the same Cattaraugus County jailer, younger and harder, had lost a Sanctuary Sleepless to a prison killing. Not again. Not in *his* jail.

Jennifer Sharifi told the lawyer to discontinue his protests.

The first day, she carefully scrutinized the four corners of her cell. The southeast corner was assigned to prayer. By closing her eyes she could see the rising sun rather than the foamstone wall; within a few days she did not need to close her eyes. The sun was there, summoned by will and belief.

The northeast corner held the sink. She washed completely twice a day, stepping out of her *abbaya* and washing that too, refusing the prison laundry and the prison garb. If the surveillance panel broadcast her daily nakedness, that was as irrelevant as the foamstone wall was to seeing the sun. Only what she did was relevant, not how subhumans viewed what she did. By their prurient viewing they had forfeited the humanity that would have allowed her to consider them.

The remaining two corners were spanned by the cot. She left the bedding folded under it, day after day, untouched. The bed itself became her place of learning. She sat on the edge, straight-backed in her still-wet *abbaya*. When hard-copies she requested were given her, erratically and intermittently, she read them, permitting herself one reading only of each tabloid, each law book, each library printout. When there was nothing to read, she learned by thinking, creating detailed scenarios covering every contingency she could imagine. She thought of the contingencies of her legal situation. Of Walcott's research. Of the future of Sanctuary. Of Leisha Camden's choices. Of the economic underpinnings of each division, each organization, each significant personal or professional relationship within Sanctuary. Each contingency branched at several places; she learned them all until she could close her eyes and see the entire great structure, decision tree after decision tree branching and rebranching, dozens of them. As new data came to her from hard-copies or from Sandaleros, she mentally redrew every affected branch. For each decision point she assigned a text from the Quran or, if there were conflicting possible applications, more than one text. When she could see the enormous balanced whole spread out behind her closed lids, she opened her eyes and taught herself to see it in three dimensions within the cell, filling the space, palpable growing branches like the tree of life itself.

"All she does is sit and stare," the matron reported to the District Attorney. "Sometimes with her eyes open, sometimes closed. Hardly ever moves."

"Does it seem to you a state of catatonia that needs medical attention?"

The matron shook her head, then nodded, then shook her head again. "How the hell would I know what one of them needs!"

The District Attorney didn't answer.

Wednesdays and Sundays were visiting days, but the only visitor

she would ever permit was Will Sandaleros, who came daily to the usually empty visiting gallery, where she sat separated from him by thick
plastiglass under a ring of surveillance panels.

"Jennifer, the grand jury returned an indictment against you."

"Yes," Jennifer said. There were no branches on her decision tree
in which the grand jury did not indict her. "Have they set a trial date?"

"December 8. Motion to reconsider bail was denied."

"Yes," Jennifer said. There had been no branches for bail, either.
"Leisha Camden testified to the grand jury." It wasn't a question.

"Yes. The testimony has been released to counsel; I'm trying to get
a hard-copy to you."

"There have been no hard-copies brought to me in two days."

"I'll move again on that. The newsgrids are about the same; you
don't want to see them."

"Yes," Jennifer said, "I do." The newsgrid hysteria was necessary:
not to her learning but to the strengthening of her prayer. "A reminder
to believers," the Quran said. "Sleepless Murder to Control World!"
"First Money—Now Blood?" "Secret Sleepless Cartel Plots Overthrow of United States—Through Murder!" "Turncoat Sleepless to
Reveal Death Total of Sanctuary Mafia." "Local Gang Claims Fatal
Beating of Teen: 'He Was Sleepless.'"

"I guess maybe you do want them," Sandaleros said. He was twenty-
five years old and had grown up in Sanctuary from the age of four, his
custody voluntarily signed over by parents who had not gotten what
they expected in a genetically-altered child. After Harvard Law, Sandaleros had returned to Sanctuary to base his practice there, leaving
only to consult with clients or appear in court. Even for that he did not
like to leave. He barely remembered his parents, and not with affection. He had been Jennifer's first choice for counsel.

"One thing more," Sandaleros said. "I have a message from your
children."

Jennifer sat very straight. Each time, this was the hardest; this was why
she disciplined herself day after night on the very edge of the hard metal
cot, back straight, mind forced into calm planning. For this. "Go ahead."

"Najla says to tell you she has finished the Physics Three software. Ricky says he found a new fish-migration pattern in the live data from the Gulf Stream, and is mapping it against his father's work in the Global Directory."

Ricky almost always found a way to include his father in his messages; Najla never did. They had been told that their father would testify against their mother in court. Jennifer had insisted that Sandaleros tell them. This was not a world in which Sleepless children could afford sheltered ignorance.

"Thank you," Jennifer said composedly. "Now tell me our defense options."

Later, after Sandaleros had gone, she sat for a long time on the edge of the cot, growing decision trees in the free spaces of her mind.

"Are you really going to do it?" Stella Bevington's pretty face on the comlink was set and cold. "You're really going to testify against one of us?"

"Stella," Leisha said, "I have to."

"Why?"

"Because she's *wrong*. And because—"

"It's not wrong to take care of your own, even if it means breaking the law! You were the one who taught me that—you and Alice!"

"This isn't the same," Leisha said, as evenly as she could. Behind Stella's head on the comlink screen were California genemod palms, long blue fronds bisected by silver. What was Stella doing in California? No outdoor link was ever adequately shielded. "Jennifer is hurting us. All of us, Sleepless and Sleeper alike—"

"Not me. She's not hurting me; *you're* doing that, by shattering the only family some of us have left. We're not all as lucky as you, Leisha!"

"I—" Leisha began, but Stella had already broken the link and Leisha was staring at a blank screen.

Adam Walcott stood in the library of Leisha and Kevin's penthouse, looking distractedly at the rows of law books, the framed holo of Kenzo

Yagai, the sculpture hewn from virgin Luna rock by Mondi Rastell. The sculpture was an androgynous human figure in a soaring heroic pose, arms stretched upward, face illuminated by intelligence. Leisha watched Walcott stand on one foot, run his left hand through his hair, run his right hand through his hair, twitch his wispy shoulders, and lower his foot. Weird—there was no other word for him. Walcott was the weirdest client she'd ever had. She couldn't even tell if he understood what she'd summoned him here to explain.

"Dr. Walcott, you understand that you can still fight the patent case against both Samplice and Sanctuary, simultaneously with the Sharifi murder case." Her voice was steady on the words. Sometimes, in the forced isolation, of her apartment, she practiced saying them aloud: *the Sharifi murder case.*

"But you won't be my lawyer," he said irritably. "You're just dropping the whole thing."

Patiently Leisha started over again. He truly didn't seem to understand. "I am in protective custody until the trial, Dr. Walcott. There have been serious threats against my life. Those aren't my bodyguards you passed in the lobby and the elevator and on the roof—those are federal marshals. I'm in custody here instead of anywhere else because the security here is better than anywhere else. Almost. But I can't represent your patent case in court, and I don't consider it advisable for you to wait until I can. In your own best interests, you should get different counsel, and I've made a list for you to consider."

She held out the hard-copy; Walcott made no move to take it. He stood on his other foot, and the intermittent strength returned to his voice. "It isn't fair!"

"Isn't . . ."

"*Fair.* For a man to work on a genetic revolution, put in his heart blood for a stinking petty company that couldn't recognize genius if it tripped over it . . . I was *promised*, Ms. Camden! Promises were made!"

She was listening intently now, despite herself. The little man's large intensity was somehow frightening. "What kind of promises, Doctor?"

"Recognition! Fame! The attention I deserve, that no one but Sleepless ever gets now!" He spread his arms wide and stood on tiptoe, his voice rising to a shriek. "I was promised!"

Abruptly he seemed aware that Leisha was studying him. He dropped his arms to his side and smiled at her, a smile of such obvious, sickly insincerity that she felt her neck prickle. It was difficult to imagine Director Lee of Samplice, a man too self-absorbed and insecure to recognize others' dreams, ever making such promises. Something was wrong here. "Who promised you those things, Dr. Walcott?"

"Ah, well," he said airily, not meeting her eyes, "you know how it is. You have youthful dreams. Life promises you. And the promise goes away."

She said, more harshly than she intended, "Everybody discovers that, Dr. Walcott. About more worthy dreams than fame and attention."

He didn't seem to have heard her. He stood staring at the portrait of Yagai, and his left arm came up behind his head to thoughtfully rub his right ear.

Leisha said, "Get another lawyer, Dr. Walcott."

"Yes," he said, almost absently, "I will. Thank you. Goodbye. I'll show myself out."

Leisha sat on the library sofa for a long time, wondering why Walcott disturbed her so much. It wasn't anything to do with this particular case; it was larger than that. Was it because she expected competence to be rational? That was the American myth: the competent man, suffused with both individualism and common sense, in control of himself and the material world. History didn't bear that myth out; competent men frequently were out of control or irrational. Lincoln's melancholy, Michelangelo's outrageous temper, Newton's megalomania. Her model had been Kenzo Yagai, but why shouldn't Yagai have been an aberration? Why should she necessarily expect the same logical and disciplined behavior from Walcott? Or from Richard, who could summon the moral strength to stop his wife's destructive and immoral behavior but who now spent his own days in protective custody sitting slumped in a corner, without the will to eat or wash or speak unless he was forced to do those things? Or from Jennifer, who used a brilliant strategic brain in the service of an obsessive need for control?

Or was it she, Leisha, who was not rational, by expecting that all these people would *not* do those things?

She got off the sofa and wandered through the apartment. All the terminals were off; there had come an hour, two days ago, when she could no longer bear the hysterical newsgrids. The windows were transluced to shut out the intermittent three-way scuffles between police and the two warring semipermanent groups of demonstrators below her window. KILL SLEEPLESS BEFORE THEY KILL US! shrilled the electronic signs of one side, answered by FORCE SANCTUARY TO SHARE PATENTS! THEY ARE NOT GODS! Occasionally the two groups, tired of fighting with police, fought with each other. The past two nights Kevin, coming home for dinner, had to run for the building between cordons of bodyguards, police, and screaming rioters, robot newsgrid holocams swooping to within inches of his face for close-ups.

Tonight he was late. Leisha found herself glancing at the clock, disliking the habit but unable to stop. This was the first time in her life she had found it hard to be alone. Or was it? Had she ever really been alone before? In the beginning there had been Daddy and Alice, then Richard and Carol and Jeanine and Tony . . . then, later, Stewart, and Richard again, and then Kevin. And always, always, there had been the law. To study, to question, to apply. The law made it possible for people of widely differing beliefs, abilities, and goals to live side by side in something more than barbarism. And Kevin had believed in his own version of that credo: that a social system was built not on the parochial limits of common culture nor the romantic ones of "the family" nor even on the contemporary manifest destiny of unlimited technological advance for all, but on the twin foundations of consensual legal and economic systems. Only in the presence of both could there be any social or personal security. Money and law. Kevin understood that, as Richard never had. It was the bond between them.

Where was he?

The terminal in the library chimed, the override code for personal calls. Leisha froze. The demonstrators, the We-Sleep fanatics, Sanctuary itself—there were so many enemies for someone like Kevin, even apart from his connection with her . . . She ran to the library.

But it was Kevin himself calling.

"Leisha—listen, honey, I'm sorry I didn't call earlier. I tried, but . . ." His voice trailed off, unlike Kevin. On the comscreen his jawline sagged slightly. He looked to her left. "Leisha, I'm not coming home. We're in the middle of an important negotiation—the Stieglitz contract, you know about it—and I have to be available. I may have to fly on very short notice to Argentina to deal with some political ramifications in their Bahia Blanca subsidiary. If I have to fight my way in and out of the apartment building, or if those crazies keep blocking air lanes on the roof . . . I can't risk it." After a moment he added, "I'm sorry."

She said nothing.

"I'll stay here at the office. Maybe when this is over . . . hell, no 'maybe' about it, when the Stieglitz contract is signed and the trial is over, then I'll come home."

"Sure, Kev," Leisha said. "Sure."

"I knew you'd understand, honey."

"Yes," Leisha said. "I do. I understand you."

"Leisha—"

"Goodbye, Kevin."

She walked from the library to the kitchen and made herself a sandwich, wondering if he would call back. He didn't. She threw the sandwich down the organic chute and went back to the library. The holo of Kenzo Yagai had shifted. Yagai bent over the Y-energy cone prototype, his dark eyes serious and intelligent, the sleeves of his white turn-of-the-century lab coat pushed above the elbows.

Leisha sat down on a straight wooden chair and put her head between her knees. But that position made her think of Richard, slumped in his room, and the thought was unbearable. She walked to the window, cleared it, and watched the street from eighteen floors above, until sudden increased agitation in the mass of distant, tiny demonstrators made it probable that someone with a zoom lens had seen her. She opaqued the windows, returned to the chair, and sat straight-backed.

Afterward, she could never remember how long she had sat there. Instead she remembered something decades old. Once, when she had been an undergraduate at Harvard, she and Stewart Sutter had gone for a walk along the Charles River. The wind had been cold and sharp, and they had run straight into it, laughing, Stewart's cheeks red as apples. Despite the cold they sat on the banks of the river, kissing, until a Mutilation Reminder had staggered, nearly naked, over the withered grass. The MuRems were a bizarre, horrifying religious sect in the service of great ideals. They mutilated their bodies to remind the world of suffering in countries under tyranny, then begged money to alleviate that global suffering. This one had amputated three of his fingers and half of his left foot. The MuRem's mangled hand was tatooed "Egypt," his bare blue foot "Mongolia," and his hideously scarred face "Chile."

He held out his begging bowl to Leisha and Stewart. Leisha, filled with the familiar shamed repugnance, had slipped in a hundred dollars. "Half for Chile, half for Mongolia. For the suffering," he had croaked; his vocal cords, too, had been offered up as a reminder. The look he gave Leisha was so crystalline, so suffused with joy, that she was unable to gaze back. She laid her head on her knees and twined her hand hard in the icy grass. Stewart had put his arms around her and murmured against her cheek. "He's happy, Leisha. He is. He's begging for a purpose, he raises a great deal of money for world suffering. He's doing what he chooses to do, and he's doing it well. He doesn't mind being mutilated. And anyway, he's going away now. He's leaving. Look—he's already gone."

12

The Profit Faire on the levee was in full swing by 8:00 P.M. Below the foamstone walls the Mississippi River slid past, dark and silent. A Y-field had been set up for security, invisible walls enclosing a bubble the diameter of a football field. The bubble covered an arc of river, a hundred yards of broad levee, and a semicircle of rough grass and dark bushes between the scooter factory and the river. From the farthest bushes came occasional giggles, accompanied by much thrashing.

On the south end of the broad levee people flocked around the refreshment kiosks, the hologame booths, the terminals where We-Sleep partially subsidized chances at major newsgrid lotteries. At the north end a noisy band whose name Jordan had forgotten blasted the night with dance music. Every thirty seconds a remote-guided holo of the We-Sleep logo, three-dimensional and six feet high, flashed in a different cubic volume of air: ten feet above the ground, two inches over the water, in the midst of the whirling dancers. Across the river, slightly blurred by the edges of the Y-bubble, the Samsung-Chrysler lights shone chastely.

"The basic flaw in your Aunt Leisha is that she belongs to the eighteenth century, not the twenty-first," Hawke said. "Have some ice cream, Jordy."

"No," Jordan said. He didn't want ice cream; even less did he want to talk to Hawke about Leisha. Again. He tried to deflect their path toward the north end of the Faire, where the dance music would drown Hawke's voice.

Hawke neither deflected nor drowned. "The ice cream's a new biopatent from GeneFresh Farms. Unbelievable in strawberry. Two cones, please."

"I don't really—"

"What do you think, Jordy? Could you ever guess they started with soybean genes? Profit margin of 17 percent last quarter."

"Amazing," Jordan said, a little sourly. He hoped the ice cream would be mediocre, but it was the best he'd ever tasted.

Hawke laughed, eyeing him keenly over his own strawberry cone. Jordan guessed that tomorrow GeneFresh Farms would be approached by a We-Sleep organizer, if they weren't already under negotiation. The Profit Faire on the levee was to celebrate companies like Gene-Fresh, which were (or would be) new cells in the We-Sleep revolution. Average profits had risen an astounding 74 percent since the Sharifi murder case had hit the media. The connection between Timothy Herlinger's death and We-Sleep buying, to Jordan as painful as it was hysterical, had brought millions of new consumers under Hawke's rhetoric. "*I knew it!*" We-Sleepers cried in triumph, fear, anger, and greed. "*The Sleepless are afraid of us! They're spooked enough to try to control us through murder!*"

In the Mississippi scooter factory, where Hawke continued to maintain headquarters in an artificially rustic manner that irritated Jordan, production had doubled before leveling off. Hawke had posted production trend charts on the factory wall, smiled one of his lavish, secret smiles, and announced the Profit Faire on the levee, "where the local politicians of my great-great-grandfather's day held their catfish fries."

Jordan, a Californian who had no idea who his great-great-grandfather was, hadn't realized unmodified catfish was edible. He looked sideways at Hawke, who laughed. "Not my Cherokee great-great-grandfather, Jordan. A different one, in a much different position. Although he wasn't one of your lords of the earth, either."

"Not 'my' lords of the earth. I don't come from that class," Jordan said, nettled. Hawke's laugh disturbed him.

"Of course not," Hawke had said, and laughed again.

Now Hawke said—just as if the discussion about GeneFresh Farms hadn't happened, just as if Jordan hadn't tried to change the subject—"The basic flaw in your Aunt Leisha is that she doesn't belong to this century at all. She belongs to the eighteenth. It's always fatal to be born out of your own time."

"Let's not talk about Leisha tonight, Hawke. All right?"

"The eighteenth-century values were social conscience, rational thought, and a basic belief in the goodness of order. With those attitudes, they were going to remake or stabilize the world, all the Lockes and Rousseaus and Franklins and even Jane Austens, who was also in the wrong century. Sound like Leisha Camden?"

"I said—"

"But of course the Romantics swept all that away, and we never worked back to it. Until the Sleepless came along. Don't you think that's interesting, Jordan? A biological innovation turning the social-value clock backwards?"

Jordan stopped walking and faced Hawke. Somewhere to his left, over the river, the We-Sleep holo appeared, shimmered, and disappeared in a burst of electronic light. "You really don't care what I say, do you, Hawke? You just steamroll right over it. Only *your* words count."

Hawke was silent, watching him keenly.

"Why did you even hire me? All you want is to snipe at me, delete my objections, have somebody to show up as stupid and—"

"All I want," Hawke said quietly, his ice cream dripping over his hands, "is for you to get angry."

"Get—"

"*Angry.* Do you think you're of any use to me when you *let* me show you up as stupid? When you don't insist on whatever you say to me? I want you to feel your own fury when somebody is stepping on you, or you'll never be any use to the Movement. What in hell do you suppose the We-Sleep idea is all about in the first place? Waking up to anger!"

There was a flaw in that someplace, something not quite right, or maybe the not-quite-right was the sight of Hawke with strawberry ice cream dripping over his hands, his words to Jordan impassioned but his eyes focused on the levee, scanning the crowd—for what? To see if he was being overheard? Only one young couple, walking toward them from the StarHolo booth, could even possibly overh—

The Mississippi exploded. Water geysered upwards, and beneath Jordan's feet the levee rocked and split. A second explosion, and the StarHolo booth crumpled. The young couple were flung to the pavement like dolls. People screamed. A fissure opened at Jordan's feet; the next moment Hawke tackled him, knocking him to safety. Even while Jordan was in the air he saw the remote-guided holo burst out above him, swollen to a monstrous ten feet visible throughout the entire Faire. But somehow it wasn't the We-Sleep logo but letters, red and gold, silhouetted against the twinkling lights across the river: Samsung-Chrysler.

No one believed it. Samsung-Chrysler, outraged, disclaimed responsibility for the attack. It was an old and honorable firm; not even the workers in the scooter factory believed S-C had set underwater explosives along the levee. The media didn't believe it; the We-Sleep Council didn't believe it; Jordan didn't believe it.

"You did it," he said to Hawke.

Hawke merely looked at him. Over his desk in the dusty factory office were spread the kiosk tabloids in hard-copy: "Sanctuary Behind Bombing of We-Sleep Faire! Sleepless Resort to Violence—Again!" The cheap paper had already curled around the tiny rips made by the kiosk printer, a flimsy We-Sleep unit built and marketed from Wichita. Two of Hawke's huge fingers worked at the largest tear. From the factory floor came irregular staccato bursts of manual machinery and shatter-rock.

"You'll use anything," Jordan said. "The media hysteria over the Herlinger murder—it's not a question of truth for you. It's just a question of taking any advantage that happens to turn up for your cause. You're no better than Sanctuary!"

Hawke said, "Nobody got hurt at the Faire."

"They might have!"

"No," Hawke said. "There was no chance of that."

It took a moment for Jordan to understand. "The ice cream melting over your hands. That was the detonator, wasn't it? A temperature-sensitive microchip just under the skin. So you could pick a time when no one would be hurt."

Hawke said softly, "Are you angry yet, Jordan? Do you want to come with me to see more babies without medical care or running water because under Yagaiism nutrition and Y-energy are basic Dole rights but medicine and plumbing fixtures are free-market contractual enterprises? Do you want to see more adults who sit around all day and rot, knowing they can't compete with automation for low-level jobs or with genemods for skilled ones? Do you want to see more toddlers with hookworm, more marauding teenagers who can have all the law they want but no real work? Are you angry yet?"

"The ends don't justify these means!" Jordan shouted.

"The hell they don't."

"You're not helping the Sleeper underclass, you're just—"

"I'm *not*? Have you talked to Mayleen lately? Her oldest kid just got accepted to RoboTech training. And she can pay for it. Now."

"You're helping, but you're stirring up more hate to do it!"

"Wake up, Jordan. No social movement has ever progressed without emphasizing division, and doing that means stirring up hate. The American revolution, abolitionism, unionization, civil rights—"

"That wasn't—"

"At least we didn't invent this particular division—the Sleepless did. Feminism, gay rights, Dole franchisement—"

"Stop it! Stop throwing sterile intellectualizations at me!"

To Jordan's astonishment—even through his anger, he felt the astonishment—Hawke grinned. His black eyes were aquiline. " 'Sterile intellectualizations'—you're one of us already. What would Aunt Leisha say, that high priestess of reason?"

Jordan said, "I quit."

Hawke didn't seem surprised. He nodded; the sharp dark gaze sliced the air like a lance. "All right. Quit. You'll be back."

Jordan started for the door.

"Do you know why you'll be back, Jordy? Because if you were to get married—say, tomorrow—and have a child, you'd alter that child's genes to be a Sleepless. Wouldn't you? And you wouldn't be able to stand yourself for doing it."

The door slid open.

Behind him Hawke said softly, "When you do come back, you'll be welcome, Jordan."

It was only outside the gates, the Mississippi sliding placidly toward the Delta, that Jordan realized there was no place else he wanted to go.

Mayleen watched him from the guardhouse. At this distance, he couldn't read her expression. He had met her oldest daughter once, a skittish girl with the same tow-headed, skinny looks as Mayleen. RoboTech school. Hookworm. Jobs.

Jordan started back toward the scooter factory. Mayleen opened the gate for him, and he went inside.

Susan Melling's wrinkled face on the comscreen was backed not by her adobe-walled study in the New Mexican desert but by a laboratory dense with terminals, plastiware, and robotic arms.

"Susan, where are you?" Leisha said.

"Chicago Med," Susan said crisply. "Research. They've given me a guest lab." The deep lines in her face pulled taut with excitement.

Leisha said slowly, "You've been working on—"

"Yes," Susan interrupted, "that genetic problem we discussed in New Mexico. The one the med school has *classified*."

The comlink, Leisha realized, was not shielded. Or else not shielded enough. She almost laughed: in the current circumstances, what could possibly constitute "enough"?

Susan said, "I just wanted you to know that we've begun, and that my distinguished Chinese colleague has arrived safely to join me."

Chinese? Susan was staring at her steadily, significantly; Leisha suddenly remembered that Claude Gaspard-Thiereux was genemod for intelligence, and that he had told Susan once, during a drunken party at an international symposium, that the genetic material woven into his had come originally from a Chinese donor. This fact had, for some reason, fascinated him. He began to collect imitation Ming vases and holopictures on the Forbidden City, which had in turn fascinated Susan. Leisha had thought the whole thing unimportant, but Susan obviously expected her to remember it now.

Gaspard-Thiereux at Chicago Med. He would have flown in from Paris only if Susan had been able to offer him proof that Walcott's findings were feasible.

Susan said crisply, "We worked through the first part of the problem, replicating earlier work in the same area, and now we've hit a sort of snag. But we're working on it, and we'll keep you informed. We're applying Mr. Wong's work to the end of the problem, rather than the beginning, because the end has the most problematical gap."

Susan was *enjoying* this, Leisha saw: not just the research but the pseudosecrecy, the theatrical code words. Her voice danced; if Leisha closed her eyes she would see the Susan of forty years ago, braids bobbing with inexhaustible energy as she led two small girls in controlled-testing "games." Sudden tenderness choked Leisha.

To say something, she said, "Starting at the end? That sounds like applying the verdict instead of the evidence to a trial brief."

"Not a justified analogy," Susan said gleefully. Her voice softened. "How are you doing, Leisha?"

"The trial starts next week," Leisha said, as if it were an answer. Which it was.

"Is Richard still—"

"No change," Leisha said.

"And Kevin—"

"He's not coming back."

"Damn him," Susan said. But Leisha didn't want to discuss Kevin. What hurt most about his defection, she'd realized, was that Kevin had betrayed the Sleepless as a group, not just her. Did that mean she no longer had personal loves, only political ones? The question was troubling.

"Susan, do you know what occurred to me yesterday? That in the whole world, there are only three people who understand why I'm testifying against a Sleepless, against what the press call 'my own kind.' Only three. You, and Richard, and . . . Daddy."

"Yes," Susan said. "Roger never felt class solidarity outweighed truth. In fact, he never felt class solidarity, period. He considered himself in a class of one. But there are undoubtedly more than three, Leisha. In the whole world."

Leisha looked across the room, at the pile of kiosk hard-copies heaped on the desk, the floor, the chair. From being unable to read them she had gone to being unable not to read them.

"It doesn't feel like more than three."

"Ah," Susan said. It was a sound Alice made, too. Leisha had never before made the connection. "Did you know that in the United States year-to-date the officially recorded number of *in vitro* genemods to produce Sleepless babies was 142?"

"That's all?"

"Down from thousands, ten years ago. Even fair and thoughtful people don't want their own children to undergo the danger and the discrimination. But if your Dr. Walcott's research . . ." She left the sentence unfinished.

"Not mine," Leisha said. "Definitely not mine."

"Ah," Susan said again, the single word a multilayered sigh.

13

The People versus Jennifer Fatima Sharifi. All rise." Leisha, seated in the witness section, rose. One hundred sixty-two people—spectators, jury, press, witnesses, counsel—rose with her, one body with one hundred sixty-two warring brains. Security fields encased the courtroom, courthouse, town of Conewango, like layered gloves. No comlinks could function through the two tightest layers. Fifteen years ago, in another of the judicial system's periodic swings between the public's right to know and the individual's right to privacy, New York State had once more banned recording devices from criminal trials. The press were all state-certified augments with eidectic memories, aural-neural bio-implants, or both. Leisha wondered cynically how many just happened to also possess unmentioned genemods.

Next to the reporters, the newsgrid holo-artists held their CAD's on their packed-together laps, minute flexes of their fingers sculpting the holos for the afternoon news. There was no identified gene site for artistic ability.

"Oyez, oyez. The Superior Court for the County of Cattaraugus, State of New York, is now in session, the Honorable Daniel J. Deepford, judge, presiding. Draw near and give your attention and you shall be heard. God save the United States and this honorable court!"

Leisha wondered if only she heard the fevered exclamation point.

It was the first day of testimony. Two and a half weeks of relentless questioning had been needed to empanel a jury: Do you, Ms. Wright, think you can make an unbiased decision about the defendant? Have you, Mr. Aratina, seen anything on the newsgrids about this case? Are you, Ms. Moranis, a member of We-Sleep? Of Awake, America! Of Mothers for Biological Parity? Three hundred eighty-nine dismissals for cause, an unthinkable number in any other *voir dire.* The jury had ended up eight men and four women. Seven white, three black, one Asian, one Latino. Five college-educated, seven with high-school certification or less. Nine younger than fifty, three older. Eight biological parents, three childless, one with legal egg-donor surrogate status. Six working, six on the Dole. No Sleepless.

"A citizen shall be tried by a jury of his peers."

"You may begin, Mr. Hossack," the judge said to the prosecuting attorney, a heavy man with thick gray hair and the considerable trial asset of being able to command attention through stillness. Like everyone else in the United States with access to a comprehensive database, Leisha now knew all about Geoffrey Hossack. He was fifty-four years old, had a win/loss ratio of 23 to 9, and had never been audited by the IRS or reprimanded by the ABA. His wife bought only real-wheat bread, three loaves a week. Hossack subscribed to two newsgrids and a private channel for Civil War buffs. His oldest daughter was failing trigonometry.

He and Judge Deepford both had records as fair, honest, and capable practitioners of the law.

Weeks ago Leisha, sitting before her terminal after her meticulous combing of Deepford's trial record, had pondered Deepford's and Hossack's dossiers. She hadn't expected that Sanctuary could manipulate the choice of either judge or prosecuting attorney; Sleepless power was mostly economic, not political. There weren't enough of them to constitute a voting bloc, and they were too resented to gain elected office. Sanctuary could of course buy individual judges, lawyers, or congressmen, and probably did, but nothing indicated that Hossack or Deepford were for sale.

More important, Deepford was not a Sleeper fanatic. Whatever his personal feelings, he had presided over nine civil suits with Sleepless litigants—there were very few criminal cases against Sleepless—and in each case Deepford's performance had been fair and reasonable. He tended to adhere closely to narrow interpretations of both the rules of evidence and the law itself, but that was the only point on which Leisha would have challenged him.

Hossack's opening statement to the jury set out his case swiftly and cleanly: Evidence existed to prove that the Y-energy deflector on Dr. Timothy Herlinger's scooter had been tampered with. Further evidence would tie this tampering to Jennifer Sharifi. "The scooter was equipped with a retina scanner, ladies and gentlemen, which showed three prints: a neighbor child who had been playing outside that morning. Dr. Herlinger himself. And the print of an adult Sleepless female. We will further demonstrate that this Sleepless woman was someone in the very highest reaches of Sanctuary power, someone who controlled the most advanced technology in the world."

Hossack paused. "We will be entering in evidence a pendant found in the parking garage at Samplice, beside the spot occupied by Dr. Herlinger's scooter. That pendant contains a microchip so advanced, so different, that government experts still can't duplicate it. We can't understand how it was made, but we *can* understand what it does. We tried it. It opens the gates of Sanctuary. In short, the State will prove that the scooter tampering was part of an elaborate illegal scheme planned and carried out by Sanctuary. We will then prove that the only person who could have masterminded this scheme was Jennifer Sharifi, creator and director of illicit power networks that include infiltration of the national banking system and even of government data storage, a concern so grave it is currently under investigation by a special task force at the United States Justice Department—"

"Objection!" Will Sandaleros called.

"Mr. Hossack," said the judge, "you are clearly beyond the boundaries of an opening statement. The jury will disregard all reference to any parallel investigations, by anybody, in this murder case."

The jury were all staring at Jennifer, straight-backed in her white *abbaya* behind a bulletproof shield. The word "power" hung in the air like a high-density charge. Jennifer never glanced sideways.

"Ms. Sharifi's motive," Hossack continued, "was to suppress patents which, if developed and marketed, would enable Sleepers to become Sleepless, with the same biological advantages as Sleepless. Sanctuary does not want us—you and me—to have these advantages. Sanctuary, led by Jennifer Sharifi, was willing to commit murder in order to prevent that."

Leisha studied the jury. They were listening hard, but she could tell nothing from the rigid Sleeper faces.

In contrast to Hossack, Will Sandaleros sailed into his opening statement in low key. "I'm at a loss to refute the prosecution's actual case," he began. His handsome, sharply-chiseled face—the Sleeper parents who rejected him, Leisha remembered, had purchased extensive appearance genemods—looked modestly bewildered. No Sleepless, Leisha well knew, could afford to approach a jury with anything that could be interpreted as arrogance. She leaned forward, ignoring the inevitable curious stares from other spectators, studying Sandaleros closely. He looked focused and energetic. He looked competent.

"The fact is," Sandaleros continued, "that there *is* no case to refute. Jennifer Sharifi is innocent of murder. The prosecution has no conclusive evidence, as I shall show, to tie Jennifer Sharifi, *or* the corporate entity of Sanctuary, to the scooter tampering, to any patent dispute, or to any murder conspiracy. What the prosecution does have, ladies and gentlemen, is a thin web of circumstance, hearsay, and forced connections. And something else."

Sandaleros moved very close to the jury box, closer than Leisha ever allowed herself to get, and leaned forward. A woman in the first row shrank back slightly. "What the prosecution has, ladies and gentlemen, is a thicker web—much thicker than its web of evidence—of innuendo, prejudice, and unwarranted connections built on hatred and suspicion of Ms. Sharifi because she is a Sleepless."

"Objection!" Hossack called. Sandaleros rolled on as if he hadn't heard.

"I say this to bring the real issues of this trial out where we all can see them. Jennifer Sharifi is a Sleepless. I am a Sleepless—"

"Objection!" Hossack called again, with real anger. "Counsel is attempting to put the prosecution on trial here. The law makes no distinction between Sleeper and Sleepless in the commission of a crime, and neither shall our use of the rules of evidence."

Every pair of eyes in the courtroom—Sleeper, Sleepless, augmented, clouded, tunnel-visioned, uncertain, fanatic—looked at Judge Deepford, who didn't hesitate. He had obviously thought this issue through beforehand. "I will allow it," he said quietly, thereby departing from his own record, and making clear how very wide a latitude he would allow Sandaleros to avoid the appearance of prejudice in his courtroom. Leisha found that the nails of her right hand were digging into her left. There was a trap here. . . .

"Your Honor—" Hossack began, very still.

"Objection overruled, Mr. Hossack. Mr. Sandaleros, proceed."

"Jennifer Sharifi is a Sleepless," Sandaleros repeated. "I am a Sleepless. This is the trial of a Sleepless accused of murdering a Sleeper, accused *because* she is a Sleepless—"

"Objection! The defendant stands accused by a grand jury's consideration of the evidence!"

Everyone gazed at Hossack. Leisha saw the moment he realized he had played into Sandaleros's hands. No matter what the evidence said, everyone in the courtroom knew that Jennifer Sharifi *had* been indicted by the twenty-three Sleepers on the grand jury *because* she was Sleepless. Fear, not evidence, had indicted her. By denying it, Hossack himself looked either dishonest or stupid. A man who could not name ugly reality. A man whose statements should be doubted.

Hossack, Leisha saw, had just had his own sense of fairness and justice used against him, to make him look like a hypocritical ass.

Jennifer Sharifi never moved.

*   *   *

The first witnesses were people who had been at the site of Timothy Herlinger's death. Hossack paraded a variety of street-team police, pedestrians, and the driver of the car, a nervous thin woman who barely restrained herself from crying. Through them, Hossack established that Herlinger had been exceeding the speed limit, had made a sharp left turn, and, like most scooter drivers, had probably relied on the automatic Y-energy deflector shield to keep him the standard foot away from anything on the other side of him. Instead he had crashed head-first into the side of the groundcar driven by Ms. Stacy Hillman, who had already started to pull forward as the traffic field changed. Herlinger never wore a helmet; deflectors made helmets superfluous. He had died instantly.

The street-team police robot had made its gross check of the scooter and discovered the failed deflector—or, rather, since deflectors never failed and such a possibility was not in its programming, it had listed the scooter as performing safely. This was so contrary to witness reports that a policeman had cautiously mounted the scooter, tried it, and discovered the failure for himself. The scooter had been sent to Forensic, Energy for expert analysis.

Ellen Kassabian, chief of Forensic, Energy, was a large woman with the slow, measured speech that juries found authoritative but which, Leisha knew, could conceal a stubborn inflexibility. Hossack questioned her closely about the scooter.

"What specifically was the nature of the tampering?"

"The shield was set to fail at the first impact at a speed above fifteen miles per hour."

"Is that an easy tampering to create?"

"No. A device was attached to the Y-cone to bring the failure about." She described the device, quickly becoming incomprehensibly technical. Nevertheless, the jury listened intently.

"Have you ever seen such a device before?"

"No. To my knowledge, it's a new invention."

"Then how do you know it does what you tell us it does?"

"We tested it extensively."

"Could you now, as a result of your testing, duplicate the device?"

"No. Oh, I'm sure someone could. But it's complicated. We had Defense Department specialists look at it—"

"We'll be calling them as witnesses."

"—and they said," Kassabian continued, undeflectable, "that it involved new technology."

"So a very sophisticated—even unusual—intelligence would be needed to engineer this tampering?"

"Objection," Sandaleros said. "Witness is being asked for her opinion."

Hossack said, "Her professional opinion is well within the ground established by her credentials."

"I'll allow it," the judge said.

Hossack repeated his question. "So a very sophisticated—even unusual—intelligence would be necessary to do this tampering?"

"Yes," Kassabian said.

"An extremely unusual person, or group of persons."

"Yes."

Hossack let that hang in the air while he examined his notes. Leisha watched how the jurors' eyes searched the courtroom for the Sleepless, an intelligent and unusual group of persons.

Hossack said, "Now let's consider the third retina print registered on the scanner the morning Dr. Herlinger died. How can you be so sure it was that of an adult Sleepless female?"

"Retina prints are scans of tissue. Like all tissue, it breaks down with age. There's what we call 'blurring,' places where cells are broken and haven't regenerated—it's nerve tissue, remember—or are malformed. Sleepless tissue doesn't do that. It regenerates, somehow—" Leisha heard the ambivalence on 'somehow,' the bitter wistfulness she had first heard twenty-one years ago from Susan Melling "—and the retina scans are very distinctive. Sharp. No blurring. The older the subject, the more surely we can identify a Sleepless print. With young children, it's sometimes hard to tell the difference, even for the computer. But this was an adult female Sleepless."

"I see. And it matches with no known Sleepless?"

"No. The print isn't on file."

"Clarify something for the court, Ms. Kassabian. When the defendant, Jennifer Sharifi, was arrested, her retina print was taken?"

"Yes."

"And does it match with the scan on Dr. Herlinger's scooter?"

"It does not."

"There is no way Ms. Sharifi tampered with that scooter herself."

"No," Kassabian said, thereby allowing the prosecution to make this point before the defense could put it to more dramatic use.

"Does the print match that of Leisha Camden, who had been in the same building with Dr. Herlinger just before his death?"

"No."

All eyes turned towards Leisha.

"But it *was* a Sleepless who bent close to that scanner—the last person to do so—sometime between the time Herlinger left home that morning and the time he died at 9:32 A.M. A Sleepless who therefore tampered with the scooter."

"Objection," Sandaleros called. "An inference on the part of the witness!"

"Withdrawn," Hossack said. He was silent a moment, again drawing all eyes to him by the profound, taut quality of his stillness. Then he repeated slowly, "A Sleepless print. A *Sleepless.*" And only then, "Nothing further."

Sandaleros was savage about the retina print. Gone was the bewildered modesty of his opening statement. "Ms. Kassabian, how many retina prints of Sleepless are stored in the law-enforcement net of the United States?"

"One hundred thirty-three."

"Only 133? Out of a Sleepless population of over 20,000?"

"That's correct," Kassabian said, and from the small shift of her weight on the witness chair Leisha saw, for the first time, that Ellen Kassabian disliked Sleepless.

"That seems a very small number," Sandaleros marveled. "Tell me, under what circumstances does a person's retina print enter the law-enforcement file?"

"When he's booked for arrest."

"That's the only way?"

"Or if he's part of the law-enforcement system itself. Police personnel, judges, prison guards. Like that."

"Attorneys, too?"

"Yes."

"So that is how, say, Leisha Camden's print was available for you to check."

"Yes."

"Ms. Kassabian, what percentage of those 133 retina prints from Sleepless belong to law-net personnel?"

Kassabian clearly didn't like answering this. "Eighty percent."

"*Eighty?* You mean, only 20 percent of 133 Sleepless—27 people—have been arrested in the nine years that retina-print records have been kept?"

"Yes," Kassabian said, too neutrally.

"Do you know what those arrests were for?"

"Three disorderly conduct, two petty larceny, twenty-two public disturbance."

"It would appear," Sandaleros said dryly, "that Sleepless are a pretty law-abiding lot, Ms. Kassabian."

"Yes."

"In fact, it would appear from the retina records that the most usual Sleepless crime is simply existing, thereby constituting a public disturbance."

"Objection," called Hossack.

"Sustained. Mr. Sandaleros, do you have any additional questions pertinent to Ms. Kassabian's actual testimony?"

And yet, thought Leisha, Deepford had allowed the introduction of the retina statistics, clearly not in proof order and only marginally relevant.

"I do," Sandaleros snapped. His whole demeanor changed; he

seemed suddenly taller, subtly fiercer. As he had with the jury, he moved slightly closer to the forensic expert. "Ms. Kassabian, can a retina scanner be loaded with a retina print by a third party?"

"No. No more than a third party could, for instance, leave your fingerprint on a gun if you were not there."

"But a third party could substitute a gun with my fingerprints for one with somebody else's. Could a scanner with prerecorded retina prints be substituted for an existing scanner, without detection, if the person doing the substitution kept his face well away from the scanner as he did so?"

"Well . . . it would be very difficult. Scanners are protected by security measures that—"

"Would it be possible?"

Kassabian said reluctantly, "Only by someone with immense engineering knowledge and experience, an unusual person—"

"May it please the Court," Sandaleros said crisply, "I would like to have replayed that portion of the record in which Ms. Kassabian discussed the qualifications of the person we *know* tampered with the scooter-deflection field."

"Recorder, search and read," Deepford said.

The computer read, "Mr. Hossack: 'So a very sophisticated—even unusual—intelligence would be needed to engineer this tampering.' Dr. Kassabian: 'Yes.' Mr. Hossack: 'An extremely unusual person, or group of persons.' Dr. Kassabian: 'Yes.' Mr. Hossack: 'How much prior—' "

"Sufficient," Sandaleros said. "So what we have here is someone who is capable of tampering with Y-energy and so must be, in your own words, Dr. Kassabian, also capable of substituting a preloaded scanner for the one already on Dr. Herlinger's scooter."

"I didn't say—"

"Is that scenario *possible*?"

"It would have to—"

"Just answer the question. Is it *possible*?"

Ellen Kassabian drew a deep breath. Her brows rushed together;

clearly, she would have liked to tear Sandaleros apart. A long moment passed. Finally she said, "It is possible."

"No further questions."

The forensic chief stared at Sandaleros in silent fury.

Leisha walked to the window of her library and looked out over the midnight lights of Chicago. The trial had recessed for the weekend and she had gone home, unable to bear the motel in Conewango longer than necessary. The apartment was very quiet. Sometime during the past week, Kevin had moved out his furniture and pictures.

She walked back to her terminal. The message hadn't changed: SANCTUARY NET. ACCESS DENIED.

"Password override, voice and retina identification, previous command."

ACCESS DENIED.

The Sanctuary net, which had always been open to every Sleepless in the world, would not even acknowledge her in stringent I.D. mode. But that was illusory. Leisha knew it; there was more Jennifer wanted her to discover than just the bald fact of her exclusion.

"Personal call, urgent, for Jennifer Sharifi, password override, voice and retina identification."

ACCESS DENIED.

"Personal call, urgent, for Richard Keller, password override, voice and retina identification."

ACCESS DENIED.

She tried to think. There was a heaviness around her skull, like being deep underwater. The newest vase of Alice's perpetual flowers filled the air with oppressive sweetness.

"Personal call, urgent, for Tony Indivino, password override, voice and retina identification."

Cassie Blumenthal, a member of the Sanctuary Council, appeared on screen.

"Leisha. I'm speaking for Jennifer, whenever you access this recorded message. The Sanctuary Council has voted in the oath of solidarity. Those who have not taken the oath are denied access to the Sanctuary net, to Sanctuary itself, and to all commerce with anyone who has taken the oath. *You* are hereby denied all such access permanently and irrevocably. Jennifer further asked me to tell you to reread Abraham Lincoln's speech to the Illinois Republican Convention of June, 1858, and to add that the historic precepts of the past have not been recalled simply because Kenzo Yagai inflated personal achievement above the value of community. As of the first of next month, all Sanctuary oath holders will begin divestiture of commercial relationships with you, with Camden Enterprises, with subsidiary holdings thereof, and with all direct and indirect holdings of Kevin Baker, including Groupnet, if he continues to refuse community solidarity. That is all."

The screen went blank.

Leisha sat still a long moment.

She directed the library bank to bring up Lincoln's speech. Words scrolled across the screen and the sonorous voice of an actor began to recite, but she needed neither; at the first words she remembered which speech it was. Lincoln, his law practice rebuilt after debts and disillusionment, accepted the Republican nomination to run for Congress against Stephen Douglas, brilliant proponent of territories' right to choose slavery for themselves. Lincoln addressed the contentious and fiery convention: *"A house divided against itself cannot stand."*

Leisha turned off the terminal. She walked to the room she and Kevin had used for their infrequent sex. He had taken the bed with him. After a while she lay down on the floor, palms flat at her side, breathing carefully.

Richard. Kevin. Stella. Sanctuary.

She wondered how much more she had left to lose.

Jennifer faced Will Sandaleros through a prison security screen that shimmered slightly, just enough to soften the hard young line of his gen-emod jaw. She said, "The evidence connecting me to the scooter tampering is mostly circumstantial. Is the jury bright enough to see that?"

He didn't lie to her. "Sleeper juries . . ." There was a long silence.

"Jennifer, are you eating? You don't look well."

She was genuinely surprised. He still thought all of that mattered—how she looked, whether she ate. On the heels of surprise came displeasure. She had thought Sandaleros was beyond that sort of sentimentality. She needed him to be beyond it, to understand that such things were perfectly irrelevant in the face of what she had to do, and what she needed him to do for her. For what else was she disciplining herself, if not for the subordination of such things as how she looked or felt? To what was really important—to Sanctuary? She was in a place now where nothing else mattered, could be allowed to matter, and she had fought very hard to get to this place. She had turned the confinement and the isolation and the separation from her children and the personal shame into roads to reach this place, and so into triumphs of will and achievement. She had thought Will Sandaleros could see that. He must travel that same road, would *have* to travel it, because she needed him at its end.

But she musn't try to bring him to that place too fast. That had been her mistake with Richard. She had thought Richard was traveling beside her, as cleanly and as swiftly, and instead he had faltered and she had not seen it, and Richard had broken. The responsibility for that was hers, because she had not seen the faltering. Richard had been tied to the Outside in ways she had overlooked: to the outside, to outworn ideals, and perhaps still to Leisha Camden. The realization brought no jealousy. Richard had not been strong enough, that was all. Will Sandaleros, raised in Sanctuary, owing his life to Sanctuary, would be. Jennifer would make him strong enough. But not too fast.

So she said, "I'm fine. What else do you have for me?"

"Leisha accessed the net last night."

She nodded. "Good. And the others on our list?"

"All but Kevin Baker. Although he did move out of their apartment."

Pleasure flooded her. "Can he be persuaded to the oath?"

"I don't know. If he can be, do you want him Inside?"

"No. Outside."

"He'll be difficult to hold under electronic surveillance. God, Jennifer, he *invented* most of that stuff."

"I don't want him under surveillance. At all. That's not the way to hold a man like Kevin. Nor is solidarity. We'll do it with economic interests and contractual rules. The tools of Yagaiism, in our own interests. And everything unguarded."

Sandaleros looked dubious, but he didn't argue. That was another thing she would have to shape in him. He must learn to argue with her. The forged metal was always stronger than the unforged.

She said, "Who else Outside has taken the oath?"

He gave her the names, with plans to move each to Sanctuary. She listened carefully; the other name she wanted to hear was not there. "Stella Bevington?"

"No."

"There's time." She bent her head, and then asked it, the one question per visit she allowed herself. The last weakness left. "And my children?"

"They're well. Najla—"

"Give them my love. Now there is something you must begin for me, Will. An important next step. Maybe the most important Sanctuary's ever taken."

"What?"

She told him.

Jordan closed his office door. Sound stopped instantly—the rat-a-tat-tat of machinery on the factory floor, the rock music, the calling voices, and—most of all—the newsgrid coverage of the Sharifi trial on the two superscreens Hawke had rented and set up at either end of the cavernous main building. It all stopped. Jordan had had his office soundproofed, paying for it himself.

He leaned against the closed door, grateful for silence. The comlink shrilled.

"Jordan, you there?" Mayleen said from the security kiosk. "Trouble in Building Three, I can't find Mr. Hawke nowhere, you better *git.*"

"What kind of trouble?"

"Fight, looks like. Screen ain't positioned well over there, somebody should take a look at it. If they don't break it first."

"I'm going," Jordan said, yanking open the door.

"So I told her—" "Hand me that there number five—" "Latest Testimony Seems to Reveal Doubts on the Part of Dr. Adam Walcott, Alleged Victim of Sanctuary Conspiracy to—" "Daaan-cing All Ni-ight with Yoooouuu—" "—Vicious Attack on Sleepless Firm of Carver & Daughter Last Night by Unspecified—"

When his vacation came, Jordan thought, he would spend all of it somewhere silent, deserted, empty. Alone.

He ran the length of the main plant, outside, and across a narrow lot—the Mississippians called it "the yard"—toward the smaller buildings used to inspect and store parts from suppliers, to stock scooter inventory, and to service equipment. Building Three was Receiving Inspection: half warehouse, half sorting station to separate incoming We-Sleep scooter parts into the defective and the usable. There were a lot of defective. Sprayfoam packing crates littered the floor. In the back, between high storage shelves, people shouted. As Jordan ran toward the sound, an eight-foot-high section of shelf crashed to the floor, scattering parts like shrapnel. A woman screamed.

Plant security was already there, two burly uniformed men restraining a man and a woman, both struggling and yelling. The guards looked bewildered; assault was rare among We-Sleep employees brought to a fever pitch of loyalty by Hawke. On the floor a third man sat moaning, holding his head. Beyond him a huge figure lay still, soaked with blood.

"What the hell happened here?" Jordan demanded. "Who's that—Joey?"

"He's a Sleepless!" the woman shrieked. She tried to kick the prostrate giant with the toe of her boot. The guard yanked her backwards. The huge bloody figure stirred.

"*Joey* a Sleepless?" Jordan said. He stepped over the moaning employee and turned the giant over; it was like turning a beached whale.

Joey—he had no other name—weighed 350 pounds and stood six feet five, a mentally retarded man of immense strength whom Hawke let live, work, and eat at the factory. Joey hauled boxes and did other menial work that at any but a We-Sleep factory would have been automated. He worked just as tirelessly as a robot, Hawke said, and he was a bona fide member of that class We-Sleep was lifting out of dependent degradation. It had struck Jordan that Joey was now as dependent on Hawke as he ever could have been on the Dole, as degraded by his coworkers' cruel jokes as he would have been in any government dorm. Jordan had kept such observations to himself. Joey seemed happy, and he was slavishly grateful to Hawke. Weren't they all?

"He's a *Sleepless!*" the woman spat. "We got no place here for his kind!"

Joey a Sleepless? That made no sense. Jordan said coldly to the man still straining against the guard's grip, "Jenkins, Security's going to let you go. If you make one move toward Joey before I get to the bottom of this, you're through here. Got that?" Jenkins nodded sullenly. To the guard Jordan said, "Report in to Mayleen that this is under control. Tell her to call for an ambulance, two patients. Now you, Jenkins, tell me what happened here."

Jenkins said, "Bastard's a Sleepless. We don't want no—"

"What makes you think he's a Sleepless?"

"We been watching him," Jenkins said. "Turner and Holly and me. He don't sleep. *Never.*"

"Spying on us!" the woman shrilled. "Prob'ly a spy for Sanctuary and that murdering bitch Sharifi!"

Jordan turned his back on her. Kneeling, he peered into Joey's bloody face. The eyelids were closed but twitching, and Jordan knew suddenly that Joey was pretending unconsciousness. The giant wore the cheapest of plastic clothing, now badly torn. With his untrimmed beard and hair, his unwashed smell, and the blood smeared across his huge body, he looked to Jordan like some cornered mangy animal, a battered bull elephant or limping bison. Jordan had never heard of a mentally retarded Sleepless, but if Joey were old enough—he looked older than God—he might have had only his sleep-regulating genes modified, without even a check on the rest. And if his natural IQ was very low . . . but why would he be *here*? Sleepless took care of their own.

Jordan's body blocked the others' view of Joey's face. The stupid woman was still shouting about spies and sabotage. Softly Jordan said, "Joey, are you a Sleepless?"

The grimy eyelids twitched frantically.

"Joey, *answer me*. Now. Are you a Sleepless?"

Joey opened his eyes; he always obeyed direct orders. Tears trickled through the blood and dirt. "Mr. Watrous—don't tell Mr. Hawke! Please, please, please don't tell Mr. Hawke!"

Pity scalded Jordan. He stood. To his surprise, Joey also staggered to his feet, steadying himself against another shelf, which shivered precariously. Joey shrank against Jordan, overwhelming Jordan with his smell. The giant was terrified. Of Jenkins, looking sullenly at the floor; of Turner, moaning and bleeding; of the filthy-mouthed Holly, who weighed maybe 105 pounds.

"Shut up," Jordan said to her. "Campbell, you stay with Turner until the ambulance gets here. Jenkins, you and she start cleaning this mess up, get someone off Station Six to make sure parts flow to the lines isn't interrupted. Both of you report to Hawke's office at three this afternoon. Joey, you go with Campbell and Turner in the ambulance."

"Nooo," Joey whimpered. He clutched Jordan's arm. Outside, ambulance sirens shrieked.

How did ambulance medics react to Sleepless?

"All right," Jordan snapped. "All right, Joey. I'll tell them to check you here."

Joey's cuts were actually superficial; there was more blood than damage. After the medics had checked him out, Jordan led Joey around the outside of the main building, in the side door, and to his own office, all the while marveling: Joey, a Sleepless? Incompetent, dirty, terrified, stupid, dependent Joey?

The soundproofed door extinguished all noise. "Now you tell me, Joey. How did you come to this factory?"

"I walked."

"I mean, why? Why did you come to a We-Sleep factory?"

"I dunno."

"Did someone tell you to come here?"

"Mrs. Cheever. Oh, Mr. Watrous, don't tell Mr. Hawke! Please, please, please don't tell Mr. Hawke!"

"Don't be afraid, Joey. Just listen to me. Where did you live before Mrs. Cheever brought you here?"

"I dunno!"

"But you—"

"I dunno!"

Jordan kept at it, gently and persistently, but Joey didn't know. Not where he was born, not what had happened to his parents, not how old he was. All he seemed to remember, repeated over and over, was that Mrs. Cheever told him never to tell anyone he was a Sleepless or people would hurt him. At night he should go away by himself and lie down. This Joey did faithfully, because Mrs. Cheever had told him to. He couldn't remember who Mrs. Cheever was, or why she'd been kind to him, or what had happened to her.

"Joey," Jordan said, "did you—"

"Don't tell Mr. Hawke!"

Mayleen's face appeared on the comlink. "Jordan, Mr. Hawke is coming in now. Holly Newman told me what happened." Her image peered curiously at Joey. "*He's* a Sleepless?"

"Don't you start, Mayleen!"

"Shit, all I said was—"

Hawke rolled into the room on a tide of sound. Immediately the office was his. He filled it with his presence, nearly as large as Joey's but so much more compelling that Jordan, who thought he was used to Hawke, felt himself dwindle once more into insignificance.

"Campbell told me what happened. Joey's a *Sleepless*?"

"Uuuunnnhhh," Joey moaned. He put his hands over his face. The fingers were like bloody bananas.

Jordan expected that Hawke would immediately grasp his mistake and remedy it. Hawke was good with people. But instead Hawke went on gazing silently at Joey, smiling faintly, not amused but oddly pleased, as if something about Joey made him feel good and there was no reason to hide that.

"Mr. Hawke, d-d-do I—" in his anguish, the giant started to stutter "—h-h-have t-to g-g-g-go . . ."

"Why no, of course not, Joey," Hawke said. "You can stay here if you want."

Hope struggled grotesquely on Joey's face. "Even if I n-n-n-never s-sleep?"

"Even if you're a Sleepless," Hawke agreed smoothly. He still smiled. "We can use you here."

Joey staggered to Hawke and fell to his knees. He threw his arms around Hawke's waist, buried his head against Hawke's hard belly, and sobbed. Hawke didn't shrink from the smell, the dirt, the blood. He went on staring down at Joey, smiling faintly.

Jordan went sick inside.

"Hawke, he can't stay here. You know that. He can't."

Hawke stroked Joey's filthy hair.

Jordan said harshly, "Joey, leave my office. This is still *my* office. Leave it now. Go—" He couldn't send Joey onto the plant floor, word would be all over the factory by now. Hawke's office was locked, the outbuildings were worse yet, there was no place at We-Sleep that Joey would be safe from his coworkers . . .

"Send him to my security shack," Mayleen's image said. Jordan had forgotten the comlink was still open. "Ain't nobody going to bother him here."

Startled, Jordan considered rapidly. Mayleen controlled weapons— but, no. She wouldn't. He heard that, somehow, in her voice.

"Go to Mayleen's guard shack, Joey," Jordan said, with as much authority as he could. "Go now."

Joey didn't move.

"Go on, Joey," Hawke said in his amused voice, and Joey went.

Jordan faced his boss. "They'll kill him if he stays here."

"You don't know that."

"Yes, I do, and so do you. You've encouraged so much hate for Sleepless. . . ." He stopped. This was what We-Sleep meant, then. Not just hatred for Kevin Baker and Leisha Camden and Jennifer Sharifi, powerful smart people who could take care of themselves, who were economic opponents with all the best economic weapons on their side. But also hatred for Joey No-Name, who wouldn't recognize an economic weapon if he tripped over it. Which he probably would.

"Don't think like that, Jordan," Hawke said quietly. "Joey is an anomaly. A blip in the Sleepless statistics. He's insignificant in the real war for justice."

"Not insignificant enough for *you* to ignore. If you really thought he was insignificant you'd send him away, to safety. They'll kill him here, and you'll let them, because that's one more way to gain the thrill of a triumph over the Sleepless, isn't it?"

Hawke sat down on Jordan's desk, with the expansive, easy movement Jordan had seen him make a hundred times before. A hundred, a thousand, counting all the times Hawke had haunted him in dreams. Hawke was settling in with his easy movements for a pleasant picking at Jordan's reasoning, a pleasant demolishment of Jordan's naive beliefs, an easy triumph over a mind that couldn't begin to match Hawke's.

Not this time.

Hawke said easily, "You're overlooking a crucial point, Jordy. The basis for any individual dignity must be individual choice. Joey *chooses* to stay here. Every proponent of human dignity, from Kenzo Yagai back through Abraham Lincoln clear back to Euripides, has argued that individual choice must supersede community pressure. Why, Lincoln himself said—I know your wonderful Aunt Leisha could supply the whole quotation—on the subject of the danger to emancipated slaves—"

Jordan said, "I quit."

Hawke smiled. "Now, Jordy, haven't we been through this before? And with what results?"

Jordan walked out. Hawke would let him, Jordan, be killed, too, in a different way. He had been doing just that, in fact, all along, and Jordan had never seen it. Or was this, too—this goading of Jordan through poor Jordy—was this, too, deliberate on Hawke's part? Did Hawke *want* him to quit?

There was no way to be sure.

The noise of the plant rushed over him. On the north superscreen was framed an aerial shot of Sanctuary, wilderness surrounding the high-tech domes of Salamanca. *"Military Buffs Have Long Enjoyed Devising Feasible Hypothetical Assaults on This Supposedly Impregnable—"* Rat a-tat-tat. *"Halooo-ooogin with My Baa-by—"* Jordan walked out the side door. Joey outweighed him by 175 pounds; there was no way Jordan could get him away from the factory by force. Joey wasn't persuadable, not by anyone but Hawke. Jordan couldn't leave him here. How?

In the security kiosk, Joey's huge body slumped against the one wall not made of transparent plastic. Mayleen cut off the comlink to Hawke's office; she must have heard the entire discussion between Jordan and Hawke. She avoided Jordan's eyes, gazing down at the unconscious Joey.

"I give him some of my great-gramama's tea."

"*Tea . . .*"

"We river rats know a lot you California boys don't never guess," Mayleen said wearily. "Git him out of here, Jordan. I done called Campbell. He'll help you load Joey into your car, if Mr. Hawke don't tell him different first. Move fast."

"Why, Mayleen? Why help a Sleepless?"

Mayleen shrugged. Then her voice turned passionate. "Shit, *look* at him! Even my baby's dirty diaper don't smell like that. You think I need to fight *that* to get somewhere in this here world? He ain't in my way, no matter if he don't need to sleep or eat or even *breathe*." Her tone changed yet again. "Poor beggar."

Jordan brought his car to the front gate. He, Mayleen, and the unsuspecting Campbell heaved Joey into it. Just before he drove away, Jordan stuck his head out the car window. "Mayleen?"

"What?" She had turned prickly again. Her colorless hair straggled into her face, disordered by the effort of hauling Joey.

"Come with me. You don't believe any more that this is right."

Mayleen's face closed. Heat into ice. "No."

"But you see that—"

"This is all I got for hope, Jordan. This. Here."

She went into the security kiosk and bent over her surveillance equipment. Jordan drove off, his captive, rescued Sleepless filling the back seat. Jordan didn't look back at the We-Sleep factory. Not this time. This time, he wasn't going back.

14

During the third week of the trial, while Richard Keller testified against his wife, activity in the press box became frantic. The holo-artists' fingers flew; the color journalists whispered subvocal notes, the men's Adam's apples working soundlessly. On a few faces Leisha saw the small, cruel smiles of small, cruel people watching pain.

Richard wore a dark suit over a black bodystretch. Leisha remembered all the light colors he'd programmed into posters and windows everywhere he'd ever lived. Sea colors, usually: green, blue, the subtle grays and creams of foam. Richard sat slumped forward in the witness box, palms flat on his knees, the courtroom light flat on skin stretched taut over broad features. His nails, she saw, were ragged, not really clean. Richard, whose passion was the sea.

Hossack said, "When did you first realize your wife had stolen Dr. Walcott's patents and filed them under the name of Sanctuary?"

Instantly Sandaleros was on his feet. "Objection! It has been established as fact nowhere—*nowhere!*—that patents were stolen, or by whom!"

"Sustained," the judge said. He looked hard at Hossack. "You know better than that, Mr. Hossack."

"When, Mr. Keller, did your wife first tell you that Sanctuary had filed patents on research to enable Sleepers to become Sleepless?"

Richard spoke in a monotone. "The morning of August 28."

"Six weeks after the actual filing date."

"Yes."

"And what was your reaction?"

"I asked her," Richard said, his hands still flat on his knees, "who in Sanctuary had developed the patents."

"And what did she answer?"

"She told me that we had taken them from Outside and had them back-filed in the United States Patent Office system."

"Objection! Hearsay!"

"Overruled," Deepford said.

"She told you, in other words," Hossack continued, "that she was responsible for both stealing and for invasion of United States datanets."

"Yes. She told me that."

"Did you question her on how this alleged theft had been accomplished?"

"Yes."

"Tell the court what she said."

This was what the press wanted; this was what the spectators jammed knee to thigh had come for. To hear the power of Sanctuary exposed from the inside, gutted by a Sleepless who was gutting himself to do it. Leisha could taste the tension. It had a coppery, salty taste, like blood.

Richard said, "I explained to Leisha Camden once that I am not a datanet expert. I don't know how it was accomplished. I didn't ask. What little I do know is on record with the United States Department of Justice. If you want to hear it, play the recording. I will not repeat it."

Judge Deepford leaned sideways over the bench. "Mr. Keller, you are under oath. Answer the question."

"No," Richard said.

"If you don't answer," the judge said, not ungently, "I'll place you in contempt."

Richard began to laugh. "Contempt? *Place* me in contempt?" He stopped laughing and raised his hands to the height of his shoulders, like a dazed boxer. His hands dropped. He let them dangle limply by his sides. No matter what was said to him, he sat unanswering, only smiling once in a while and murmuring "Contempt," until the judge declared an hour's recess.

When court reconvened, Deepford looked tired. Everyone but Will Sandaleros looked tired. Dismembering a man, Leisha thought numbly, was hard work.

Will Sandaleros looked on fire.

Hossack dangled a pendant by its gold chain in front of the witness. "Do you recognize this, Mr. Keller?"

"Yes." The skin on Richard's face looked puffy, like old dough.

"What is it?"

"It's a micro-power controller keyed to Sanctuary's Y-field."

The jury stared at the pendant in Hossack's hand. A few leaned forward. One man slowly shook his head.

The pendant was tear-shaped, of some smooth, opaque substance the green of fresh apples. According to the testimony of the surly garage attendant, he had found the thing near Dr. Herlinger's scooter slot just moments after seeing a figure, masked and gloved, run out a side entrance. The shield on the entrance had been taken down: "So it don't record my every little coming and going all day, you know?" the attendant said. Surveillance tape verified this testimony. Leisha hadn't doubted it in the first place. Long experience had taught her to recognize a witness too uninterested in justice to care about perverting it.

The green pendant swung gently in Hossack's fingers.

"Who owns this device, Mr. Keller?"

"I don't know."

"The Sanctuary pendants aren't individualized in any way? With initials, or by color, or anything at all?"

"No."

"How many exist?"

"I don't know."

"Why is that?" Hossack said.

"I wasn't in charge of their manufacture or distribution."

"Who was?"

"My wife."

"You mean the defendant, Jennifer Sharifi."

"Yes."

Hossack let that hang there while he consulted his notes. *My wife.* What, Leisha could almost hear the jury think, does it take to make a husband condemn his wife? Her fingers tightened against each other.

"Mr. Keller, you are a member of the Sanctuary Council. Why don't you know how many of these pendants exist?"

"Because I didn't want to know."

If she had been Richard's lawyer, Leisha thought, she would never have let him say that. But Richard had refused all counsel. She wondered suddenly if he had a pendant of his own. Did little Najla? Ricky?

Hossack said, "Wasn't the reason you didn't want to know anything about the pendants because your wife's other activities appalled you so much?"

"Objection!" Sandaleros cried furiously. "Not only is Mr. Hossack feeding the witness prejudicial opinions, but—as I've repeatedly tried to point out—this entire line of evidence has not been tied directly to my client and is in fact irrelevant. Opposing counsel knows there are at least twenty other people with those pendants; he agreed to that stipulation. If Mr. Hossack thinks he can milk irrelevant circumstances for their thrill value—"

"Your Honor," Hossack said, "we're establishing that the link between Sanctuary and the scooter tampering is an unequivocally clear one that—"

"Objection! Do you think that even if that amulet could be shown to belong to a member of Sanctuary, that any Sleepless would be so stupid as to *drop* it? This is clearly a frame, and Ms. Sharifi—"

"Objection!"

"Counsel will approach the bench!"

Sandaleros made a visible effort to control himself. Hossack sailed forward, all grave mass. Deepford leaned over the bench toward them, his face rigid with anger. But he was not as angry as Sandaleros when the two lawyers returned. Leisha closed her eyes.

She knew now what to expect when Sandaleros cross-examined. She hadn't been sure, before. Now she knew.

It wasn't long coming. "And so you are telling this court, Mr. Keller," Will Sandaleros began with clear disbelief, "that your motive for betraying your wife by going to Leisha Camden—"

"Move to strike," Hossack said wearily. " 'Betrayal' is clearly an inflammatory word."

"Sustained," the judge said.

"So you are telling this court that your motive for revealing to Leisha Camden your wife's alleged surveillance activities and alleged theft—your motive for this was concern for her under a law that had not protected your business from being ruined by prejudice on the part of Sleepers, had not protected your friend Anthony Indivino from being murdered by Sleepers, had not—"

"Objection!" Hossack cried.

"I'll allow it," Deepford said. His face sagged.

"—had not protected your children from being dangerously menaced by a We-Sleep mob at Stars and Stripes Airport, had not protected your marine-research ship from being sunk by parties unknown but allegedly Sleepers—after all these failures of the law to protect you in these circumstances, your motive for turning in your wife was concern for her under the law?"

"Yes," Richard said hoarsely. "There was no other way to stop Jennifer. I told her—I begged her—I went to Leisha before I knew about Herlinger . . . I hadn't . . . Leisha didn't tell me—"

Even Judge Deepford glanced away.

Sandaleros repeated scathingly, "And your motives for exposing your wife to Ms. Camden were conjugal concern and good citizenship. Very commendable. Tell me, Mr. Keller, were you and Leisha Camden ever lovers?"

"Objection!" Hossack all but screamed. "Irrelevant! Your Honor—"

Deepford studied his gavel. Leisha, through her numbness, saw that he was going to allow the question. Out of a concern for fairness to the minority, the persecuted, the habitually discriminated against.

"Overruled."

"Mr. Keller," Sandaleros said between clenched teeth; he was becoming, Leisha saw, the avenging angel, layer by layer, cell by cell. Gene by gene. The original Will Sandaleros was almost gone. "Were you and Leisha Camden, the woman to whom you exposed your wife's alleged wrongdoing, ever lovers?"

"Yes," Richard said.

"Since your marriage to Jennifer Sharifi?"

"Yes," Richard said.

"When?" Kevin's face was quiet on the hotel comscreen.

Leisha said carefully, "Before you and I started living together. Jennifer was obsessed with Tony's memory, and Richard felt—it doesn't matter, Kevin." As soon as the words were out, she knew how stupid they were. It mattered profoundly. To the trial. To Richard. Perhaps—even, still—to Jennifer, although how could Leisha guess what mattered to Jennifer? She didn't understand Jennifer. Obsession fell within Leisha's comprehension; obsessive secrecy, the preference for dark and silent plotting rather than lighted battles, did not. "Jennifer knows. She knew at the time. Sometimes it almost seemed . . . as if she *wanted* me to reach out to Richard."

Kevin said, as if it were an answer, "I'm taking the Sanctuary oath."

It was a moment before Leisha answered. "Why?"

"I can't do business otherwise, Leisha. Baker Enterprises is too deeply meshed with Donald Pospula's firm, with Aerodyne, with half a dozen other Sleepless companies. My losses would be enormous."

"You don't know the first thing about real losses!"

"Leisha, it isn't a personal decision. Please try to see that. It's purely financial—"

"Is that the only thing that matters?"

"Of course not. But Sanctuary isn't asking for anything immoral, only for community solidarity based firmly on economic solidarity. That isn't—"

Leisha broke the comlink. She believed Kevin; his decision was purely economic, within boundaries he could construe as moral. Emotional obsession like Jennifer's would never move him, never touch that smooth clear face, nor the smooth, clear brain beneath it. Obsessions like Jennifer's—and like her own for the necessity of law.

Days ago, she had asked herself what she had left to lose. Now, she knew.

Security encoded in secret pendants. Oaths of fealty. Planted evidence—because Will Sandaleros was right, no Sleepless would have ever left that pendant there. They were, all of them, too careful. But that fact would not be admissible in court. Generalities—even if profoundly true, even if crucial—never were.

Leisha sat on the edge of the hotel bed. It dominated the room, that bed. She had assumed, on first checking in at Conewango, that that was because sex was so important to the business of hotels. Wrong assumption. Reasoning from parochial experience.

It was sleep that was central. To everyone's assumptions.

It wasn't that she expected the practice of law to be clean. No trial lawyer expected that, not after years of plea bargains and perjury and crooked cops and political deals and misapplied statutes and biased juries. But she had believed that the law itself, apart from its practice, was, if not clean, at least large. Large enough.

She remembered the day she had realized that Yagaiist economics were not large enough. Their stress on individual excellence left out too many phenomena, too many people: those who had no excellence and never would. The beggars, who nonetheless had definite if obscure roles to play in the way the world ran. They were like parasites on a mammal that torment it to a scratching frenzy that draws blood, but whose eggs serve as food for other insects that feed yet others who fatten the birds that are prey for the rodents the tormented mammal eats. A bloody ecology of trade, replacing the linear Yagaiist contracts occurring in a vacuum. The ecology was large enough to take Sleepers and Sleepless, producers and beggars, the excellent and the mediocre and the seemingly worthless. And what kept the ecology functioning was the law.

But if the law itself was not large enough?

Not large enough to take in what a Sleepless would do, unprovable but clear as air? To take in what had happened between Richard and her. To take in not only what Jennifer had done, but why. Most of all, to take in that ineffable envy, as potent as genetic structure itself but not able to be spliced, altered, engineered out of existence. Envy for the powerful. The law had never been able to take that in. It had created endless civil rights legislation to correct prejudice against the biologically identifiable: Blacks. Women. Chicanos. The handicapped. But never before in the United States had the objects of envy and the objects of biological prejudice been the same group. And United States law was not large enough to take that in.

Leisha put her head between her knees. It was clear how the rest of the trial would go. Her own testimony would be discredited by Sandaleros as maneuverings by a jealous other woman against the legal wife. Richard would be discredited. Hossack would hit hard on his strong point: Sanctuary's power. Sleepless power. Sandaleros would not allow Jennifer to testify; her composure would look like coldbloodedness to a jury of Sleepers, her desire to protect her own like an attack on the Outside—

Which it had been.

The jury could go either way: acquit on the supposed love triangle, and then Jennifer would escape the law. Or convict because she was a powerful Sleepless, and then Jennifer would never survive her fellow inmates. Sanctuary would withdraw deeper into itself, a powerful spider spinning electronic webs for its own protection around a country of Sleepers increasingly filled with fear of people they seldom saw, never netted with, and would not buy from lest the Sleepless ruin the economy of which they were either shadow or source, no one could tell for sure. *They control things secretly, you know. They want to enslave us. They work with international competitors to bring us to our knees. And they don't stop at murder.*

And so prove that all along Jennifer had been right to protect her own.

It was a snake swallowing its own tail. Because the law, in its striving to be fair and treat all equally, left too much out. It was not large enough. It was not as large as the genetic and technological future which, outgrowing it, would be lawless.

Sitting on the edge of the bed in the dark hotel room, Leisha could feel her belief in the law leave her, as if the air itself were being sucked out of the room. She was choking, falling into a vacuum of cold and dark. The law wasn't large enough. It couldn't hold Sleeper and Sleepless together after all, couldn't provide any ethical way to judge behavior, and without judgment there was nothing. Only lawlessness and the mob and the void—

She tried to stand, but her knees buckled. Nothing like this had happened to her before. She found herself on the floor, on her hands and knees, and a still-rational part of her mind said, *heart attack.* But it couldn't be. Sleepless hearts did not give out.

Cold—

Blackness—

Emptiness—

Daddy—

The opening of the hotel-room door brought her back. It opened from the outside, without alarms. Leisha staggered to her feet. Across the room, beyond the bed, a figure stood silhouetted in the doorway, a thick figure carrying something even thicker. Leisha didn't move. Her own people—Kevin's people—had installed the security for this room, making it identical to her apartment in Chicago. No one in Conewango had the entry codes.

If it was a stranger, if Sanctuary was organized for assassination as well as theft . . .

The assassin would at least be good. Sleepless always were.

An arm stretched out from the dark figure. A hand fumbled for the manual switches.

"Lights on," Leisha said clearly.

The blocky shape was a suitcase. Alice stood blinking in the sudden light. "Leisha? Are you sitting in the *dark*?"

"*Alice!*"

"Your apartment codes opened both doors . . . don't you think you should change them? There's a bunch of reporters in the lobby—"

"*Alice!*" Then she was across the room, sobbing—she, who never cried—in Alice's arms.

"Didn't you know I'd come?" Alice said.

Leisha shook her head against Alice's chest.

"*I* knew." Alice released her, and Leisha saw that Alice's face shone with some strong emotion. "*I* knew that this would be the night for you. The night you'd fall into the Hole. I knew it yesterday—I *felt* it." She laughed suddenly, very shrill. "I felt it, Leisha, do you understand? It was like being hit with a load of bricks. I felt that you'd be in your worst trouble tonight, and I knew I had to come."

Leisha stopped sobbing.

"I felt it," Alice said yet again. "Across 3,000 miles. Just the way it's happened to other twins!"

"Alice—"

"No, don't say anything, Leisha. You weren't there. I know what I felt."

Leisha saw that the powerful emotion blazing on Alice's face was triumph.

"I knew you needed me. And I'm here. It's all right, Leisha, honey, I know about the Hole, I've been there—" She reached again for Leisha, putting her arms around her, laughing and crying. "I know, honey, it's all right. You're not alone. I've been there, I know . . ."

Leisha hung onto her sister with all her strength. Alice was pulling her back from the dark place. The void, the Hole. Alice, whose bulk anchored Leisha short of the edge, solid as earth. Alice, who now would never be unreachable again. Not now that Alice had known something before Leisha did. Not now that Alice had saved Leisha by becoming the one thing she hadn't lost.

"I *knew,*" Alice whispered. And then, stronger, "Now I can stop sending all those damn flowers."

* * *

It wasn't until later, after they'd talked for hours and Alice was starting to look sleepy, that the comlink shrilled. Leisha had turned it off; only a priority override could get through. She turned her head toward the screen. Two passwords flashed there. The link's fuzzy logic had admitted them simultaneously, apportioning one voice per speaker:

"Susan Melling here. I must—

"This is Stella Bevington. I just accessed the nets. The—"

"—talk to you *immediately.* Call—"

"—pendant the newsgrids say was—"

"—me on a shielded—"

"—found at that parking garage—"

"—line as soon as you can!"

"—is mine."

"We've finished our research," Susan's image said on the comscreen. Her gray hair straggled in greasy strands from a careless bun; her eyes burned. "Gaspard-Thiereux and I. On Walcott's Sleepless redundancy codes in DNA."

Leisha said evenly, "And?"

"Is this an unshielded line? Hell, forget that. Let the press tap. Let Sanctuary tap. Hey, Blumenthal—you listening?"

"Susan, please—"

"No please about it. No thank you, no nothing. That's why I wanted to tell you this myself. No nothing. The equations can't work."

"Can't—"

"There's a gap that can't be closed between shutting down the sleep mechanism at the preembryonic genetic level and trying to do the same thing after the brain has begun to differentiate at roughly eight days. The reasons the gap can't be closed are quite clear, quite specific, quite biologically final. They have to do with the tolerance of genetic noise in those genetic texts that are repetitions of regulatory systems. You don't need the details—the result is that we will never be able to convert a Sleeper into a Sleepless. Never. No one. Not Walcott, not the superbrains at Sanctuary, not all the king's horses and all the king's men. Walcott is lying."

"I . . . I don't understand."

"He made the whole thing up. It's very plausible, plausible enough to take good researchers a while to check. But essentially it's a lie, and there's no way a scientist with his famous withheld final step could not know that. Walcott knew. His research is a lie. He came to you with this stupendous discovery he *knew* would be shown to be a lie, and Sanctuary committed fraud for patents that are a lie, and Jennifer Sharifi is being tried for murder because of a lie."

Leisha couldn't take it in. None of it made any sense. She was very aware of Alice across the room, standing completely still. *"Why?"*

"I don't know," Susan said. "But it's a lie. You hear that, press? You hear that, Sanctuary? It's a lie!"

She started to cry.

"Susan . . . oh, Susan . . ."

"No, no, don't say anything. I'm sorry. I didn't mean to cry. That's the one thing I didn't mean to do. . . . Who's that with you? You're not alone?"

"Alice," Leisha said. "She—"

"It's just that I thought maybe I could become what I created. Stupid idea, huh? All of literature shows that the creators can't become the creations."

Leisha said nothing. Susan stopped crying as abruptly as she had started, tears drying on her old, soft, wrinkled skin. "After all, Leisha, that wouldn't do, would it? For the creators to become the creations? Who would there be to go on perfecting the art if we all got to be patrons?" Then, in a different voice, she said, "Bring Walcott down, Leisha. Like any other quack who sells worthless hope to the dying. Bring the bastard down."

"I will," Leisha said. But she didn't mean Walcott. In a sudden dizzying rush, she saw who it was that had been committing theft, and how, and why.

15

Jordan opened his apartment door, sleepy and Astonished. It was 4:30 in the morning. Leisha Camden stood there with three silent bodyguards.

"Leisha! What . . ."

"Come with me. Quick—by now I'm sure Hawke knows I'm here. There was no way to tell you I was coming that he wouldn't intercept. Get dressed, Jordan. We're going to the We-Sleep factory."

"I—"

"Now! Hurry!"

Jordan thought of telling her that he wasn't going to the factory—not now, not ever. But another look convinced him that Leisha would go there alone, and he suddenly didn't want that. Leisha wore a long blue sweater over a black bodystretch. Blue shadows pooled in the hollows under her eyes. She leaned a little forward on the balls of her feet, as if she were leaning into him, and it suddenly occurred to Jordan that she needed him with her. Not for physical protection—the three bodyguards collectively massed 640 pounds, not counting weapons—but for some other, edgy reason Jordan couldn't define.

"Let me get dressed," he said.

In the dark hallway Joey raised his head from his oversized cot. "Go back inside," Jordan said. "It's all right." Leisha, in need of him.

There was a plane, apparently folded in on itself in some state-of-the-art way that let it land vertically, in the apartment-house parking lot. But this was no aircar—it was a definite plane. The control panel bore no identifying marks. In the air it unfolded itself and shot over the sleeping town toward the river.

"All right, Leisha. Tell me what this is all about."

"Hawke killed Timothy Herlinger."

Something shifted inside Jordan. He knew what it was: truth. Tiny, deadly, like one of those poison pellets that dissolve in the heart of suicides. All you had to do was swallow it and the hard part was over, the rest inevitable and unstoppable. Jordan felt it move, and knew it had already been there before Leisha spoke. It had been there in the Profit Faire, in Jordan's ambiguous admiration of Hawke, in the argument over Joey, even in Mayleen's new toilet and her lace tablecloth. It was in the We-Sleep Movement itself.

He looked at Leisha. She seemed to radiate light, a hard lurid light like the Y-fields designed to alert people to dangerous machinery. She said again, "Hawke killed Dr. Herlinger. He set it up."

Jordan heard himself say, "And you're glad."

She turned a shocked face toward him. They regarded each other in the small cockpit of the plane, the three bodyguards a motionless blur behind them. Jordan had not meant to say it, but when the words were out he knew they, too, were true. She was glad. That it was Hawke and not a Sleepless. Gladness. That was the source of the lurid light, and of her need to have him with her.

"Witness for the persecution," he said, in a voice so unlike his own that Leisha said, "What?"

"Never mind. Tell me."

She didn't even hesitate. "The retina print on the scanner will match Stella Bevington's. Hawke must have taken it at your mother's party for Beck, at the new house, when everybody was drinking and careless. The party he bullied you into bringing him to. And that's when he got Stella's pendant, too. Jennifer sent her one; she wanted Stella in

Sanctuary and was trying to force Stella to choose. Stella was wearing the pendant but she took it off at the party because she saw all over again the kindness, the tolerance of Sleepers like your mother" . . . *oh, Daddy, the specialness of Alice!* . . . "Hawke took the pendant from her purse. She reported the loss to Jennifer but with no details; that was because of me. . . ."

Leisha turned her head. Jordan allowed himself no sympathy, no compassion. Leisha, he thought, was losing nothing. The murderer was a Sleeper.

"Jennifer knew nobody would be able to figure out by accident what the pendant did, and it would self-destruct if they tried, so she wasn't really worried that Stella lost it. Jennifer had already taken Hawke's bait on the patents. Jordan, there never was any process to alter Sleepers to Sleepless. Hawke hired Walcott and Herlinger to pretend there was, make a false lead look scientifically plausible. . . . God, he arranged the whole thing in detail. So Sanctuary would break into the government nets and back-file. Then he could use Walcott to report the theft, set the press going, and even without an indictment Sanctuary would take a beating. We-Sleep membership would soar."

Which was exactly what had happened, Jordan thought. Hawke was always a good planner. The little plane began its descent over the factory.

"But then Herlinger changed his mind. He had a flash of conscience and was going to expose Walcott and Hawke. So Hawke had him killed."

And that was typical of Leisha, too, Jordan thought. She didn't think: *Herlinger was trying to blackmail his partners, so they had him killed. Or, Herlinger got into a power struggle with Hawke and Hawke had him killed.* No, she assumed a flash of conscience, even in this situation. She assumed the public-minded and decent cause. "An eighteenth-century sensibility," Hawke had said. With scorn.

Jordan said, "You don't know that you're right. And if what you say is true and Hawke has me under such surveillance that he already knows we're coming . . . there will be no evidence left when we get there."

Leisha turned on him a brilliant gaze. "There wouldn't have been anyway. Not discoverable evidence."

"Then why are we going there?"

She didn't answer.

The gate of the factory was unshielded. The guard—not Mayleen—waved them through.

Hawke waited in his office, leaning casually against the front of his desk, palms flat on the wooden surface behind him. The desk held the full parody display: the Cherokee dolls, the Harvard coffee mug, the model We-Sleep scooter, the pile of misspelled mail from grateful workers at their first job in years, the plaques and pen sets and gilded statuettes from We-Sleep businesses. Some of them Jordan had never seen; Hawke must have taken them out, item by item, and arranged them carefully on the desk so his big body would not block the sight of them from the door. All the cheap accolades from hard-scrabble businesses, all the totems of contradictory successes. Looking at them, Jordan felt coldness slide over him. It was real, then. Not just true, but real. Hawke had killed.

"Ms. Camden," Hawke said.

Leisha wasted no words. Her voice was controlled, but the lurid light was still on her. "You killed Timothy Herlinger."

Hawke smiled. "No. I did not."

"Yes, you did," Leisha said, but it didn't sound to Jordan as if she were arguing, or trying to force agreement. "You set up Walcott's phony research to fan the hatred toward Sleepless, and when you saw a chance to accuse a Sleepless of murder, you did that, too."

"I don't know what you're talking about," Hawke said pleasantly.

As if he hadn't spoken, Leisha went on. "You did it to increase We-Sleep profits. Or rather, you think you did it for that reason. But profits were increasing anyway. You really did it because you're not a Sleepless, and never can be, and you're one of the haters that always moves to destroy any superiority he can't have."

The flesh above Hawke's collar started to redden. This was evidently not what he'd expected to hear. Jordan said, "Leisha . . ."

"It's all right, Jordan," she said clearly. "The three bodyguards are highly trained, the plane is equipped with surveillance equipment trained on my body, I am recording, and Mr. Hawke knows all this. There is no danger." She turned to Hawke. "Not to you, either, of course. Nothing is provable. Not against you, not against Jennifer once the retina print is identified as Stella Bevington's, because she can explain not only how she lost the pendant but where she was the morning Herlinger died. She was in a corporate meeting with fourteen executives in Harrisburg, Pennsylvania. You knew all that would surface, didn't you, Mr. Hawke, as soon as the pendant was introduced in evidence and Stella realized it was hers. You knew the trial would fail, and no one would be convicted. But the hatred would have been inflamed a little more, and that's what mattered to you."

"You're talking garbage, Ms. Camden," Hawke said. Jordan saw that he was again in control of himself, his big body relaxed and powerful as he leaned against the desk. "But I'll respond to your last statement anyway. I'll tell you what matters. *This*—" he picked up the sheaf of letters behind him "—matters. Gratitude from people who did not have the dignity of work before, and because of We-Sleep have it now. This matters."

"Dignity? Based on fraud and theft and murder?"

"The only theft I know of was committed by Sanctuary, stealing Walcott's patents. At least, so I hear on the newsgrids."

"Ah," Leisha said. "Then let me tell you of one more theft, Mr. Hawke. Just so you understand. You stole something else, and you stole it from my sister Alice, and from my friend Susan Melling, and from every other Sleeper who believed there was a chance at the long life and increased powers that come with Sleeplessness. They believed that, for a little while. They *hoped* that, in those hours of the night when Sleepers lie awake and think about living and dying and not sleeping. You wonder how I know that. Let me tell you how I know. I know because Susan Melling is dying of an inoperable brain condition, and knows it, and wants desperately not to die. I know because my sister said to me during the trial—the trial you engineered for your own aggrandizement— she said, 'The hardest thing I ever learned, Leisha, wasn't to raise

Jordan alone or earn a living or to accept that Daddy didn't love me. The hardest thing I ever learned was that even if I blamed you, I was still going to have to do all those things. The hardest thing I learned was that there's no way out.' You held out the promise of a way out, Mr. Hawke, and then robbed Alice of it. Alice and Susan and every other Sleeper who doesn't take hatred as a way out. You didn't rob the haters. You robbed the others, the people who try to be too decent for hatred. That's what you stole and who you stole it from."

Hawke's smile was stiff. There was a long silence. Finally he said mockingly, "Very pretty, Ms. Camden. You could easily find a job writing greeting cards."

Leisha's expression didn't change. She turned to go, and in that single contemptuous movement Jordan suddenly saw how little she had expected from this meeting. She had not confronted Hawke expecting to change him, or to learn anything from him, or even to discharge her rage. Those were not the reasons she had come, or the reason she had needed Jordan to come with her.

No one stopped them as they left the factory. No one spoke until the plane skimmed over the dark fields sliced by the darker river. Jordan looked at his aunt. She didn't know about Joey, didn't know that Jordan had already left Hawke. "You came here for me. So I would see what Hawke is."

Leisha took his hand. Her fingers were cold. "Yes, I came for you. That's all there is, Jordan. You. And you and you and you and you and you. I thought there was something more, something larger, but I was wrong. One by one. That's all there is."

"Community," Jennifer Sharifi said calmly to Najla and Ricky, "must always come first. That's why Daddy won't be coming home again. Daddy broke his solidarity with his community."

The children looked at their shoes. They were afraid of her, Jennifer saw. That was not bad; fear was only the ancient word for respect.

Najla finally said in a small voice, "Why do we have to leave Sanctuary?"

"We aren't leaving Sanctuary, Najla. Sanctuary goes with us. Wherever the community is, that's Sanctuary. You'll like the new place we're taking Sanctuary. It's safer for our people."

Ricky raised his eyes to his mother. Richard's eyes, in Richard's face. "When will the orbital be ready for us?"

"Five years. We must plan it, construct it, pay for it." Five years would be faster than an orbital had ever been constructed before, even given that they had purchased an existing shell from a Far East government that now would have to build itself another one.

Ricky said, "And we'll never come back to Earth again?"

"Certainly you'll come back to Earth," Jennifer said. "On business, when you're grown. Much of our business will still be here, among those few Sleepers who are not beggars or parasites. But we'll conduct business from the orbital, and we'll find ways to use genemods to build the strongest society ever known."

Najla said doubtfully, "Is that legal?"

Jennifer rose, the folds of her *abbaya* falling around her sandals. The two children rose as well, Najla still looking doubtful, Ricky troubled. "It will be legal," Jennifer said. "We'll make it legal for you, and for all the children to come. Legal, and solid, and safe."

"Mother—" Ricky said, and stopped.

"Yes, Ricky?"

He looked at her, and a shade passed over his small face. Whatever he had been going to say, he decided to keep it to himself. Jennifer bent and kissed him, kissed Najla, and turned to start toward the house. She would talk again to the children later, explaining to them in small doses they could absorb, making it all clear. Later. Right now there was so much else to do. To plan. To keep in control.

16

usan Melling and Leisha Camden sat in lawn chairs on the roof of Susan's house in the New Mexico desert and watched Jordan and Stella stroll toward a huge cottonwood beside the creek. Overhead the summer triangle, Vega and Altair and Deneb, shone faint beside a brilliant full moon. On the western horizon the last red faded from low clouds. Long darknesses moved over the desert toward the mountains, whose peaks still glowed with unseen sun. Susan shivered.

"I'll get your sweater," Leisha said.

"No, I'm fine," Susan said.

"Shut up."

Leisha climbed down the ladder from the roof, found the sweater in Susan's cluttered study, and stopped a moment in the living room. All the polished skulls were gone. She climbed the ladder and put the sweater around Susan's shoulders.

"Look at them," Susan said, with pleasure. Just before the deeper darkness of the cottonwood, the silhouette that was Jordan blended with the shadow that was Stella. Leisha smiled; Susan's eyes, at least, were still sharp.

The two women sat in silence. Finally Susan said, "Kevin called again."

"No," Leisha said simply.

The old woman shifted her slight, painful weight in her chair. "Don't you believe in forgiveness, Leisha?"

"Yes. I do. But Kevin doesn't know he's done anything that requires it."

"I take it he doesn't know either that Richard is here with you."

"I don't know what he knows," Leisha said indifferently. "Who can tell anymore?"

"Like you, for instance, couldn't tell that Jennifer Sharifi was innocent of murder. And you won't forgive yourself any more than you forgive Kevin."

Leisha turned her head away. Moonlight ran up her cheek like a scalpel. From the cottonwood came low laughter. Leisha said suddenly, "I wish Alice were here."

Susan smiled. The smile was strained; her painkillers needed to be increased again. "Maybe she'll just show up again if you need her hard enough."

"That's not funny."

"You don't believe it happened, do you, Leisha? You don't believe Alice had a paranormal perception about you."

"I believe she believes it," Leisha said carefully. Everything was different now between her and Alice, and the difference was too precious to risk. Alice was the only thing she'd gotten back from this year of cataclysmic loss. Alice and Susan, and Susan was dying.

Still, she had always been able to be honest with Susan. "You know I don't believe in the paranormal. The normal is difficult enough to understand."

"And the paranormal disturbs your world view a lot, doesn't it?" After a minute Susan added in a softer tone, "Are you afraid Alice will disapprove of Jordan and Stella? A Sleepless and a Sleeper?"

"God, no. I know she'd approve." She gave a sudden bark of harsh laughter. "Alice may be one of the twelve people in the world who would."

Susan said, as if it were relevant, "You also got calls from Stewart Sutter, Kate Addams, Miyuki Yagai, and your secretary, what's-his-name. I told them all you'd call back."

"I won't," Leisha said.

"There are more than twelve," Susan said. Leisha didn't answer.

Below them, Richard emerged from the front door and walked toward the distant mesa. He moved slowly, limply, as if the direction
didn't matter to him. Leisha thought it probably didn't. Very little did.
That he was here at all was due only to Jordan, who had not hesitated
but simply put Richard in the car and brought him. Jordan seldom hesitated any more. He acted. A moment later the huge figure of Joey, who
loved walking anywhere, shambled happily after Richard.

Susan said, "You think the Sharifi trial ended all chance of real
integration—Sleepers and Sleepless, We-Sleep and mainstream economy, have and have-nots."

"Yes."

"There's never a last chance for anything, Leisha."

"Really? Then how come you're dying?" After a moment Leisha
added, "I'm sorry."

"You can't hide here forever, Leisha, just because you're disillu-
sioned with law."

"I'm not hiding."

"What do you call it?"

"I'm living," Leisha said. "Just living."

"The hell you are. Not like this, not you. Don't argue with me—I
have the insight of the almost-eternal."

Despite herself, Leisha laughed. The laugh hurt.

Susan said, "Damn right it's funny. So call Stewart and Kate and
Miyuki and that secretary."

"No."

Richard disappeared into the darkness, followed by Joey. Jordan
and Stella, holding hands, started back toward the house. Susan said,
with apparent guilelessness, "*I* wish Alice were here."

Leisha nodded.

"Yes," Susan said artlessly, "it would be good to collect your entire
community."

Leisha looked at her, but Susan was absorbed in studying the
moonlight on the desert, while below them some small animal scurried
by unseen and overhead the stars came out one by one by one by one.

BOOK THREE

DREAMERS

2075

"*The dogmas of the quiet past are inadequate to the stormy present. The occasion is piled with difficulty, and we must rise with the occasion. As our case is new, so we must think anew, and act anew. We must disenthrall ourselves.*"

—ABRAHAM LINCOLN,
MESSAGE TO CONGRESS,
DECEMBER 1, 1862

17

On the morning of her sixty-seventh birthday, Leisha Camden sat on the edge of a chair in her New Mexico compound and contemplated her feet.

They were narrow and high-arched, the skin healthy and fresh right up to the toes, which were strong and straight. The toenails, cut straight across, glowed faintly pink. Susan Melling would have approved. Susan had set great store by feet: their strength, the condition of their veins and bones, their general usefulness as a barometer of aging. Or not aging.

It made her laugh. *Feet*—to be remembering Susan, dead for 23 years, in terms of feet. And not even Susan's feet, which might be logical, but Leisha's own feet, which was ridiculous. *In memoriam bipedalis*.

When had she begun to find funny such things as feet? Not, certainly, when she was young, in her twenties or thirties or fifties. Everything had been so serious then, of such world-shaking consequence. Not just the things that actually might have shaken the world, but everything. She must have been very tiresome. Perhaps there was no way for the young to be serious without being tiresome. They lacked that all-important dimension of physics: torque. Too much time ahead, too little behind, like a man trying to carry a horizontal ladder with a grip at one end. Not even an honorable passion could balance very well. And while jiggling hard to just keep your balance, how could anything ever be funny?

"What are you laughing at?" Stella said, coming into Leisha's office after only the most peremptory knock. "That reporter is waiting for you in the board room."

"Already?"

"He's early." Stella sniffed; she hadn't wanted Leisha to talk to any reporters. *"Let them have their tricentennial without us,"* she had said. *"What does it have to do with us? Now?"* Leisha hadn't had an answer, but she'd agreed to see the reporter anyway. Stella could be so incurious. But, then, Stella was only fifty-two and found hardly anything funny.

"Tell him I'm coming," Leisha said, "but not until I check on Alice. Give him some coffee or something. Let the kids play him their flute solo; that ought to keep him enthralled." Seth and Eric had just learned to make flutes from animal bones they scavenged in the desert. Stella sniffed again and went out.

Alice had just awoken. She sat on the edge of her bed while her nurse eased the nightgown over her head. Leisha ducked back into the hall; Alice hated to have Leisha see her naked body. Not until Leisha heard the nurse say, "There, Ms. Watrous," did she come back into the room.

Alice wore loose, cotton pants and a white top cut wide enough for her to put on herself with just her right arm; the left was useless since her stroke. Her white curls had been combed. The nurse knelt on the floor, easing her charge's feet into soft slippers.

"Leisha," Alice said, with pleasure. "Happy birthday."

"I wanted to say it to you first!"

"Too bad," Alice said. "Sixty-seven years."

"Yes," Leisha said, and the two women held each other's gaze, Leisha straight-backed in her white shorts and halter, Alice steadying herself with one veined hand on the footboard of the bed.

"Happy birthday, Alice."

"Leisha!" Stella again, in top managerial mode. "You have a com-link conference at nine, so if you're going to see that reporter . . ."

From the right side of her mouth, so softly that Stella couldn't hear, Alice murmured, "My poor Jordan . . ."

Leisha murmured back, "You know he loves it," and went to the board room to meet the reporter.

He surprised her by looking about sixteen, a lanky boy with too-sharp elbows and bad skin, dressed in what must be the latest adolescent fashion: balloon-shaped shorts and plastic blouse trimmed with tiny dangling plastic scooters in red, white, and blue. He perched nervously in a chair while Eric and Seth danced around him playing flutes, badly. Leisha sent her grandnephews from the room. Seth went cheerfully; Eric scowled and slammed the door. In the sudden quiet Leisha sat down across from the boy.

"What newsgrid did you say you represent, Mr. . . . . Cavanaugh?"

"My high school net," he blurted. "Only I didn't tell the lady that when I made the appointment."

"Of course not," Leisha said. Forget her feet—*this* was funny. The first interview she had granted in ten years, and it turned out to be to a kid for his high-school grid. Susan would have loved it.

"Well, then, let's begin," she said. She knew the boy had never spoken to a Sleepless before. It was written all over him: the curiosity, the uneasiness, the furtive assessment. But no envy, in any of its virulent forms. That was the remarkable thing: its absence in this unremarkable boy.

He was better organized than he looked. "My mom says it used to be different than it was now. She says donkeys and even Livers hated Sleepless. How come?"

"How come you don't?"

The question seemed to genuinely surprise him. He frowned, then looked at her with a sideways embarrassment that told Leisha, more clearly than words, how decent he was. "Well, I don't mean to offend you or anything, but . . . why would I hate you? I mean, donkeys are the ones—Sleepless are really just sort of super-donkeys, aren't they?— who have to do all the work. We Livers just get to enjoy the results. To live. You know," he said, in a burst of ingenuous confiding, "I can never figure out why donkeys don't see that and hate *us*."

"Plus ça change, plus c'est la même chose."

"What does that mean?"

"Nothing, Mr. Cavanaugh. Are there any donkeys in your school?"

"Nah. They have their own schools." He looked at Leisha as if she was supposed to know that, which of course she did. The United States was a three-tiered society now: the have-nots, who by the mysterious hedonistic opiate of the Philosophy of Genuine Living had become the recipients of the gift of leisure. Livers, eighty percent of the population, had shed the work ethic for a gaudy populous version of the older aristocratic ethic: the fortunate do not have to work. Above them—or below—were the donkeys, genetically-enhanced Sleepers who ran the economy and the political machinery, as dictated by, and in exchange for, the lordly votes of the new leisure class. Donkeys managed; their robots labored. Finally, the Sleepless, nearly all of whom were invisible in Sanctuary anyway, were disregarded by Livers, if not by donkeys. All of it, the entire trefoil organization—id, ego, and superego, some wit had labeled it sardonically—was underwritten by cheap, ubiquitous Y-energy, powering automated factories making possible a lavish Dole that traded bread and circuses for votes. The whole thing, Leisha thought, was peculiarly American, managing to combine democracy with materialism, mediocrity with enthusiasm, power with the illusion of control from below.

"Tell me, Mr. Cavanaugh, what do you and your friends do with all your free time?"

"Do?" He seemed startled.

"Yes. Do. Today, for instance. When you're done recording this interview, what will you do?"

"Well . . . drop off the recording at school. The teacher will put it on the school newsgrid, I guess. If he wants to."

"Is he a Liver or a donkey?"

"A Liver, of course," he said, a little scornfully. Her stock, Leisha saw, was dropping rapidly. "Then I might work on reading till school's out at noon—I can almost read, but not quite. It's pretty useless, but my mom wants me to learn. Then there's the scooter races at noon, I'm going with some friends—"

"Who pays for and organizes those?"

"Our local assemblyman, of course. Cathy Miller. *She's* a donkey."

"Of course."

"Then some friends are having a brainie party, our congressman passed out some new stuff from Colorado or someplace, then there's this virtual-reality holovid I want to do—"

"What's that called?"

"*Tamarra of the Martian Seas.* Aren't you going to see it? It's agro."

"Maybe I'll catch it," Leisha said. Feet, reporters, Tamarra of the Martian Seas. Moira, Alice's daughter, had emigrated to a Martian colony. "You know there aren't really any seas on Mars, don't you?"

"That so?" he said, without interest. "Then some friends and I are going to play ball, then my girl and I are going to fuck. After that, if there's time, I might join my parents at my mom's lodge, because they're having a dance. If there's not time—Ms. Camden? Is something funny?"

"No," Leisha gasped. "I'm sorry. No eighteenth-century aristo could have had a fuller social schedule."

"Yeah, well, I'm an agro Liver," the boy said modestly. "But I'm supposed to ask you questions. Now, is . . . no, wait . . . what's this—foundation you run? What does it do?"

"It asks beggars why they're beggars and provides funding for those who want to be something else."

The boy looked bewildered.

"If, for instance," Leisha said, "you wanted to become a donkey, the Susan Melling Foundation might help send you to school, finance augments for you, whatever was necessary."

"Why would I ever want to do that?"

"Why indeed?" Leisha said. "But some people do."

"Nobody *I* know," the boy said decidedly. "Sounds a little wormy to me. One more question: Why do *you* do it? Run this foundation thing?"

"Because," Leisha said with precision, "what the strong owe beggars is to ask each one why he is a beggar and act accordingly. Because community is the assumption, not the result, and only by giving nonproductiveness the same individuality as excellence, and acting accordingly, does one fulfill the obligation to the beggars in Spain."

She saw that the boy had understood not one word of this. Nor did he ask. He stood, picked up his recording equipment with obvious relief—the day's work over—and held out his hand. "Well, I guess that's it. The teacher said four questions are enough. Thanks, Ms. Camden."

She took his hand. Such a polite boy, so devoid of envy or hatred, so satisfied. So stupid. "Thank you, Mr. Cavanaugh. For answering my questions. Will you answer one more?"

"Sure."

"If your teacher does put this interview on the student newsgrid, will anybody watch it?" He looked away; she saw he didn't want to embarrass her with the answer. Such a polite boy. "Do you watch the newsgrids at all, Mr. Cavanaugh?"

Now he did meet her eyes, his young face shocked. "Of course! My whole family does! How else would my mom and dad know which donkeys would give us the most for our vote?"

"Ah," Leisha said. "The American Constitution at work."

"And next year's the tricentennial year," the boy said proudly; Livers were all patriots. "Well, thanks again."

"Thank *you*," Leisha said. Stella, stern at the doorway, ushered the boy out.

"Your comlink call is in two minutes, Leisha, and right now there's a—"

"Stella—how many applications has the Foundation processed this quarter?"

"One hundred sixteen," Stella said precisely. She kept all Foundation records, including financials.

"Down what percentage from last quarter?"

"Six percent."

"And from last year-to-date?"

"Eight percent. You know that." Leisha did; Stella would have more to occupy her if the Foundation were still running at the heady pace of its first years. She wouldn't be trying to make secretarial and maternal duties fill up a first-rate brain, leaning on everybody else in the process. Stella must have guessed what Leisha was thinking. She said suddenly, "You could go back to law. Or write another book. Or start another corporation, if you'd even consider competing with the donkeys at what you do even better."

"Sanctuary competes," Leisha said mildly. "And the new economic order isn't based on competition anyway, it's based on quality living. A young man just told me so. Don't badger me, Stella, it's my birthday. What's all that noise out there?"

"That's what I've been trying to *tell* you. There's a child out beyond the gate, screaming his head off to see you and nobody but you."

"A Sleepless child?" Leisha asked, her blood quickening. It still happened, sometimes: an illegal genemod, a confused child learning slowly over years that he was different, that the scooter races and holovids and brainie parties somehow weren't enough for him as they were for his friends. Then there would be the chance learning of the Susan Melling Foundation, usually from a kind donkey, and the scary, determined journey in search of his own kind even before he knew what it meant to belong to his own kind. Taking these Sleepless children or teenagers or sometimes even adults inside the compound, helping them to become what they were, had been Leisha's sweetest pleasure during her two and a half decades in the isolated desert.

But Stella said, "No. Not a Sleepless. He's about ten years old, a dirty kid yelling his head off that he has to see you and nobody else. I sent Eric out to tell him you had open reception tomorrow, but he socked Eric in the eye and said he couldn't wait."

"Did Eric flatten him?" Leisha said. Stella's twelve-year-old son had strength mods. And karate lessons. And a disposition no Sleepless should have.

"No," Stella said, with pride, "Eric's growing up. He's learned not to hit unless there's a clear physical need for defense."

Leisha doubted this. Eric Bevington-Watrous troubled her. But all she said was, "Let the boy in. I'll see him now."

"Leisha! Tokyo is on the comlink this very minute!"

"Tell them I'll call back. Humor me, Stella—it's my birthday. I'm old."

"*Alice* is old," Stella said, altering the mood instantly. After a moment she said, "I'm sorry."

"Let the kid in. At least it will stop that yelling. What did you say his name was?"

"Drew Arlen," Stella said.

In orbit over the Pacific Ocean, the Sanctuary Council broke into spontaneous applause.

Fourteen men and women sat around the polished metal table shaped like a stylized double helix in the Council dome. A plastiglass window three feet above the floor ran around the entire dome, occasionally crossed with thin metal support struts. The dome itself sat as close as possible to one end of the cylindrical orbital, so the view from the conference room, which neatly occupied half the Council dome, was appealingly varied. To the "north" stretched agricultural fields, dotted with domes, curving gently upward until lost in the hazy sky. To the "south" was space, uncompromising in the relatively thin layer of air that lay between the Council dome and the plastiglass end of the orbital cylinder. To the north, a warm and sunny "day" as sunlight streamed into the orbital through the long unopaqued window sections; to the south, endless night, filled variously with stars or an oppressively huge Earth. The uneven curvature of the conference table and the chairs bolted to the floor meant that six Council members faced stars, eight faced sun.

Jennifer Sharifi, permanent Council leader, always faced north, toward the sun.

She said, pleasure sparkling in her dark eyes, "All the brain scans, fluid analyses, spinal cartography results, and of course DNA analyses indicate nothing but success. Doctors Toliveri and Clement are to be warmly congratulated. And so, of course, are Ricky and Hermione." She smiled warmly at her son and daughter-in-law. Ricky smiled back; Hermione ducked her head and a spasm crossed her extravagantly beautiful face. About half of Sanctuary's families no longer altered genes, content with the intellectual and psychological benefits of Sleeplessness and wanting to preserve family resemblances. Hermione, violet-eyed and sleek-limbed, belonged to the other half.

Councilor Victor Lin said eagerly, "Can't we see the baby? Certainly the environment has to be sterile enough." Several people laughed.

"Yes, please," Councilor Lucy Ames said, and blushed. She was only twenty-one, born on the orbital, and still a little overwhelmed that her name had come up for a Council term in the citizen lottery. Jennifer smiled at her.

"Yes, of course. We can all see the baby. But I want to repeat what you have been told before: This round of genetic alteration has gone far beyond anything that any of us are privileged to enjoy. If we wish to keep our advantage over the Sleepers on Earth, we must explore every avenue of superiority open to us. But there are sometimes minor, unavoidable prices to pay as we move forward."

This speech sobered everyone. The eight councilors with lottery terms, those not of the Sharifi family that controlled 51 percent of Sanctuary financially and hence 51 percent of Council votes, glanced at each other. The six permanent councilors—Jennifer, Ricky, Hermione, Najla, Najla's husband Lars Johnson and Jennifer's husband Will Sandaleros—went on smiling determinedly. Except for Hermione.

"Bring in the baby," Jennifer said to her. Hermione left. Ricky reached out a tentative hand as his wife passed, but didn't touch her. He drew his hand back and stared out the dome window. Nobody spoke until Hermione returned with a wrapped bundle.

"This," Jennifer said, "is Miranda Serena Sharifi. Our future."

Hermione put the baby on the conference table and unwrapped its yellow blanket. Miranda was ten weeks old. Her skin was pale, without rosiness, and her hair was a thick mat of black. She gazed around the conference table from bright, very dark eyes. The eyes bulged in their sockets and darted constantly, unable to remain still. The strong, tiny body twitched ceaselessly. The minute fists opened and closed so fast it was hard to count her fingers. The baby radiated a manic vitality, an overwrought tension so intense it seemed her gaze would bore a zigzag hole in the dome wall.

Young Councilor Ames put her fist to her mouth.

"At first glance," Jennifer said in her composed voice, "you might think that our Miranda's symptoms look like certain nervous-system disorders the unaltered beggars are prey to. Or perhaps symptoms of para-amphetamines. But this is something *very* different. Miri's brain is operating at three or four times the speed of ours, with superbly enhanced mnemonic capacities and equally enhanced concentration. There is no loss of nerve-tissue control, although there is some minor loss of motor control as a side effect. Miri's genemods include high intelligence, but what the changes to her nervous system will do is give her ways to *use* that intelligence that we cannot now predict. This genemod is the best way around the well-known phenomenon of intellectual regression to the mean, in which superior parents have children of only normal intelligence, providing a lesser platform from which new genemods can launch."

A few people around the table nodded at this lecture; a few more, familiar with the lesser accomplishments of Najla and Ricky compared to Jennifer herself, looked down at the table. Councilor Ames continued to stare at the twitching infant, her eyes wide and her hand to her mouth.

"Miranda is the first," Jennifer said. "But not the last. We in Sanctuary represent the best minds of the United States. It is our obligation to keep that advantage. For all our sakes."

Councilor Lin said quietly, "Our usual Sleepless, genemod babies are already doing that."

"Yes," Jennifer said, smiling brilliantly, "but at any time the beggars on Earth could decide to reverse their shortsighted policy and begin to do that again themselves. We need more. We need everything we can create for ourselves from the genetic technology we dare to use to its fullest and they do not—mind, technology, defense—"

Will Sandaleros put his hand lightly on her arm.

For a second fury blazed in Jennifer's eyes. Then it was gone, and she smiled at Will, who gazed at her tenderly. Jennifer laughed. "Was I orating again? I'm sorry. I know you all understand the Sanctuary philosophy as well as I do."

A few people smiled; a few shifted uneasily around the polished table. Councilor Ames went on staring, wide-eyed, at the convulsing baby. Hermione caught the young woman's horrified gaze; immediately she wrapped Miranda in her blanket. The thin yellow material jerked and twitched. Along the hem were embroidered white butterflies and dark blue stars.

Drew Arlen stood before Leisha Camden with his legs braced firmly apart. Leisha thought that she had never seen such a contrast as this child with the teen-age reporter who had just left, and whose name she had already forgotten.

Drew was the filthiest ten-year-old she had ever seen. Mud caked his brown hair and smeared the remains of his plastic shirt, pants, and torn Dole-issue shoes. So much dirt clung to a deep scratch on his exposed left arm that Leisha thought it must surely be infected; the skin had a red, angry look around elbow bones like chisels. One tooth had been knocked out of a face that was remarkable only for eyes as green as Leisha's own and a sort of stubborn eagerness, as if Drew were prepared to fight for something with every fiber of his dirty, skinny, clearly non-donkey self.

"I'm Drew Arlen, me," he said. It might have been a fanfare.

"Leisha Camden," Leisha said gravely. "You insisted on seeing me."

"I want to be in your Fountain."

"Foundation. Where did you hear about my Foundation?"

Drew waved this away as of no consequence. "From somebody. After he told me, I done come a long way to get here, me. From Louisiana."

"On foot? By yourself?"

"I stole rides when I could," the boy said, again as if this were not worth mentioning. "It took a long time. But now I'm here, me, and I'm ready for you to start."

Leisha said to the household robot, "Bring sandwiches from the refrigerator. And milk." The robot glided soundlessly away. Drew watched it with total absorption until it left the room. He turned to Leisha. "Is that the kind that can wrestle with you? For muscle training. I see them on the newsgrids, me."

"No. It's just a basic retrieve-and-record 'bot. Now what is it you're ready for, Drew?"

He said impatiently, "To get started. Your Fountain. Making me into somebody."

"And just what does that mean to you?"

"*You* know—You're the Fountain lady! Get cleaned up, me, and educated, and be somebody!"

"You want to become a donkey?"

The boy frowned. "No, but thass where I got to start, me, don't I? Then go on from there."

The robot returned. Drew looked longingly at the food; Leisha gestured and he fell on it like a filthy little dog, tearing at the sandwiches with teeth on the left side of his face and wincing with pain whenever the sore, empty hole on the right came in contact with bread or meat. Leisha watched.

"When did you eat last?"

"Yesterday morning. Thass good."

"Do your parents know where you are?"

Drew picked up a crumb from the floor and ate it. "My mom don't care. She's at brainie parties, her, all the time now. My daddy's dead." He said this last harshly, looking straight at Leisha from his green eyes, as if she should know already about his father's death. Leisha pulled the terminal from the wall.

"Won't do no good to call them," Drew said. "We got no terminal, us."

"I'm not going to call them, Drew. I'm going to find out something about you. Where in Louisiana did you live?"

"Montronce Point."

"Personal bio search, all primary databanks," Leisha said. "Drew, what's your Dole security number?"

"842-06-3421-889."

Montronce was a tiny Delta town, no donkey economy to speak of. One thousand nine hundred twenty-two people, school with 16 percent attendance for students, 62 percent for volunteer teachers, who kept the building open fifty-eight days a year. Drew was one of the 16 percent, off and on. His medical history was nonexistent, but those of his parents and two younger sisters were recorded. Leisha listened to it all, and grew very still.

When the terminal was done, she said, "Your grades, even in what passes for a school in Montronce, weren't terrific."

"No," the boy agreed. His eyes never left her face.

"You don't seem to have unusual abilities in athletics, music, or anything else."

"No, I don't, me."

"And you don't really want to be educated for a donkey job."

"Thass all right," he said aggressively. "I can do that."

"But you don't really want to. The Susan Melling Foundation exists to help people become what they want to become. What is it you want your future to hold?" It seemed an absurd question to ask a ten-year-old, especially this ten-year-old. Poorer than even most Livers. Not particularly talented. Scrawny. Smelly. A Sleeper.

And yet not ordinary, either—the bright green eyes looked at Leisha with a directness most adult Sleepers never managed, not even in the relaxed, hedonistic tolerance of the tricentennial social climate. In fact, Leisha thought, there was more than directness in Drew's eyes: There was a confidence in her help that Foundation applicants almost never had. Most of them looked at her with uncertainty ("Why should you help me?") or suspicion ("Why should you help me?") or a nervous obsequiousness that inevitably reminded her of groveling dogs. Drew looked as if he and Leisha were business partners in a sure thing.

"You heard the terminal say how my Grampy died, him."

Leisha said, "He was a workman building Sanctuary. A metal strut tore loose in space and ripped his suit."

Drew nodded. His voice held the same buoyant confidence, without grief. "My Daddy was a little boy then. The Dole didn't hardly provide nothin' then."

"I remember," Leisha said wryly; what the Dole had provided, courtesy of basic cheap Y-energy and social conscience, was nothing compared to what donkeys and government now provided, courtesy of the need for votes. Bread and circuses, saved from Roman barbarism only by that same cheap affluence. Comfortable and courted, Livers lacked the pent-up rage for the arena.

She had expected Drew to pass over her reference to remembering his father's era; most children regarded the past as irrelevant. But he surprised her. "You remember, you? How it was? How old you be, Leisha?"

He doesn't know any better than to use my first name, Leisha thought indulgently—and immediately saw, for the first time, Drew's gift. His interest in her was so intense, so fresh and real shining from the green eyes, that she was willing to indulge him. He carried blamelessness on him like a scent. She began to see how he could have made the trip from Louisiana to New Mexico still healthy: people would help him. In fact, the blood on his arm was fresh and so was the knocked-out tooth; it was possible he had met with nothing but help until he encountered Eric Bevington-Watrous outside Leisha's walls.

And he was only ten years old.

She said, "I'm sixty-seven."

His eyes widened. "Oh! You don't look like an old lady, you!"

You should see my feet. She laughed, and the child smiled. "Thank you, Drew. But you still haven't answered my question. What is it you want from the Foundation?"

"My daddy grew up without his daddy and so he grew up rough, him, drinking too much," Drew said, as if it were an answer. "He hit my mom. He hit my sisters. He hit me. But my mom told me he wouldn't a been like that, him, if his daddy had lived. He'd a been a different man, him, kind and nice, and it warn't his fault."

Leisha could see it: The abused mother, not yet thirty herself, exonerating the man to his abused children, and eventually coming to believe the excuse herself because she too needed an excuse, to keep from leaving. *It wasn't his fault* becomes *It isn't my fault. She spends all her time at brainie parties,* Drew had said. There were brainies and there were brainies: Not all met the FDA's guidelines for either mildness or non-accumulation of side effects.

"It warn't my Daddy's fault," Drew repeated. "But I figure, it warn't mine, neither, me. So I had to get out of Montronce."

"Yes, but . . . what do you *want*?"

The green eyes changed. Leisha wouldn't have thought a child could look like that. Hatred, yes—she had seen children's eyes full of hate. But this wasn't hate, or anger, or even childish aggrievement. This was a completely adult look, such as not even adults wore much anymore, an old-fashioned look: icy determination.

Drew said, "I want Sanctuary."

"Want it? What do you mean, you want it? To get even? To destroy it? To hurt people?"

The green eyes softened; they looked amused, an even more adult look, even more disconcerting. Leisha stood up, then sat down again.

"'Course not, silly," Drew said. "I wouldn't hurt nobody, me. I don't want to destroy Sanctuary."

"Then—"

"Someday, me, I'm gonna *own* it."

The alarm sounded all over the orbital, loud and unmistakable. Technicians grabbed suits. Mothers picked up the babies shrieking at the noise, and instructed terminals in voices that trembled almost enough to obscure identification. The Sanctuary Exchange immediately froze all transactions; no one would profit from any dimension of the disaster, whatever it was.

"Get a flyer," Jennifer said to Will Sandaleros, already in his contamination suit. She pulled on hers and ran out of their dome. This one could be it. Any one of them could be it.

Will lifted the flyer. As they approached the free-fall zone along the orbital's center axis, the comlink said, "Fourth panel. It's a projectile,

Will. 'Bots thirty-three seconds away; tech crew a minute and a half.
Watch the vacuum pull—"

"We won't get there fast enough for that," Will said crisply. Under
the crispness Jennifer heard the satisfaction. Will didn't like her to
rush personally to damage sites. To keep her away, he'd have to tie her
down.

She could see the hole now, a ragged gash in an agricultural panel.
The robots were already there, spraying the first coat of tough plastic
over the breach, anchored against the outrush of Sanctuary's precious
air by Y-powered suction cups that could have held asteroids together.
When a robot had to move, the suction simply cut off in alternate feet.
The tech crew flyers spun in gracefully, and the crew in their sanitary
suits were out in seconds, spraying the crops in a wide semicircle with a
different sealant, one that would not harm anything organic until it
could be analyzed at the DNA level, for whatever might be there.

Weapons were only half the danger; the worse half was contamination. Not all the nations of Earth placed sanctions on genetic research.

"Where's the projectile?" Jennifer said over the comlink to the
tech chief. His suit had audio only, but he didn't have to ask who was
speaking.

"H section. They've got it sealed. It dented the panel on impact but
didn't puncture." That was good; the projectile was available for analysis without retrieving it from space. "What does it look like?"

"Meteor."

"Maybe," Jennifer said and Will, beside her, nodded. She was glad
it was Will. Sometimes it was Ricky when damage happened, and that
was always tiresome.

Will flew more slowly back across the orbital. He was a good pilot,
and proud of his skill. Below them Sanctuary stretched—fields and
domes, roads and power plants, window panels continuously cleaned
by the tiny 'bots that did nothing else. Bright warm artificial sunshine
suffused the air with golden haze. As they landed, the spicy smell of
soyflowers, the newest decorative edible, wafted toward Jennifer.

"I want the Council assembled to hear the lab reports," she said.

Will, out of his helmet, looked first startled, then comprehending. "I'll call them."

You could never rest. The Quran and United States history agreed on at least that one point: "And they who fulfill their covenant and endure with fortitude misfortune, hardship, and peril—these are they who are true in their faith." And then, "The price of liberty is eternal vigilance."

Not that Sanctuary had genuine liberty.

Jennifer stood before her Council. Ricky looked at her face, and his own grew set. Najla stared out the window. Councilor Lin leaned forward; Councilor Ames held her hands tightly clasped together on the metal table.

"The lab reports are all negative," Jennifer said. "This time. The composition of the projectile is consistent with J-class meteors, although that of course does not rule out its capture and subsequent use as a weapon. It appeared to contain no active microbes, and such spores as were found are consistent with J-class. The soil does not contain any foreign microbes, genetically altered or otherwise, that we could identify, although of course that doesn't mean they aren't there, hidden through DNA mimicry with gene triggers for later activation."

"Mother," Ricky said carefully, "nobody but us is capable of that level of genetic work. And even we're not very good at it yet."

Jennifer smiled brilliantly at him. "No one we know about."

"We monitor every lab on Earth, practically, through data-tapping—"

"Note the word 'practically,'" Jennifer said. "We don't actually know we have them all, do we?"

Ricky shifted position in his chair. He was thirty-one, a stocky man with thick hair over a low brow and dark eyes. "Mother, this is the sixteenth damage alert in two years, and not one of them has been an attack. Eight meteor hits, with three punctures. Three temporary malfunctions, almost immediately corrected. Two spontaneous microbe mutations from the space radiation we can't do a thing about. One—"

"Sixteen we *know* about," Jennifer said. "Can you guarantee that right now there are not DNA-mimetic microbes in the air you're breathing? That your baby is breathing?"

Councilor Ames said timidly, "But in the absence of proof—"

"Political proof is a beggar concept," Jennifer said. "You don't know that, Lucy, because you've never been on Earth. The concept of scientific proof is perverted there, used selectively to advance whatever cause the government is espousing to make claims on its betters. They can 'prove' anything, in their courts of law, in their newsgrids, in their financial dealings. What were your taxes last year to the IRS, Lucy? To New York State? And what did you get back in return? Yet the president of the United States would offer you proof that you have an obligation to support the weak by paying them, and further proof that if you don't, his military has the right to seize or destroy the very facilities you use to support your life and the life of your community."

"But," Councilor Ames said, bewildered, "Sanctuary pays its taxes. They're unfair, but we pay them."

Jennifer did not answer. After a moment Will Sandaleros said smoothly, "Yes. We do."

Ricky Keller said, "The point is, none of these damage incidents have been attacks. Yet our assumption always is that they are, and even evidence to the contrary is suspect. Have we carried this paranoia too far?"

Jennifer looked at her son. Strong, loyal, productive, a member of the community to be proud of. She was proud of him. She loved him and Najla as much as when they had been children, but her love had done them a disservice. She knew that now. Through her protection, her fierce shielding of them from what the beggars could do, they had grown up too secure. They didn't understand how it was, outside this enclave where community was strength, safety, survival, and where strength and safety and survival let a person use his talents for the fulfillment of his life. Her children did not understand the clawing, hot-eyed hatred the beggars felt toward that attitude, because beggars could never fulfill their own lives without looting the lives of their betters. Ricky and Najla had seen that only secondhand, in newsgrid broadcasts from Earth, and then usually contemporary broadcasts. Like wild animals who have eaten to satiety, the beggars were relatively quiet now under the Dole, under the absence of Sleepless before their very eyes. They dozed in the sun of cheap Y-energy, and it was easy to forget how dangerous they really were. Especially if, like her children, you had spent most of your life in safety.

Jennifer would never forget. She would remember for all of them.

She said, "Vigilance is not paranoia. And trust outside the community is not a survival skill. It could endanger us all."

Ricky said nothing more; he would never endanger the community. None of them, Jennifer knew, would ever do that.

"I have a proposal to put in front of you," Jennifer said. Will, the only one who knew what she was going to say, grew taut. Ready.

"All our safety measures are defensive. Not even retaliatory defensive, merely damage-control defensive. But the core of our existence is the survival of the community and its rights, and among the rights of the community is self-defense. It's time for Sanctuary to develop bargaining power through defensive weapons. We've been prevented from doing that by the careful international monitoring of every Sanctuary transaction with Earth, no matter how covert. The only way we've kept the beggars out of here for twenty-four years is by never giving the slightest legal excuse for the issuance of a search warrant."

Jennifer searched her audience's faces, tallying: Will and Victor Lin solidly with her—that was good, Lin was influential; three more listening with receptive body language; three closed and frowning; eight with the faces of surprise or uncertainty, including young Lucy Ames. And both her children.

She went on composedly, "The only way to both prevent penetration of Sanctuary by Sleepers and to create defensive weapons is through the use of our one undeniably superior technology: genetics. We've already done that with the new genemods for Miranda and the other children. Now we need to think about using our strength to create defensive weapons."

A storm of protest broke out. She and Will had expected this. Sanctuary, a refuge, had no military tradition. They listened carefully, not so much for the arguments as for the alliances. Who might be persuaded, who would never be, who was open to what moves along the decision tree. All the moves would be open and legitimate: community above all. But communities changed. The eight non-family councilors held their seats for only two years. And even family composition was open to change. Lars Johnson was Najla's second husband; she might have a third, or Ricky might have a new wife. And at sixteen, the next generation would take voting seats on the Council. Sixteen, for a genemod Sleepless, was old enough to make intelligent choices; Miranda's choices would be superintelligent.

Jennifer and Will could wait. They would force no one. That was the way a community worked. Not among the beggars, but here, in Sanctuary, that was the way the community worked. It worked through the slow shaping of consensus among the members, the productive who were entitled to their individual viewpoints because they *were* productive. Jennifer could wait for her community to take action.

But the Sharifi Labs research facilities did not belong to the community. They were hers, built and financed with her money, not the Sanctuary Corporation funds. And what was hers could begin work immediately. That way, the biological weapons would be ready when the community needed them.

"I think," Najla said, "that we should discuss this in terms of the next generation. What relationships will we have with the federal government twenty years down the line? If we feed all the variables into the Geary-Tollers social-dynamics equations . . ."

Her daughter. Bright, productive, committed. Jennifer smiled across the table at Najla with love. She would protect her daughter.

And start the research on genemod bioweapons.

Drew had two problems at Leisha's place in the desert: Eric Bevington-Watrous and food.

The way he figured it, nobody but him even knew these were

problems. On the other hand, they thought he had all kinds of problems that Drew himself didn't see as bothersome at all. They thought he was worried by the strange manners, the confusing number of people to keep straight, the donkey talk he'd never heard before, the need to sleep that only a few others shared, and the time he had to wait, doing nothing until September when they shipped him off to the donkey school they were paying for.

None of these were problems for Drew, especially the doing nothing. Nobody in his short life had ever done otherwise. But doing nothing, he saw on the first day, was not going to keep the scooter up in this place. Not here. These people were afraid of doing nothing.

So he kept busy, and made sure everybody saw him keeping busy, at all the things they thought were his problems. He learned the names of everybody in the compound—that's what they called it, a "compound," which up till that very minute Drew had thought was a double fuck at a brainie party, something he had once observed with great interest. He learned how they were related: Leisha and her sister, the old lady with a stroke who was a Sleeper, and her Sleeper son Jordan and his Sleepless wife Stella, whom Drew saw pretty quick he had better call "Mr. Watrous" and "Mrs. Bevington-Watrous." That's just the way they were. They had three kids, Alicia and Eric and Seth. Alicia was grown-up— she might be as old as eighteen—but not married, which Drew thought strange. In Montronce, women of eighteen usually had their first baby. Maybe donkeys were different.

There were other people, too, mostly Sleepless but not always, who lived there. Drew learned what all these people did—law and money and donkey things like that—and he tried to stay interested. When he couldn't stay interested he tried to at least stay useful, running errands and asking people if they needed anything. "Obsequious little lackey," he heard Alicia say once, but then the old lady cut her off pretty sharp by saying, "Don't you dare misunderstand him, young lady. He's doing the best he can with the genes he's got, and I won't have you trampling on his feelings!" Drew hadn't felt trampled; he didn't know what either "obsequious" or "lackey" meant. But he'd learned that the old lady liked him, and after that he spent a lot of time doing things for her, who after all needed it the most anyway since she was so old.

"Are you by any chance a twin, Drew?" she asked him once. She was working, very slowly, at a terminal.

"No, ma'am," he answered promptly. The idea gave him crawlies. Nobody else was like him!

"Ah," the old lady said, smiling a little. "Determinedly discontinuous."

They used a lot of words he didn't understand: words, ideas, manners. They talked about the shift of electoral power—what kind was that? Was it different from Y-energy? About genemod diatoms feeding Madagascar, about the advantages of circumlunar orbitals compared to the older circumterrestial ones. They told him to cut his meat with fork and knife, not talk with his mouth full, say thank you even for stuff he didn't want. He did it all. They told him he had to learn to read, and he worked at the terminal every day, even though it was slow scooting and he didn't see how he would ever use it. Terminals spoke you whatever you wanted to know, and when there were words on the screen there wasn't as much room for graphics. Graphics made more sense to Drew than words anyway. They always had. He *felt* things in graphics, colors and shapes in the bottom of his brain that somehow floated up to the top and filled his head. The old lady was a spiral, brown and rust-colored; the desert at night filled him with soft sliding purple. Like that. But they said to learn to read, so he did.

They said to get along with Eric Bevington-Watrous, too, but that was harder than the reading. And it was Eric who first noticed Drew's problem with the food. He was smart; they were all so fucking *smart*.

"Having trouble with real food, aren't you," Eric taunted him. "Used to that Liver soysynth stuff, and real food rips at your gut. Why don't you shit it out right here, you mannerless little vermin?"

"What's your problem, you?" Drew said quietly. Eric had followed him to the enormous cottonwood by the creek, a place Drew liked to be alone. Now he stood, tensed, and started a slow turn to get the water at his back.

"You're my problem, vermin," Eric said. "You're a parasite here. You don't contribute, you don't belong, you can't read, you can't even eat. You aren't even clean. Why don't you just take a walk into the ocean and let the waves wipe your ass!"

As Drew slowly turned, Eric did too. That was good: Eric might have twenty pounds and two years on him, but he didn't know how to maneuver for fighting advantage. The sun appeared over Drew's left shoulder. He kept turning.

He said, "I don't see *you* contributing so fucking much, you. Your grandmom says you're the biggest worry she got, her."

Eric's face turned purple. "You never talk about me with my own family!" he yelled, and charged forward.

Drew dropped to one knee, ready to leverage Eric over one shoulder and throw him into the creek. But just before Eric reached Drew, he leapt into the air, a controlled leap that brought instant sickening waves through Drew's chest: he had made a bad mistake. Eric was trained; it was just a kind of training Drew hadn't recognized. The toe of Eric's boot caught Drew under the chin. Pain exploded through his jaw. His head whipped backward and he felt something snap in his spine. The force of the kick hurtled him backward, over the shallow embankment into the creek.

Everything went wet and red.

When he came to, he lay on a bed. Wires and needles ran from his body to machines that whirred and hummed. His head whirred and hummed, too. He tried to raise it from the pillow.

His neck wouldn't move.

Instead, he turned it slowly to the side as far as it would go, a few inches. A bulky figure sat in a chair beside his bed: Jordan Watrous.

"Drew!" Jordan jumped up from his chair. "Nurse! He's awake!"

There were a great many people in his room, then, most of them not in Drew's careful catalog of compound-dwellers. He didn't see Leisha. His head hurt, his neck hurt. "Leisha!"

"I'm here, Drew." She came around to his head. Her hand was cool on his cheek.

"What happened . . . me?"

"You had a fight with Eric."

He remembered. Looking at Leisha, he was astonished to see that there were tears in her eyes. Why was she crying? The answer came, slowly—she was crying over *him*. Drew. Him.

"I hurt."

"I know you do, honey."

"I can't move my neck, me."

Leisha and Jordan exchanged looks. She said, "It's strapped down. There's nothing wrong with your neck. But your legs—"

"Leisha—not yet," Jordan begged, and Drew turned his head slowly, painfully, toward Jordan. He had never heard that kind of voice from a grown man. From his mom or his sisters, after Daddy whomped them good, but not from a grown man.

Something in his head whispered, *this is important*.

"Yes, now," Leisha said steadily. "The truth is best, and Drew's tough. Honey—something broke in your spine. We did a lot of repair work, but nerve tissue doesn't regenerate . . . at least not in people like . . . the doctors did muscle augments, other things. I know you don't understand what that means yet. What you can understand is that your neck is all right, or will be in a month or so. Your arms and body are all right. But your legs . . ." Leisha turned her head. The harsh overhead light made her tears shiny. "You won't walk again, Drew. The rest of your body functions normally, but you won't walk. You'll have a powerchair, the best we can buy or build or invent, but . . . you won't walk."

Drew was silent. It was too enormous; he couldn't take it all in. Then, abruptly, he could. Colors and shapes exploded in his mind.

He said fiercely, "Does this mean I can't go to no school in September, me?"

Leisha looked startled. "Honey, it's past September. But yes, of course you can still go to school, next term, if you want to. Of course you can." She looked across the bed at Jordan, and her look held so much pain that Drew looked too.

Jordan looked burned. Drew knew what it was to look burned—he had seen it on men whose scooters, illegally modified, went up in flames and took part of them with it. He had seen it on a woman whose baby had drowned in the big river. He had seen it on his mom. It was a look not to get yourself any feelings about, because the feelings would hurt so bad you couldn't help nobody. Not even yourself. And that look should mean some help for somebody, Drew had always thought, or how come people had to go through having it gnaw at their faces?

He said, "Mr. Watrous, sir—" he had learned that word, they liked it here "—it warn't Eric's fault. I started it."

Jordan's face changed. First the look went away, then it came back, then it hardened into something else, and then it came back again, worse than before.

Leisha said, "We know that's not true. Eric told us what happened."

Drew thought about that; maybe it was true. He didn't understand Eric all the way through, him, he'd already known that. And if things had been backside-to, so that Drew had been the one to make it so Eric couldn't walk . . .

Couldn't walk.

"Honey, don't," Leisha said, and now she was begging, too. "I know it seems terrible, but it isn't the end of the world. You can still go to school, learn to 'be somebody' the way you said. . . . Be brave, Drew. I know you *are* brave."

Well, he was. He was a brave kid, him, everybody always said that, even in stinking Montronce. He was Drew Arlen, who was going to own Sanctuary someday. And he would never, ever, ever look as burned as Mr. Watrous did now. Not Drew Arlen, him.

He said to Leisha, "Will the powerchair be the kind that can float three inches above the floor and go down stairs?"

"It will be the kind that can fly to the moon if you want it to!"

Drew smiled. He made himself smile. He saw something now, sitting clean in front of him, like a big shimmery bubble he didn't know how he'd missed before. It was big and warm and shining, and he not only saw it, he *felt* the bubble in every little bone in his body. Mr. Watrous said brokenly, "Drew, nothing can make this up to you, but we'll do everything we can, everything. . . ."

And they would. That was the bubble. Drew hadn't had words for it before—he somehow never had words till somebody gave them to him—but that was the bubble. Right there. He didn't have to run errands for the old lady anymore or learn the manners they shoved at him or even eat the real food. He would go on doing these things because some of them he wanted to learn and some of them he liked. But he didn't *have* to. They would do anything for him, now. They would have to. Now and for the rest of his life.

He had them.

"I know you will, you," he said to Jordan. For a long moment the bubble held him, while Leisha and Jordan exchanged startled looks above his head. Then the bubble burst. He couldn't hold it. It wasn't gone entirely, it was still true and would come back, but he couldn't hold it now. His legs were broken, and he would never walk again, and he started to cry, a ten-year-old strapped immobile on a hospital bed in a room with strangers who never slept.

18

oming next: A Nation Becalmed: The United States at its Tri-centennial," said the newsgrid announcer. "A special CNS broadcast in depth."

"Hah," Leisha said. "They couldn't report in depth on a soysynth cooking bee."

"Hush, I want to hear it," Alice said. "Drew, hand me my glasses from the table."

They formed a semicircle around the hologrid, twenty-six assorted people sitting or standing or leaning against the adobe walls. Drew handed Alice her glasses. Leisha spared a minute from the ridiculous broadcast to glance at him. Drew had been a year in his powerchair, and he maneuvered it as unthinkingly as a pair of shoes. In the months away at school he had grown taller, although no less skinny. He was quieter, less open, but wasn't that normal for a boy approaching ado-lescence? Drew seemed all right: he was used to his chair, adjusted to his new life. Leisha turned her attention back to the hologrid.

It represented state-of-the-art donkey technology, a flattened rec-tangle fastened to the ceiling, pocked by various apertures and bulges. It projected the broadcast in three-dimensional holograms five feet high on the holostage below. The color was more vivid than reality, the outlines less vivid, so that all images took on the bright, soft look of children's drawings.

"Three hundred years ago today," said the preternaturally hand-some narrator, obviously genemod, dressed in a spotless uniform of George Washington's army, "the founders of our country signed the most historic document the world has ever known: The Declaration of Independence. The old words still move us: 'When in the course of human events, it becomes necessary for one people to dissolve the po-litical bonds which have connected them with another, and to assume among the Powers of the earth, the separate and equal station to which the Laws of Nature and Nature's God entitle them, a decent respect to the opinions of mankind requires that they should declare the causes which impel them to the separation. We hold these truths to be self-evident, that all men are created equal—' "

Alice snorted. Leisha glanced at her, but Alice was smiling.

" '—that they are endowed by their Creator with certain unalien-able rights, that among these are Life, Liberty, and the pursuit of Happiness—' "

Drew frowned. Leisha wondered if he knew what the words even meant; his grades at school had not been spectacular. A thin blanket covered his legs. Across the room Eric, subdued and sullen, lounged against a wall. He never looked directly at Drew but Drew, Leisha had noticed, almost seemed to go out of his way to power his chair up to Eric, talk to him, turn on him Drew's dazzling smile. Revenge? But surely that was too subtle for an eleven-year-old. Reconciliation? Need? "All three," Alice had said crisply. "But, then, Leisha, you never were very sensitive to theater."

The picturesque narrator finished the Declaration of Indepen-dence and vanished. Scenes followed of July Fourth celebrations across the country: Livers roasting soysynth barbeque in Georgia; red-white-and-blue scooters parading in California; a donkey ball in New York, with the women in the new severe gowns that were stark straight falls of silk but were worn with elaborate collars and arm cuffs of heavy, jewel-studded gold.

The voice-over was electronically enhanced: "Independence indeed—from hunger, from want, from the factionalism that divided us for so long. From foreign entanglements—as George Washington advised 300 years ago—from envy, from class conflict. From innovation—it has been a decade since the United States has pioneered a single important technological breakthrough. Contentment, it seems, breeds comfort with familiarity. But was this what the founding fathers intended for us, this sweet comfort, this undisturbed political balance? Does the Tricentennial find us at a destination, or becalmed in stagnant waters?"

Leisha was startled: When was the last time she had heard even a donkey newsgrid ask the question? Jordan and Stella both leaned forward.

"And what effect," the voice-over went on, "is this mellow balance having on our young? The working class—" scenes of the New York Stock Exchange, Congress in session, a meeting of Fortune 500 CEO's—"still hustles. But the so-called Livers, the eighty percent of the population who control elections through sheer numbers, represent a shrinking pool from which to draw the best and the brightest to create America's future. Becoming the best and the brightest must be preceded by a *desire* to excel—"

"Aw, switch the grid," Eric said loudly. Stella glanced at him, her eyes angry; Jordan looked down at the floor. This middle child was breaking both their hearts.

"—and perhaps adversity itself is necessary to create that desire. The all-but-discredited ideals of Yagaiism that held such strong sway forty years ago when—"

Wall Street and scooter races vanished. The narrator went on, describing holoscenes that were not there, but the stage filled with a projection of dense blackness. "What the—" Seth said.

Stars appeared in the blackness. Space. The narrator's voice went on describing the Tricentennial party at the White House. In front of the stars appeared an orbital, spinning slowly, and beneath it a banner with a quote from a different president in a different time—Abraham Lincoln: "No man is good enough to govern another man without that other's consent."

Babble filled the room. Leisha sat a moment, stunned, but then she understood. This was not a general broadcast. Sanctuary maintained a number of communications satellites, monitoring Earth broadcasts and conducting datanet business. They were capable of focused, very narrow beam frequencies. The image of Sanctuary was intended for no place else but the compound, for no one else but her. It had been twenty-five years since Leisha had communicated with Sanctuary, or its overt holdings, or its shadowy, covert business partners. That lack of communication, with its myriad ramifications, had forced all their idleness, their becalmed stagnation: hers and Jordan's and Jordan's children. Twenty-five years. Hence this broadcast.

Jennifer just wanted to remind her that Sanctuary was still there.

Miri's earliest memory was stars. Her second earliest memory was Tony.

In the stars memory, her grandmother held her up to a long curved window, and beyond the window was black dotted with steady lights: glowing, wonderful lights, and as Miri watched, one of them flew past. "A meteor," Grandma said, and Miri reached out her arms to touch the beautiful stars. Grandma laughed. "They're too far for your hand. But not for your mind. Always remember that, Miranda."

She did. She always remembered everything: every bit of what happened to her. But that couldn't be true because she didn't remember a time without Tony, and Mommy and Daddy told her there had been a whole year without him, before he was born to them just the way she had been. So there must be at least a year she didn't remember.

She did remember when Nikos and Christina Demetrios came. And soon after the twins, Allen Sheffield came, and then Sara Cerelli. Six of them, tumbling around the nursery under the watchful eye of Ms. Patterson or Grandma Sheffield, going home to their domes with their parents for visits, playing games with the electrodes on their heads for Dr. Toliveri and Dr. Clement. They all liked Dr. Toliveri, who laughed easily, and they even liked Dr. Clement, who didn't. They all liked everything, because everything was so interesting.

Their nursery was in the same dome as another one, and for part of every "day"—Miri wasn't sure what that word meant yet except that it had something to do with counting something, and she liked counting—the plasti-wall between them was opened. The kids in the other nursery rushed into Miri's, or the other way around, and Miri tumbled over the floor with Joan or tussled over toys with Robbie or piled blocks on top of each other with Kendall.

She remembered the day that stopped.

It started with Joan Lucas, who was bigger than Miri and had curly, bright brown hair shiny as stars. Joan said to her, "Why do you wiggle all over like that?"

"I d-d-d-don't kn-know," Miri said. She had noticed of course that she and Tony and the others in her nursery twitched, and Joan and the others in hers did not. And Joan never stuttered, either, the way Miri and Tony and Christina and Allen did. But Miri hadn't thought about it. Joan had brown hair; she had black; Allen had yellow. Twitching seemed like that.

Joan said, "Your head is too big."

Miri felt it. It didn't feel bigger than before.

"I don't want to play with you," Joan said abruptly. She walked away. Miri stared after her. Ms. Patterson was there immediately. "Joan, do you have a problem?"

Joan stopped walking and stared at Ms. Patterson. All the children knew that tone. Joan's face crumpled.

"You are being silly," Ms. Patterson said. "Miri is a member of your community, of Sanctuary. You will play with her now."

"Yes, ma'am," Joan said. None of the children was exactly sure what a community was, but when the adults said the word, they obeyed. Joan picked up the doll she and Miri had been trying to dress. But Joan's face stayed crumpled, and after a while Miri didn't want to play anymore.

She remembered this.

They had lessons every "day," three nurseries of kids learning together in a community. Miri remembered vividly the moment she realized that a terminal was not just to watch or listen to; you could

make it *do* things. You could make it tell you things. She asked it what a
"day" was, why the ceiling was up, what Tony had for breakfast, how
old Daddy was, how many days till her birthday. It always knew; it knew
more than Grandma or Mommy or Daddy. It was very wise. It told you
to do things, too, and if you did them right it made a smiling face and if
you didn't you got to try again.

She remembered the first day she noticed that sometimes the terminal was wrong.

It was Joan who made Miri see it. They were working on a terminal
together, which everyone had to do part of each day—Miri knew the
word, now—because they were a community. Miri didn't like working
with Joan; Joan was very slow. Left alone, Joan would still be on the
second problem when Miri was on the tenth. She sometimes thought
Joan didn't like working with her either.

The terminal was in visual mode only: they were practicing reading.
The problem was "doll:plastic baby:?" Miri said, "M-m-my t-t-turn,"
and typed in "God." The terminal flashed a frowning face.

"That's not right," Joan said, with some satisfaction.

"Y-y-yes, it is," Miri said, troubled. "The t-t-t-terminal's wr-
wrong."

"I suppose you know more than the terminal!"

"G-God is *r-r-r-right*," Miri insisted. "It's f-f-four st-str- strings
d-d-down."

Despite herself, Joan looked interested. "What do you mean, 'four
strings down'? There's no strings in this problem."

"N-n-not in the p-p-p-p-problem," Miri said. She tried to
think how to explain it; she could *see* it in her mind, but explaining it
was harder. Especially to Joan. Before she could begin, Ms. Patterson
was there.

"Is there a problem here, girls?"

Joan said, not nastily, "Miri has a wrong answer, but she says it's
right."

Ms. Patterson looked at the screen. She knelt down beside the children. "How is it right, Miri?"

Miri tried. "It's f-f-four l-l-l-little str-strings down, M-M-Ms. P-P-Patterson. S-s-s-see, a 'd-doll' is a 't-t-t-toy'—the f-f-first string g-goes f-from d-d-doll t-to t-t-toy. A t-toy is f-f-f-for 'p-pretend,' and one thing w-w-we p-p-p-pretend is th-that a shooting st-st-st-star is a r-r-real st-st-star, so you c-can p-put 'sh-sh-sh-shooting star' n-next in the f-f-f-irst string. T-t-to m-make the p-p-p-pattern w-w-w-w-work." So many words was hard work; Miri wished she didn't have to explain so hard. "Th-Then a shooting st-s-st-star is *r-really* a m-m-m-meteor, and you have to m-m-make the str-string g-g-g-go r-real now b-b-because b-b-before you m-m-made it p-pretend, so the end of the f-f-first str-string, f-four l-l-little str-strings d-down, is 'm-m-m-m-meteor.' "

Ms. Patterson was staring at her. "Go on, Miri."

"Th-then for 'p-plastic,' " Miri said, a little desperately, "the f-f-first string l-l-leads t-t-to 'invented.' It *h-h-h-has* to, you s-see, b-b-because 't-toy' led t-t-t-t-to 'p-pretend.' " She tried to think of a way to explain that the fact that the little strings were one place off from each other was part of the whole design, echoed in the inversion she was going to make of the same words between substrings two and three, but that was too hard to explain. She stuck to the strings themselves, not the overall design, which troubled her because the overall design was just as important. It just took too long to explain in her stammering speech. " 'Invented' g-g-goes t-t-to 'p-p-people,' of c-course, b-because p-people invent things. The p-p-people st-string l-leads to 'c-c-community,' a l-l-lot of p-people, and that st-string has to g-g-go t-to 'orbital,' b-b-because then the t-t-two str-strings l-l-lined up n-next t-t-to each other m-make the p-problem s-s-s-say 'm-m-meteor: orbital.' "

Ms. Patterson said in a funny voice, "And that's a reasonable analogy. Meteor *does* bear a definable relationship to orbital: one natural and inhuman, one constructed and human."

Miri wasn't sure what all Ms. Patterson's words meant. This wasn't going right. Ms. Patterson looked a little scary, and Joan looked lost. She plunged ahead anyway. "Th-then f-f-for 'b-b-baby,' the f-f-first str-string l-l-leads to 'sm-small.' Th-that leads t-t-to 'p-protect,' l-l-like I d-do T-T-Tony, b-b-b-because he's sm-smaller than m-m-m-m-me and m-might g-get h-h-hurt if he c-climbs t-t-too h-h-h-high. Then the l-l-little str-string g-goes to 'c-c-community' b-b-because the c-community pr-protects p-p-p-p-people, and the f-fourth little str-str-string h-has to g-g-go t-to 'p-people' b-because a c-c-community *is* p-people, and b-b-b-because it w-was that w-way upside d-d-down under 'pl-plastic,' and a l-l-l-lot of our orbital is m-m-m-made of p-plastic."

Ms. Patterson still had her funny voice. "So at the end of three sets of four strings—Joan, don't change the terminal screen just yet—at the end of these strings of yours, the problem reads 'meteor is to orbital as people is to blank.' And you typed in 'God.'"

"Y-y-yes," Miri said, more happily now—Ms. Patterson did understand!—"b-b-because an orbital is an in-invented c-c-community, wh-while a m-m-meteor is j-just b-bare r-rock, and G-G-God is a pl-planned c-c-community of m-m-m-m-minds, while p-p-people alone are j-j-just one by one b-bare."

Ms. Patterson took her to Grandma. Miri had to explain the whole thing all over again, but this time it was easier because Grandma drew the design while Miri talked. Miri wondered why she hadn't thought of this herself. The drawing let her put in all the cross-connections and it was much clearer that way, even if some of the lines she drew were wobbly because the light pen in her fist wouldn't go as straight as the picture in her mind.

When she was done, the drawing looked very simple to her. But, then, it *was* simple, just a little set of strings to practice reading:

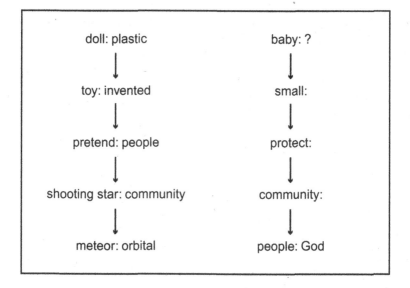

Afterward, Grandma was quiet a long time.

"Miri, do you always think this way? In strings that make designs?"

"Y-y-yes," Miri said, astonished. "D-d-don't y-you?"

Grandma didn't answer that. "Why did you want to type in the analogy that exists four little strings down on the terminal?"

"Y-you m-m-mean instead of ei-eight or t-t-ten str-strings d-d-down?" Miri said, and Grandma's eyes got very wide.

"Instead of . . . of no strings down. The one the terminal wanted. Didn't you know that was what it wanted?"

"Y-yes. B-but . . ." Miri squirmed in her chair ". . . I g-g-g-get b-bored with the t-t-top str-strings. S-s-sometimes."

"Ah," Grandma said. After another long silence she said, "Where did you hear that God is a planned community of minds?"

"On a n-n-newsgrid. M-M-Mommy w-was pl-playing it wh-wh-when I w-was h-h-h-home for a v-v-visit."

"I see." Grandma stood. "You are very special, Miri."

"T-T-Tony is t-t-too. And N-N-Nikos and Ch-Christina and Al-Al-Allen and S-Sara. G-G-Grandma, w-will the n-n-new b-baby

M-M-Mommy w-wants to h-h-have be sp-special wh-when it's b-b-b-born?"

"Yes."

"W-will it t-t-twitch l-like we d-d-d-do? And st-st-stutter? And eat s-s-so m-m-m-much?"

"Yes."

"And th-think in str-str-strings?"

"Yes," Grandma said, and Miri always remembered the expression on her face.

There were no more newsgrid broadcasts from Earth. They had never come into the nursery, only into Mommy and Daddy's dome, but now Miri never saw them there either. "When you are older," Grandma said. "There are beggar ideas you'll have to encounter soon enough, but not just yet. Learn first what's right."

It was Grandma, or sometimes Grandpa Will, who decided what was right. Daddy was gone a lot on business. Mommy was often there, but sometimes it seemed to Miri she didn't want to be. She would turn her head away from Miri and Tony when they entered a room.

"It's b-b-because w-we t-tw-twitch and st-stutter," she said to Tony. "M-M-M-Mommy d-d-doesn't-like us."

Tony started to cry. Miri put her arms around him and cried too, but she wouldn't take the words back. They were true; Mommy was too beautiful to like anyone who twitched and stuttered and drooled, and truth was paramount to a community. "I'm y-your c-c-c-community," she told Tony, and that was an interesting sentence because it was both true and of limited truth, with substrings and cross-connections that went down sixteen strings and formed a pattern that drew on what she had been learning in mathematics and astronomy and biology, a glorious pattern intricate and balanced as the molecular structure of a crystal. The pattern was almost worth Tony's tears. Almost.

As she grew older, however, Miri began to feel there was something missing in her patterns. She couldn't tell what. She had drawn a number of them for Grandma and Dr. Toliveri, until they got so complicated she knew she was leaving things out. Besides, every time she drew a string pattern, thinking and drawing it made new patterns, each with multilevel strings and crosshatching of their own, and there was no way to draw those, too, because if she did, drawing them would just generate *more*. Drawing and explaining could never keep up with thinking, and Miri grew impatient with the attempts to try.

She understood, by the time she was eight, the biology of what had been done to her and the others like her. SuperSleepless, they were called. She understood, too, that it must never be allowed to interfere with the twin truths Sanctuary was built on: productivity and community. To be productive was to be fully human. To share your productivity with the community in strict fairness was to create strength and protection for all. Anyone who would try to violate either truth—to reap the benefits of community without in turn contributing productively to it—was obscene, an inhuman beggar. Miri recoiled from the thought. No one could be that morally repulsive. On Earth, yes, which was full of what Grandma called beggars in Spain, some of whom were even Sleepless. But never in Sanctuary.

The alterations to her nervous system—to Tony's, Christina's, Allen's, Mark's, Joanna's—were to make her more productive, more use to the community and herself, more intelligent than humans had been before. They were all taught that, even the non-Supers, and eventually they all accepted it. Joan and Miri played together, now, every day. Miri was filled with gratitude.

But much as she liked Joan, much as she admired Joan's long brown curls and ability to play the guitar and high sweet laugh, Miri knew that it was with her own kind, the other Supers, that she felt the most community. She tried to hide this; it was wrong. Except for Tony, of course, who was her brother, and who one day would, with her and baby Ali— who had turned out to not be a Super after all, despite what Grandma said—join the Sharifi voting block that controlled 51 percent of Sanctuary stock, plus the family economic holdings. These were the things that guaranteed they were not beggars.

The economic structure of Sanctuary interested her. Everything interested her. She learned to play chess, and for a month refused to do anything else—the game let you make dozens of generations of strings, all intricately knotted to your opponent's string! But after a month, chess palled. There were, after, all, only two sets of strings involved, even though they got very long.

Neurology interested her more. The brain had a hundred billion neurons, each with multiple receptor sites for neurotransmitters, of which there were so many variants that the strings you could construct were nearly infinite. By the time Miri was ten she was conducting experiments in neurotransmitter dosage, using herself and the willing Tony as primary subjects, Christina and Nikos as controls. Dr. Toliveri encouraged her. "Soon you will be contributing yourself, Miranda, to the next generation of Supers!"

But it was all not enough. There was still something missing in her strings, something Miri felt so obscurely she could not discuss it with anyone but Tony, who, it turned out, didn't know what she was talking about.

"Y-y-you m-mean, M-Miri, s-some str-str-strings h-have weak p-p-p-places d-due to insufficient d-d-databases t-to draw c-concepts fr-fr-from?"

She heard the spoken words, but she also heard more: the strings that came with them, the Tony-strings in his own head, which she could guess at because she knew him so well. He sat supporting his big head in his hands, as they all frequently did, his mouth and eyelids and temples twitching, the thick dark hair jerking rhythmically over his forehead with the convulsions of his body. His strings were lovely, strong and sharp, but Miri knew that they were not as long as hers, or as complex in their crosshatching. He was nine years old.

"N-n-no," she said slowly, "n-not insufficient d-d-databases. M-more l-l-l-like—a s-space where another d-d-d-dimension of st-strings should g-g-go."

"A th-third d-d-dimension of thought," he said, with pleasure. "G-g-great. B-but—wh-wh-why? It all f-fits in t-t-two d-dimensions. S-s-s-simplicity of d-design is s-s-s-superiority of design."

She heard the strings on that one: Occam's razor, minimalism, program elegance, geometric theorems. She waved her hand, clumsily. None of them were physically very deft; they tended to avoid research that required handling many materials, and to spend time programming robowaldos when such handling couldn't be avoided. "I d-d-d-don't kn-know."

Tony hugged her. No words were necessary between them, and that was a third language, an addition to the simplicity of words and the complexity of strings, and better than either.

Jennifer for once looked shaken.

"How could it happen?" Councilor Perrilleon said. He looked as white as Jennifer.

The doctor, a young woman still in recyclable steriles, shook her head. Blood stained the front of her smock. She had come right from the hospital delivery room to Jennifer, who had called an emergency Council session. The doctor looked close to tears. She had returned to Sanctuary only two months ago from the Earth medical training that was still mandatory, much thinner than when she had left.

Perrilleon said, "Have you filed the birth certificate yet?"

"No," the doctor said. She was intelligent, Jennifer thought, as well as capable. The horror around the table did not lessen, but over it crept an almost imperceptible relaxation. There was no official transmission yet to Washington.

"Then we have a little time," Jennifer said.

"If we weren't still tied to the New York State and United States governments, we'd have more time," Perrilleon said. "Filing birth certificates, receiving a security Dole number—" he snorted "—being entered in the tax rolls—"

"None of that counts just now," Ricky said, a little impatiently.

"Yes, it does," Perrilleon insisted. Jennifer saw his long face set into stubborn lines. He was seventy-two, just a few years younger than she, and had come from the United States in the first wave of settlement. He knew, had seen, how it was there—unlike the Sleepless born in

Sanctuary—and he remembered. His votes had been useful to Jennifer's goals for Sanctuary. She would miss him when his term ended.

"The question we have to face," Najla said, "is what to do about this . . . baby. And we don't have much time. If there's an anomaly in the birth-certificate filing, some damned agency or other might get a search warrant."

It was what they all dreaded—a legal reason for Sleepers to come to Sanctuary. For twenty-six years they had made sure no such legal reason existed, by scrupulously meeting every single bureaucratic requirement of both the United States and the New York State governments; Sanctuary, as the property of a corporation registered in New York State, fell under its legal jurisdiction. Sanctuary filed its legal motions there, licensed its lawyers and doctors, paid its taxes, and each year sent more of its lawyers to Harvard to learn how to keep "there" and "here" legally separate.

This new baby could shatter that separation.

Jennifer had regained her composure. She was still very pale, but her head with its crown of black hair was held high. "Let's start by stating the facts. If this baby should die, its body would be shipped to New York for autopsy, as they all are."

Perrilleon nodded. He already knew where she was going. His nod was support.

She went steadily on. "If that happens, the Sleepers might have a legal reason to enter Sanctuary. Charges of murder."

No one mentioned that other travesty of a murder trial, thirty-five years ago. This one would be different. Sanctuary would be guilty.

"On the other hand," Jennifer said in her clear voice, "it might be medically possible that the baby would appear to die of Sudden Infant Death Syndrome, or some other clearly unassailable cause. Or, if the baby lives, then we will have to raise it. Here, with our own. In its . . . condition, with all that implies." She paused. "I think our choice is clear."

"But how could it happen!" Councilor Kivenen burst out. She was very young, and inclined to be weepy. Jennifer wouldn't miss her when her term ended.

Dr. Toliveri said, "We don't know as much as we would like about genetic information transmission over time. There have only been two naturally-born generations of Sleepless . . ." His voice trailed off. It was obvious that in some way he blamed himself, Sanctuary's Chief Geneticist. This was so clearly unfair that Jennifer felt anger. Raymond Toliveri was a superb geneticist, responsible for creating her precious Miranda. . . . Already this baby was causing disruption and strife in the community.

But didn't they always?

Councilor Kivenen said to the young doctor, "Tell us once more what happened."

Her voice had steadied. "The delivery was normal. A nine-pound boy. He cried right away. The nurse wiped him off and took him to the McKelvey-Waller scanner for the neonatal brain scan. It takes about ten minutes. While he was lying there in the padded basket under the scanners, the baby, he . . . went to sleep." There was a moment of silence. Finally Dr. Toliveri said, "RNA regression to the mean . . . we know so little in the area of redundant coding . . ."

Jennifer said crisply, "It's not your fault, Doctor." She let that sink in, so they could all see the guilt a Sleeper—even an infant Sleeper—could bring to blameless people. Then she started the debate.

The Council explored all possible legal scenarios: What if they filed a birth certificate but falsified it, checking the box for "Sleepless" rather than "Sleeper"? It might be eighty years before the child died of a premature old age and the government demanded an autopsy. But the child would have to take the mandatory New York State Board of Education tests at age seven. How much norm data did the beggars really have for those tests—enough to differentiate Sleepers from Sleepless? And there was the retina scan, virtually proof positive of sleep identity, although not for very small children. . . . What if . . .

Over and over again Jennifer, with the help of Will and Perrilleon, dragged the argument back to the real issue: The good of the community versus the good of one who would be forever an outsider. Not only an outsider but also a point of disruption, a potential point of legal entry for foreign governments, a person who could never produce on the level of the rest of them, who would forever take more than he gave.

A beggar.

The vote was eight to six.

"I won't be the one to do it," the young doctor said suddenly. "I won't."

"You don't have to be," Jennifer said. "I am Chief Executive Officer; mine is the signature that would have been on a falsified birth certificate; I will do it. Are you sure, Dr. Toliveri, that the injection will create conditions indistinguishable from SIDS?"

Toliveri nodded. He looked very pale. Ricky looked down at the surface of the table. Councilor Kivenen stuck her fist in her mouth. The young doctor looked in pain.

But none of them protested aloud after the vote was taken. They were a community.

Later, afterward, Jennifer cried. Her tears humiliated her, hot scant tears like boiling salt. Will held her and she could feel his stiffness even as he patted her back. This wasn't what he expected from her. It wasn't what she expected, either.

But he tried. "Dearest one—there was no pain. The heart stopped immediately."

"I know," she said coldly.

"Then . . ."

"Forgive me. I don't mean to do this."

Later, when she had come back to herself, she didn't apologize again. But she said to Will, as they walked together under the curved arc of agricultural and technical panels that was the sky, "The fault is with the government regulations that force us into deceit no matter what we do. It's just one more example of what we've said before. If we were not part of the United States . . ."

Will nodded.

They walked first to visit Miranda in the children's dome, and then to Sharifi Labs, Special Enterprises Division, as important as Miranda and under the tightest private-property security anywhere under Sanctuary's solid, productive sky.

Spring had come to the desert. Prickly pear bloomed with yellow flowers. Along the washes, cottonwoods glowed greenly. Sparrow hawks, solitary most of the winter, perched in twos. Leisha watched this flowering, so much more austere and rocky than along Lake Michigan, and wondered sardonically if the desert's modesty was as much a draw for her as was its isolation. Here, nothing was genetically modified.

She stood in front of her work terminal, munching an apple and listening to the program recite the fourth chapter of her book on Thomas Paine. The room glowed with sunlight. Alice's bed had been dragged to the window so she could see the flowers. Leisha hastily swallowed a bite of apple and addressed the terminal.

"Text change: 'Paine rushing to Philadelphia' to 'Paine's rushing to Philadelphia.'"

"Changed," the terminal said.

Alice said, "Do you really think anyone still cares about those old rules for verbals?"

"*I* care," Leisha said. "Alice, you haven't touched your lunch."

"I'm not hungry. And you don't care about verbals; you're just filling time. Listen, there's a whole lot of commotion in the front of the house."

"Hungry or not, you have to eat. You *have* to." Alice was seventy-five but looked much older. Gone was the stocky figure that had plagued her all her life; now her skin stretched thin over bones revealed as delicate wirework. She had had another stroke, and after that she'd put away her terminal. Leisha, in desperation, had even suggested that Alice resume her work on twin parapsychology. Alice had smiled sadly—the twin work was the only thing they had never been able to really discuss—and had shaken her head. "No, dear. It's too late. To convince you."

But the stroke hadn't impaired Alice's love for her family. She grinned as the commotion from the front of the house exploded into the room.

"Drew!"

"I'm home, Grandma Alice! Hey, Leisha!"

Alice held out her arms hungrily, and Drew powered his chair to go into them. Unlike Alice's grandchildren, with their own perfect health, Drew was never repulsed by the frozen left side of Alice's face, the spittle at the left corner of her mouth, the slightly slurred speech. Alice hugged him tightly.

Leisha put down her apple—it lacked flavor anyway; whatever the agrogene combines had done this time was a step backward—and tensed on her toes, waiting. When Drew finally turned to her she said, "You've been kicked out of another school."

Drew started his ingratiating grin, got a closer look at Leisha's face, and stopped smiling. "Yes."

"What for this time?"

"Not grades, Leisha. This time I studied."

"Well, then?"

"Fighting."

"Who's hurt?"

He said sullenly, "A son of a bitch named Lou Bergin."

"And I presume I'll be hearing from Mr. Bergin's lawyer."

"He started it, Leisha. I just finished it."

Leisha studied Drew. He was sixteen, and despite the powerchair—or because of it—he exercised fanatically, keeping his upper body superbly conditioned. She could well believe he was a lethal fighter. His adolescent features didn't yet fit together: nose too big, chin too small, skin spotted by acne where it wasn't still rounded by baby fat. Only his eyes were handsome, vivid green fringed by thick black lashes, with a concentrated gaze that could still make almost anyone think that Drew found him completely fascinating. Leisha was an exception. For the past two years there had been antagonism between them, periodically mitigated by clumsy attempts on his part to remember how much he owed her, and on hers to remember the engaging child he had been.

This was the fourth school that had expelled him. The first time, Leisha had been indulgent: He was a small crippled Liver, and the intellectual demands of a school full of donkey children, most genetically modified for intelligence and physical health, must have been overwhelming for him. The second time she had been less indulgent. Drew had failed every single subject, simply ceasing to go to class at all, spending solitary hours with his semiautomatic guitar or games terminal. No one had disturbed him. The school expected its students, most of whom would run the country someday, to be self-motivated.

Leisha sent him next to the most structured school she could find. Drew loved it immediately; he discovered the drama program. He was the star of his acting class. "I've found my destiny!" he said on a com-link call home. Leisha winced; Alice laughed. But four months later Drew was home, bitter and silent. He had failed to get a part in either *Death of a Salesman* or *Morning Light*. Alice asked gently, "Was it because they didn't want a Willy Loman or Kelland Vie in a powerchair?" "It was donkey politics," Drew spat. "And it always will be."

Leisha then searched hard for a school with an untaxing academic program, a strong artistic one, a structured school day, and as high a percentage as possible of students from families without much political clout, impressive financial connections, or illustrious histories. She found one that seemed to qualify in Springfield, Massachusetts. Drew had seemed to like the school and Leisha had thought things were going well. Yet here he was again.

"Look at your face," Drew said sullenly. "Why don't you say it aloud? 'Here's Drew back again, fucked-up Drew who thinks he's going to be somebody but can't finish anything. What the shit should we do about poor little Liver Drew?' "

"What *are* we going to do?" Leisha said cruelly.

"Why don't you just give up on me?"

Alice said, "Oh, no, Drew."

"Not you, Grandma Alice. *Her*. Her that insists that people be wonderful or they don't exist."

Leisha said, "As opposed to thinking they're wonderful just because they exist, but do nothing to fulfill their own existence?"

Alice rapped out, "That's enough, you two!"

It wasn't enough for Leisha. Drew's goading had hurt parts of her she hadn't known still existed. She said, "Now that you're home, Drew, you'll want to see Eric. He's straightened himself out wonderfully and is making genuine progress with global atmospheric curves. Jordan is immensely proud of him."

Drew's green eyes blazed. Leisha turned her back. She was suddenly, sickeningly, ashamed of herself. She was seventy-five years old—an incredible fact in itself; she never felt seventy-five—and this boy was sixteen. Unmodified, a Sleeper, not even drawn from the donkey class . . . As she got older, she lost compassion. Why else was she shut away from the world in this New Mexico fortress, in retreat from a country she had once hoped to help improve for everyone? Youthful dreams.

Dreams which Drew didn't even have.

Alice said wearily, "All right, Leisha. Drew, Eric asked me to give you a message."

"What?" she heard Drew snarl. But it was a softened snarl; he could never stay angry at Alice. Not at Alice.

Alice said, "Eric said to tell you that as part of his studies he walked into the Pacific and got his ass wiped. What does that mean?"

Drew laughed. "Really? *Eric* said that? I guess he has changed." The brooding bitterness returned to his voice.

Stella ran into the room, looking distracted. She had put on weight and now looked like a painting by Titian, with plump, healthy flesh under youthfully red hair. "Leisha, there's a—Drew! What are you doing home?"

"He's visiting," Alice said. "There's a what, dear?"

"There's a visitor to see Leisha. Actually, three visitors." Stella smiled, and her chins wobbled with excitement. "Here they are!"

"Richard!"

Leisha catapulted across the room into his arms. Richard caught her, laughing, then let her go. Leisha turned immediately to his wife, Ada, a slim Polynesian girl who smiled shyly. Ada still had trouble with English.

When Richard had first brought Ada to the New Mexico compound, after twenty years of solitary, aimless wandering around the globe, Leisha had been wary. She and Richard had never again been lovers; Leisha had recoiled from the thought of sleeping with Jennifer's husband. And Richard had never asked. He had grieved for years for his lost children, Najla and Ricky, a silent bitter grieving so unlike a Sleepless that Leisha had not known how to respond. She had been relieved when he traveled for years at a time, disappearing with only his credit ring and the clothes on his back into India, Tibet, the Antarctic colonies, the central South American desert—always somewhere technologically backward, as close to primitive as a world fueled by Kenzo Yagai still possessed. Leisha never asked him about his journeys; he never volunteered information. She suspected he passed as a Sleeper.

Then four years ago he had returned for one of his infrequent stays bringing Ada. His wife. She came from one of the South Pacific voluntary cultural preserves. Ada was slim and brown, with long lustrous black hair and a habit of ducking her head when anyone addressed her. She spoke no English. She was 15 years old.

Leisha had welcomed her, set about learning Samoan, and tried to hide the fact that she was hurt to the heart. It wasn't that Richard had rejected her; it was that he had rejected all the choices of being Sleepless. Choosing accomplishment. Choosing ambition. Choosing the mind.

But gradually Leisha had come to understand. The point for Richard was not only that Ada, with her shy smiles and halting speech and youthful adoration of Richard, was so different from Leisha. It was that Ada was so different from Jennifer Sharifi.

And Richard seemed happy. He had done what Leisha had not, and had made his own kind of peace with their Sleepless past. And if that peace looked like a surrender, could Leisha say that her own solution—the moribund Susan Melling Foundation, which had had all of ten applicants last year—was really any better?

"I see you, Leisha," Ada said in English. "I see you gladly."

"And I see you gladly," Leisha said warmly. For Ada, this was a long speech of great intellectual power.

"I see you gladly, *Mirami* Alice." *Mirami,* Richard had once said, was

a term of great respect for the honored old. Ada had flatly—shyly and
sweetly, but flatly nonetheless—refused to believe that Alice and Leisha
were twins.

"And I see you gladly, dear," Alice said. "You remember Drew?"

"Hey," Drew said, smiling. Ada smiled slightly and looked away, as
was proper for a married woman to an unrelated man. Richard said genially, "Hey, Drew," which was such a change from the usual shadowed
pain in his eyes when he spoke to Drew that Leisha blinked. She had
never really understood that pain: Drew was a generation younger than
Richard's lost son. And, of course, he was a Sleeper.

Alice's voice quavered, which meant she was tiring. "Stella said
three visitors . . ."

Stella entered then, carrying a baby.

"Oh, Richard," Leisha said. "Oh, Richard . . ."

"This is Sean. After my father."

The baby looked absurdly like Richard: low brow, thick dark hair,
dark eyes. Only his coffee-colored skin proclaimed Ada's genes. They
had evidently not had him modified at all. Leisha took the infant in her
arms, not sure what she felt. Sean gazed at her solemnly. Leisha's heart
turned over.

"He's beautiful . . ."

"Let me hold him," Alice said hungrily, and Leisha surrendered the
baby. She was glad for Richard, who had always wanted a family, an an-
chor, an intimate community. . . . Two years ago Leisha had medical
tests to confirm that her own eggs were inert. Gametes, Susan had
warned her decades ago, did not regenerate.

Kevin Baker, the only prominent Sleepless left in the United States,
had four children by his young Sleepless wife.

Jennifer Sharifi, she knew from consulting United States birth records, had two children and four grandchildren.

Alice may have lost Moira, emigrant to Mars colony, but she had
Jordan and his three children.

Stop it, she told herself, and did.

The baby was passed around. Stella bustled in with cookies and coffee. Alice, tired, was wheeled to her room to sleep. Jordan came in from a field he was cultivating with experimental genemod sunflowers. Richard talked, seemingly freely and yet with something odd in his manner, about his and Ada's wanderings through the Artificial Islands Game Sanctuary off the African coast.

"Hey," Drew said, and at the sound in his voice everybody looked up. "Hey—this baby's *sleeping*."

Leisha sat still. Then she stood, walked to Drew's chair, and stared down at the infant carryall parked at Drew's feet. Sean lay with his tiny fists flung above his head, asleep. His closed eyelids fluttered. Leisha's stomach clenched. Richard had felt such hatred of his own kind, his own people, that he had had *in vitro* genemod to *reverse* sleeplessness.

He was gazing at her. "No, Leisha," he said quietly. "I didn't. It's natural."

"*Natural . . .*"

"Yes. That's where we've been the last month, after the Artificial Islands—Chicago Medical Institute. Looking for answers to a spontaneous regression. But there's nobody there who's doing more than cookbook carrying out of old discoveries—hell, there's no geneticists left anywhere who can do more than that, except in agribusiness." He fell silent; Leisha and he both knew this was not true. There was Sanctuary.

Leisha said thickly, "Do they know at least if it's widespread, or on the increase . . . statistical parameters . . ."

"It seems to be pretty rare. Of course, there's so few Sleepless now they can't construct any statistical profiles."

Again that silence, heavy with the unnamed.

It was Ada who broke the silence. She couldn't have followed much of the conversation between Leisha and her husband, but she rose gracefully to move beside Leisha. Ada stooped and picked up her baby. Gazing tenderly down at him, she said, "I see you gladly, Sean. I see you sleep," and then her gaze rose to meet Leisha's directly, for the first time that Leisha could ever remember.

Even when everything in the country had changed, nothing had changed.

ennifer, Will, the two geneticists, Doctors Toliveri and Blure, and their technicians stood watching the creation of a miniature world.

Five hundred miles away in space, a plastic bubble floated. As the Sanctuary team watched via screen in Sharifi Labs, Special Enterprises Division, the bubble reached maximum inflation. Inside it, thousands of plastic membranes pulled taut. The interior was a honeycomb of thin-walled tunnels, chambers, and diaphragms, some with pinhole pricks, some as porous as standard Earth building materials, some open. None was more than four inches high. When the bubble was fully inflated with standard atmospheric mix, the hologrid in the lab's ceiling projected downward a transparent, three-dimensional model of the bubble and its internal partitions.

From each of four chambers on the outside of the bubble, five mice were released. The mice squeezed through the tunnels, whose low height prevented free fall, squeaking hysterically. On the hologrid model twenty black dots traced their path. A screen on another wall displayed twenty sets of readings from the biometers implanted in each mouse.

The mice ran free for ten minutes. Then from a single source inside the bubble was released the genemod organism, distantly related to a virus, that Toliveri and Blure had spent seven years creating.

One by one, the biometer readings faltered and the squeaking, amplified on audio, disappeared. The first three ceased transmitting within three minutes; the next six a few minutes later; five more within ten minutes. The last six transmitted for nearly thirty-one minutes.

Dr. Blure fed the data into an extrapolation program. He frowned. He was very young, no more than twenty-five, and since he was very blond the beard he seemed trying hard to grow was a soft stubble, like down. "No good. At that rate, the configurations of the smallest orbital project at over an hour. And of a beggar city, on a still day, over five hours for saturation."

"Too slow," Will Sandaleros said. "It won't convince."

"No," Blure said. "But we're closer." He glanced again at the flat bioreadings. "Imagine people who would actually use such a thing."

"The beggars would," Jennifer Sharifi said.

No one contradicted her.

Miri and Tony sat in their shared lab in Science Dome Four. Ordinarily children used school laboratories, not professional ones, for their learning projects; space on an orbital was too precious to dole out indiscriminately. But Miri and Tony Sharifi were not ordinary children and their projects were not just learning experiences. The Sanctuary Council, Sharifi Labs, and the Board of Education had held a meeting to explore the issues: Should Miri's neurological experiments and Tony's datasystems improvements be considered class projects, patentable private enterprises, or work for hire for Sanctuary Corporation? Should any potential profits belong to the family business, to the corporation, or to a trust fund arranged for Miri and Tony until they were no longer minors under New York State law? Everyone at the meeting had smiled, and the discussion had been happy; they were all too proud of the Supers to fight over them. The decision had been that their work belonged to Sanctuary with a 60 percent royalty share to the children themselves of any commercial applications, plus college credit. Miri was twelve, Tony eleven.

"L-l-look at th-this," Tony said. Miri didn't answer for forty-five seconds, which meant she was at a crucial point in thought-string construction and the string Tony's words had started was knotted in only at the periphery. Tony waited cheerfully. He was usually cheerful, and Miri could seldom detect any black strings among the thought edifices he mapped for her on his hologrid. That was his current project: mapping how the Supers thought. He had started with one sentence: "No adult has an automatic claim on the production of another; weakness does not constitute a moral claim on strength." Tony had spent weeks eliciting from twelve Supers every string and cross-string this sentence evoked, entering each into a program he had written himself.

It had been slow work. Jonathan Markowitz and Ludie Calvin, the youngest Supers in the experiment, had lost patience with the opaque, stammering slowness of spoken words and had twice flounced out of Tony's dogged sessions. Mark Meyer's strings had been so bizarre that the program refused to recognize them as valid until Tony rewrote sections of the code. Nikos Demetrios had clear strings and cooperated eagerly, but in the middle of his interrogation he caught cold, was quarantined for three days, and came back with such different strings for the same phrases that Tony threw out all his data for contamination by artistic rearrangement.

But he had persisted, sitting at the holoterminal across from Miri's even longer hours than she did, twitching and muttering. Now he smiled at her. "C-c-come s-s-see!"

Miri walked around their double desk to Tony's side. The holoterminal's three-dimensional display had been opaqued on the side facing her. When she finally got to see his preliminary results, Miri gasped in delight.

It was a model of *her* strings for Tony's research sentence, each concept represented by a small graphic for concretes, by words for abstracts. Glowing lines in various colors mapped first-, second-, and third-level cross-references. She had never seen such a complete representation of what went on in her mind. "It's b-b-beautiful!"

"Y-y-yours are," Tony said. "C-c-c-compact. El-elegant."

"I kn-know that sh-shape!" Miri turned to the library screen.

"T-T-Terminal on. Open L-Library. Earth b-b-bank. Ch-Chartres C-C-C-Cathedral, F-F-France, R-R-R-Rose W-W-Window. G-G-G-Graphic d-d-d-display."

The screen glowed with the intricate stained-glass design from the thirteenth century. Tony studied it with the critical eye of a mathematician. "N-n-noo . . . n-not r-really the s-s-s-s-same."

"In *f-f-feel* it is," Miri said, and the old frustration teased her, making limp spiraling strings in her mind: There was some essential connection between the Rose Window and Tony's computer model that wasn't obvious but was *there*, somehow, and of tremendous unseen importance. But her thinking couldn't express it. Something was missing in her thought strings, had always been missing.

Tony said, "L-l-look at J-J-Jonathan." Miri's thought model vanished and Jonathan's appeared. Miri gasped again. "H-h-how c-can he think l-like th-that!"

Unlike Miri's, Jonathan's model wasn't a symmetrical shape but an untidy amoeba, with strings shooting off in all directions, petering out, suddenly shooting back for weird connections Miri didn't immediately understand. How did the Battle of Gettysburg connect to the Hubble constant? Presumably Jonathan knew.

Tony said, "Th-those are the only t-t-two I've d-d-done s-s-so far. M-m-mine is n-next. Then the p-program will s-s-superimpose them and l-look for c-c-communication p-principles. S-s-someday, M-M-Miri, b-b-besides f-furthering c-c-communications science, we c-c-could use t-terminals to t-t-talk to each other w-without this f-f-f-fucking one-d-d-dimensional sp-sp-speech!"

Miri looked at him with love. His was work with a genuine contribution to the community. Well, maybe some day hers would be, too. She was working on synthetic neurotransmitters for the speech centers of the brain. Someday she hoped to create one that, unlike any the scientists had tried so far, would produce no side effects while it inhibited stuttering. She reached out and caressed the side of Tony's big head, lolling and jerking on his thick neck.

Joan Lucas burst into their lab without knocking. "Miri! Tony! The playground's open!"

Instantly Miri dismissed neurotransmitters and communications science. The playground was open! All the children, Norms and Supers alike, had waited for this for weeks. She grabbed Tony's hand and scampered after Joan. Outside, Joan, long-legged and fleet, easily outdistanced her, but no child in Sanctuary needed directions to the new playground. They just looked up.

In the core of the cylindrical world, anchored by tough thin cables, the inflated plastic bubble floated at the orbital's axis. Gravity here was so thin it approximated free fall, at least enough for the children. Miri and Tony crowded into the elevator that took them up, slipped on velcro mittens and slippers, and screamed in delight as they were dumped inside the huge bubble. The inside was crossed by translucent pink plastic struts, all with elastic give, with opaque boxes for hiding in, with pockets and tunnels that ended in midair. Everything was dotted with soft inflated hand-holds and velcro strips. Miri launched herself headlong into the air, flew across a plastic room, and launched herself back, crashing into Joan. Both girls giggled, and drifted slowly downward, clutching at each other and squealing when Tony and a boy they didn't know tore by overhead.

Miri's strings rippled in her mind with chaos theory, with mythic images, with angels and flyers and Icarus and acceleration ratios and Orville Wright and Mercury astronauts and membraned mammals and escape velocities and muscle-strength-weight ratios. With delight.

"Come inside here," Joan shouted over the shrieking. "I have a secret to tell you!" She grabbed Miri, stuffed her into a translucent suspended box, and crowded in after her. Inside it was marginally less noisy.

Joan said, "Miri, guess what—my mom's pregnant!"

"W-w-wonderful!" Miri said. Joan's mother's eggs were Type r-14, difficult to penetrate even *in vitro.* Joan was thirteen; Miri knew she had wanted a baby sister or brother with the same tenacity that Tony wanted a Litov-Hall auto-am. "I'm s-s-s-so g-g-g-glad!"

Joan hugged her. "You're my best friend, Miri!" Abruptly she launched herself out of the box. "Catch me!"

Miri never would, of course. She was too clumsy, compared to Joan's Norm agility. But that didn't matter. She hurtled herself after Joan, shrieking with the others just for the pleasure of making noise, while below her the world tumbled over and over in patterns of hydrofields and domes and parks as beautiful as strings.

The Tuesday after the playground opened was Remembrance Day. Miri dressed carefully in black shorts and tunic. She could feel the somber shape of her strings, shifting with her thoughts in compact, flattened ovals as dark as everyone's clothes. Religious holidays in Sanctuary varied from family to family; some kept Christmas, Ramadan, Easter, Yom Kippur, or Divali; many kept nothing at all. The two holidays held in common were the Fourth of July and Remembrance Day, April 15.

The crowd gathered in the central panel. The park had been expanded by covering surrounding fields of super-high-yield plants with a temporary spray-plastic latticework strong enough to stand on and large enough to accommodate every person in Sanctuary. Those few who could not leave their work or had temporary illnesses watched on their comlinks. A temporary platform for the speaker loomed above the crowd. High above the platform floated the deserted playground.

Most people stood with their families. Miri and Tony, however, clustered with the other Supers who were older than eight or nine, half hidden in the shadows of a power dome. The Supers were happier apart from crowds of Norms, whom they couldn't keep up with physically, and happier together. Miri didn't think her mother had even looked for her or Tony or Ali. Hermione had a new baby to whom she was devoted. No one had explained to Miri why this one, like little Rebecca, was a Norm. Miri hadn't asked.

Where was Joan? Miri twisted and turned, but she couldn't see the Lucas family anywhere.

Jennifer Sharifi, wearing a black *abbaya,* mounted the platform.

Miri's heart swelled with pride. Grandma was beautiful, more beautiful even than Mother or Aunt Najla. She was as beautiful as Joan. And on Grandma's face was the composed, set look that always evoked in Miri strings and cross-references of human intelligence and will. There was no one like Grandmother.

"Citizens of Sanctuary," Jennifer began. Her voice, amplified, carried to every corner of the orbital without once being raised. "I call you that because although the United States government calls us citizens of that country, we know better. We know that no government founded without the consent of the governed has the right to claim us. We know that no government without the ability to recognize the reality of men having been created unequal has the vision to claim us. We know that no government operating on the principle that beggars have a right to the productive labor of others has the morality to claim us.

"On this Remembrance Day, April 15, we recognize that Sanctuary has the right to its own consenting government, its own clear-eyed reality, the fruits of its own productive labor. We have the right to these things, but we do not yet possess the actualities. We are not free. We are not yet allowed the 'separate and equal station to which the Laws of Nature and of Nature's God entitle' us. We have Sanctuary, thanks to the Sleepless vision of our founder Anthony Indivino, but we do not have freedom."

"Y-y-yet," Tony whispered grimly to Miri. She squeezed his hand and stood on tiptoe to search the crowd for Joan.

"And yet we have created for ourselves as much of the measure of freedom as we can," Jennifer continued. "Assigned without our consent to a New York State court jurisdiction, we have never in thirty-two years either filed or incurred a lawsuit. Instead, we have set up our own judicial system, unknown to the beggars below, and administered it ourselves. Assigned without our consent to licensing regulations for our brokers, doctors, lawyers, even teachers of our own children, we have complied with all the regulations. We have done this even when it means living for awhile among the beggars. Assigned to comply with meaningless statistical regulations that number us equal with beggars, we have counted and measured and tested ourselves as required and then dismissed the result as the irrelevant pap it surely is."

Miri spotted Joan. She was pushing through the crowd, heedlessly elbowing people, and Miri was shocked to see that Joan hadn't changed into Remembrance Day black. She wore a forest-green halter and shorts. Miri raised her arm as far as she could beyond the shadow of the power dome and waved frantically.

"But there is one requirement of the beggars we cannot dismiss," Jennifer said. "Beggars do not work to support their own lives; they depend, snarling, on their betters to do that. To support the millions of nonproductive 'Livers' in the United States, Sanctuary—as an entity and as individuals—is forcibly robbed of a total of 64.8 percent of its annual productivity through the legal thievery of state and federal taxes. We cannot fight this, not without risk to Sanctuary itself. We cannot resist. All we can do is remember what this means—morally, practically, politically, and historically. And on April 15 of every year, as our resources are taken from us with nothing given in return, we do remember."

Joan's pretty face was puffy and streaked—she had been *crying*. Miri tried to remember the last time she had seen someone as old as Joan cry. Little children cried, when they fell down or couldn't do a terminal problem or fought with each other over toys. But Joan was thirteen. Adults, catching sight of her face as Joan elbowed through the crowd, tried kindly to question her. Joan ignored them, pushing toward Miri.

"We remember the hatred toward Sleepless on Earth. We remember—"

"Come with me," Joan said fiercely to Miri. She grabbed her friend and half-dragged her around the power dome, until the curved black surface completely hid Jennifer from view. Jennifer's voice, however, floated toward them, as clear as if she stood beside Joan's trembling body. Strings exploded in Miri's mind. She had never seen a Norm twitch.

"Do you know what they've done? *Do* you, Miri?"

"Wh-who? Wh-wh-wh-what?"

"They've killed the baby!"

Blackness swept through Miri. Her knees gave way and she sank to the ground. "The b-b-b-beggars? H-h-h-how?" Joan's mother had been only a few weeks pregnant and she hadn't left Sanctuary; did that mean there were beggars *here*. . . .

"Not the beggars! The Council! Led by your precious grandmother!"

Strings unraveled, and ripped. Miri gripped the ends firmly. Her nervous system, always revved up to the edge of biochemical hysteria, began to slide over that edge. Miri closed her eyes and breathed deeply until she was in control.

"Wh-what h-happened, J-J-J-Joan?"

Miri's calm, fragile as it was, seemed to calm Joan. She slid to the grass beside Miri and wrapped her arms around her knees. There was a scratch, not yet fully regenerated, on her left calf.

"My mother called me in to her study just before I was going to change for Remembrance Day. She'd been crying. And she was lying on the pallet she and Daddy use for sex."

Miri nodded; her mind made strings of why a Sleepless would be in bed if she were not having sex or injured.

Joan said, "She told me that the Council had made the decision to abort the baby. I thought that was strange—if the prefetal tests show DNA failure in a major area the parents naturally abort. What does the Council have to do with it?"

"Wh-wh-what d-d-do they?"

"I asked where the DNA failure was. She said there wasn't one."

Around them floated Jennifer's voice: "—the assumption that, *because* they are weak, they are automatically owed the labor of the strong—"

"I asked my mother why the Council ordered an abortion if the baby was normal. She said it wasn't an order but a strong recommendation, and she and Daddy were going to comply. She started crying again. She told me the gene analysis showed that the baby is . . . was . . ."

She couldn't say it. Miri put her arm around her friend.

". . . was a Sleeper."

Miri took her arm away. The next minute she regretted it, bitterly, but it was too late. Joan scrambled to her feet. "You think Mom should abort too!"

Did she? Miri wasn't sure. Strings whirled in her head: genetic regression, DNA information redundancy, spiraling children in the playground, the nursery, the lab, productivity . . . beggars. A baby, soft in Joan's mother's arms. She remembered Tony in her own mother's arms, her grandmother holding Miri up to see the stars . . .

Jennifer's voice came louder: "Above all, to remember that morality is defined by what contributes to life, not what leeches from it . . ."

Joan cried, "I'll never be friends with you again, Miranda Sharifi!" She ran away, her long legs flashing under the green shorts she should not have been wearing on Remembrance Day.

"W-w-wait!" Miri cried. "W-wait! I think the C-C-Council is wr-wr-wrong!" But Joan didn't wait.

Miri would never catch her.

Slowly, awkwardly, she got up from the ground and went to the lab in Science Dome Four. Her and Tony's work terminals were both on, running programs. Miri turned them off, then swept all the hard-copy off her desk with one lash of her arm.

"D-d-damn!" The word was not enough; there must be more such words, must be . . . something to do with this pain. Her strings were not enough. Their incompleteness taunted her yet again, like a missing piece of an equation you knew was missing even though you had never seen it before, because otherwise there was a hole in the center of the idea. There was a hole in Miri, and a Sleeper baby spiraled through it— Joan's Sleeper brother, who by this time tomorrow wouldn't exist any more than the missing piece of the thought equation existed, had ever existed, was ever out there somewhere. And now Joan hated her.

Miri curled herself under Tony's desk and sobbed.

Jennifer found her there two hours later, after the Remembrance Day speeches were over and the huge chunk of credit, the equation for productive labor, had been transmitted to the government which gave nothing back in return. Miri heard her grandmother pause in the doorway, then unhesitatingly cross the room, as if she already knew where Miri was.

"Miranda. Come out from there."

"N-n-no."

"Joan told you that her mother is carrying a Sleeper fetus that must be aborted."

"N-n-not 'm-must.' The b-b-baby c-could l-l-l-live. It's n-normal in every other w-w-way. And th-th-they *w-want* it!"

"The parents are the ones who made the decision, Miri. No one else could make it for them."

"Then wh-wh-wh-wh-*why* are J-Joan and her m-mother c-c-c-crying?"

"Because sometimes necessary things are hard things. And because neither of them has yet learned to accept hard necessity without making it worse by regret. That's a vital lesson, Miri. Regret is not productive. Nor is guilt, nor grief, although I have felt both over the five Sleeper fetuses we've had in Sanctuary."

"F-f-five?"

"So far. Five in thirty-one years. And every set of parents has made the decision Joan's parents have, because every set saw the hard necessity. A Sleeper child is a beggar, and the productive strong do not acknowledge the parasitic claims of beggars. Charity, perhaps—that is an individual matter. But a claim, as if weakness had the moral right over strength, were somehow superior to strength—no. We don't acknowledge that."

"A S-S-Sleeper b-baby would be p-p-productive! It's n-n-normal otherwise!"

Jennifer sat down gracefully on Tony's desk chair. The folds of her black *abbaya* trailed on the ground beside Miri's crouching body. "For the first part of its life, yes. But productivity is a relative thing. A Sleeper may have fifty productive years, starting at, say, twenty. But unlike us, by sixty or seventy their bodies are weakened, prey to breakdowns, wearing out. Yet they may live for as many as thirty more years, a burden on the community, a shame to themselves because it is a shame to not work when others do. Even if a Sleeper was industrious, amassed credit against his old age, purchased robots to care for him, he would end up isolated, not able to take part in Sanctuary's daily life, degenerating. Dying. Would parents who loved a child bring it into such an eventual fate? Could a community support many such people without putting a spiritual burden on itself? A few, yes—but what about the principles involved?

"A Sleeper raised among us would not only be an outsider here— unconscious and brain-dead eight hours a day while the community goes on without him—he would also have the terrible burden of know- ing that someday he will have a stroke, or a heart attack, or cancer, or one of the other myriad diseases the beggars are prone to. Knowing that he will *become* a burden. How could a principled man or woman live with that? Do you know what he would have to do?"

Miri saw it. But she would not say it.

"He would have to commit suicide. A terrible thing to force onto a child you loved!"

Miri crawled out from under the desk. "B-b-but, G-G-Grandma— w-w-we all m-m-must d-die s-s-s-someday. Even y-y-y-you."

"Of course," Jennifer said composedly. "But when I do, it will be after a long and productive life as a full member of my community— Sanctuary, our heart's blood. I would want no less for my children or grandchildren. I would settle for no less. Neither would Joan's mother."

Miri considered. Complex nets of thought knotted themselves in her head. Finally, painfully, she nodded.

Jennifer said, just as if she had not won, "I think, Miri, that you are old enough to start viewing broadcasts from Earth. We made the rule about being fourteen because we thought it would be best to form your principles first, you and the other children, before showing you their violation on Earth. Perhaps we were wrong, especially with you Supers. We're still groping our way with you, dear heart. But perhaps it would be best if you saw the kind of wasted, parasitic lives that beggars—they call themselves 'Livers' now—actually prefer."

Miri felt a strange reluctance to watch the Earth broadcasts, a re- luctance she certainly had not felt before today. But again she nodded.

Her grandmother smelled of some scented soap, light and clean; her long hair, bound in a twist, gleamed like black glass. Miri put one hand shyly on Jennifer's knee.

"And one more thing, dear heart," Jennifer said. "Twelve is too old to cry, Miri, especially over hard necessity. Survival alone demands too much of us for tears. Remember that."

"I w-w-will," Miri said.

The next day she saw Joan, walking from her parents' dome to the park. Miri called to her, but Joan kept walking and didn't turn her head. After a moment, Miri lifted her chin and walked in the other direction.

20

The five young men crept toward the chain-link fence, keeping to the shadows of unpruned bushes, trees, and an abandoned and sagging bench in what might once have been a park. The moon rode high in the east, gilding the fence with silver. The fence links were wide apart, worked in scrolls that were both uneven and insubstantial; the fence was undoubtedly only a marker, with a Y-field providing the real security. If so, the field's faint shimmer wasn't visible in the darkness and there was no way to assess its height.

"Throw high," Drew whispered from his powerchair to the boy next to him, whoever it was. All five wore dark plasti-suits and black boots. Drew could only remember three of their names. He had met them this afternoon at a bar, shortly after he'd drifted into town. He guessed they were younger than his nineteen; it didn't matter. They had Dole credits for liquor and brainies, so why should it matter? Why should anything matter?

"Now!" somebody yelled.

They rushed forward. Drew's chair caught on a clump of tough, uncut weeds and he pitched forward. The straps caught him and the chair righted itself and drove on, but the others reached the Y-shield first. They hurled their makeshift bombs, made with gasoline foraged from an abandoned field-style farm. No one but Drew had known what the stuff was, just as no one but Drew had ever heard of a "Molotov cocktail." He was the only one who could read.

"Shit!" screamed the youngest boy. His bomb hit what might have been the top part of the energy fence, exploded, and rained fire and plastic back onto the dry grass. It caught. Two of the other bombs did the same; the fourth boy dropped his and ran screaming. His shirt had caught fire from an exploding fragment.

Drew raced his chair to six feet from the fence, pulled back his arm, and threw. His heavily muscled arms, the result of unremitting exercise, sent the bomb sailing over the top of the Y-fence. Grass on both sides of the shield blazed.

"Karl's hit!" someone yelled. The three other boys rushed back toward their scooters. One of them tackled Karl and rolled him, screaming, in the grass. Drew sat in his chair, unmoving, watching the fire and listening to the alarm shriek even louder than the burning boy.

"Someone to get you out, fartsucker," the deputy sheriff said. He released the Y-lock and banged the jail door open. Drew looked up insolently from the foamstone cot, a look that vanished when his rescuer entered.

"You! What for?"

"Expecting Leisha again?" Eric Bevington-Watrous said. "Too bad. This time you get me."

Drew drawled, "She get tired of bailing me out?"

"If she isn't, she should be."

Drew studied him, trying to match Eric's cool contempt. The furious boy who had fought him beside the cottonwood might never have existed. Eric wore black cotton pants, ruffled bodystretch, and a black bias-cut coat, all conservative but fashionable. His boots were Argentinian leather, his hair barbered, his skin glowing. He looked like a handsome, decisive donkey used to running things, while Drew knew he looked like a Liver gone too bad to do any Living. Which he was. Stepping outside his own field of vision, which was the only way he cared to see anything these days, Drew saw Eric and himself as a smooth cool ovoid floating beside a ragged misshapen pyramid, every point dented or spiked or saw-toothed.

Who had done the misshaping in the first place? Who had crippled him? Whose fucking charity had shown him just how worthless he was next to all the fartsucking donkeys in the world?

"What if I don't want to be bailed out?"

"Then rot here," Eric said. "*I* don't care."

"Why should you? In your take-charge donkey suit and your Sleepless superiority and your aunt's money?"

Eric was beyond that kind of taunt. "My money, now. I earn it. Unlike you, Arlen."

"It's a little harder for some of us."

"Oh, and aren't we supposed to feel sorry for you because of that? Poor Drew. Poor stinking crippled petty-criminal Drew." Eric said this in a disinterested tone, so adult that Drew blinked. Eric was only two years older than Drew; not even Leisha managed that much detachment.

Would either of them be here in this cell if she did?

The thought was a spiny worm, sliding through his mind, leaving a trail of slime that glowed even in the dark.

"Jailer," Eric said, "we're going."

No one answered. No one mentioned criminal charges, lawyers, bail money, the whole legal system that was supposed to function with equal justice for all men fucking-shit equal.

Drew dragged himself on his elbows across the floor and climbed into his chair, parked just beyond the bars. No one helped him. He followed Eric—why not? What the fuck did it matter if he were in jail or out, rotting in this one-scooter town or rotting somewhere else? By his sheer indifference he demonstrated the stupidity of either choice.

"If you really thought that, you'd stay here," Eric said over his shoulder, not breaking stride, and Drew had his face rubbed in it all over again: They were just smarter. They knew. Fucking Sleepless.

A groundcar waited. Drew turned his chair in another direction, but before he moved it Eric had slapped a Y-lock over the control panel on the chair's arm.

"Hey!"

"Shut up," Eric said. Drew aimed a right cross but Eric was quicker, and had the advantage of mobility. His fist caught Drew under the chin, not hard enough to break his jaw but sufficient to send pain lancing through his face clear to the temples. When the pain receded slightly, Drew was manacled.

He started cursing, summoning every filth he had learned in eighteen months on the road. Eric ignored him. He picked Drew out of his chair and threw him in the back seat of the car, already occupied by a bodyguard who righted Drew, looked him deeply in the eyes, and said simply, "Don't."

Eric slid behind the wheel. This was new among donkeys: driving themselves. Drew ignored the guard and raised both arms, manacled together, over his head to bring them down hard on Eric's neck. Eric never even turned around. The guard caught Drew's arms at the top of their swing and did something so painful to his shoulder that he collapsed, blinded by agony, in the back seat. He started to sob.

Eric drove.

They took him to a Liver motel, the kind rented for brainie or sex parties on Dole credit. Eric and the guard stripped him and dumped him into the cheap, oversized bathtub meant for four. Drew's head went under. He breathed water until he could pull himself up; neither of them helped him. Eric poured a half bottle of genemod dirt-eaters into the water. The bodyguard stripped, climbed in with Drew, and started to scrub him down.

Later, there were straps on the bed.

Tied down, helpless without his chair, Drew lay cursing his own tears while Eric loomed above him and the bodyguard took a walk.

"I don't know why she wants to bother with you, Arlen. I do know why *I'm* here. First, because otherwise she would have to be, and second, because otherwise you would be on your feet and I could knock you down the way you deserve. You've been given every opportunity, every consideration, and you burned them all. You're stupid and you're undisciplined and at nineteen years old you don't have even the minimum ethics that would let you ask what happened to your friend back there who got set on fire by your pointless destruction. You're a disaster as a human being, even a Liver human being, but I'm giving you one more chance. Note this well: None of what's going to happen to you is Leisha's idea. She doesn't even know about it. This is my present to you."

Drew spat at him. The spittle fell short, landing on the foamstone floor. Eric didn't even grimace before he turned away.

They left him there, tied, all night.

The next morning the bodyguard fed Drew from a spoon, like a baby. Drew spat the food back in his face. The bodyguard, expressionless, slugged him in the jaw, to the right of where Eric had hit him, and threw the rest of the breakfast in the disposal chute. He threw Drew a clean set of jacks, the cheapest possible Dole clothing, drawstring pants and loose shirt in undyed, biodegradable gray. Drew struggled to pull on the pants only because he suspected they would otherwise throw him into the car naked. He couldn't manage the shirt over his manacles. He clutched it to his chest as the bodyguard carried him, barefoot, outside.

They drove for four or five hours, stopping once. Just before they stopped, the guard blindfolded Drew. He listened intently as Eric got out of the car, but all he heard was soft murmuring in what might or might not have been Spanish. The car started again. Eventually the guard removed the blindfold; the flat desert countryside hadn't changed. Drew's bladder ached, until he finally just let go in the car. Neither of the others commented. The plastic pants held the piss against his skin.

They stopped again in front of a low, large, windowless building like a sealed airport hangar. Drew didn't know what town they were in, what state. Eric had said nothing the entire morning.

"I'm not going in there!"

"Strip off those wet pants first, Pat," Eric said, with disgust. The bodyguard grabbed the hem of his pants and yanked. Drew struggled, but his ineffective thrashing stopped when a roadrunner walked casually across his line of vision. A snake dangled from the roadrunner's beak, half eaten. The snake's skin was green, with orange letters spelling out "*puta.*"

They were someplace where illegal genetic engineering didn't even have to be hidden from the cops.

Inside were endless gray corridors, each blocked with a Y-field. At each checkpoint Eric stepped up to the retina scanner and was cleared without saying a word. This, whatever it was, had all been arranged.

The fear in Drew was a gray spreading ooze, shapeless, and its lack of shape was what made it fearsome.

A small room, finally, with a clean white stretcher. Pat dumped him onto it. Drew rolled off, hitting the floor with an unprotected splat. He tried to drag himself, naked, toward the door. Pat scooped him up effortlessly—augmented muscles—threw him back on the gurney, and strapped him down. Someone he couldn't see touched his head with an electrode.

Drew screamed. The room turned orange, then red with bright hot dots, each a burn on flesh. But that was in his mind, nothing had touched him yet but cold metal. But they were going to, they were going to burn out his mind—

"Drew," Eric said softly, very close to his ear, "listen to me. This is not an electronic lobotomy. This is a new genemod technique. They're going to infect your brain with an altered virus that will make it impossible for you to block the flow of images to the cortex from the limbic. That's the older, more primitive part of the brain. Then biofeedback adjusts your brainwaves until the cortex learns the pathways for processing the images into theta activity. Do you understand?"

He understood nothing. The fear engulfed the rest of his mind, gray bubbling ooze shot through with hot red burns, and when someone screamed he was flooded with shame that it was himself. Then the machine turned on, and the room was gone.

He lay on the stretcher for six days. An IV dripped nutrients into his arm; a catheter removed urine. Drew was aware of neither. For six days subtle electrochemical pathways in his brain were reinforced, widened as a highway is widened by a road crew that builds sturdily but doesn't know what will march over the road. Images flowed freely, without chemical inhibitors, from Drew's subconscious mind, from his racial memory, from the older reptilian parts of the brain to the newer, society-conditioned cortex, which usually received them unfiltered through dreams and symbols and would have broken down in shrieking confusion without the strong scaffolding of genemod drugs holding it together.

He crouched on a rock in the sunlight and he had claws, teeth, fur, feathers, scales. His jaws tore and rendered the thing wailing helplessly, and the blood flew in his face, snout, crown. The blood-smell excited him, and the wordless rushing in his ears said, "Mine, mine, mine, mine . . ."

He reared up on his hind legs, powerful as pistons, and brought the rock down again on the other's head. His father, writhing in the vomit of his last drunk, held up clasped hands and pleaded for mercy. Drew brought the rock down hard, and in the corner of the den his mother crouched, her fur glistening with brainies, waiting for the penis that was already engorged with killing. . . .

They were chasing him, all of them, Leisha and his father and the howling things that wanted to cut his throat, and he was running running through a landscape that kept shifting: trees that would not hold still, bushes that opened jaws and snapped at him, rivers that tried to suck him under into blackness . . . then the landscape became the desert compound and Leisha was there; too, screaming at him that he was a failure and he deserved to die because he could never do anything right, could not even stay awake the way real people could. He grabbed Leisha and threw her down and with the action came such astonishing freedom, such an exultant state of potency that he laughed out loud and then both he and Leisha were naked and she was tied up and he looked around her study and said gloatingly "All of this is mine, mine, mine. . . ."

"He isn't in pain," the doctor said. "The writhing is no more than stepped-up muscular reflexes in response to cortical bombardment. Not unlike dreaming."

"Dreaming," Eric repeated, staring at Drew's writhing body. "Dreaming . . ."

The doctor shrugged, a gesture not of indifference but of tremendous tension. This was only the fourth time the experimental psychiatric technique had been used. The other three people had had no powerful relatives, or whatever this Mr. Smithson was to Bevington-Watrous. The doctor didn't care what he was. They were outside United States borders, and in Mexico the genemod laws functioned by expensive permits. The doctor had a permit. Not to do what he was doing, of course, but then who ever had that sort of permit? He shrugged again.

"It's been three days," Eric said. "When does this phase . . . stop?"

"We start the artificial reinforcement this afternoon. We—yes, nurse, what is it?"

"Comlink for Mr. Bevington-Watrous." The young Mexican nurse sounded scared. "It's Ms. Leisha Camden."

Eric turned slowly. "How did she find us?"

"I don't know, sir. Will you . . . will you come to the terminal?"

"No," Eric said.

The nurse was back in ninety seconds. "Sir, Ms. Camden says if you don't talk to her she'll be here in two hours."

"I won't talk to her," Eric said stubbornly, but the pupils of his eyes widened, making him suddenly look much younger. "Doctor, what happens if this treatment is interrupted now?"

"It cannot be interrupted now. We don't know exactly how the—but there would certainly be grave mental consequences. Certainly."

Eric went on staring at Drew.

The images became shapes. In doing that they didn't lose identity but gained it: The shapes were the images plus more. The shapes were the essence of the images, and they were both Drew's and not Drew's: both his personal angels, demons, heroes, fears, yearnings, drives, and everyone's. No one saw them but him, no one had ever seen them, but they were his translations of universals: he knew that. Even through the strange drugs and electrodes and semitrance state, a part of his conscious mind knew that. It recognized the images and Drew knew he would never forget them, and that he was not done with making them.

"We're introducing theta activity now," the doctor said. "We're electronically forcing his cortex into brain waves characteristic of slow-wave sleep."

Eric said nothing. A clock on the wall flashed the time, and he seemed unable to take his eyes off it.

"Of course, Mr. Bevington-Watrous, you signed all the legal waivers for this treatment for Mr. Smithson, but you also assured us that if there were extradition ramifications you are in a position to—"

"Not all Sleepless are equally powerful, Doctor. I, for instance, am as powerful as the extradition authorities, but not as powerful as my aunt. You might as well accept that fact now. Because she'll make sure we both do."

Drew slept. And yet it was not sleep. The images kept marching over the reinforced highway from the limbic to his accessible mind, and he saw them, and he knew them. But now he moved among them, Drew, a sleepwalker with a sleepwalker's privileged duality: asleep and yet in control of his muscles. He moved among the shapes, and he changed them, remade them, and shaped them through lucid dreaming.

"The EEG shows delta activity because he's deeply rooted in slow-wave sleep now," the doctor said. It wasn't clear whether he was talking to Eric or himself. "Most dreaming goes on during REM sleep, but some goes on during SWS, and that's very important. This whole treatment is based on the fact that decreased SWS is associated with schizophrenia, with histories of violence, with poor sleep regulation in general. By forging artificial pathways between unconscious impulses and the state of SWS, we force the brain to confront and subdue those impulses that create disordered behavior. The theory says that the result is a state of heightened tranquility, a tranquility without the logy aspects of the usual depressant drugs, in fact a *true* tranquility based on the brain's new connection among its warring—no one can get past the Y-field security on this building, Mr. Bevington-Watrous."

"Who designed the security?"

"Kevin Baker. Through a blind subsidiary of ours, of course."

Eric smiled.

Drew breathed evenly and deeply, his eyes closed, his powerful torso and wasted legs still.

He was master of the cosmos. Everything in it moved through his mind, and he shaped them through lucid dreaming, and they were his. He, who had possessed nothing, been nothing, was master of it all.

Dimly, through dreams, Drew heard the first alarm chime.

It had taken her four days to trace them. She had only succeeded because she had, finally, called Kevin. And asked for his help.

Staring at Drew strapped into machines, at Eric clutching one elbow with the opposite palm like a defiant schoolboy, Leisha thought: now *we can't ever go back.* The thought was clear, cold, deliberate, and she didn't care that it was both theatrical and vague. Alice's grandson stood over the Sleeper he had used, as if Drew were a lab rat or a defective chromosome, as if Eric were any of the haters that for three-quarters of a century had seen Sleepless as experiments or defects. As if Eric were Calvin Hawke, or Dave Hannaway, or Adam Walcott. Or Jennifer Sharifi.

Alice's grandson. A Sleepless.

Drew lay naked. With the bitterness smoothed out of his face by sleep, he looked younger than nineteen, more like the child who had first come to her in the desert compound full of swaggering confidence. *"I'm gonna own Sanctuary, me."* The wasted legs didn't seem to belong to the muscled, adult torso. There was a knife scar on his chest, a fresh burn on his right shoulder, bruises on his jaw. Leisha knew she and hers were responsible for all of it. Better to have left Drew alone, turned him away nine years ago, never tried to make him something he could never be. *"Daddy, when I'm grown up I'm going to find a way to make Alice special, too!" And you've never stopped trying, have you, Leisha? With all the Alices, all the have-nots, all the beggars who would have been better off if you'd left them, in your hubristic specialness, alone.*

Tony—you were right. They're too different from us.

Tony . . .

To Eric she said coldly, "Tell me exactly what you've done to him. And why."

The little doctor said eagerly, "Ms. Camden, this is an experiment—"

"You," Leisha said to Eric. "You tell me." Bodyguards stepped between her and the doctor, cutting him off. The room was full of bodyguards.

Eric said shortly, "I owed him."

"This?"

"A last chance to be human."

"He was human! How can you experiment on—"

"We're experiments, and we worked out all right," Eric said, with a faith in the logic of reduction that took her breath away. Had she ever been that young?

Eric went on. "You always expect the worst, Leisha. I took a chance, yes, but four other experimental patients have benefited—"

"A chance! With a life not your own! This isn't even a licensed medical facility!"

"Excuse me," the doctor said, "I have a permit that—"

"How many experimental ones are, anymore?" Eric said. "The donkeys don't allow it. They cut off genemod research before it could turn into an even bigger weapon to blast away at their status quo that isn't—Leisha, the other four patients for this operation are doing well. They're calmer, they seem to have more control of their own emotions that—"

"Eric, *this was not your decision to make.* Do you hear me? Drew didn't choose this!"

For a moment Eric looked again the sulky, angry child he had been. "I didn't ask to be the way I am, either. Dad chose that for me by marrying a Sleepless. Who ever gets to choose?"

Leisha stared at him. He didn't see the distinction—he truly did not. Alice's grandson, both privileged and outcast all his life, who thought those conditions had conferred wisdom.

But hadn't they all thought that? From Tony onward?

Drew's lips made soft movements in his profound sleep, sucking at a nonexistent breast.

* * *

The room brightened slowly: First gray shadows, then pearly haze through which shapes moved dimly, and then light, clean and pale. Drew tried to move his head. He felt spittle trickle from his mouth.

There was something moving inside his head, several somethings, of utmost importance. Drew turned his attention away from them. He could afford to do that; he knew, with complete confidence, that whatever the new thing was inside his head, it wasn't going to leave before he examined it. It wasn't ever going to leave. He had it; it *was* him. What he didn't have was knowledge of this room. What had happened in it. Who was here. Why.

Someone in white said, "He's awake."

Faces blossomed above him, an amorphous mass that only slowly separated. Nurses' faces, glancing sideways at each other. A short, olive-skinned doctor, his left eye twitching frantically. The twitch reached Drew: He saw the man's nervousness, his fear, as a jagged red line that suddenly grew, took three-dimensional shape, and as it did the other thing in Drew's head moved gracefully forward to meet it. It met, too, the shapes of fear and guilt from the corners of his mind, detached from him and yet still his. The shapes of the doctor's fear and of Drew's merged—*Eric, the Molotov cocktails, Karl burning*—and Drew looked at those shapes, and felt them, and he knew that he knew this man. This doctor, who all his life took chances on the edge of fear not for the good fortune the chances might bring, but to escape the nothingness he carried inside. This man for whom success was never enough—could I have done it better? Will someone else do it better?— but for whom failure was annihilation. Drew saw the shapes for how the doctor would have reacted to a failed test in medical school, to an appointment that went to someone else, to an arrest for this facility here, now. The first two were the defeated hunched shapes of failure; the third was a burning glee in failure that he had not caused himself, that had been inflicted on him from the outside. And so it was a kind of triumph, and Drew saw the shapes for that too, shapes without words, that fastened not on his heart—he felt no particular sympathy—but through the successive layers of his mind, like a plant putting down very deep roots. An unshakable tree. The tree of knowledge, wordless, as all trees are wordless against a still sky.

Drew blinked. It had all taken only a moment. And he would know it forever.

"Lift your head," the doctor said harshly, as if Drew had been the one to injure him and not the other way around, and Drew saw the shapes for the harshness, too. Other shapes from deep in himself drifted toward it, merged with it. Drew watched. The shapes were him, but he was something else, too, something separate, something that watched and understood.

He lifted his head. A screen to his right began to beep softly, in an atonal pattern. The doctor studied the screen intently.

Leisha rushed into the room.

At the sight of her, so many shapes exploded in Drew's head that he couldn't speak. She bent over him, glancing at the screen, putting a cool hand on his forehead. "Drew . . ."

"Hello, Leisha."

"How . . . how are you feeling?"

He smiled, because the question was so impossible to answer.

She said tightly, "You're going to be all right, but there's a lot you have a right to know," and Drew saw how clearly the words took the shape of Leisha herself: *a right to know*. He saw the shape, the intricate balance, of all the questions of rights and privileges she had struggled with all her life, had made into her life. He saw the clean, basically aus- tere shape of Leisha herself, struggling with the messy other shapes that sent off shoots and pseudopods and could not be captured, as she consistently struggled to do, in principles and laws. The struggle itself had a shape, and he groped to find a word for it, but the words were not there. For him, the words had seldom been there. The closest word he could find was an antique one—*knight*—and it was wrong, was too pale for the intense poignancy of the shape of Leisha struggling to cod- ify the lawless world. The word was wrong. He frowned.

Leisha said "Oh—don't cry, Drew, dear heart!"

He had been nowhere near crying. She didn't understand. How

could she? He didn't understand himself this thing that had happened to him, or been done to him, or whatever it was. Eric had wanted to hurt him, yes, but this wasn't hurt, this was only making Drew more himself, like a man who had been able to run two miles and now could run ten. Still himself—his muscles, his bones, his heart—but more so, and that more moved him from something ordinary to something . . . else. Extraordinary. He seemed to himself extraordinary.

Leisha said, "Doctor, he can't speak!"

"He can speak," the doctor said shortly, and briefly his shapes came to Drew again: the hysterical pumped-up excitement that was fear, the triumph of not showing it. "The brain scans show no impairment in the speech centers!"

"Say something, Drew!" Leisha begged.

"You are beautiful."

He had never seen it before: how could he not have seen it? Leisha bent above him, her hair golden as a young girl's, her face stamped with the decisive power of a woman in her prime. Drew saw the shapes that had formed that power: they were the shapes of intelligence and suffering. How could he not have seen it before? Her breasts swelled softly under the thin fabric of her shirt; her neck rose from the shirt like a warm column, white hollowed delicately with blue. And he'd never seen it before. Not at all. How beautiful Leisha was.

Leisha drew back slightly, frowning. She said, "Drew—what year is it? What town were you arrested in?"

He laughed. The laugh hurt his chest, and he realized for the first time that there was tape across his ribs, and that his arms were still strapped down. Eric entered the room and stood at the foot of Drew's bed, and at the sight of Eric's rigid face more shapes crowded Drew's head. He saw why Eric had done what he had done, all of it, clear back to the day by the cottonwood when two boys had fought to what would have been the death if either of them had been strong enough to make it so. Following that came the shapes for Drew's father, beating his children in a drunken rage, and for Karl pierced and burning from the bomb he had failed to hurl high enough. They were all, in fact, the same shape, and so ugly that for the first time Drew felt the other, separate self, the self who watched the shapes, burned by them. He closed his eyes.

"He's fainted!" Leisha said, and the doctor snapped back, "No, he hasn't!" and even with his eyes closed Drew saw the shapes he and Eric had made, so there was no point in keeping his eyes closed. He opened them. He knew now what the point *was*. Would have to be.

"Leisha . . ." His voice surprised him: it came out weak and faint. Yet he didn't feel weak. He tried again. "Leisha, I need . . ."

"Yes? What? Anything, Drew, anything."

That other day came back to him, the day he had been crippled. Lying on the bed just like this, Eric's father bending above him saying, "We'll do everything we can . . . everything," and himself thinking, *now I've got them*. The same shapes. Always, throughout a man's life—and more than his own life—testified deep shapes stirring far down in his mind, flicking tails and fluttering gills, more than his own life.

"*What,* Drew? What do you need?"

"A Staunton-Carey programmable hologram projector."

"A—"

"Yes," Drew whispered with the last of his strength. "Now. I need it now."

21

iri was thirteen. For a year she had been watching the Sleeper broadcasts, on both the Liver and the donkey news-grids. The first few months the grids were absorbing because they raised so many questions: Why were scooter races so important? Why did the beautiful young men and women on *Bedtime Stories* change sex partners so often when they seemed so ecstatic with the ones they already had? Why did the women have such huge breasts, the men such big penises? Why should a congresswoman from Iowa make a resentful speech about the spending of a congressman from Texas when, it seemed, the congresswoman was spending just as much herself, and they weren't members of the same community anyway? At least, they didn't seem to define themselves that way. Why did all the newsgrids praise the Livers for doing nothing—"creative leisure"—and hardly mention the people who worked to run things, when it turned out the people who ran things also ran the newsgrids?

Eventually Miri discovered answers to these questions, either by databank research or by talking with her father or grandmother. The trouble was, the answers weren't very interesting. Scooter races were important because Livers thought they were important—was that all? Was there no standard except what pleased at the moment?

Her mind created long strings out of this question, pulling in the

Heisenberg Principle, Epicurus, a defunct philosophy called existentialism, the Rahvoli constants for neural reinforcement, mysticism, epileptic storms in the so-called "visionary" centers of the brain, social democracy, the utility of the social organism, and Aesop's fables. The string was a good one, but the part supplied by the Earth newsgrid was still essentially uninteresting.

The same was true for the answers to the rest of Miri's questions. Political organization and resource allocation depended on a precarious balance between Liver votes and donkey power, and that balance seemed to be the results of a haphazard social evolution, not of planning or principles. Things in the United States were the way they were because they were the way they were. If there was more depth than that, the newsgrids didn't reveal it.

She decided it was just the United States, coddled by cheap Y-energy, rich from licensing those same patents abroad, as decadent as her grandmother had always said. She learned Russian, French, and Japanese and spent a few months watching newsgrids in those languages. The answers were different but no more interesting. Things happened because they happened; they were the way they were because that was the point they'd come to. Minor border wars were fought, or they weren't. Trade agreements were signed, or they weren't. Important Sleepers died, or they had operations and recovered. A French broadcaster, one of the most prominent, always closed his broadcast the same way: *Ça va toujours.*

Nowhere on the popular newsgrids could Miri find any mention of scientific research or breakthroughs that were not clear sensationalism, of political excitement, of complex musical sounds like the Bach or Mozart or O'Neill in the library banks, of ideas as complex as those she discussed with Tony every day.

After six months, she stopped watching the newsgrids.

One thing had changed, however. Often her grandmother was busy, spending more and more time in the Sharifi Labs, and it was her father whom Miri took questions to. He didn't have all the answers, and the ones he did have made short, lopsided strings in her mind. He had left Earth, he told her, when he was ten, and although he sometimes went there on business, he seldom spent much time with Sleepers. Usually he did business through a middleman, a Sleepless who nonetheless lived on Earth, a man named Kevin Baker.

Miri knew about Baker; he was extensively documented in the databanks. She wasn't much interested in him. He seemed faintly contemptible to her: A man who lived alone with the beggars, profited from them, and preferred those profits—which were apparently huge—to the connections of community. But she listened while her father talked, because through the newsgrids she had become interested in her father. Unlike her mother, he could look directly at Miri's twitching face and oversized head, her jerking body, without looking away. He could listen to her stutter. He sat, a dark low-browed man with his hands resting quietly on his knees, and listened to her patiently, and in his dark eyes was something she couldn't name, no matter how many strings she wrapped around it. All the strings started with pain.

"D-D-Daddy, wh-wh-wh-where were y-y-you?"

"Sharifi Labs. With Jennifer." Her father, unlike Aunt Najla, often referred to his mother by her name. Miri wasn't sure when that had started.

She looked at him. There was a light sweat on his forehead, although Miri thought her lab was cool. His face looked shaken. Miri's strings included seismic tremors, adrenalin effects, the compression of gases that form the ignition of stars. She said, "Wh-wh-wh-what are the L-L-L-L-L-Labs d-doing?"

Ricky Keller shook his head. He said abruptly, "When do you join the Council?"

"S-sixteen. T-two years and t-t-two m-months."

Her father smiled, and the smile started a string that spun itself, surprisingly, to a Sleeper newsgrid she had seen months ago and had not thought of since: a story, evidently fiction, from a mystic book central to several Sleeper religions. A man called Job had been looted of one possession after another without either fighting in his own defense or devising ways to regain or replace them. Miri had thought Job spineless, or stupid, or both, and had lost interest in the broadcast before it was over. But her father's smile reminded her now of the actor's resigned face. All her father would say, however, was, "Good. We need you on the Council."

"Wh-wh-wh-why?" Miri said sharply, hating that it took so long to get the word out, even while she was warmed by his need.

He didn't answer.

Will Sandaleros said, "Now."

Jennifer leaned forward, staring at the three-dimensional holographic bubble. A thousand miles away in space, the original inflated, pressurized with standard air, and released the mice from their semi-hypothermic state. Tiny drip-patches on their collars brought their biological systems back to full functioning in minimum time. Within minutes the biometers on their collars showed them dispersed throughout the interior of the bubble, which was a complex internal topography mathematically congruent to Washington, D.C.

"Ready," Dr. Toliveri said, "Stand by. Six, five, four, three, two, one, go."

The genemod viruses were released. Air currents matched to winds five miles per hour from the southwest wafted through the temperature-controlled bubble. Jennifer shifted her attention to the biometer read-out screen on the far wall. Within three minutes, it showed no activity.

"Yes," Will said. He wasn't smiling, but he took her hand. "Yes."

Jennifer nodded. To Toliveri, Blure, and the three technicians she said, "A superb job." She turned to Will. Her beautiful, composed voice was very low. "We're ready for the next stage."

"Yes," he said again.

"Start the purchase negotiations for Kagura orbital. Don't go through Kevin Baker. Keep it blind."

Will Sandaleros looked as if he didn't mind being told what had actually been decided between them years earlier. He looked as if he understood his wife's need to issue orders. Then he looked again at the biometer, his eyes gleaming.

Miri opened the door to Tony's lab. He had moved to his own work quarters in Science Building Two six months ago, when there was no longer room in one lab for both their projects. Every time Miri looked at his half of the partners' desk she felt sad, although she thought perhaps part of the sadness came from her own work's going so badly. In two years she had modeled every genetic modification she could think of, without coming closer to any that would correct the stutters and twitches of all the Supers' hyped-up electrochemical processes. The work had begun to feel sterile to her, to remind her of the missing component, whatever it was, of the strings themselves. Elusive, sterile, and nonproductive. Today had been another failure. She was in a terrible mood, a terrible, fast-moving, chaotic-string, sterile mood. She wanted Tony's comfort and encouragement. She wanted Tony.

His lab door was locked, but Miri's retina print was in the authorized file and the STERILE ENVIRONMENT light was off. She placed her right eye to the scanner and pushed open the door.

Tony lay on the floor, twitching and jerking, on top of Christina Demetrios. Over his thrusting body Miri saw Christy's eyes widen, then darken. "Oh!" Christy said. Tony said nothing; possibly he hadn't heard Miri, or even Christina. His naked buttocks contracted powerfully and his whole body shuddered with orgasm. Miri backed out of the lab, closed the door, and ran to her own lab.

She sat with her hands clasped, twitching, on her desk, her head bowed. Tony hadn't told her—well, why should he tell her? It was his business, not hers; she was only his sister. Not his lover—his sister. Strings formed and reformed in her head: For the first time, various ancient and obscure stories, which she had remembered only because she remembered everything, made sense to her. Hera and Io. Othello and Desdemona. She knew the entire physiology of sex—hormone-influenced secretions, vascular engorgement, pheromone triggers. She knew everything. She knew nothing.

Jealousy. One of the most community-destroying emotions there was. A *beggar* emotion.

Miri stood up and paced distractedly. No. She would not give in to the degradation of jealousy. She was better than that. Tony deserved better than that of his sister. Idealism. (Stoicism, Epicureanism "We are shaped and fashioned by what we love," Tony's butt pumping away in Christina . . .) She would solve this problem her own way (darkness, fullness, the throbbing ache, gravitational pressure to ignite gases into thermonuclear reactions, cepheid variables . . .).

Miri washed her face and hands. She put on a clean pair of white shorts and tied a red ribbon in her dark hair. Her lips, despite their constant twitching, set together hard. She didn't have to think whom to approach; she already knew, and knew that she knew, and knew all the implications of already knowing (darkness, fullness, lying on her belly on her lab floor or under the genemod soy plants that met in a concealing arc, her hands between her legs).

His name was David Aronson. He was three years older than she, a Norm but fairly intelligent, an intense believer in the Sanctuary Oath and in her grandmother's leadership. He had dark curling hair, as dark as Miri's own, but very light eyes of clear, black-lashed gray. His legs were long, his shoulders at eighteen were as broad and powerful as a grown man's. His mouth was generous, wide mobile lips of an almost molded firmness. Miri had spent the past six months looking at David's mouth.

She found him where she expected to: at the orbital's shuttle port, poring over CAD displays of machinery. In two months he would leave for a doctoral program in engineering at Stanford, his first trip to Earth.

"Hello, Miri." He had a deep voice, a little rough. Miri liked the roughness. She could find no reason why.

"D-D-David. I w-w-w-want t-to ask you s-s-something."

He looked slightly to one side of her, at the CAD holo. "What?"

She had no trouble being direct; all her life, the trouble in communication had come from the difficulty and simplicity of speech compared to

the enormous complexity of her thoughts. She was used to simplifying
things for Norms as much as possible. This was already a simple thing; it
seemed to her to fit admirably, as almost nothing else did, to the limitations of language.

"W-w-will y-you have s-s-s-sex with m-m-m-me?"

David straightened. Color mounted in his cheeks. He continued to
look past her. "I'm sorry. Miri, but that's not possible."

"Wh-wh-why n-not?"

"I already have a lover."

"Wh-wh-who?"

"Don't you think that's my business?"

He sounded cold; Miri couldn't see why. Noncommercial information, surely, was for community use, and what information could be
more public? She was used to having questions answered. If they were
not, she was used to exploring why not. "Wh-wh-why w-w-won't you
t-t-tell me who?"

David bent ostentatiously closer to his screen. His beautiful mouth
set. "I think this conversation is over, Miri."

"Wh-wh-why?"

He didn't answer her. The strings of her thoughts suddenly tangled,
tightened around her like a noose. "B-b-bec-c-cause I'm ugly? I t-t-
t-t-twitch?"

"I said I didn't have anything else to say!" Frustration, or embarrassment, or anger, overcame courtesy, and he finally looked directly at
her before stalking off. Miri recognized the look: She had often seen it
on her mother's face before Hermione turned to fiddling with a screen,
or a cup of coffee, or anything handy. Miri recognized, too, that she
was the reason for the frustration or embarrassment or anger, and that
she had somehow contributed enough of it to justify the discourtesy.
He didn't want her, and she had had no right to press him—but all she'd
wanted was answers. By pressing him, she'd only humiliated herself.
He didn't want her. She twitched, her head was too big, she stuttered,
she wasn't pretty like Joan was. No Norm would want her.

She walked carefully, as if she were a chemical compound that shouldn't be jarred, back to her laboratory. Sitting at her desk, she again clasped her hands—jerking, twitching—and tried to calm herself. To think. To construct orderly, balanced nets of thought that would hold everything useful to the problem, everything relevant—intellectually, emotionally, biochemically—everything productive. After twenty minutes, she got up again and left the lab.

Nikos Demetrios, Christina's twin, was fascinated by money. Its international flow, fluctuations, uses, changes, symbolism were, he had once told Miri, more complex than any natural Gaea patterns on Earth, just as useful to biological survival, and more interesting. At fourteen, he'd already made suggestions about international trading to the adult Norms with seats on the Sanctuary Exchange. They purchased his suggestions on investment opportunities around the globe: new wind-shear-detection technology under development in Seoul, a catalytic antibody application marketed in Paris, the embryonic Moroccan aerospace industry. Miri found him in the central communications building, in his tiny office ringed with datascreens.

"N-N-N-Nikos . . ."

"H-h-h-hello, M-M-M-M-Miri."

"W-w-will you have s-s-s-s-sex with m-me?"

Nikos regarded her steadily. Mottled color swept from his neck to his forehead. Miri saw that, like David Aronson, Nikos was embarrassed, but unlike David he didn't seem embarrassed by the directness of the question. She could only think of one other reason he could be embarrassed. She turned and stumbled from the office.

Nikos called, "W-w-w-wait! M-Miri!" His voice sounded genuinely distressed; they had been playmates their entire lives. He couldn't coordinate his movements even as well as she could. She easily outdistanced him.

Back in her lab, door locked and STERILE ENVIRONMENT seal activated, Miri sat, fiercely willing herself not to cry. Her grandmother had been right: There were hard necessities to face. One did not cry.

After that she was courteous and distant with Nikos, who didn't seem to know what to do about that. Eventually she saw him with a Norm, a pretty fourteen-year-old named Patricia who seemed fascinated by Nikos's skill with money. Miri had never talked much with Christina; now she talked less. David she never saw. With Tony she was the same as always: he was her workmate, friend, beloved confidant. Her brother. Now there was just this one area where the confiding didn't extend, was all. It was unimportant. She wouldn't let it be important. Hard necessity.

Two weeks later, Miri resumed watching the newsgrids from Earth, but only the sex channels. There were a lot of them. She found one she liked, removed all retina prints except her own from her lab-door programming, and learned to masturbate efficiently. She did it twice a day, her neurochemical responses being as hyped in this area as every other. She never permitted herself to think about Tony while she did it, and Tony never asked her why he could no longer enter her lab unannounced. There was no need. He knew. He was her brother.

Seating herself in the chair Drew indicated, Leisha had a funny thought: *I wish I smoked.* She remembered her father smoking, reaching for his monogrammed gold cigarette case, making a ritual out of lighting a cigarette. His eyes would half-close and his cheeks would hollow with the first long inward drag. Roger always said it relaxed him. Even then Leisha had known he was lying: It revitalized him.

Which did she want now, tranquility or revitalization? It seemed she was in need of both, and that what Drew would offer her would provide neither.

He had insisted on her being the first one, and alone. "A new art form, Leisha," he'd said, with that peculiar intensity that had marked him since Eric's illegal experimentation. Drew had always been intense, but this was different. He looked at Leisha from under those thick dark lashes, and she was afraid for him. This, then, was what it felt like to be a parent, this fear that your child was not going to be able to obtain what he'd set his heart on. That he would fail, and you would hurt for him more than you ever did for your own failures. How had Alice stood it? How had Stella?

But not Roger. He had been sure, from the beginning, that his child would not fail. *Surprise, Daddy. Look at me now,* sulking idly in the desert for twenty years, an Achilles whose Agamemnon was fighting her own stupid war while Leisha raised a son whose major talent was petty crime and who was not, in fact, even hers.

She said to Drew, not gently, "You should know that I've never been particularly sensitive to art, in any form. Maybe somebody else—"

"I know you're not. That's why I want it to be you."

She settled herself into the chair. "All right. Let's start." It sounded more resigned than she'd intended.

"Lights off," Drew said. The room in the New Mexico compound, fitted over the past seven months with a half-million dollars of theatrical equipment, darkened. Leisha heard Drew's chair move across the floor. When the holograph projector on the ceiling came on, he was seated directly beneath it, the console on his lap. Around him was nothing: not floor or walls or ceiling, just Drew suspended in the velvety blackness of a fairly standard null-projection.

He started to talk in a low voice. For a moment, all Leisha heard was the voice itself, calm and musical: She had never realized that Drew had such a beautiful voice. In normal surroundings, you didn't notice it. Then the words penetrated. Poetry. Drew—*Drew*—was reciting an old poem, something about golden groves unleaving . . . Leisha knew she had heard it before but couldn't think of the author. She was a little embarrassed for Drew. His voice was beautiful and soothing, but reciting poetry to holographic illustrations was about as juvenile artsy as you could get. Her heart tightened. Another false step, another failure . . .

Shapes swam toward her out of the darkness.

They weren't quite identifiable, and yet she recognized them. They passed above Drew, behind him, in front of him, even through him, while he finished the poem and started it again. The same poem. At least she thought it was the same poem. Leisha wasn't sure because it was hard to concentrate on the words; she had never much liked poetry anyway but even if she had it would be hard to concentrate. She couldn't take her eyes off the shapes. They slipped behind Drew and she tried to follow them with her eyes, see through him to see them, but she couldn't. The effort was tiring. When the wavering shapes emerged again from behind Drew, they were different. She strained forward to make out exactly what they were . . . she recognized them . . .

Drew started the poem a third time. " 'What, Margaret, are you grieving over golden groves unleaving . . .' "

She was grieving, but not over leaves. The shapes slid in and out of her mind and suddenly Drew had vanished. . . . He must be good to have programmed that . . . and the grief welled and filled her. She recognized a shape, finally: It was her father. *Roger.* He stood in the old conservatory in the house on Lake Michigan, the house that had been torn down twenty-six years ago. He was holding an exotic in his hands, thick-petaled and creamy white, with a flushed pink center. She cried out and he said clearly, "You haven't failed, Leisha. Not with Sanctuary, not with trying to make Alice special too, not with Richard, not with the law. The only failure is to not use your individual capacities, and you have done that. All your life. You tried."

Leisha gave a little scream and rose from her chair. She walked toward her father and he didn't vanish, not even when she stood with him directly under the holographic projection equipment. But the flower in his arms vanished and he took both her hands, saying gently, "You were the whole point of my individual striving," and Leisha shook her head violently. There was a blue ribbon on her head: She was a child again. Mamselle came in with Alice, and Alice said, "You never wronged me, Leisha. Never. There's nothing to forgive." Then Alice and Roger both vanished and Leisha was running through a forest filled with sunshine, green and golden slanting bars of light pouring through the trees. She was laughing, and in the light was the warmth of living plants and the scent of spring and the taste of forgiveness. Never had Leisha felt so free and joyous, as if she were doing exactly what she had always been meant to do. She laughed again and ran harder, because at the end of the sunlit, flowered path was her mother, holding out her arms and laughing too, her face alight with love.

There were tears on her cheeks. She sat in her chair in the adobe room. The lights were on. Immediately nausea hit her.

Drew said eagerly, "What did you see?"

Leisha doubled over, fighting her stomach. Finally she gasped, "What . . . did you do?"

"Tell me what you saw." He was inexorable: the young artist.

"No!"

"It was powerful, then." He leaned back in his wheelchair, smiling.

Leisha straightened slowly, hanging onto the back of her chair. Drew's face was triumphant. She said, more calmly now, "What did you do?"

He said, "I made you dream."

Dream. Sleep. Six teen-agers in the woods, and a vial of inter-leukin-1 . . . but this had been nothing like that. Nothing.

What this had been like was the night Alice had come to her in the Conewango hotel room, during Jennifer Sharifi's trial. The night Leisha had lost her belief in the power of the law to create a common commu-nity, and had stood trembling at the edge—

Darkness—

The void—

But this dream of Drew's had been *light,* not darkness. Yet it was the same. Leisha was sure of it. The edge of something vast and lawless, something that could swallow the tiny careful light of her reason . . . And then Alice had come. Across that vast unknown, Alice had some-how heard Leisha, in some way that had nothing to do with the careful light. *I knew,* Alice had whispered. And she had gone straight to Leisha, against all reason.

And now Drew, against all reason, had somehow manipulated an unknown part of her mind. . . .

Drew said eagerly, "It starts with a kind of hypnosis, but one that reaches around the cortex to call on universal . . . shapes I call them. They're more than that. But I don't have the words, Leisha, you know I never did. I just know they're in me and everybody else. I bring them out, *call* them out, so that they can take their own shapes in the person's dream. It's a kind of lucid dreaming, semidirected, but more than that. It's new." He sucked in a deep breath. "It's mine."

Logical questions calmed her. "Semidirected? You mean you determined what I would . . . dream?" But she couldn't maintain the detached tone. She was feeling too many things, not all of them good. "Drew—that's what dreaming is like? That's what Sleepers *do*?"

He shook his head. "No. Not often. I guess—I don't really know yet what happened. You're the first, Leisha!"

"I . . . *dreamed* about my father. And my mother."

His eyes gleamed. "Good, good. I was working with shapes from my parents." His young face suddenly darkened, lost in some private memory Leisha suddenly didn't want to share. Dreaming . . . this was too public. Too irrational. Too much a letting go, a surrender. But if it were a surrender to sunlight, to sweetness . . . No. It wasn't reality. Dreams were escape, she had always known that, she who had never dreamed. Dreams were as much an evasion of the real world as Alice's Twin Group pseudoscience. But what she'd just experienced from Drew . . .

"I'm too old to have my world turned inside out like a sock!"

Drew suddenly grinned, a smile of such pure triumph unmixed with frustration or arrogance that Leisha was dazzled. But she held onto her reason, hard. She said, "Drew, the other four patients who had the same operation as you in that Mexican clinic—they didn't come out of it with anything like this, any sort of change, any . . ." She couldn't find the word.

"But they weren't artists," he said, with the absolute conviction of the reborn young. "I am."

"But—" Leisha began, and got no farther because Drew, still smiling—still triumphant—leaned far over from his chair and kissed her hard on the mouth.

Leisha sat very still. She could feel her body respond, for the first time in . . . how long? Years. Her nipples hardened, her belly tightened . . . he smelled male, of male skin and hair. Her mouth opened of its own volition. Leisha drew sharply back.

"No, Drew."

"Yes!"

She hated to spoil his triumph, his terrifying achievement—she had been *dreaming.* But about this she was sure. "No."

"Why not?" He was pale now, but steady. His pupils were huge.

"Because I'm seventy-eight years old and you're twenty. I know it doesn't look that way to you, but to my mind—my *mind,* Drew—you're a child. And you always will be to me."

"Because I'm a Sleeper!"

"No. Because I've lived fifty-eight years you haven't."

"Don't you think I know that?" Drew said fiercely.

"No. I don't. You have no idea what it means." She covered his hand with her own. "I think of you as a son, Drew. A son. Not a lover."

He looked her straight in the eyes. "And what did your dream tell you about mothers and fathers and children that was so terrifying?"

For a moment she felt the dream again, and she glimpsed something behind the dream, some obverse side of the sunlit path, the smiling Roger with his hands full of exotics, the loving Elizabeth as Elizabeth had never really been, not to her. Leisha couldn't quite see that obverse side but it was there, deep in her mind, a way of ordering the world that had nothing to do with the law or economics or political integration or all the other things she had given her life to, not necessarily a worse way, or a better one, but different, *alien* . . . the glimpse slipped away.

She said, with all the compassion she could, "I'm sorry, Drew."

As she left the room he said quietly after her, "I'll get better at my art, Leisha. I'll draw out more from your preconscious, I'll show you things you never even . . . Leisha!"

She couldn't answer him. It would only make it worse. She went out and softly closed the door.

By evening, when she had figured out how to discuss it with him, what to say to put the whole dizzying episode into rational perspective, Stella told her Drew had packed and was gone.

Miri took her seat in the Council dome. It was a new seat, added to the room at her sixteenth birthday, the fifteenth chair bolted to the floor

around the polished metal table. From now on, the 51 percent of Sanctuary stock owned by the Sharifi family would be voted in seven equal
blocks. Next year, when Tony took his seat, there would be eight. The
chair squeaked slightly as Miri sat in it.

"The Sanctuary Council is proud to welcome Miranda Serena
Sharifi as a voting member," Jennifer said formally. The councilors applauded. Miri smiled. Her grandmother had for a moment eased the
tension in the room, so thick its currents could have been graphed on a
Heller matrix. Miri glanced around the table from under lowered eyes;
she habitually ducked her head now, since in her mirror that seemed to
minimize her twitching and jerking. Her mother applauded without
looking directly at Miri. Her father smiled with that resigned melancholy that was always in his eyes now. Beautiful Aunt Najla, pregnant
with another Super, stared at Miri with unblinking determination.

The term councilors smiled, but she didn't know them well enough
to know what the smiles meant. She wondered if they were jealous of
her sudden power. The Sanctuary charter, she knew from the library,
was far more generous within the family than any family corporation on
Earth would be. And on the newsgrid "dramas," usual community procedure on Earth seemed to be for young males to kill the fathers who
ran business empires or ranches or orbital corporations, in order to
gain power. Then they apparently married their dead fathers' young
third wives. This was such a barbaric and appalling social system that
Miri concluded it couldn't be the way the beggars really ran things; they
must like their "dramas" to explore situations that bore no relation to
reality. This was such a silly idea that for the second time she had given
up the dramas in disgust and returned to the sex channels.

"We have a full agenda," Jennifer said in her graceful voice. "Councilor Drexler, will you start with the treasurer's report?"

The treasurer's report, routine and positive, did nothing to reduce
the tension. Miri, unobserved now, studied one face after another from
under her lowered brow. Something was very wrong. What?

The agricultural, legal, judicial, and medical committee heads
made their reports. Hermione twisted a strand of her honey-colored

hair (when was the last time Miri had touched her mother's hair? Years) around one finger, transferred the curl to a second finger, around and around. Twist, twist. Najla rubbed her swollen belly. Councilor Devore, a thin young man with large soft eyes, looked as if he were sitting on hot coals.

Finally Jennifer said, "One more addendum to the medical report, which I asked Councilor Devore to leave to general discussion. As most of you know, we have had an accident." Abruptly Jennifer lowered her head, and Miri saw with astonishment that Jennifer needed a moment before she could go on. Miri was used to thinking of her grandmother as invulnerable.

"Tabitha Selenski, of Kenyon International, was repairing a power-conversion input in Business Building Three and received a power charge that . . . Her gross tissues are regenerating, very slowly. But parts of her nervous system are so destroyed there's nothing to regenerate. She won't ever be fully conscious again, although there's partial consciousness, at about the level an animal might have . . . She will need constant care, including such basic tasks as diaper changes, feeding, restraint. Moreover, she will never again be a productive member of the community."

Jennifer looked at each Council member in turn. Miri's strings knotted themselves into horrible nets. To be helpless, dependent on others for everything, a drain on someone else's time and resources without giving anything back . . .

A beggar.

She saw what the issue was, and her stomach lurched.

"I once knew a woman on Earth," Jennifer said, "when I was a child. A friend's mother. After my friend, the woman had another child, one with a profound neural disorder. As part of its so-called treatment, the mother was required to move its arms and legs in the rhythmic patterns of crawling, trying to impress those patterns on the brain and so stimulate brain development. She had to do this for an hour, six times every day. Between sessions, she fed the child, washed it, suctioned wastes from its colon, played prescribed tapes to stimulate its senses, bathed it, and talked to it nonstop for three half-hour sessions equally spaced around the clock. This woman had once played the piano professionally, but now she never touched it. When the child was four, its doctors added more to the treatments. Four times a day the mother was required to wheel the child around the yard for exactly fifteen minutes, encountering the same objects in the same order but under different weather conditions, again to build certain response patterns into the brain. My friend helped with all this, but after years of it, she hated to even go home. So did the woman's husband, who eventually didn't go home at all. Neither of them was there the day the mother shot both herself and her child."

Jennifer paused. She picked up a paper. "The Council has a petition from Tabitha Selenski's husband, to end her suffering. We must decide now."

Councilor Letty Rubin, a young woman with angular features that could have been turned on a lathe, said passionately, "Tabitha can still smile, still respond a little. I visited her and she tried to smile at the sound of my voice! She has a right to her life, whatever it is now!"

Jennifer said, "My friend's mother's child could smile, too. The real question is, do we have the right to sacrifice someone else's life to the care of hers?"

"It wouldn't have to be a sacrifice of one life! If we divide up the caretaking, in for instance two-hour shifts, the burden would be spread among so many that nobody would really be sacrificed."

Will Sandaleros said, "The principle would still be there. A claim on the strong by the weak *because* of weakness. A beggar's claim, that says the fruits of a person's labor belong to whoever can't labor for himself. Or won't. We don't recognize that weakness has a moral claim on competency."

Councilor Jamison, an engineer nearly as old as her grandmother whose only genemod was Sleeplessness, shook his head. He had a long, plain face with a sharp knobby chin. "This is a human life, Councilor Sandaleros. A member of our community. Doesn't the community owe its members full support?"

Will said, "But what constitutes a member of a community? Is it automatic—once you have joined, you are included for good? That leads to institutional morbidity. Or does being a member of a community mean that you continue to actively support the community, and actively contribute to it? Would, for instance, your insurance company, Councilor Jamison, continue to include a subscriber in the client list if he stopped paying his premiums?"

Jamison was silent.

Letty Rubin cried, "But a community is not congruent with a business arrangement! It must mean more!"

Jennifer's voice cut sharply across her last words. "What it *should* mean is that Tabitha Selenski shouldn't want to be a burden on her community. She should have the principles and dignity to not want to continue so-called life as a beggar, which means she should have included the standard life-termination clause in her will. I have, Will has, *you* have, Letty. Since Tabitha didn't, she's abandoned the principles of this community and declared herself no longer a member."

Ricky Sharifi said, "Self-preservation is an innate drive, Mother."

Jennifer said, "Innate drives can be modified for the good of civilization. This happens all the time. Sexual fidelity, formal laws to settle disputes, incest taboos—what are they but modifications imposed by will for the good of all? The innate drives would be to kill for revenge or to fuck our brains out whenever the urge struck."

Miri stared at her grandmother—never, never had she heard Jennifer use language like that. Her grandmother's speech was always formal, almost pedantic. The next moment she saw that it had been deliberate, theatrical, and she felt a slight distaste, followed by renewed stomach churning. Her grandmother did not trust her arguments alone to convince the Council to kill Tabitha Selenski.

To kill.

Strings whirled in her head.

Jean-Michel Devore said nervously, "What are the Sleepless except modifications of innate drives?"

Jennifer smiled at him.

Najla Sharifi said, "The definition of a community is key here. I think we all agree on that. Our definition seems to involve certain traits—like Sleeplessness—certain abilities, and certain principles. Which of these are crucial? Which are optional?"

"A good place to start," Will Sandaleros approved.

Jennifer said, "A member of the community must possess all three. The trait of Sleeplessness, the ability to contribute to the community rather than drain it, the principles to value the community's profound good above his own immediate preferences. Anyone who does not possess these things is not only too different from us but an active danger." She leaned forward, palms flat on the table. "Believe me, *I know.*"

There was a little silence.

Into the silence Hermione said quietly, "Anyone who thinks too differently from us is not really a member of our community."

Miri's head jerked up. She stared at her mother, who didn't look back. All the strings in Miri's head turned over once, slowly, inside out. For a moment she couldn't breathe.

But her mother had meant anyone who thought differently about *principles . . .*

Words from two dozen languages weaved themselves into her strings: *Harijan. Proscrit. Bui doi. Inquisición. Kristalnacht. Gulag.*

"A c-c-c-community d-d-d-d-" she couldn't, in her emotion, get the damn words out, "*d-divided* on f-f-f-fundamentals w-w-will d-destroy itself."

"Which is why we must not divide into the able and the parasitic," Jennifer said swiftly.

"Th-th-that's not whh-wh-wh-what I m-m-meant!"

They argued for five hours. Only Najla, her back aching from pregnancy, left, making over her proxy to her husband. In the end, the vote was nine to six: Tabitha Selenski must leave the community. She could, if her husband wished, be sent to Earth, among the beggars.

Miri had voted with the minority. So, to her surprise, had her father. The majority decision upset her, although of course she would abide by it. Sanctuary was owed her allegiance. But she felt confused and she wanted to discuss it all with Tony, as only they could, in the full depth and breadth of all the cross-references, tertiary associations, strings of meaning. Tony's computer program was a success. The Supers now used it routinely for communication among themselves, exchanging massive programmed edifices of meaning without the everlasting barricades of speech. She hurried to Tony.

Outside the Council dome, her father stopped her. Ricky Keller had hollows under his eyes. It occurred to Miri that seeing him sit in Council beside his mother, most people would conclude that Jennifer was the younger. Each year Ricky's manner became gentler. He said now, one hand on Miri's shoulder, "I wish you had met my father, Miri."

"Y-y-y-your f-father?" No one ever spoke of Richard Keller. Miri had been told about the trial; what he had done to Jennifer, his wife, was monstrous.

"I think in many ways you're like him, despite being a Super. Genetic inheritance is trickier than we know, despite our smugness. It's not all in quantifiable chromosomes."

He walked away. Miri didn't know whether to be pleased or insulted. Richard Keller, the traitor to Sanctuary. People usually said she was like her grandmother, "a strong-minded woman." But her father's eyes had been soft under their melancholy. Miri stared after his retreating, stooped figure.

The next day, Tabitha Selenski died by fatal injection. A persistent rumor circulated that Tabitha had injected the dose herself, but Miri didn't believe that. If Tabitha had been capable of doing that, the Council wouldn't have voted as it did. Tabitha had been nearly a vegetable. That was the truth. Miri's grandmother had said so.

BOOK
FOUR

BEGGARS

2091

*"No man is good enough
to govern another man
without that other's consent."*

—ABRAHAM LINCOLN, PEORIA,
OCTOBER 16, 1854

22

The 152nd Congress of the United States faced an annual trade deficit that over the past ten years had increased six-hundred percent, a federal debt that had more than tripled, and a fiscal debt of twenty-six percent. For nearly a century, Y-energy patents had been licensed by Kenzo Yagai's heirs exclusively to American firms, as specified in Yagai's eccentric will. This had fueled the longest economic climb in history. Through Y-technology, the United States had pulled out of a dangerous turn-of-the-century international slump and an even more dangerous internal depression. Americans invented and built every known application of Y-energy, and everyone wanted Y-energy. American-designed and fueled orbitals circled the Earth; American-built aircraft spanned the skies; American-built weapons traded on the illegal arms market of every major nation in the world. The colonies on Mars and Luna survived on Y-generators. On Earth, a thousand engineering applications cleaned the air, recycled the wastes, warmed the cities, fueled the automated factories, grew the genetically-efficient food, powered the institutionalized Dole, and kept the expensive information flowing to the corporations that each year became richer, more shortsighted, and more driven, like an earlier age's bloated aristocrats popping buttons off their waistcoats as they wagered fortunes at faro or E.O.

In 2080, the patents ran out.

The International Trade Commission opened international access
to Y-energy patents. The nations that had nibbled at the crumbs of
American prosperity—building the machine housings, sublicensing
the less profitable franchises, surviving as middlemen and brokers—
were ready. They had been ready for years, the factories in place, the
engineers trained at the great American donkey universities, the designs prepared. Ten years later the United States had lost sixty percent
of the global Y-energy market. The deficit climbed like a Sherpa.

Livers didn't worry. That was what they elected their congressmen
and women to do: to worry. To scramble in their donkey working fashion and find solutions, to take care of the problem, if there was a problem. The citizenry, those that were listening at all, didn't see any
problem. The public scooter races and Dole allotments and newsgrid
entertainment and politically-funded mass rallies, with plenty of food
and beer, and district building and energy grants continued to grow.
And in districts where they didn't grow, of course, the politicians just
didn't get returned. Votes, after all, had to be earned. Americans had
always believed that.

The domestic deficit became critical.

Congress raised corporate taxes. Again in 2087, and then again in
2090. The donkey firms that sent daughters and fathers and cousins to
Congress protested. By 2091 the issue could no longer be ignored. The
House debate, which lasted six days and nights and revived the art of
filibuster, was carried on the newsgrids. Hardly anyone outside of
donkeys watched it. One of the few who did was Leisha Camden. Another was Will Sandaleros.

At the end of the sixth day, Congress passed a major tax package.
Corporate taxes were recalibrated to the steepest sliding scale the
world had ever seen. At the top of the scale, corporate entities that
qualified were taxed at ninety-two percent of gross profit, with strict
limitations on expense claims, as their share of governing America. At the
next bracket, corporations were taxed at seventy-eight percent. After
that, the brackets descended rapidly.

Of corporations taxed at seventy-eight percent, fifty-four percent were based on Sanctuary Orbital. Only one corporation met the ninety-two percent tax criteria: Sanctuary itself.

Congress passed the tax package in October. Leisha, watching a newsgrid in New Mexico, glanced involuntarily out the window, at the sky. It was blue and empty, without a single cloud.

Will Sandaleros made a full report to Jennifer Sharifi, who had been away from Sanctuary on Kagura Orbital, concluding a vital arrangement there. Jennifer listened calmly, the folds of her white *abbaya* falling gracefully around her feet. Her dark eyes glistened.

"Now, Jenny," Will said. "Starting January 1."

Jennifer nodded. Her eyes went to the holoportrait of Tony Indivino, hanging on the dome wall. After a moment they returned to Will, but he was bent over the hard-copy of projected Sanctuary tax figures, and had not noticed.

Miri couldn't get Tabitha Selenski's death to move from the front of her mind. No matter what she was thinking about—her neurochemical research, joking with Tony, washing her hair, anything—Tabitha Selenski, whom Miri had never met, tangled, knotted, tied herself into Miri's strings and choked there.

Choked. She had researched the injection from which Tabitha had died; it would have stopped the heart instantly. Without the heart to pump, the lungs could not draw in air. Tabitha would have choked on her own already-breathed air, except of course she wouldn't have known it because the injection had also immediately paralyzed what was left of her brain.

Miri sat alone in the suspended bubble playground at Sanctuary's core and thought about Tabitha Selenski. Miri was too old for the playground. Still, she liked to go there when it was empty, sailing slowly from one handhold to another, her clumsiness canceled by the absence of both gravity and observers. Today her thought strings seemed as solitary as the playground.

No, not solitary—five other people, including her father, had voted with her to let Tabitha live in Sanctuary even as a beggar. But there was a difference in their votes, their reasons, their arguments for compassion. Miri felt the difference but she couldn't name it, neither in words nor strings, and that was intensely frustrating. It was the old problem; something was missing from her thoughts, some unknown kind of association or connection. Why couldn't she spin out an exploratory string about the difference between her vote and the others', and so learn what that difference was? Explain it, examine it, integrate it into the ethical system that Tabitha Selenski's accident had charred just as surely as it had charred her mind. There was something missing here, something important to Miri. A hole where an explanation should be.

She looked at the fields and domes and pathways below. Sanctuary was beautiful in the soft, UV-filtered sunlight. Clouds drifted at the far end; the maintenance team must be planning rain. She would have to check the weather calendar.

Sanctuary. (Refuge> churches> law> the protection of person and property> the balance of the rights of the individual with those of society> Locke> Paine> rebellion> Gandhi> the lone crusader on a higher moral plain . . .) Sanctuary was all of that for the Sleepless. Her community. Why, then, did she feel as if Tabitha's death had pushed her to a place where the refuge was violated (Becket in the cathedral, blood on the stone floor . . .)? To a place where nothing was safe after all?

Slowly Miri climbed down from the playground bubble to look for Tony, who would not have the answers either but would understand the questions. He would understand as far as she did herself, anyway, which suddenly didn't seem very far. Something vital was missing.

What?

In late October Alice had a heart attack. She was eighty-three years old. Afterward she lay quietly in bed, pain masked by drugs. Leisha sat by her bedside night and day, knowing it couldn't be long. Much of the time Alice slept. Awake, she drifted in drugged dreams, and often there was a small smile on her wizened face. Leisha, holding her hand, had no idea where her sister's mind wandered until the night Alice's eyes cleared and focused and she gave Leisha a smile of such warm sweetness that Leisha caught her breath and leaned forward. "Yes, Alice? Yes?"

Alice whispered, "Daddy is w-watering the plants!"

Leisha's eyes prickled. "Yes, Alice. Yes, he is."

"He gave me one."

Leisha nodded. Alice relapsed into sleep, smiling, in that place where a small girl had her father's love.

She woke a second time a few hours later to clutch Leisha's hand with unexpected strength. Her eyes were wild. She tried to sit up, gasping. "I made it! I made it, I'm still here, I didn't die!" She fell back on the pillows.

Jordan, standing by Leisha at his mother's bedside, turned his face away.

The last time Alice woke, she was lucid. She looked at Jordan with love, and Leisha saw that she would say nothing to him, because nothing was necessary. Alice had given her son everything she had, everything he needed, and he was safe. To Leisha she whispered, "Take . . . care of Drew."

Of Drew, not Jordan or Eric or the other grandchildren. Alice knew, somehow, where need was greatest. Hadn't she always known?

"Yes, I will. Alice—"

But Alice had already closed her eyes, and the smile was back on lips that twitched in private dreams.

Afterward, while Stella and her daughter pinned up the sparse gray hair and called the state government for the special permit for private burial, Leisha went to her own room. She took off all her clothes and stood in front of the mirror. Her skin was clear and rosy, her breasts sagged slightly from decades of gravity but were still full and smooth, the muscles in her long legs flexed when she pointed her toe. Her hair, still the bright blond Roger Camden had ordered, fell around her face in soft waves. She thought of seizing a scissors and hacking the hair into ragged chunks, but she felt too old, too tired, for theatrical gestures. Her twin sister was dead of old age. Asleep for good.

Leisha pulled on her clothes, not looking again at the mirror, and went to help Stella and Alicia with Alice's body.

Richard and Ada and their son came to New Mexico for the funeral. Sean was nine now, an only child—was Richard afraid that a second baby might be Sleepless? Richard looked content, looked as settled as his and Ada's wandering life could be, looked no older. He was mapping ocean currents in a highly-farmed section of the Indian Ocean, just off the continental shelf. The work was going well. He put his arms around Leisha and said how sorry he was about Alice. Leisha knew that Richard meant it, and through her grief a part of her mind reflected that this had been the most important man in her adult life and that as he held her she felt nothing. He was a stranger, linked to her only by the biology of parental choice and the past of finite dreams.

Drew, too, came home for the funeral.

Leisha had not seen him in four years, although she had followed his spectacular career on the newsgrids. She met him in the stone-floored courtyard, bright with cactuses kept in forced bloom and exotics under humidified, transparent Y-bubbles. He drove his chair up to her without hesitation. "Hello, Leisha."

"Hello, Drew." He still had the same intense green gaze, although in every other way he had changed yet again. Leisha thought of the dirty, skinny ten-year-old, the gawky teen trying hard to be a donkey in coat and tie and borrowed manners, the drama major with clipped hair and retro lace-cuffed clothing, the bearded drifter with sullen eyes and weak, dangerous resentments. Now Drew wore quiet, expensive clothes, except for a single, flashy, giveaway diamond arm cuff. His body had filled out, his face had matured. He was, Leisha saw without desire, a handsome man. Whatever else he was he had learned to keep hidden.

"I'm so sorry about Alice. She had the most generous soul I've ever known."

"You knew that about her? Yes, she did. And she created it for herself, with very little help from those who should have helped her."

He didn't ask what she meant by that; words had never been Drew's medium.

He said, "I'll miss her tremendously. I know I haven't been here in years." He spoke without a tremor of embarrassment. Drew had apparently made his peace with the final awkward scene between him and Leisha. But if so, why stay away for four years? Leisha had sent enough messages inviting him home. "But even though I wasn't here, Alice and I talked on comlink every Sunday. Sometimes for hours."

Leisha hadn't known that. She felt a flash of jealousy. But was she jealous of Drew, or of Alice?

She said, "She loved you, Drew. You were important to her. And you're in her will, but that can all wait until after the funeral."

"Yes," Drew said, without apparent interest in his inheritance. Leisha warmed to that. The child Drew was still there, under the flashy arm cuff and the strange career neither of them mentioned. And yet she should mention it, shouldn't she? This was Drew's work, his achievement, his individual excellence.

"I've followed your career on the grids. You've been very successful, and we're proud of you."

A light kindled in his eyes. "You watched a grid performance?"

"No, not a performance. Just the reviews, the praise . . ."

The light went out. But his smile was still warm. "That's all right, Leisha. I knew you couldn't watch it."

"Wouldn't," she said, before she could stop herself.

He smiled. "No—couldn't. It's all right. Even if you never let me put you into lucid dreaming again, you're still the single most important influence on my work that I'll ever have."

Leisha opened her mouth to reply to this—to the sentiment, to the sting below the sentiment, to the stubborn ambivalence below both—but before she could speak Drew added, "I've brought someone with me for Alice's funeral."

"Who?"

"Kevin Baker."

Leisha's awkwardness vanished. Drew might confuse her still, this son she had not birthed who had become something she could neither envision nor understand, but Kevin was a known quantity. She had known him for sixty years—since before Drew's father had been born.

"Why is he here?"

"Why don't you ask him yourself," Drew said shortly, and Leisha knew that Drew had learned, from Kevin or the datanets or somewhere, everything that had happened between her and Kevin. Sixty years' worth of everything. Time just piled up, Leisha thought. Like dust.

"Where is Kevin now?"

"On the north patio." Drew added to her back as she left the courtyard, "Leisha—one more thing. I haven't changed. About what I want, I mean."

"I'm not sure what you mean," she said, although she did, and berated herself for petty cowardice.

He made an impatient gesture—exactly how old was he now? Twenty-five. "I don't believe you, Leisha. I want what I've always wanted. You and Sanctuary."

That did catch her by surprise—half of it, anyway. Sanctuary. It had been a decade since Drew had so much as mentioned it to her. Leisha thought the childish dream of revenge or justice or conquest, or whatever it was, had faded long ago. Drew sat in his chair, a powerfully-built man despite the crippled legs, and his eyes didn't falter when they met hers. Sanctuary.

He was a child still, in spite of everything.

She went to the north patio. Kevin stood there alone, examining a stone shaped by desert wind into a long, tapered shape like a sandstone tear. At the sight of him Leisha realized that she felt no more than she had at the sight of Richard. Age had killed Alice's body; it seemed to have worked instead on Leisha's heart.

"Hello, Kevin."

He turned quickly. "Leisha. Thank you for inviting me."

So Drew had lied to him. It didn't seem to matter. "You're welcome."

"I wanted to pay my last respects to Alice." He stood awkwardly, and finally smiled ruefully. "Sleepless aren't very good at this, are we? At death, I mean. We never think about it."

"I do," Leisha said. "Would you like to see Alice now?"

"Later. First there's something I want to say to you, and I don't know if I'll get another chance. The funeral's in an hour, isn't it?"

"Kevin—listen. I don't want to listen to any apologies or explanations or reconstructions of events forty years old. Not now. I just don't."

"I wasn't going to apologize," he said, a little stiffly, and Leisha suddenly remembered herself saying to Susan Melling, on the roof of this same house, *Kevin doesn't see there's anything to forgive.* "What I wanted to say to you was on a different topic altogether. I'm sorry to bring it up just before the funeral but as I said, there might not be another time. Has Drew told you what business I handle for him?"

"I didn't know you handled any business for him."

"Actually, I handle it all. Not his tour bookings—there's an agency that does that—but his investments and security needs and so forth. He—"

"I should think the amount Drew makes would be pretty small compared to your usual corporate clients."

"It is," Kevin said, without self-consciousness, "but I do it for you. Indirectly. But what I wanted to say was that he insists I secure his investments exclusively in funds or speculations traded through Sanctuary."

"So?"

"Most of my business is with Sanctuary anyway, but on their terms. Dealing Earth-side when they don't want their own people to come down, and especially doing the security on their Earth-side transactions. There are still a lot of people out there who hate Sleepless, despite the benevolent social climate on the grids. You'd be surprised how many."

"No, I wouldn't," Leisha said. "What is it you want to tell me?"

"This: There's something starting to happen on Sanctuary. I don't know what it is, but I'm in a unique position to see the outer fringes of their planning for whatever it is. Especially through Drew's tiny investments because he wants them as close into the heart of Sanctuary dealings as they'll permit. Which, incidentally, was never very close, and now it's getting even more distant. They're liquidating whenever they can, converting investments not to credit but to equipment and to tangibles like gold, software, even art. That's what my watchdog program flagged in the first place: There's never been a Sleepless who collected art seriously. We're just not interested."

This was true. Leisha frowned.

Kevin continued, "So I went on digging, even in areas I don't handle. The security is harder to crack than it used to be; they must have some very good younger wizards up there, although there's no formal record of it anywhere. Sanctuary's spent the last year moving all investment it doesn't liquidate into holdings outside the United States. Will Sandaleros bought a Japanese orbital, Kagura, a very old one with a lot of internal damage, used mostly for genetic breeding experiments on altered meat animals for the luxury orbital trade. Sandaleros bought it in the name of Sharifi Enterprises, not of Sanctuary. They've acted strange with it—they evicted all the tenants but there's no record of moving out any of the livestock. Not so much as a single disease-resistant goatow. Presumably they brought their own people in to care for the animals, but I can't crack any of those records. And now they've started to move all their people on Earth back up to Sanctuary. The kids at grad school, the doctors doing residencies, the business liaisons, even the occasional kook who's down here slumming. They're all going back to Sanctuary, by ones and twos, inconspicuously. But they're all going back."

Leisha frowned. "What do you think it means?"

"I don't know." Kevin put down the wind-sculpted stone. "I thought you might be able to guess. You knew Jennifer better than any of us left here."

"Kev, I don't think I ever really knew anybody in my life." It just slipped out; she hadn't planned to say anything so personal. Kevin smiled thinly.

Drew drove his chair onto the patio. His eyes were red. "Leisha, Stella wants you."

She went, her mind full of Sanctuary's movements, of Alice's death, of the exploitive congressional tax package, of Drew's investing in Sanctuary, of Kevin's concern, of her irrational fear of Drew's art—it was irrational, she knew that. She didn't seem to have the energy to stay rational that she'd had when she was younger. There was no way to think about so many things at once. They were too different. The human mind could not encompass them. A different way of thinking was needed. *Daddy, you failed—you should have provided that in the genemod, too. A better way of integrating thought, not just better thoughts.*

Leisha smiled, without mirth. Poor Roger. Blamed for everything Alice wasn't, everything Leisha was, everything Leisha wasn't. It was funny, in a way. But only in the unhumorous way anything recent was funny. In another eighty years, maybe she would find it hilarious. All it took was enough time, piling up like dust.

"Ashes to ashes, dust to dust . . ."

It was Jordan who had chosen the beautiful, painful, sentimental words, Drew knew. Drew had never heard the funeral service before and he wasn't sure what all the archaic phrases meant, but looking at the faces gathered around Alice Camden Watrous's grave, he was sure that Jordan had chosen the words, Leisha disliked them, and Stella was impatient with them. And Alice? She would have liked them, Drew knew, because her son had chosen them. That would be enough for Alice. And so for Drew, too.

Shapes slid quietly in and out of his conscious mind.

For he knoweth our frame; he remembereth that we are dust. As for man, his days are as grass: as a flower of the field, so he flourisheth. For the wind passeth over it, and it is gone; and the place thereof shall know it no more.

It was Eric who read the words—Alice's grandson, Drew's old enemy. Drew looked at the handsome, solemn man Eric had become, and the shapes in his mind deepened, slithered faster. No, not shapes, this

time he wanted the word. He was determined to find the word for
Eric, who might be dust but if so only a high-quality real-leather
solid-platinum dust that would never be passed over and known no
more because Eric was a Sleepless, born to ability and power, no matter how much youthful rebellion he had acted out once. Drew wanted
the word for Richard, eyes downcast beside his Sleeper wife and little
boy, pretending he was like them. The word for Jordan, Alice's son,
torn in two all his life between his Sleeper mother and brilliant Sleepless aunt, defended only by his own decency. The word for Leisha, who
had loved—if what Kevin Baker had told Drew was true—Sleepers far
more than she had ever loved any of her own kind. Her father. Alice.
Drew himself.

He couldn't find the right word.

Jordan was reading now, from some different old book, they all
knew so many old books: "Sleep after toil, port after stormy seas, ease
after war, death after life . . ."

Leisha looked up from the coffin. Her face was set, unyielding.
Light from the desert sky washed over the planes of her cheeks, the pale
firm lips. She didn't look at Drew. She glanced at the wind-smoothed
stones on either side of Alice's in the little plot, BECKER EDWARD WA-
TROUS and SUSAN CATHERINE MELLING, and then straight forward, at
nothing. At air. But even though no glance passed between them, Drew
suddenly knew, from the fluid shapes inside his mind and the rigid
shape of Leisha outside it, that he would never bed her. She would never
love him as anything but a son, because a son was how she had seen him
first, and she didn't change her major shapes. She couldn't. She was
what she was. So were most people, but for Leisha it was even more
true. She didn't bend, didn't flex. It was something in her, something
from the sleeplessness—no, it was something *not* in her. Something the
very fact of sleeplessness left out. Drew couldn't define what. But the
Sleepless all had it, this inflexibility, this inability to change categories,
and because of it Leisha would never love him the way he loved her.
Never.

Pain clutched him, so strong that for a moment he couldn't see

Alice's coffin below him on the ground. Alice, whose love had let Drew grow up in a way Leisha's never could. His vision cleared and he let the pain flow freely, until it became another shape in his mind, jagged with lacerations but more than itself, more than himself. And so, bearable.

He could never have Leisha.

Then all that was left was Sanctuary.

Drew looked again around the circle. Stella had her face hidden against her husband's shoulder. Their daughter Alicia rested both hands on the shoulders of her small daughters. Richard had not raised his head; Drew couldn't see his eyes. Leisha stood alone, the clear desert light revealing her young skin, unlined eyes, rigidly compressed lips.

The word came to Drew, the word he had been hunting for, the word that fit them all, Sleepless mourning their best beloved who had not been one of them and for that very reason *was* their best beloved:

The word was "pity."

Miri bent furiously over her terminal. Both the display and the readout said the same thing: This synthetic neurochemical model performed worse than the last one. Or the last two. Or the last ten. Her lab rats, their brains confused by what was supposed to be the answer to Miri's experiment, stood irresolutely in their brain-scan stalls. The smallest of the three gave up: He lay down and went to sleep.

"T-t-t-terrific," Miri muttered. What ever made her think she was a biochemical researcher? "Super"—yeah. Sure. Super-incompetent.

Strings of genetic code, phenotypes, enzymes, receptor sites formed and reformed in her head. None of it was any good. Waste, waste. She threw a calibration instrument clear across the lab, guaranteeing it would have to be recalibrated.

"Miri!"

Joan Lucas stood in the doorway, her pretty face twisted as rope. She and Miri had not talked in years. "Miri . . ."

"Wh-wh-what is it? J-J-J-Joan?"

"It's Tony. Come right now. He . . ." Her face twisted even more. Miri felt the blood leave her heart.

"Wh–wh–what?"

"He fell. From the playground. Oh, Miri, come—"

From the playground. From the axis of the orbital . . . no, that wasn't possible, the playground was sealed, and after a fall from that height there would be nothing left—

"From the elevator, I mean. The outside. You know how the boys dare each other to ride the outside of the elevator, on the construction ribs, and then duck in the repair hatch—"

Miri hadn't known. Tony hadn't told her. She couldn't move, couldn't think. She could only stare at Joan, who was crying. Behind Miri, one of the genemod rats gave a soft squeak.

"Come on!" Joan cried. "He's still alive!"

Barely. The medical team had already reached him. They worked grimly on the smashed legs and broken shoulder before they moved him to the hospital. Tony's eyes were closed; one side of his skull was covered with blood.

Miri rode in the emergency skimmer the short distance to the hospital. Doctors whisked Tony away. Miri sat unmoving, unseeing, looking up only when her mother arrived.

"Where is he!" Hermione cried, and a small, cruel part of Miri's mind wondered if Hermione would finally look directly at her oldest son, now when everything that made looking worthwhile was gone. Tony's smile. The expression in his eyes. His voice, stammering out his words. Tony's words.

The brain scan showed massive damage. But, miraculously, consciousness survived. The drugs that dulled his pain also dulled what made him Tony, but Miri knew he was still there, somewhere. She sat by his side, holding his limp hand, hour after hour. People came and went around her but she spoke to none of them, looked at none of them.

Finally the doctor pulled a chair close to hers and put a hand on her shoulder. "Miranda."

Tony's eyelids fluttered more that time; she watched carefully—

"Miranda. Listen to me." He took her chin gently in his hand and pulled her face toward his. "There's nervous system damage beyond what can regenerate. There might be—we can't be sure what we're looking at. We've never seen this pattern of damage."

"N-n-not even on T-T-T-Tabitha S-Selenski?" she said bitterly.

"No. That was different. Tony's Mallory scans are showing highly aberrant brain activity. Your brother is alive, but he's suffered major, nonreparable damage to the brain stem, including the raphe nuclei and related structures. Miranda, you know what that means, you research in this area, I have the readouts here for you—"

"I d-d-d-don't w-w-want to s-s-s-see th-them!"

"Yes," the doctor said, "You do. Sharifi, talk to her."

Miri's father bent over her. She hadn't realized he was there. "Miri—"

"D-d-d-don't d-d-do it! N-n-no, D-D-Daddy! N-not to T-T-T-Tony!"

Ricky Keller didn't pretend to not understand her. Nor did he pretend to a strength Miri knew, under the chaotic horrible strings in her mind, he didn't possess. Ricky looked at his broken son, then at Miri, and slowly, shoulders stooped, he left the room.

"G-g-get out!" Miri screamed at the doctor, at the nurses, at her mother, who stood closest to the door. Hermione made a small gesture with her hand and they all left her. With Tony.

"N-n-n-no," she whispered to Tony. Her hand tightened convulsively in his. "I w-w-w-won't—" The words would not come. Only thoughts, and not in complex strings: in the straight linear narrowness of fear.

I won't let them. I'll fight them every way I can. I'm as strong as they are, smarter, we're Supers, for you I'll fight; I won't let them; they can't stop me from protecting you; no one can stop me—

Jennifer Sharifi stood in the doorway.

"Miranda."

Miri moved around the foot of the bed, between her grandmother and Tony. She moved slowly, deliberately, never taking her eyes off Jennifer.

"Miranda. He's in pain."

"L-l-l-life is p-p-pain," Miri said, and didn't recognize her own voice. "H-h-hard n-n-n-n-necessity. Y-y-you t-t-t-t-taught m-me that."

"He won't recover."

"Y-y-you d-d-don't kn-know that! N-n-not y-y-y-yet!"

"We can be sure enough." Jennifer moved swiftly forward. Miri had never seen her grandmother move so fast. "Don't you think I feel it as passionately as you do? He's my grandson! And a Super, one of the precious few we have, who in a few decades are going to make all the difference to us, when we need it most, when we have fewer and fewer resources from Earth to draw on and will have to invent our own from sources not even dreamed of yet. Our resources and genemod adaptions and technology to leave this solar system and colonize somewhere finally safe for us. We needed Tony for that, for the stars—we need every one of you! Don't you think I feel his loss as passionately as you do?"

"If y-y-y-you k-k-k-k-kill T-T-T-T-T-" she couldn't get the words out. The most important words she had ever said, and she *couldn't get them out—*

Jennifer said, with pain, "No one has a right to make claims on the strong and productive because he is weak and useless. To set a higher value on weakness than on ability is morally obscene."

Miri flew at her grandmother. She aimed for the eyes, curving her nails like claws, bringing up her knee to drive as hard as she could into Jennifer's body. Jennifer cried out and went down. Miri dropped on top of her and tried to get her trembling, jerking hands around Jennifer's throat. Other hands grabbed her, pulled her off her grandmother, tried to pin Miri's arms to her sides. Miri fought, screaming—she had to scream loud enough for Tony to hear, to know what was happening, to make Tony wake up—

Everything went black.

Miri was drugged for three days. When she finally awoke, her father sat beside her pallet, his shoulders hunched forward and his hands dangling between his knees. He told her Tony had died of his injuries. Miri stared at him, saying nothing, then turned her face away to the wall. The foamstone wall was old, speckled with motes of black that might have been dirt, or mold, or the negatives of tiny stars in a galaxy flat and two-dimensional and dead.

Miri would not leave her lab, not even to eat. She locked herself in and for two days ate nothing. The adults couldn't override the locking security, which Tony had designed, but neither did they try. At least Miri didn't think they tried; she didn't really care.

Her mother initiated contact once over the comlink. Miri blanked the screen, and her mother didn't try again. Her father tried several times. Miri listened, stone, to what he had to say, in one-way mode so he could neither see nor hear her. There was nothing to hear anyway. She didn't answer. Her grandmother did not try to call Miri.

She sat in a corner of the lab, on the floor, her knees drawn up to her chest and her thin, twitching arms clasped around her knees. Anger raged through her, storms of anger that periodically swept away all strings, all thought, swept away everything ordered and complex in torrents of primitive rage that did not frighten her. There was no room for being frightened. The anger left no room for anything else except a single thought, at the edge of what had been her previous self: *The hypermods apply to emotions as much as to cortical processes.* The thought didn't seem interesting. Nothing seemed interesting except her fury at Tony's death.

Tony's murder.

On the third day an emergency override brought every screen in her lab alive, even those that couldn't receive local transmissions. Miri looked up and clenched her fists. The adults were better than she had thought if they could get the computer system to do that, if they could override Tony's programming . . . But they couldn't, nobody had been as good with systems as Tony, nobody . . . *Tony* . . .

"M-M-M-Miri," said Christina Demetrios's face, "l-l-l-let us in. P-p-p-please." And when Miri didn't answer, "I l-l-l-l-l-loved h-him t-t-too!"

Miri crawled to the door, where Tony had installed a complex lock combining manual and Y-fields. Crawling nearly made her faint; she hadn't realized her body was quite so weak. A hyped metabolism ordinarily consumed huge amounts of food.

She opened the door. Christina came in, carrying a large bowl of soypease. Behind her were Nikos Demetrios and Allen Sheffield, Sara Cerelli and Jonathan Markowitz, Mark Meyer and Diane Clarke, and twenty more. Every Super over the age of ten in Sanctuary. They crowded the lab, jerking and twitching, the broad faces on their large, slightly misshapen heads streaked with tears, or set with fury, or blinking frantically with hyped thought.

Nikos said, "Th-they d-d-d-d-did it b-b-b-b-because he w-w-w-was one of us."

Miri turned her head slowly to look at him.

"T-T-T-T-T-Tony w-w-w-w-w-w-" The word wouldn't come. Nikos jerked over to Miri's terminal and called up the program Tony had designed to construct strings according to Nikos's thought patterns, and the conversion program to Miri's patterns. He typed in the key words, studied the result, altered key points, studied and altered again. Christy wordlessly held out a bowl of soypease to Miri. Miri pushed it away, looked at Christy's face, and ate a spoonful. Nikos pressed the key to convert his string edifice to Miri's. She studied it.

It was all there: The Supers' documented conviction that Tony's death had been different from Tabitha Selenski's. The medical differences were there: Tabitha had been proven cortically destroyed, but Tony's brain scans and autopsy records showed only an uncertain degree of disablement, the readouts inconclusive about the amount of personality left. They were completely clear, however, about the destruction of certain brain-stem structures which regulated the production of genemod enzymes. Tony might or might not have still been Tony; he might or might not have still had his mental abilities intact; there had not been enough time allowed to find out. But either way he would, without doubt, have spent some unknown part of each day asleep.

The medical evidence, obtained from the Sanctuary hospital records without even a trace that they had been entered, didn't stand alone on Miri's hologrid. It was knotted into strings and cross-strings of concepts about community, about the social dynamics of prolonged organizational isolation, of xenophobia, of incidents that Miri recognized between the Supers and the Norms in school, in the labs, in the playground. Mathematical equations on social dynamics and on psychological defenses against feelings of inferiority were tied to Earthside historical patterns: Assimilation. Religious zeal against heretics. Class warfare. Serfdom and slavery. Karl Marx, John Knox, Lord Acton.

It was the most complex string Miri had ever seen. She knew without being told that it had taken Nikos the entire day since Tony's autopsy to think through, that it represented the thoughts and contributions of the other Supers, and that it was the most important string she had ever studied—thought or felt—in her life.

And that something—still, *always*—was missing from it.

Nikos said, "T-T-T-Tony t-t-t-t-t-taught m-m-m-m-me h-h-h-how." Miri didn't answer. She saw that Nikos said that sentence, which was already self-evident, to keep from saying the other one that every element in the complex molecule of his string implied: *The Norms think we Supers are so different from them that we are a separate community, created by them to serve the needs of their own. They don't know they think this way, they would deny it—but they do it nonetheless.*

She looked around at the faces of the other children. They all understood. They were not children, not even the eleven-year-olds, not even in the sense Miri had been a child at eleven. Each new genemod had opened the potential to more pathways in the brain. Each new genetic modification had expanded use of those cortical structures once only available in times of intense stress or intense insight. Each new modification had created more differences from the adult Norms who fashioned them. These Supers—especially the youngest—were children of the Normals only in the grossest biological sense.

And she, Miri herself, how much was she the child of Hermione

Wells Keller, who could not bear to even look at her? The daughter of
Richard Anthony Keller, whose intelligence was in defeated thrall to his
mother? The granddaughter of Jennifer Fatima Sharifi, who had killed
Tony for a community that was defined only as she chose to define it?

Christina said softly, "M-M-M-M-Miri, eat."

Nikos said, "W-w-w-w-we m-m-m-m-m-m-*must* n-not l-l-l-
let them d-d-d-d-do it ag-g-g-gain."

Allen said, "W-we c-c-c-c-c-c-" He jerked his shoulders in
frustration. Speech had always been harder for Allen than even for
the rest of them; sometimes he didn't talk for days. He pushed Miri
from the console, called up his own string program, keyed rapidly,
and converted the result to Miri's program. When he was done she
saw, in beautifully ordered and composed strings, that if the Supers
made blanket assumptions about Norms, they would be as ethically
wrong as the Sanctuary Council. That each person, Super and Normal, would have to be judged as an individual, and that this might
have to be carefully balanced with the need for security. They could
already ensure complete, covert control of the Sanctuary systems, if
necessary for their own defense, but they could not ensure complete
control of the Norms they included in their defenses against never
letting another Super be killed by the Council. It was a risk, to be
balanced by the moral dilemma of becoming that which they were
condemning in the Council. The moral factors glinted and dragged
throughout Allen's strings; they were unquestioned assumptions in
Nikos's.

Miri studied the projection, the strings in her own mind knotting
and forming faster than they had ever done in her life. She didn't feel
moral; she felt hatred for everyone who had killed Tony. And yet she
saw Allen was right. They could never just turn on their own parents,
grandparents, other Sleepless—their community. They just couldn't.
Allen was right.

Miri nodded.

"D-d-d-d-defense. Ours," Allen got out.

"Inc-c-c-cludĩng N-N-N-Norms who are . . . r-r-r-r-r-right," Diane Clarke said, and the others intuited the strings she meant by the word "right."

Jonathan Markowitz said, "S-S-S-S-Sam S-S-S-S-Smith."

Sarah Cerelli said, "J-J-J-Joan L-Lucas. H-her unborn b-b-b-b-b-baby b-b-b-b-b-brother." Miri again saw herself and Joan crouched by the power dome on Remembrance Day, heard again her own narrow hardness about Joan's grief over the abortion of her Sleeper brother. Miri winced. How could she have been so hard on Joan? How could she not have *seen*?

Because it hadn't yet happened to her.

"W-w-w-we n-n-n-n-need a n-n-n-name," Diane said. She took Allen's place in front of the console and called up her own string program. When she made room for Miri to see the results, Miri saw a complex thought edifice about the power of names for self-identification, of self-identification for community, about the Supers' position in the Sanctuary community if the need for their own defense never arose again. It might not. It might happen that no one of their number was ever again hurt or endangered by the Norms, and the two communities could exist for decades side by side, with only one of them actually knowing there were two. The power of a name.

Miri's mouth twisted. She said, "A n-n-n-n-name."

"Y-yes. A n-name," Diane said.

She looked at them all. Diane's strings flowed in holographic projection, detailing both their separateness and the complex limits of their physical and emotional dependency. A name.

"The B-B-B-B-Beggars," Miri said.

"I had no choice," Jennifer said. "I had no choice!"

"No, you didn't," Will Sandaleros said. "She's just too young to hold a Council seat, Jenny. Miri hasn't learned yet to control herself, or to direct her talents toward her own good. She will. In a few years you can restore her seat. It was just a misjudgment, dear heart. That's all."

"But she won't talk to me!" Jennifer cried. In another moment she had regained control of herself. She smoothed the folds of her black *abbaya* and reached to pour herself and Will more tea. Her long slim fingers were steady on the antique pot; the fragrant stream of singleaf tea, a genemod developed on Sanctuary, fell unwaveringly into the pretty alloy cups Najla had molded for her mother's sixtieth birthday. But sharp lines ran from Jennifer's nose to her mouth. Looking at his wife, Will realized that pain could look like age.

"Jenny," he said gently, "give her more time. She had a bad shock and she's still a child. Don't you remember yourself at sixteen?"

Jennifer gave him a penetrating look. "Miri is not like us."

"No, but—"

"It's not only Miri. Ricky refuses to talk to me either."

Will put down his teacup. His words had the careful sound of a courtroom statement. "Ricky has always been a little unstable for a Sleepless. A little weak. Like his father."

Jennifer said, as if it were an answer, "Ricky and Miri will both have to recognize what Richard never could: The first duty of a community is to protect its laws and its culture. Without the willingness to do that, without that patriotism, you have nothing but a collection of people who happen to live in the same place. Sanctuary must protect itself." After a moment she added, "Especially now."

"Especially now," Will agreed. "Give her time, Jenny. She's your granddaughter, after all."

"And Ricky is my son." Jennifer rose, lifting the tea tray. She didn't look at her husband. "Will?"

"Yes?"

"Put Ricky's office and Miranda's lab under surveillance."

"We can't. Not Miri, anyway. The Supers have been experimenting with security. Whatever Tony designed isn't breakable. Not by us, anyway, without leaving obvious traces."

At Tony's name, fresh grief broke into Jennifer's eyes. Will rose and put his arms around her, despite the tea tray. But her voice was composed.

"Then move Miri to a different lab, in a different building. Where we can effect surveillance."

"Yes, dear heart. Today. But Jenny—it *is* just childish grief and shock. She's a brilliant girl. She'll come around to right and necessity."

"I know she will," Jennifer answered. "Move her today."

23

A week after Tony's death, Miri went in search of her father. Orbital Facilities had thrown her out of her lab—hers and Tony's, where he had once worked and laughed and talked with her—and moved Miri to a new lab in Science Building Two. That same afternoon Terry Mwakambe had come to her lab. Terry was the most brilliant of all the Supers at systems control, better even than Tony, but he and Tony had seldom worked together because Terry's strings made communication difficult. Radical genemod add-on's, with neurochemical consequences not yet fully understood, made him strange even to other Supers. Most of his strings consisted of mathematical formulas based on chaos theory and on the newer disharmony phenomena. He was twelve years old.

Terry spent hours at Miri's terminals and wall panels, his eyes blinking furiously and his young mouth a thin, twitching line. He said nothing at all to Miri. Eventually she realized that his silence was a fury as great as her own. Terry loved his parents, Norms who had altered his genes to create his weird, extraordinary intelligence, his Super abilities that now those same Norms were putting under surveillance as if Miri, one of his own, were some looting beggar. Terry's sense of betrayal filled the lab like heat.

When he was done, the Council surveillance equipment worked perfectly. It showed Miri playing endless games of chess against her terminal. A defense against grief. An assertion of power by someone who had discovered she was powerless against death. Miri's body, tracked on infrared scanner, slumped over the hologram board, taking a long time to make each move. Systems surveillance programs made available every move in every game. Miri won them all, although she made an occasional sloppy defense.

"Th-th-*there*," Terry said, and slammed out of the lab. It was the only word he'd spoken.

Miri found her father sitting in the park beneath the spot where the playground had floated. His and Hermione's second Norm child sat on his lap. The baby was almost two, a beautiful boy named Giles, with genemod chestnut curls and wide dark eyes. Ricky held him as if he might break, and Giles squirmed to get down.

"He doesn't talk yet," was the first thing Ricky said to Miri. She ran through the implications of this remark.

"H-h-he w-w-w-will. N-N-N-Norms s-sometimes just s-s-save it up and then s-start t-t-t-talking in s-s-sentences."

Ricky clutched the fretting baby tighter. "How do you know that, Miri? You're not a mother; you're still a child yourself. How do you all know?"

She couldn't answer him. Without strings and edifices of thought, the answer to his real question—*how do you think, Miri*—would be so incomplete it would be worthless. But her father couldn't comprehend strings. He couldn't ever understand.

She said instead, "*You* l-l-l-l-loved T-T-Tony."

He looked at her over the baby's head. "Of course I did. He was my son." But a moment later he added, "No. You're right. Your mother didn't love him."

"N-n-n-nor m-m-m-me either."

"She wanted to." Giles began to whimper. Ricky loosened his grip slightly but did not put Giles down. "Miri—your grandmother has had you dropped as a Council member. She introduced a motion to raise the age for Council participation for family members to twenty-one, the same as it is for term Council members. The vote passed."

Miri nodded. She wasn't surprised. Of course her grandmother would want her dropped from the Council now, and of course the Council would agree. There had always been those who resented different criteria for Sharifi voting shares than for general shares, although how the Sharifi family apportioned its votes was its own business. Or perhaps the resentment over her seat had arisen from the same source as the justification: She was a Super.

Giles gave a tremendous kick of his sturdy legs and started to howl. Ricky finally put him down, and smiled wanly. "I guess I thought if I held him long enough, he'd come out with a complete sentence. Something like, 'Please, father, let me down to explore.' At two, you would have."

Miri touched Giles, now happily investigating the genemod grass. The grass's ion pump operated so efficiently it needed only minute nutrients. Giles's hair felt soft and silky. "H-h-he's n-n-n-not m-m-m-me."

"No. I'll have to remember that. Miri, what were you and all the other Supers doing meeting in Allen's lab the other night?"

Alarm ran through her. If Ricky had noticed and speculated, had other adults? Could speculation alone harm the Beggars? Terry and Nikos said no one could crack the security they had set up, but anyone could wonder why such heavy security existed in the first place. Would wonder be enough to trigger retaliation? What did Miri, or any other Super, know about how Norms really thought?

"I think," Ricky said carefully, "that you were all mourning, in your own way, and in privacy. I think that if you all happen to meet again, and if any Norms ask what you're doing, that's what you'll tell them."

Miri let go of Giles's hair. She slipped her hand into her father's. Her fingers, the blood racing hot and fast from her Super metabolism, the muscles jerking, twitched against his cold ones.

"Y-y-y-y-yes, D-D-D-Daddy," she said. "W-w-we w-w-will."

It took them a month and a half to program hidden overrides into Sanctuary's major systems: life-support, external defense, security, communications, maintenance, and records. Terry Mwakambe, Nikos Demetrios, and Diane Clarke did most of the work. There were a few program failsafes they couldn't crack, mostly in external defense. Terry worked doggedly, twenty-three hours a day, under cover of a surveillance-cheat program of his own devising. Miri wondered what it showed him doing, but she didn't ask. Terry's wordless frustration at not being able to crack the last few failsafes was almost a physical entity, like air pressure. Miri, in contrast, was surprised how quickly the Beggars had, in essence, taken over the orbital, even though they had as yet actually changed nothing. Perhaps they never would. Perhaps they wouldn't have to.

At the start of the second month, Terry broke a major failsafe. He and Nikos called a meeting in Nikos's office. Both boys were pale as salt. A web of red capillaries pulsed in Terry's forehead above his mask. In the last month a dozen of the Supers had taken to wearing these masks, molded plasper that covered the bottom half of their faces, chin to eyes, with a hole left for breathing. A few of the girls decorated their masks. The children closest to their Norm parents, Miri noticed, didn't wear masks. She didn't know if anyone had questioned those who did, or had connected the appearance of the masks with Tony Sharifi's death.

"Sh-Sh-Sh-Sharifi L-L-L-L-L-L-L-" Terry made a slashing gesture that meant, roughly, "Fuck it." In the past month their nonverbal signals, always a part of Super communication, had become more violent.

Nikos tried. "Sh-Sh-Sharifi L-Labs has m-m-m-made and st-st-stored a f-f-f-f-f-" He, too, was too agitated. Terry called up the string on his terminal; like most of Terry's strings, it was incomprehensible to anyone but Terry. Nikos then created a string in his own program and converted it to Miri's, still the format most accessible to the group as a whole. The twenty-seven children crowded near.

Sharifi Labs had developed and synthesized an instantly fatal, airborne, highly communicable genemod organism, built from the code of a virus but highly different in important phenotypes. Packets of the

organism, in a frozen state that could be unfrozen and dispersed by remote control from Sanctuary, had been installed in the United States
by selected Sleepless graduate students studying on Earth. There were
packets secreted in New York, Washington, Chicago, Los Angeles, and
on Kagura orbital, which Sharifi Labs now owned. The packets were
virtually undetectable by conventional methods. The virus could kill
every aerobic organism evolved enough to possess a nervous system
before the organism's own brief life cycle ended, in roughly seventy-
two hours. Unlike every other virus that had ever existed, this one could
not reproduce itself indefinitely. All copies self-destructed seventy-
two hours after being unfrozen. It was a gorgeous piece of genemod
engineering.

Nobody said anything.

Finally Allen stammered, "F-f-f-f-for d-d-d-d-defense.
N-n-not t-t-t-t-to b-be used except if S-S-S-S-S-Sanctuary is
att-tt-ttacked f-first! N-n-n-never p-p-p-p-pre-emptive—"

"Y-y-yes!" Diane said eagerly. "Only f-f-f-for d-d-defense! It
h-h-h-has t-to b-b-b-be. W-w-w-we w-w-w-wouldn't—"

Christy said desperately, "L-l-l-like *us*. L-like the B-B-Beggars
are d-d-doing."

Voices broke out, stammering and shouting. They all wanted to believe that Sanctuary was doing no different from they themselves, setting up secret self-defense mechanisms the Council would never need to
actually use. The packets existed for verbal bargaining, for posturing
threats that were, after all, the only thing Sleepers understood. Everybody knew that. Sleepless had a right to self-defense if Sanctuary were
directly attacked. Sleepless were not killers. The Sleepers were the
killers. Everybody knew that, too.

Miri looked first at Terry's face, then Nikos's, then Christy's, then
Allen's. She looked back at her grandmother's biological weapon, secret even from the Sanctuary Council, known only to the handful of
Sharifi Lab partners who had developed, synthesized, and secreted it
in cities full of other children.

Did her father know?

Miri thought suddenly, inanely, that she, too, would make herself a molded plasper mask.

In the end, after hours of agitated discussion, the Beggars did nothing about the biological weapon. There was nothing they could do. If they told the Council what the Supers knew, the Council would guess their real abilities. If they disabled the remote mechanisms, the adults would also guess. If that happened, the Beggars would lose the covert chance to protect their own—as they had not been able to protect Tony. And anyway, if the virus was only for defense, created in the fervent hope it would never be needed, then how was what Sharifi Labs did different from what the Beggars themselves were doing?

The children couldn't think of anything to do beyond installing defensive overrides, so they did nothing.

Miri walked slowly back to her own lab, and Terry's surveillance-cheat program kicked in to show her winning game after game of non-existent chess.

The Beggars' discovery agitated Miri for days. She tried to work on her old neurological research to inhibit stammering. She broke a delicate bioscanner, misspoke a vital piece of code into the work terminal, and threw a beaker across the room. She kept seeing her father, with Giles squirming on his lap. Ricky loved her. He loved her enough to suspect the Supers were withdrawing into their own community and to not . . . what? What could he do anyway? What did he want to do?

Strings blew through her mind, like clouds swirled from maintenance jets: Loyalty. Betrayal. Self-preservation. Solidarity. Parents and children.

The comlink chimed. Despite her agitation, Miri went as still as possible when she saw Joan Lucas's face appear.

"Miri. If you're there, will you turn on two-way?"

Miri didn't move. Joan had brought her the news of Tony's death, crying herself. Joan was a Norm. Was Joan her old friend? Her new enemy? Categories no longer held.

"Either you're not there, or you don't want to talk to me," Joan said.

She had grown even prettier over the past year, a seventeen-year-old genemod beauty with a strong jaw and huge violet eyes. "That's all right. I know you're still . . . hurting over Tony. But if you *are* there, I wanted to tell you to access newsgrid twenty-two from the United States. Right now. There's an artist on that I watch sometimes. He helped me with . . . some problems I was having in my mind. It might help you to watch him, too. It's just a thought." Joan glanced down, as if she were weighing words carefully and did not want Miri to see the expression in her eyes. "If you do access, don't let it record on the master log. I'm sure all you Supers know how to do that."

For the first time, Miri realized that Joan had been calling on a scrambled-code link.

Miri stood irresolutely, chewing a strand of unkempt hair, a habit she had started since Tony's death. How could watching an "artist" from Earth help Joan with "problems in her mind"? And what kind of problems would someone like Joan, perfectly fitted to her community, have anyway?

Nothing in common with Miri's.

She picked up the beaker she had hurled, and washed and disinfected it. She went back to the DNA code for a synthetic neurotransmitter modeled on her work terminal, and resumed the tedious task of computer-testing minute hypothetical pinpoint alterations in this formula, which might or might not even be the right starting point. The program wouldn't run, there was a glitch someplace. Miri banged on the side of the terminal. "F-f-f-f-fuck!"

Nikos or Terry would have known how to fix it instantly. Or Tony.

Miri collapsed onto a chair. Waves of grief washed through her. When the worst had passed, she turned again to the terminal. Even with the maintenance program, she couldn't find the glitch.

She turned to the comlink and accessed U.S. newsgrid twenty-two.

It was completely black. Another glitch? Miri had leaped up to shove her fist into the miniature holographic stage and pound on its floor when the stage center suddenly brightened. A man in a chair, eight inches high, started to speak.

" 'Happy those early days when I/ Shined in my Angel-infancy!/ Before I understood this place . . .' "

This? A man in a chair reciting some kind of beggar poetry? Joan broke years of virtual silence to tell Miri to watch *this?*

As the man began to speak, the blackness behind him took shape. No—shapes came out of it, repetitive but also subtly different, oddly compelling. Strings formed in Miri's head, and she saw that they, too, although made of the most mundane thoughts, were also subtly different from her usual strings, the overall shape not unlike the ones slithering past the man reciting from the wheelchair. Maybe Diane should see this: She was working out equations to describe the formation of thought strings, building on the work Tony had done before he died.

" 'But felt through all this fleshly dress/ Bright shoots of everlastingness,' " the man said. Miri realized suddenly that his chair was technologically enhanced, and that he must be somehow damaged or deformed. Not normal.

The strings in her mind grew flatter, calmer. The shapes in the hologrid had changed. She heard the man's words, and yet she didn't; the words were not what was really important. And wasn't that right? Words had never been important, only strings, and the strings had shapes like—but not like—the ones around the man. Only the man had disappeared, too, and that was all right because she, Miri, Miranda Serena Sharifi, was disappearing, was sliding down a steep long chute and each meter she traveled she became smaller and smaller until she had disappeared and was invisible, a weightless transparent ghost that neither twitched nor stammered, in the corner of a room she had never seen before.

Below it, she knew, were other rooms. It was a deep building— deep, not tall—and each room was like this one, filled with light so palpable it was almost alive. In fact, it *was* alive, forming suddenly into a beast with fifteen heads. Miri held a sword. "No," she said aloud, "I'm transparent, I can't use a sword," but this apparently made no difference, because the beast started toward her, roaring, and she hacked at a head. It fell off, and only then did she see it was her grandmother's.

Jennifer's head lay on the floor, and as Miri watched in horror a hole opened in the floor and the head, smiling faintly, slid down it. Miri knew it was going to another, deeper room—this whole place was room after room, opening off each other—but the head wouldn't vanish entirely. Nothing ever vanished entirely. The beast attacked again and she cut off another head, which dropped just as serenely through the floor. It had been her father's.

Suddenly fury filled her. She hacked and hacked. Some of the heads she recognized as they burrowed deeper into the building, others she didn't. The last one was Tony's, and instead of vanishing it grew a body—not Tony's but David Aronson's genemod-perfect body, the body she had tried to seduce three years ago when he had rejected her. Tony/David started undressing her, and she immediately became excited. "I always wanted you," she said. "I know," he replied, "but I had to stop twitching first." He entered her and the world above their heads exploded into strings of thought.

"No, wait a minute," Miri said to Tony, "those aren't the right strings." She looked up, concentrated, and changed the strings at several points. Tony waited, smiling with his beautiful mouth on the motionless body. When Miri was done changing the strings, he reached out to hold her again and such tenderness, such peace flooded Miri that she said joyously, "It doesn't matter about Mother!" "It never did," Tony said, and she laughed and stroked him and—

—woke up.

Miri started in terror. The lab swam back into existence around her. It had been *gone,* been replaced by—

She had been asleep. She had been dreaming.

"N-n-n-no," Miri moaned. How could she have been asleep? *She?* Dreams were what Sleepers had, dreams were thought-construct described in theoretical brain studies . . . The holoterminal was once more dark. Slowly the man faded back in.

The shapes. His equipment had projected shapes, and then there had been answering shapes in her mind. Like thought-string edifices—but not. From a different part of her brain, perhaps, not cortical? But the feeling of peace, of joy, of tremendous oneness with Tony, that could only have come from her cortex. She had dreamed it. He had—she dredged up the Earth word—"hypnotized" her with his mind shapes, his poetry on aloneness, and then the shapes in the hologram had drawn forth her own dreaming shapes . . .

But there had been more. Miri had changed the dream. She had concentrated on the strings above her and Tony's heads and *changed* them, deliberately. She could see both versions now, in memory.

Miri sat very still, as still as she had in the dream.

"Drew Arlen," a too-hearty voice was saying over the holo of the man in the chair, "Lucid Dreamer. The new art form that has taken the country by flash! This is a nonreplicable program, Livers out there in Holo-Land, so to purchase your own copy of one of Drew's six different Lucid Dreaming performances—"

Miri pressed Tony's code to replicate. The man in the chair froze in time.

She put her head between her knees, still dazed. She had been dreaming. She, Miranda Sharifi, Sleepless and Superbright. She could see Tony still, feel his arms around her, feel the depth of the building below her, its endless rooms. She could still see the thought strings, solid as matter, that she had reached up and changed.

Miri raised her head from her knees and went to her work terminal. She fixed the program glitch. It was easy; all she had to do was follow the strings she had seen in the dream, the ones she had changed. She typed in the pinpoint DNA code she had been hunting for three years and had never really seen. The program ran it against her parameters, probability tables, and neurochemical interactions. The comparisons and modeling would take a while to complete, but Miri already knew— the genemods were the right ones. They were the ones she had been searching for, had been circling around, but had not seen until a part of her dreaming mind had looked in a different way at the facts in her thought strings, and added what was missing.

That was right; her mind had added what was missing, what had always been missing, all her life. The ideas—not linear, not knotted into strings, not connected in perceptible ways—from the missing part of her mind. The dreaming part. No—the *lucid dreaming* part, which reached into a universe deeper than one story, to pull out things she had never guessed were there and yet were indubitably hers. Things she—the conscious Miri—could partially manipulate in the dream world.

Miri looked at the frozen holo of the artist in the chair. He was smiling faintly; unseen light glinted on his glossy hair. He had bright green eyes. She felt again the dream orgasm with Tony. Every fiber of her fierce, young, single-minded personality knotted itself around the figure of Drew Arlen, who had given her this gift, this redemption.

Lucid dreaming.

Miri rose. She wanted to synthesize her neuorological compound, test it, and take it. She knew it would work. It would inhibit the stuttering and stammering and twitching of the Supers without impairing their superabilities. It would let them be themselves, only with an added dimension.

Like lucid dreaming. Oneself, only more so.

But there was something else to do first. She called up the library program and set it for the widest possible preliminary search parameters: all data in Sanctuary records, in legal Earth databanks for which Sanctuary paid stiff fees, in illegal Earth ones for which they paid even stiffer fees. She added the search programs Tony had designed and taught her to use, the ones that accessed databanks their owners thought completely secure. Miri added anything else she could think of. She wanted wanted to know everything there was to know about Drew Arlen. Everything.

And then she would figure out how to get to him.

The Beggars crowded into Raoul's lab, sitting on benches, the desk, the floor. They talked softly, as they usually did to each other, allowing a long time for the words to come out. Most of the time they didn't look directly at each other. Nearly all wore masks now, some elaborately ornamented.

Miri's mask was undecorated. She wasn't going to wear it long.

"N-n-n-nucleid p-p-p-p-p-prot-teins—"

"—f-f-f-found a n-new r-r-ribbon fl-flow—"

"—t-t-t-two p-pounds h-h-h-heavier—"

"M-my n-n-n-new si-si-sister—"

"C-C-C-C-C-C-C-C—" A grunt of frustration. The first terminal came out to call up a string program.

"Wait a minute before you turn to string communication," Miri said. "I have something to show you."

The room fell into frozen silence. Miri took off her mask and brushed her long bangs from her eyes. She gazed at them serenely from a face that didn't twitch, or jerk, or tremble.

"Uhn-n-n-n-n," someone said, as if punched in the stomach.

"I found the pinpoint code," Miri said. "The enzyme is easily synthesized, has no predicted side effects and none observed in myself— so far anyway—and can be delivered by slow-drip subcutaneous patch." She rolled up her sleeve to show them the slight scar, rapidly regenerating, on her upper left arm.

"The f-f-f-f-f-*formula*!" Raoul, the other biological researcher, demanded hungrily.

Miri called up the string edifice on her work terminal. Raoul pasted himself in front of it.

Christy said, "Wh-Wh-When?"

"I put the patch in three days ago. Since then I haven't left the lab. No one has seen it but you."

Nikos said, "D-d-d-d-do m-m-m-m-me!"

Miri had prepared twenty-seven subcutaneous patches. The Beggars formed an assembly line, with Susan disinfecting the upper arm of each of them, Raoul making the incision, Miri inserting the patch, and Diana bandaging tightly. There was no need for stitches; the skin would regenerate.

"It takes a few hours for the effects to kick in," Miri said. "The enzyme has to direct the manufacture of a sufficient amount of neurotransmitter."

The Supers looked at Miri with shining, twitching eyes. She leaned forward. "Listen—there's something else we have to talk about.

"You know I've been searching for this genemod for nearly four years; well, in the first two I was still exploring the problem. But I don't think I would have found the solution at all if I hadn't learned to do something else. It's called lucid dreaming."

She had their complete, formidable attention.

"It sounds like something Sleepers do, and a Sleeper led me to it. Through Joan Lucas. But we can do lucid dreaming, too, and although I don't have any brain-scan data yet, I think we might do it differently from Sleepers. Or even from Norms." Miri explained about Joan's call, about Drew Arlen, about seeing her own research string in the lucid dream and reaching up to change it.

"It's as if strings are one kind of thinking, one that effectively unites associative and linear thought, and lucid dreaming is some other kind. It uses . . . *stories*. Pulling from the unconscious, maybe, the way Sleeper dreams are supposed to do. But Sleepers don't have string edifices to put together with the stories. They can't—I don't know!— maybe they can't shape the lucid dreaming as well because they don't have such coherent shapes to work with in the first place. Or maybe they can shape the dream, but without the visualized complexity of strings, the shaping only operates on an emotional level." Miri shrugged. Who could say how Sleepers' minds worked?

"Anyway, lucid dreaming is like . . . being reborn. Into a world with more dimensions than this one. And I want you to all try it."

From the pocket of her shorts Miri pulled the program cartridge of her favorite of Drew's performances, the second. Recording the entire series of six had been no challenge for Tony's programs, no matter what the newsgrids claimed.

Terry Mwakambe had thrown one of his impenetrable security fields around Raoul's lab before the meeting began. Miri inserted her cartridge into Raoul's holoterminal. She turned her back to the miniature stage; she didn't want to fall asleep herself, not this time. She wanted to watch the others.

One by one their eyes glazed, although they didn't close. Drew Arlen's musical voice licked at their eyelids, reciting words, suggesting ideas. The Supers dreamed.

When it was over, they awoke almost simultaneously. They laughed, and cried, and talked excitedly about their dreams—all but Terry, the most genetically modified, the most different. He sat slumped in a corner, his head bent so that all Miri could see was hair.

Somewhere in the middle of the laughing and exclaiming, Miri's synthetic enzyme stimulated sufficient production of three different, interdependent brain chemicals to change the subtle, genetically-coded composition of cerebrospinal fluids.

Terry stood. His thin body and large head were held very still. He looked at all of them from eyes that neither blinked nor twitched.

He said, "I know how to remove the last Sharifi Labs failsafes. And I know what's behind them."

24

On New Year's Day Leisha walked along the creek, under the cottonwoods. A light snow glistened on the ground. She looked up to see Jordan, coatless, puffing toward her. The lines and wrinkles on his sun-battered face—he was sixty-seven—were pulled taut as wires.

"Leisha! Sanctuary has seceded from the United States!"

"Yes," Leisha said, without surprise. She had decided shortly after Alice's funeral that this must be Jennifer's intent. It fit. It occurred to her that she and Kevin Baker were probably the only two people in the country who were not surprised. Or maybe Kevin was surprised. She had not talked to him since Alice's funeral.

Leisha bent to pick up a stone: it was almost a perfect oval, polished by patient wind and ancient water. Under her fingers the stone felt icy. "Yes," she said to Jordan. "I know."

"Well, aren't you coming in to watch the grids?"

"Don't we always?" Leisha said, and at her tone, Jordan stared.

Sanctuary made its declaration at 8:00 A.M. January 1, 2092. The statement, released simultaneously to the country's five most important newsgrids, the president, and the Congress of the United States, none of whom were fully functional at that hour on New Year's Day, was not negotiable:

When in the course of human events it becomes necessary for one people to dissolve the political bands which have connected them with another, and to assume among the powers of the earth, the separate and equal station to which the laws of nature and of nature's God entitle them, a decent respect to the opinions of mankind requires that they should declare the causes which impel them to the separation.

We hold these truths to be self-evident to the examining eye: That all men are *not* created equal. That all are entitled to life, liberty, and the pursuit of happiness, but that none are guaranteed these at the expense of others' freedom, others' labor, or others' pursuit of their own happiness. That governments instituted among men to secure these rights derive their just powers from the consent of the governed. That a government which both fails to protect the rights of a people *and* to secure their consent has become destructive of those ends and it is the right of that people to alter or abolish it, and to institute new government, laying its foundation on such principles and organizing its powers in such form as to them shall seem most likely to effect their safety and happiness.

This should not be undertaken for light and trivial causes, but when a long train of abuses and usurpations evinces a design to deprive a people of what is rightfully theirs, it is their duty to throw off such a government. The history of the present government of the United States is such a history of repeated injuries and usurpations. To prove this, let the facts be submitted to a candid world.

The United States has effectively denied to Sanctuary representation in any legislature or lawmaking body, due to widespread and ignorant hatred by Sleepers of the Sleepless.

The United States has levied ruinous taxes on Sanctuary, thus bringing about *de facto* taxation without representation, and thus also taking by the threat of force the fruits of the labor of Sanctuary's citizens.

In return for such taxes, the United States has provided no protection, social benefits, legal representation, or trade advantages to Sanctuary. No citizen of Sanctuary uses federal or state roads, schools, libraries, hospitals, courts, police protection, fire protection, Dole benefits, public entertainment designed to gain voting representation, or any other governmental service. Such citizens of Sanctuary as attend graduate institutions in the United States fully pay their own fees and expenses, waiving public charity.

The United States has erected trade barriers against the business establishments of Sanctuary in the form of unequal taxes and trade quotas, forcing Sanctuary to trade with foreign powers or else to trade on terms which harass our people and eat out their substance.

The United States has obstructed the administration of justice by refusing assent to laws for establishing judiciary powers on Sanctuary itself, so that we are deprived of the basic judicial right to trial by a jury of our peers.

Finally, the United States has used against Sanctuary the threat of military force if Sanctuary should not comply with all these unjust and immoral conditions, in effect abdicating true government on Sanctuary and waging war against us.

We therefore, the representatives of Sanctuary, in General Council assembled, appealing to the Supreme Judge of the World for the rectitude of our intentions, do, in the name and by the authority of the people of Sanctuary, solemnly publish and declare that this orbital colony is, and of right ought to be, a free and independent state; that we are absolved of all allegiance to the United States of America, and that all political connection between them and the United States is and ought to be dissolved. As a free and independent state, Sanctuary possesses the power to levy war, conclude peace, contract alliances, establish commerce, and do all other acts which independent states have a right to do. We of Sanctuary further declare that our first act as an independent state is to throw off the yoke of foreign tribute in the form of ruinous and unequal Quarterly Estimated Corporate taxes unfairly levied January 15 of this year 2092, followed by other such taxes as the United States may try to impose to our ruin and detriment April 15 of this year.

In support of this Declaration we, the duly elected and appointed representatives of Sanctuary, mutually pledge to each other our lives, our fortune, and our sacred honor.

The newsgrid facsimile bore fourteen signatures, led by a large, scrawled *Jennifer Fatima Sharifi*. Jennifer's usual handwriting, Leisha remembered, was small and neat.

Stella said, "They did it. They really did it."

Jordan said, "Leisha—what will happen now?"

"The IRS will wait for the nonpayment of the January 15 taxes. When it doesn't come, they'll attach a jeopardy assessment to Sanctuary. That means they'll have the right to physically seize the material assets to hold as protection against getting their money."

"Physically seize *Sanctuary*? Without even a hearing or something?"

"Jeopardy assessment puts the seizure first, the hearing second. That's probably why Jennifer chose this course of action. Everybody will have to move very fast. Half of Congress is away for the holidays." Leisha noted how detached she sounded, how calm. How amazing.

Stella said, "But seizing Sanctuary—how, Leisha? With the army? An assault?"

Jordan said, "They could blow it out of the sky with a single Truth missile."

"But they won't," Stella argued, "because that would just destroy the property the IRS is trying to seize. It'll have to be a . . . an invasion. But that would be just as hard on Sanctuary—orbital environments are *fragile*. Leisha, what the hell is Jennifer thinking of?"

"I don't know," Leisha said. "Look at the signatures. Richard Anthony Keller Sharifi, Najla Sharifi Johnson, Hermione Wells Keller—Richard's children have married. I don't think Richard knows that."

Stella and Jordan looked at each other. "Leisha," Stella said in her acerbic way, "doesn't it seem to you this is more than a matter of *family news*? It's a civil war! Jennifer has finally succeeded in separating virtually all the Sleepless from the rest of the country, from the mainstream of American society—"

"And are you going to tell me," Leisha asked, smiling without amusement, "that the twelve of us sitting out here in this forgotten compound in the desert haven't done exactly the same thing?"

Neither of the others answered her.

"Do you think," Stella said finally, "that Sanctuary is a match for the *United States*?"

"I don't know," Leisha said, and Stella and Jordan stared at each other, aghast. "I'm not the right person to ask. I've never once, in my entire life, been right about Jennifer Sharifi."

"But, Leisha—"

"I'm going down to the creek," Leisha said. "Call me if we go to war."

She left Stella and Jordan staring at each other, bewildered and angry at her, unable to see the distinction between criminal indifference and what, to Leisha, was even worse: criminal uselessness.

The United States Congress, from the first, took Sanctuary's secession threat seriously. This was *Sleepless*. Senators and congressmen who had scattered to their constituencies for the winter holidays hastily reassembled in Washington. President Calvin John Meyerhoff, a big slow-moving man dubbed in the newsgrids "Silent Cal II," nonetheless possessed a sharp brain, finely tuned to foreign policy. If it struck Meyerhoff as ironic that the major foreign crisis of his waning first term involved a section of the United States technically part of Cattaraugus County, New York, the irony was not present in any of the press releases from the Oval Office.

The Liver newsgrids, however, saw the Sanctuary threat as hysterically funny, raw material for the two-minute comedy sketches that were the favorite form of entertainment. Few Livers had ever dealt with, heard of, or known any Sleepless, whose dealings were with the donkey class that ran the businesses that ran the country. A Liver newsgrid gleefully made the prediction: "Next to Secede—Oregon! Inside story!" The sketch was dramatized with holoactors with taped-up eyelids standing in downtown Portland and ranting that it was necessary for Oregon people "to dissolve the political bands that connect them with another people." FREE OREGON banners suddenly appeared at scooter races, at brainie parties, at the free dance palaces. A racer named Kimberly Sands won the Belmont Winter Race in a scooter painted with the Oregon flag superimposed over the United States flag.

On January 3, the White House issued a statement that Sanctuary had in effect made a statement of both sedition and terrorism, declaring its "power to levy war" while conspiring to overthrow the United States government as it pertained to a section of New York State. Neither terrorism nor sedition could be tolerated in a free democracy. The National Guard was put on alert. Sanctuary was told, in a statement released to the press as well, that on January 10 a delegation consisting of members from both the State Department and the IRS—a coupling seldom seen before in American diplomacy—would dock at Sanctuary "for discussion of the situation."

Sanctuary replied that if any shuttle or other space-going vessel approached the orbital, Sanctuary would open fire.

Congress met in emergency session. The IRS levied a jeopardy assessment against all assets held by Sanctuary, Inc., and its principal shareholders, the Sharifi family. The tabloid newsgrids, more interested in drama than in federal tax procedure, whooped that the IRS would sell Sanctuary at an auction to pay the taxes and penalty: "Anybody want to buy a used shuttle? A slightly dented orbital panel? Oregon?" WBRN, "the Brainie Channel," held a mock auction in which Oregon was won by a couple in Monterey, California, who announced that Crater Lake National Park wished to secede from Oregon.

On January 8, two days before Sanctuary was to receive the federal delegation, the *New York Times,* Newsgrid Division, in conjunction with its venerable donkey newspaper, offered an editorial called "Why Keep

Oregon?" The newsgrid version was spoken on all six daily holobroad-casts by the leading anchorman; the hard-copy version was centered, alone, on the editorial page.

WHY KEEP OREGON?

In the past week the country has been offered both a serious se-cession threat by Sanctuary, stronghold of American Sleepless, and a sideshow by the so-called tabloid newsgrids. Sideshows can, depending on your taste, be amusing, vulgar, demeaning, or trivial. This one, however, centering as it does on the lighthearted "Free Oregon" movement, actually serves a useful purpose in aid-ing understanding of the nature of the threat from Sanctuary.

Suppose it **were** Oregon that was trying to secede from the union? Suppose further that a thoughtful, objective person—assuming there are any left in the general Liver hoopla—wished to set forth genuine, thoughtful arguments against Oregon's right to do so. What might those arguments be?

The first point to note is that such arguments must start from a parallel with the American Revolution, not the Civil War, in which eleven Confederate States tried to depart the union. In-deed, in all the fun that irresponsible newsgrids are having with this issue, we don't remember hearing one reference to Fort Sumter or Jeff Davis. The parallel with the Revolution is implied in the borrowed language of Sanctuary's so-called Declaration of In-dependence. Clearly, Sanctuary considers itself as much an op-pressed colony as did the original thirteen American colonies, and a thoughtful rebuttal to the Sanctuary document must start with an examination of that parallel.

It is not very convincing. Our first argument against allowing Oregon—or Sanctuary—to secede is that of **no contest**. The case does not admit of enough evidence to warrant admission to seri-ous decision, because the parallels between 1776 and 2092 are so weak. The American colonies had had foreign rule forced on them without representation, foreign soldiers quartered among them, second-class status with a first-class mother country. Sanctuary, on the other hand, has had no federal official so much as enter the place since its initial inspection 36 years ago. Sanctuary is represented in the New York State legislature, in the federal Congress, and in the person of the president—all through the absentee ballot, which Sanctuary residents receive as a matter of course for each election and which are, according to reliable sources, never returned.

It is true that Sanctuary is taxed very heavily in the new tax package approved last October by Congress. But Sanctuary is also the richest entity in not only the United States, but the world. A sliding tax scale is appropriate. Unlike the American colonies, Sanctuary does not hold second-class, exploited economic status in the world. If the entire economic truth could ever be pieced together from investment records around the world, we might very well find that Sanctuary enjoys **more** financial status in the global economy than the United States; certainly its international bond rating is higher. We might find that Sanctuary actually possesses more opportunity to exploit rather than be exploited. Certainly the Sanctuary annual deficit—if one exists at all—is less than the United States government's. It is as if Oregon had decided that because its use of federal services and its payment of federal taxes are both less than, say, Texas's, it may secede. Wrong.

No, by the criteria of the original Declaration of Independence, Oregon and Sanctuary must both remain in the Union.

Another argument to keep Oregon is **negative precedent.** If Oregon could secede, why not California? Why not Florida? Why not Harrisburg, Pennsylvania? The Balkanization of the Union was settled in that other conflict 225 years ago, that conflict Sanctuary is so careful not to mention in its secession document.

Third, Oregon may not secede because of the argument of **violated relationship.** It is through United States resources, including the struggle of United States citizens, that Oregon was settled, was built to economic prosperity, was enabled to become the center of the fur trade in the nineteenth century and of Class E comlink production in the twenty-first. Oregon must honor that reciprocal relationship even if she is tired of it, just as a child who has been put through law school by her parents must, in keeping with the Civil Rights Act of 2048, support her elderly parents in the amount needed to maintain the same standard of living she enjoyed at law school. She cannot shuck them off just because she is now more successful than they. She cannot secede from the relationship that established her in her current enviable position. Nor could Oregon.

Finally, Oregon must not be allowed to secede because it is, simply and finally, **illegal**. Defiance of United States sovereignty, refusal to pay taxes, threats of maintaining independence by aggression—all are outlawed by the United States Code. For Oregon to attempt secession is an illegal act; for her to be allowed to succeed would be a slap in the face to every law-abiding citizen, state, and organizational entity in the country.

Why keep Oregon? For reasons of no contest, negative precedent, violated relationship, and legality.

And as it is for Oregon, so it is for Sanctuary.

No matter who lives there.

Drew arrived at the New Mexico compound the evening of January 6. The day had been unusually cold; he had wrapped a red muffler around his throat and a matching blanket over his legs. Both, Leisha noted, were of fine Irish wool. He powered his chair across the large open living room, built to provide a gathering place for seventy-five and lately never holding more than ten or twelve. Alice's daughter Alicia and her family had moved back to California, Eric was in South America, Seth and his wife in Chicago. Drew, Leisha saw, had once more changed.

The strident flamboyance of the newly successful artist, a little too self-conscious, had softened. Success did that. Looking up at her face, greeting her, Drew's gaze was open but in no way needy—not even of attention. He was sure, now, of what he was, without her confirmation.

Nor did his gaze shut her out as automatically of less interest than himself, the way so many celebrities did. Drew still looked at the world as if willing to be interested, with the addition of a faint smiling challenge that said continued interest would have to be earned.

It was the look Leisha remembered, always, as her father's.

"I thought I should come home," Drew said, "in case this political situation becomes really tense."

"You think it won't?" Leisha said dryly. "But, then, you never knew Jennifer Sharifi."

"No. But you did. Leisha—tell me. What's going to happen to Sanctuary?"

In Drew's intonations—*Sanctuary*—she heard all the old obsession. What did he himself make of that childish obsession now, in his strange adult profession? Did Sanctuary, transformed into the shapes of desire, fuel his lucid dreaming?

Leisha said, "The military won't blow Sanctuary out of orbit, if that's what you mean. They're civilians up there, even if terrorist civilians, and about a fourth of them are children. Any weapons they have could be deadly, but Jennifer always had too much political acumen to cross the line where she could be hit back really hard."

"People change," Drew said.

"Maybe. But even if obsession has eroded Jennifer's judgment, she has others up there to counteract it. A very smart lawyer named Will Sandaleros and Cassie Blumenthal and of course her children must be over forty by now—"

Abruptly Leisha remembered Richard saying, forty years ago, *"You become different, walled away with only other Sleepless for decades . . ."*

Drew said, watching her, "Richard's here, too."

"Richard?"

"With Ada and the kid. Stella was fussing over them when I came in. Apparently Sean has a flu or something. You seemed surprised that Richard's here, Leisha."

"I am." She suddenly grinned. "You're right, Drew—people change. Don't you think that's kind of funny?"

"I never thought you had much of a sense of humor, Leisha. With all your other wonderful qualities, I never suspected that one."

She said sharply, "Don't try to bait me, Drew."

He said, "I wasn't," and she saw in his private smile that he meant it: He had never thought she had much of a sense of humor. Well, maybe their ideas of humor were very different. Along with so much else.

Richard came in, alone. He was abrupt. "Hello, Leisha. Drew. Hope you don't mind the unannounced visit. I thought . . ."

She finished the thought for him. "That if Najla or Ricky had any communication to make to you, it would be through me? Richard, dear . . . I think Kevin would be a more likely choice. Sanctuary deals with him . . ."

"No. They wouldn't use Kevin," Richard said, and Leisha didn't ask how he knew. "Leisha, what's going to happen with Sanctuary?"

Everyone asked her that. Everyone assumed she was the political expert. She, who had sat—"sulked," Susan Melling had called it—thirty years idle in the desert. What went on in people's minds, even her own people? "I don't know, Richard. What do *you* think Jennifer will do?"

Richard didn't look at her. "I think she'd detonate the world if she thought it would finally make her feel safe."

"You're saying—do you know what you're saying, Richard? That all of Sanctuary's political philosophy still comes down to one person's personal needs. Do you believe that?"

"I believe it about all political philosophies," Richard said.

"No," Leisha said, "Not all."

"Yes," and it was not Richard who made the rebuttal, but Drew.

"Not the Constitution," Leisha said, surprising herself.

"We'll see," Drew said, and smoothed the fine, expensive Irish wool over his withered legs.

Sanctuary, without night or day, without seasons, had always kept eastern standard time. This fact, as familiar to Jennifer as the feeling of her own blood flowing through her veins, suddenly struck her as grotesque.

Sanctuary, the refuge and homeland of the Sleepless, the pioneer in the next stage of human evolution, had all these years been tied to the outworn United States by the most basic of man-made shackles, time. Standing at the head of the Sanctuary Council table at 6:00 P.M. EST, Jennifer resolved that when this crisis was over, those shackles would be cut. Sanctuary would devise its own system of measuring time, free from the planet-based idea of day and night, free from the degrading circadian rhythms that bound Sleepers. Sanctuary would conquer time.

"Now," Will Sandaleros said. "Fire."

None of the Council was seated; they all stood, palms flat on the polished metal table or clenched at their sides, eyes turned to the screens at one end of the room. Jennifer scanned each face: excited or determined or pained. But the few that were pained were also resolute, with the pain that accepts the necessity for the surgery. She had had the lottery system replaced by elections—that alone had taken nearly a decade. Then, she had maneuvered a long time for this particular Council. She had talked people into delaying candidacy, sometimes for decades. She had lent subtle support here, subtle discouragement there. She had reasoned, traded, probed, waited, accepted delays and indecision. And now she had a Council—all but one—capable of supporting her at the decisive moment for Sleepless everywhere, for all time, as time was described by the worn-out country that had ceased to matter to human evolution.

Robert Dey, seventy-five years old, the respected patriarch of a large and rich Sanctuary family, who had passed on to all of them, for decades, stories of Sleepless abused and hated in the United States of his childhood.

Caroline Renleigh, twenty-eight, a brilliant communications expert with a fanatic belief in Sleepless Darwinian superiority.

Cassie Blumenthal, with Jennifer since the earliest days of Sanctuary and instrumental in the events leading up to Jennifer's trial—events considered ancient history on Sanctuary but still very real to Cassie's tenacious mind.

Paul Aleone, forty-one, a mathematician-economist who had not only foreseen the collapse of the Y-energy-based American economy when the international patents expired, but had created a program that predicted exactly the past ten years' worth of legerdemain and folly, even as the United States tried to deny that its bluebird of illusionary prosperity had in fact flown. Aleone had worked out the economic future of Sanctuary as an independent state dealing with other independent states more prudent than the United States.

John Wong, forty-five, a lawyer who was also Appeals Justice of Sanctuary's seldom-used court system, proud of the fact that Sleepless, except for routine contract interpretations, seldom used it. There was little violence, little vandalism, less theft on Sanctuary. But Wong, a historian, understood the power of the judiciary among a law-abiding people in times of controversial change, and he believed in change.

Charles Stauffer, fifty-three, head of Sanctuary external security. Like all good soldiers, he was constantly prepared for attack, constantly ready to have his preparations justified. It was not such a long step, Jennifer thought, from preparation to actuality, from ready to eager.

Barbara Barcheski, sixty-three, the silent, thoughtful head of a firm dealing in corporate information modeling. For a long time Jennifer had been unsure about Barcheski. She was a student of political systems, coming over decades to believe that unlimited technological progress and community loyalty were basically incompatible, a premise she heavily supported by studies of societies in flux, from Renaissance Venice to the industrial revolution to the early orbital utopias. Study of a paradox, Jennifer knew, leads almost inevitably to evaluation—but not necessarily negative evaluation. She waited. Eventually Barbara Barcheski made up her methodical mind: When a society must choose, community loyalty carried the better long-term odds for survival than even technological progress. Barbara Barcheski loved Sanctuary. She supported Jennifer.

Dr. Raymond Toliveri, sixty-one, the brilliant chief researcher of Sharifi Labs. Jennifer had never questioned his support for this project;

he'd created it. What had been difficult was to get Toliveri, whose fanatical work schedule made him a virtual recluse, elected to the Council. That had taken Jennifer a long time.

Then there were Will Sandaleros, Najla and her husband Lars Johnson, and Hermione Sharifi. All stood taut and proud, knowing fully the consequences of what they were about to do, and accepting those consequences without evasion, without weakness, without excuses.

Only Ricky stood slumped against the far wall of the Council dome, his eyes on the floor, his arms folded across his chest. Hermione, Jennifer saw, would not look at her husband. They must have fought over this. And it was Hermione—only Jennifer's daughter-in-law, not her genetic son—who supported the side of justice. A complex emotion kindled in Jennifer—anger and pain and aching maternal guilt—but she pushed it away. There was no more time for Ricky's failures. It was Sanctuary's time.

"Now," Will said, "Fire," and he activated the all-Sanctuary communications net, comlink screens and holostages inside, speakers outside. Jennifer smoothed the folds of her white *abbaya* and stepped forward.

"Citizens of Sanctuary. This is Jennifer Sharifi, speaking to you from the Council dome, where the Sanctuary Council is in full emergency session. The United States has answered our Declaration of Independence as we expected, with the announcement of a Sleeper invasion tomorrow morning. This *must not be allowed to happen.* To permit this delegation to dock at Sanctuary would say that we permit negotiation where no negotiation is possible, would signal irresolution where we are resolute, would allow for the possibility of economic and judicial punishment where we are morally and evolutionarily right. The delegation must not dock at Sanctuary.

"But to try to stop the beggars by force might endanger or harm them. This too would send to the United States a false statement. Sleepless do not attack where there has been no attack. We understand self-defense, and we accept its necessity, but we do not want war. We want to be left alone, to pursue in our own way the lives, liberty, and pursuit of happiness by our own labors that until now have been denied us.

"No, the most we can do to stop the beggars is give them a show of that force we will not use unless we are pressed to do so in defense. Accordingly, the following demonstration, created by the authority of all members of the Sanctuary Council, is being broadcast simultaneously to major United States newsgrids, overriding their own broadcasts."

Caroline Renleigh keyed manual codes into her console. Will Sandaleros spoke on a closed link to Sanctuary internal security, a group so seldom used that most people had forgotten it existed—which had allowed Will free rein in building it up. On every comlink in Sanctuary, and every comlink on Earth turned to the five serious donkey newsgrids, there appeared an image of the decaying habitat Sanctuary had purchased from the Japanese, Kagura Orbital, whose name meant "god music."

Jennifer's voice spoke over the image. "This is the Sanctuary Council. The United States government has announced an invasion of Sanctuary tomorrow morning, in the form of a so-called peace-keeping delegation. But there can be no true peace where there is physical and economic coercion. We have not agreed to host this delegation. We are a peace-loving people who wish to be left alone. If the United States does not honor this wish, it in effect will be launching the first attack. We will not permit Sanctuary to be attacked.

"For the purpose of deterring this attack, and as a demonstration of the lengths to which we will go to protect our home, Sanctuary offers the following demonstration. The United States press has speculated on what weapons Sanctuary could possibly bring to bear to defend itself. We don't want this to be a speculative question. We don't want our secession from the United States to be tarred with any imputation of withholding vital information. We *do* want to avoid war by the illustration of how terrible such a war would be.

"This is Kagura Orbital, which Sanctuary now owns. There are no humans left on the orbital. Animal life does remain here: domestic livestock, insects used for pollination, birds and reptiles used for eco-logical balance, and miscellaneous rodents."

Each holostage or comlink screen showed the interior of Kagura, first in a long pan and then in close-ups of grazing goatows and bicat-tle. The Japanese had fewer restraints on genetic engineering than the United States; the meat stock was thick, slow, juicy, contented, and stupid. The robot cameras followed the flight of a bird, the scuttle of an insect on a leaf.

"In a single hidden packet on this orbital is an organism developed by Sanctuary genetic engineers. It is wind-borne. Its genetic code in-cludes a built-in seventy-two-hour destruct from the time it is re-leased. This packet will now be released by remote from Sanctuary."

The view of the orbital showed no change in sound or light. A gentle breeze created by maintenance ruffled some leaves. The meat animal munching them, a bicow, rolled its eyes. It made a single anguished, painful sound and crumpled.

Birds fell from the skies. The drone of insects stopped. Within two minutes nothing moved except the leaves, rustling in the lethal breeze.

Jennifer's voice said quietly, "Kagura Orbital is open to any scien-tific expedition that wishes to verify this phenomenon. Wear full con-tamination suits if you arrive before seventy-two hours have passed, and exercise utmost caution. We advise you to wait until after that time.

"There are similar packets, in multiples, throughout the cities of New York, Washington, Chicago, and Los Angeles.

"Do not attempt to dock any delegation at Sanctuary tomorrow, or to fire upon Sanctuary in any way. If you do so, we will consider our-selves justified in retaliating. The retaliation will take the form you've just seen.

"We in Sanctuary leave you with a thought from one of your own great statesmen, Thomas Paine: 'We fight not to enslave, but to set a country free, and to make room for honest men to live.' "

Caroline Renleigh terminated the broadcast.

Immediately the Council screens filled with scenes from inside Sanctuary. People streamed into the central park where Remembrance

Day speeches were held. The lattices had not been put up over the growing plants and Jennifer, watching intently, thought it a good sign that no one trampled any plants. Her people were angry, but not destructive. She looked from face to face, cataloging the anger.

No one in Sanctuary had been told about the Kagura demonstration except the Council, which had voted for it, the carefully-chosen graduate students who had planted the packets on Earth, and Will Sandaleros's equally-carefully chosen security force. The secrecy had been a hard fight for Jennifer. The elected councilors, fiercely committed to their community, had wanted to discuss the weapon with their constituents. Jennifer had invoked her own trial, when someone inside the old Sanctuary in Cattaraugus County, someone never identified, had mailed the Sanctuary Oath to Leisha Camden before the Council was ready to release it. The same thing could happen again. And Richard Keller—Najla looked fiercely out the window, Ricky at his feet—had taken information about their operations to that same Leisha Camden, imperiling them all. The same thing could happen again. The Council had finally, reluctantly, agreed to secrecy.

"Sanctuary is not a military machine!" a face now shouted into the comlink. It was Douglas Wagner, an original settler, in his youth a peace activist. He had formidable organizational skills; he could be very powerful.

Will said, "I'll sequester him and later I'll talk to him myself."

"Take him quietly," Jennifer said, so softly that no one but Will heard. "Don't create a rallying point." She tried to watch all the screens at once.

"We should have been told!" a woman cried. "How is Sanctuary different from the beggars' society if decisions are made for us, about us, without our knowledge or consent? We aren't dependents, and we aren't killers! This was no part of the independence plan we were told about!" A small crowd gathered to listen to the woman.

"I know her," Councilor Barcheski said. "Will, have her brought here to a meeting room. I'll talk to her."

A face on Will's security comlink said, "All quiet in B section, Will.

People seem to agree that the demonstration was necessary, if distasteful."

"Good," Will said.

Councilor Dey said, "Here they come."

A group of citizens stalked purposefully toward the Council dome, which had been opaqued. The surveillance screen showed the citizens try the door, try again, and realize that the dome was locked. A computer voice said smoothly, "The Council wants to hear all your opinions on the controversial demonstration of Sanctuary power, but right now we must concentrate on the reactions from Earth. Please come back later." The Sleepless looked at each other: Indignation. Resignation. Anger. Fear. Jennifer studied their faces.

After ten minutes of loud protests, they went away.

The broadcasts from Earth began.

". . . unprecedented terrorist threat from a quarter long suspected by many to be not only disloyal but dangerous . . ."

"Instant crisis in the developing standoff between the Sanctuary Orbital and the United States government from which it is trying to secede . . ."

". . . dangerous panic in the four cities allegedly mined with deadly viruses, although officials are . . ."

". . . a mistake to believe that just because a threat has been made the capability to carry out that threat necessarily exists. American gen-emod expert Dr. Stanley Kassenbaum is here with us now to . . ."

"Ladies and gentlemen, the president of the United States!"

The donkey grids were fast. Jennifer would give them that. She wondered if the other grids would continue their inane jokes about Oregon.

President Meyerhoff spoke in his slow, rich, reassuring voice, reassuring in part because it was heard so seldom and had therefore taken on the value of a scarce luxury, like three-carat natural diamonds.

"My fellow Americans, as most of you know, the United States has received a terrorist threat from Sanctuary Orbital. They claim the capability to cause serious harm to four major American cities through illegal genetically modified viruses. They threaten to release these viruses if the scheduled federal delegation attempts to dock at Sanctuary tomorrow. This situation is intolerable for several reasons. The long-standing policy of the United States has been to never bargain with terrorists, under any circumstances. At the same time, however, absolutely paramount must be the safety and well-being of our citizens. That is never negotiable.

"To the citizens of New York and Chicago, of Washington and Los Angeles, I say this: Do not panic. Do not leave your homes. The United States will allow no action that will imperil your safety. Even as I speak to you, expert teams of biological warfare specialists are securing the safety of our cities. Even as I speak to you, every attention is being given to this intolerable and cowardly threat. I repeat: The best thing you can do is remain in your homes . . ."

The newsgrids continued to show people fighting to leave Washington, Chicago, New York, and Los Angeles. Aircars streamed above ground; super-rail cars were jammed; groundcars clogged the highways.

The White House broadcast never directly answered the question: Will the delegation attempt to dock at Sanctuary tomorrow morning?

"Keeping their options open," Councilor Dey said grimly. "A mistake."

"They're Sleepers," Councilor Aleone said, with contempt. But his breath came quickly.

An hour after the Kagura orbital demonstration, Sanctuary received a focused, high-powered communication from the White House, demanding immediate surrender of all illegal weapons, including the alleged criminal possession of biologicals. Sanctuary sent back a quote from Patrick Henry this one recognizable even to some of the Livers: "Give me liberty or . . ."

Two hours after the demonstration, Sanctuary sent another multi-channel conventional broadcast, audio only. It announced that the deadly genemod virus packets were cached not in Washington, New

York, Los Angeles, and Chicago, but in Washington, Dallas, New Orleans, and St. Louis.

People started to stream out of St. Louis, and to riot in New Orleans. The evacuation didn't slow from Chicago, New York, or Los Angeles.

A hysterical woman in Atlanta reported that all the pigeons on her terrace had just died all at once. People began to leave Atlanta, while a team in contamination suits rushed out from the CDC. They found the pigeons had eaten rat poison, but by that time the newsgrids had replaced the story with one about dead cattle near Fort Worth.

Jennifer leaned closer to the screen. "They can't plan. Can't coordinate. Can't *think.*"

The protests within Sanctuary had reached a peak and subsided. All its spontaneous leaders were either locked in rational argument with councilors, were "sequestered" in the building quietly prepared by Sandaleros's security force, or were busy collecting signatures on the official petitions that were Sanctuary's usual answer to dissent. Always before, it had been a sufficient answer.

"The beggars can't plan *at all,*" Jennifer repeated. "Not even when it's in their own best interests."

Will Sandaleros smiled at her.

"Leisha," Stella said timidly, "do you think we should do anything about . . . about security?"

Leisha didn't answer. She sat in front of three comlinks, each turned to a different newsgrid. She sat easily, without strain, but with a stillness that not even Stella's timidity—Stella! timid!—could penetrate.

"I should have thought of that!" Jordan said. "I didn't . . . I mean, it's been so long since anybody hated Sleepless . . . Stell, who's here this week? Maybe we can set up a rotating guard, in case we need it, I mean . . ."

Drew said, "There's a Class Six Y-field around the compound, patrolled by three armed guards."

Stella and Jordan stared at him. Drew added, "Since this morning. I'm sorry I didn't tell you. I hoped I was wrong and Sanctuary wouldn't do this."

"How did you even guess they *would*?" Stella snapped, her tartness back.

"Kevin Baker. He guessed."

"He would," Stella sniffed.

Jordan said, "Thank you, Drew," and Stella had the grace to look slightly ashamed.

And Leisha said nothing, completely still.

"We have no choice," Miri said to Nikos. They huddled in Raoul's lab, eight Supers, all that had made for the same place when the announcement of the Kagura Orbital demonstration struck like a meteor. Some of the others had run to Miri's lab, dodging protesters and uniformed security forces—since when had Sanctuary had *uniforms*? Some had run to Nikos. An official "stay-inside" command had come over all audio channels—since when had Sanctuary had official commands? The children activated the comlinks between the three buildings.

All the normal comlinks in Sanctuary were dead.

Miri looked at Terry Mwakambe a second before the Super exploded in words Miri had never heard put together before. A detached corner of her mind, a part not whirling with chaotic strings, noted that cursing combinations must have some relationship to mathematical progressions for Terry to do it so naturally.

He immediately activated the hidden communications net the Supers had spent two months programming into every function of Sanctuary, a shadowy second orbital command so well hidden it could not be detected by the first.

"Nikos? Are you there? Who's with you?"

Nikos's face came on-line. "Diane, Christy, Allen, James, Toshio."

"Where's Jonathan?"

"With me," Mark said, cutting in on the link. "Miri, it's happened. They did it."

"What are we going to do?" Christy said. She had her arm tightly around Ludie, one of the eleven-year-olds, who was crying.

"We can't do anything," Nikos said. "That's not our agreement. They're not harming the Supers, they're trying to get Sanctuary free for all of us."

"They're going to get all of us killed!" Raoul cried. "Or else they're going to kill hundreds of thousands of other people in our name. Either way, we're definitely harmed!"

"It's an external defense issue," Nikos argued. "Not one for the Beggars."

"It's a betrayal," said Allen coldly. "And not just of us. Uniformed guards, stay-inside orders, cutting communications—Christ, they're *arresting* people out there! I saw a guard *drag* Douglas Wagner into a building. For the crime of thinking differently! How is that different from killing Tony for becoming different? The Council has betrayed the citizens of Sanctuary, including us. But the others can't do anything about it and we can!"

"They're our *parents* . . ." Diane said, in anguish, and Miri heard all the strings in Diane's voice.

Miri said, as resolutely as she could, "What we're going to do first is link with all the Beggars, wherever they are. I don't see Peter—does anybody know where he is? Terry, find him and link, unless he's with Norms. Then we're going to discuss this. Thoroughly. Everybody's opinions. Then we're going to make a group decision."

For *our* good, she added to herself. But not aloud.

Three hours after the Kagura Orbital demonstration, Sanctuary broadcast to the United States that the same remote capabilities that could release and disperse the genemod virus in major American cities could also destroy the viruses completely before release. Sanctuary was eager to do so, if Congress agreed to a presidential order that the corporate entity of Sanctuary Inc. was no longer part of the United States for purposes of governance, taxation, or citizenship, and would henceforth have the same status as other independent nations.

Those other nations took various stances. Those allied most closely with the United States issued official statements condemning the "rebels" for terrorist acts, but refused to enforce trade embargos. The White House did not push for this. Foreign commentators pointed out, with various degrees of candor, that White House pushing might lead to a too-frank disclosure of just how heavily American allies depended on the pervasive international financing and genemod research controlled from Sanctuary.

Those countries currently not allied with the United States issued statements condemning both sides as moral barbarians with no respect for even their own laws or citizens, a line so expected and so familiar it roused little attention. Only Italy, once more socialist with the peculiarly chaotic, fatalistic flamboyance of Italian socialism, managed an original position. Rome announced that the Sleepless were the leaders in a new liberation of the working classes oppressed by American media governance, and that Sanctuary would lead the world in a new era of responsible use of newsgrids in the service of labor. This puzzling statement went largely unanswered, except in Italy.

A shuttle containing an international scientific coalition launched toward Kagura. Immediately demonstrators in the United States screamed that it not be allowed to return to Earth.

A Sleepless living alone in New York, an inoffensive little man who had shunned other Sleepless for fifty years, was dragged from his apartment and beaten to death.

Sanctuary beamed another message to the United States: " 'No man is good enough to govern another man without that other's consent'—A. Lincoln."

"That was for you," Stella said angrily. "The Lincoln quote—it's the wrong war. They've been mangling the Revolution, not the Civil War. Jennifer just put the Lincoln in there because you're a Lincoln scholar!"

Leisha didn't answer.

*   *   *

"For us to take over the orbital—just take it over, with no warning— would be as bad as Sanctuary's releasing the virus on Earth with no warning," Nikos said. He sent his string program to the other three buildings where Supers had gathered. The string was surprising for Nikos, who usually thought in bold strings with strong, clear cross- references. This string was delicately balanced, ethics and history and community solidarity carefully balanced, opposing values so al- most equal that the shape was fragile with internal tension. The string was almost more characteristic of Allen than of Nikos. Miri studied it carefully. She approved of its pressured delicacy.

It meant Nikos was not that strongly committed to opposing her.

Christy said, "What if we gave them a warning?"

The idea had come up over an hour ago. But Christy's string had new elements in it, drawn from military justification: Pre-emptive strikes versus clear-cut alternatives. The burden of blame in courts of war balanced with the options explored for peace. The weight of moral effort on the perceived extent of permissive force: Pearl Harbor. The Israeli homeland. Hiroshima. General William Tecumseh Sherman. The Paraguay Standoff. The Supers' strings seldom included military history; Miri hadn't known Christy's memory had indexed these mili- tary stories enough to build strings on them.

"Yeeesss," Nikos said slowly. "Yeessss . . ."

Ludie, only eleven, said, "I can't threaten my *mother*. Not even in- directly!"

I could, Miri thought, and watched Nikos, and Christy, and Allen, and the unpredictable Terry.

"Yeeessss," Nikos said. "And if—"

Strings of probability looped and knotted and spun.

"Will, there's another group of citizens demanding admittance to the Council dome," Councilor Renleigh said.

Sandaleros turned. "How did they get this far against the stay- inside order?"

"How?" Councilor Barcheski said, with some disgust; tensions were developing in the Council. "They *walked.* How many enforcers do you think you've got out there? And how afraid do you think our own citizens are of the ones you do have?"

Jennifer said calmly, "No one wants our people afraid."

"They're not," Barbara Barcheski said. "They're demanding to come in and talk to you."

"No," Sandaleros said. "When this is over, when we've got the independence from Earth—then we'll talk."

"When nobody cares what you did to get it," Ricky Sharifi said. It was the first time he had spoken in three hours.

Caroline Renleigh said, "They've got Hank Kimball with them. I've worked with him on systems. The security field around the Council dome may not stand."

Cassie Blumenthal looked up from her terminal. Her yellowish teeth gleamed. "It'll stand."

After a while, the protesters went away.

"Jennifer," John Wong said, "Newsgrid Four is agitating heavily for a single nuclear surgical strike, blowing up Sanctuary and our 'alleged detonators' in one clean blow."

Jennifer said, "They won't do that. Not the United States."

Ricky Sharifi said, "You're relying on the decency of the beggars to win your war for you."

"I think, Ricky," Jennifer said composedly, "that if you remembered the events Will and I remember, you would not talk about the decency of the beggars. I think, too, that you should keep your further opinions silent."

If her voice splintered a little, it was only a very little, and no one heard it but Ricky and Jennifer herself. Or, at least, no one acted as if they'd heard it.

Richard Keller had entered the holoroom so silently the others didn't realize at first that he was there. He stood behind Stella and Jordan, far back against the wall, his dark eyes above the heavy beard deep and shadowed. Drew noticed him first. Drew had never much liked

Richard, who seemed to him to have given up, retreated, although Drew couldn't say from what. Richard, after all, had married again, had another child, traveled around the world, learning and working. Leisha, on the other hand, did none of these things. Yet it still seemed to Drew that Leisha, walled up in the desert, had not given up, and Richard had.

That made no sense. Drew wrestled with the abstractions a while longer and then, as usual, abandoned the attempt to think it out in words. Instead, he let cool shapes that were, and were not, Richard and Leisha slide through his mind.

Richard slouched against the wall, listening to strident newsgrid announcers scream for the death of the children he had not seen in forty years.

If the government blew up Sanctuary, Drew thought suddenly, Richard would still have Ada and Sean. And if Sean died in, say, some sort of accident—in Drew's experience kids frequently died in accidents—then would Richard have another child, either with Ada or with somebody else? Yes, he would. And if that kid died, Richard would replace it with still another child. He would. And then another . . .

Drew began to see what it was that Richard, unlike Leisha, had given up.

"This is the president of the United States addressing Sanctuary, Incorporated." Meyerhoff's face, larger than life, filled the Sanctuary screen. Typical of Sleepers, Jennifer thought—they enlarged images, thinking that enlarged reality. In the Council dome, everyone not engaged in crucial monitoring gathered quickly around the screen. Najla bit her bottom lip and took a step toward her mother. Paul Aleone folded his hands tightly together.

It was a two-way link. "This is Jennifer Sharifi, chief executive officer of Sanctuary, Incorporated, and president of the Council of Sanctuary Orbital. We are receiving you, Mr. President. Please proceed."

"Ms. Sharifi, you are in criminal violation of the United States Code. You must know that."

"We are no longer citizens of the United States, Mr. President."

"You are also in violation of the United Nations Accordance of 2042 and the Geneva Convention."

Jennifer was silent, waiting for the president to realize that he had just implied to Sanctuary the status of independant nation. She saw the moment he did, although he was good at keeping the slip to just one moment. She said, "Put a resolution before Congress that Sanctuary is an entity independent of the United States, and there will no longer be a situation for the two of us to consider."

"The United States is not going to do that, Ms. Sharifi. Nor will we negotiate with terrorists. What we will do is prosecute the Sanctuary Council, every member, to the fullest extent of the law, for treason."

"It is not treason to seek independence from tyranny. Mr. President, if you have nothing new to say, I see no reason to continue this conversation."

The president's voice hardened. "I have this to say, Ms. Sharifi. Tomorrow morning the United States will attack Sanctuary with every means at our disposal if you do not, by midnight tonight, reveal to the secretary of state the location of every alleged weapon of biological warfare planted by Sanctuary in the United States."

"We will not do that, Mr. President. Nor will your conventional means of detection—with which we are quite familiar—succeed in locating them. They are made of materials, and by methods, not available to the United States. In fact, Mr. President—"

Alarms sounded outside the Council dome. Cassie Blumenthal looked up, incredulous. The Y-field security had been breached. Will Sandaleros lunged to clear the windows. Before he could, the Council dome door opened and Miranda Sharifi entered at the head of a line of Superbright children.

"—we have nothing else to discuss at this time," Jennifer finished. She had seen the president's expression sharpen at the clearly audible alarms. She broke the comlink; Cassie Blumenthal quickly blacked out all transmissions to and from Earth.

The Supers kept crowding into the dome, twenty-seven of them.

Will Sandaleros said harshly, "What are you doing here? Go home!"

"No," Miri said. A few of the adults glanced at each other; none of them was yet accustomed to the lack of stuttering and twitching. It made the children seem not less alien, but more.

"Miranda, go home!" Hermione thundered. Miri didn't even glance at her mother. Jennifer moved swiftly to take charge of the situation, which must not be allowed to get out of control. *Must* not.

"Miranda, what are you doing here? You must know it's both inappropriate and dangerous."

"You're the one that's caused the danger," Miri said. Jennifer was horrified at the look in the child's eyes. She didn't let her horror show.

"Miranda, you have two choices. You can either all leave now, immediately, or the guards will remove you by force. This is a war room, not a school room. Whatever you have to say to this Council can wait until this crisis is over."

"No, it can't," Miri said. "It's about the crisis. You threatened the United States without the consent of the rest of Sanctuary. You convinced the rest of the Council, or bullied them, or bribed them—"

"Remove the children," Jennifer said to Will. Guards in their unfamiliar uniforms had already crowded into the packed dome. A woman seized Miri's arms. Nikos said, very loudly, "Don't do that. We Superbrights have complete control of all Sanctuary systems. Life support, communications, defense, everything. There are hidden programs you can't begin to understand."

"Any more than the Sleepers could understand your genemod viruses," Miri said.

The woman holding Miri's arms looked confused. Dr. Toliveri said, outraged, "That's impossible!"

Nikos said, "Not for us."

Jennifer scanned the children, her mind racing. "Where's Terry Mwakambe?"

"Not here," Nikos said. He spoke into his lapel link. "Terry—take control of Cassie Blumenthal's terminal. Link her to Charles Stauffer's external defense system."

At her terminal, Cassie Blumenthal made a quick, choked sound. She spoke commands at her console, then switched to manual and keyed rapidly. Her eyes opened wide. Charles Stauffer sprang forward. He keyed what Jennifer, numb, thought must be override codes. Jennifer kept her voice calm.

"Councilor Stauffer?"

"We've lost control. But the missile bays are opening . . . Now they're closing."

Miranda said, "Tell the United States you'll destroy the packets of viruses on Earth in exchange for immunity for the rest of Sanctuary, except for the Council members. Tell them you'll destroy the organisms, give the United States the locations, and open Sanctuary to federal inspection. Or if you don't do those things . . . then we Supers will."

Robert Dey drew in a quick breath. "You can't."

Allen said, with utter conviction, "Yes. We can. Please believe it."

"You're children!" someone said, with such harshness it took Jennifer a minute to identify the voice. Hermione.

"We are what you made us," Miri said.

Jennifer looked at her granddaughter. This . . . child, this girl who had never been spat upon because she was Sleepless . . . never locked in a room by a mother who was putrid with jealousy of a beauty her daughter would never lose, even as the mother's beauty was inexorably fading . . . never locked in a cell away from her children . . . never betrayed by a husband who hated his own sleeplessness . . . this spoiled and pampered child who had been given everything was attempting to thwart her, Jennifer Sharifi, who had brought Sanctuary into its very being by the force of her own will. This petty child would undo everything Jennifer had worked for, suffered for, planned for a lifetime devoted to her people, to the well-being and independence of the Sleepless . . . No. No girl gone rotten and selfish at the core was going to ruin the future for her own people, the future Jennifer had fought for. Had created. Had *willed*, by her own spirit moving across what had been a hopeless void. No.

She said to the guards, "Take them all. Carry them to the detention building and put them in a secure room. Remove every bit of technology from every one of them first." She hesitated, but only for a moment. "Strip search them for hidden technology, and let them have nothing, not even clothing that looks harmless. Nothing."

"Jennifer—you can't do that!" Robert Dey said. "They're our—your—our children!"

"Make your choice," Miranda said. "Or is that it?"

It had been years since Jennifer had allowed herself to feel hatred. It came surging up, black and viscous, from all those places in her mind she never allowed herself to go . . . For a moment she was so horrified she couldn't see. Then her vision cleared and she could do the rest of it. "Find Terry Mwakambe. Immediately. Put him with the others. Be especially careful that he doesn't have anything with him, not so much as a scrap of harmless-looking clothing."

"Jennifer!" John Wong cried.

"You know, don't you," Miri said directly to Jennifer. "You know what Terry is. Even more than what I am, or Nikos, or Diane . . . or you *think* you know. You think you understand us the same way the Sleepers always thought they understood you. They never gave you credit for basic humanity, did they? You were different, so you weren't part of their community. You were evil, scheming, cold—and much, much better than they were. And you did think you were better, all you Sleepless, that's why you called them beggars. But *we're* better than you are, and so you killed one of us because you could no longer control him, didn't you? And now we're capable of things you never even imagined. Who are the beggars now, Grandmother?"

Jennifer said, in a voice she didn't recognize—but calm, *calm*—"Strip them now. All technology, even if you don't recognize it. And . . . And detain my son, too. With them."

Ricky Sharifi only smiled.

Miri began taking off her own clothes. After a stunned moment and a quick command from Nikos—a command Jennifer didn't understand, did they have their own *language?*—the other children began to undress as well. Allen Sheffield tossed his lapel comlink on the polished metal table; it made a clink loud in the paralyzed silence, and Allen smiled. Not even the youngest of the Supers cried.

Miri pulled her shirt over her head. "You've given your life to your community. But we Supers aren't in that community now, are we? And you killed the one of us who might have made a bridge between your community and ours, the best and most generous of us all. You killed him because he didn't fit your definition of a community any more. And now we don't, either. For one thing, we dream. Did you know that, *Jennifer*? Lucid dreaming. Taught to us by a Sleeper." Miri kicked off her sandals.

Cassie Blumenthal said, panic in her voice, "I can't regain control of the communications system."

"Stop this," Charles Stauffer said. "Children, put your clothes back on!"

"No," Miri said. "Because then we'd look like members of your community, wouldn't we, Jennifer? And we're not. We never can be again."

Someone said over a comlink, "We have Terry Mwakambe. He's not resisting."

Miri said, "And not even your own community really matters to you. Otherwise you would have taken us up on the choice we offered you. That way only you would have faced trial for treason. The beggars below would have granted the rest of the Council immunity. Now they'll all be indicted for conspiracy to treason. You could have saved them and you didn't, because that would have meant giving up your own control over who is in your community and who is out, wouldn't it? Well, you lost it anyway. The day you killed Tony." Miri yanked down her shorts. She stood naked, the other Supers behind her. Some of the girls covered their budding breasts with crossed arms; a few of the boys held hands in front of their genitals. But none of them cried. They stared at Jennifer with cold, unchildlike eyes, as if she had confirmed something for them, as if they were thinking . . . thinking unknowable things . . . Miri stood uncovered, the nipples on her small breasts erect, her dark pubic hair as thick as Jennifer's own. Her large misshappen head was held high. She smiled.

Ricky came forward, holding his own shirt. He put it around Miri's shoulders and drew it closed across her breasts, and for the first time the girl looked at someone else besides Jennifer. She glanced at her father, blushed painfully, and whispered, "Thank you, Daddy."

Cassie Blumenthal said tiredly, "A delayed-timing broadcast just left for the White House. There's a duplicate here. It contains all the locations and neutralizing procedures for every virus packet we planted in the United States."

Charles Stauffer said, "None of the Sanctuary external defenses are operative."

Caroline Renleigh said, "Emergency security on the detention dome is down. Overrides don't regain control . . ."

Cassie Blumenthal said, "Second delayed-timing broadcast beamed at . . . at *New Mexico* . . ."

Only Miranda said nothing. She was sobbing, an overwrought sixteen-year-old girl, on her father's shoulder.

25

Leisha watched the hologrids of the rioting in Atlanta over dead pigeons, the rioting in New York over clogged ground traffic leaving the city, the rioting in Washington over rioting. All the old banners had come out—NUKE THE SLEEPLESS!—did they just keep the placards and banners in some dusty basement between crises thirty or forty years apart? All the old rhetoric was out, all the old attitudes, even—on the worst of the Liver grids—all the old jokes. "What do you get if you cross a Sleepless with a pit bull? A set of jaws that *really* never let go." Leisha had heard that one when she was at Harvard. Sixty-seven years ago.

She said out loud, "And I looked and saw that there was nothing new under the sun, and the race was not to the swift, nor the battle to the strong, nor favor to men of skill . . ." Jordan and Stella watched her worriedly. It wasn't fair to worry them with melodramatic tag lines. Especially not after hours of silence. She should talk to them, explain to them what she was feeling . . .

She was so tired.

For more than seventy years she had seen the same things, over and over, starting with Tony Indivino. "If you walked down a street in Spain and a hundred beggars each asked for a dollar and you wouldn't give it to them so they jumped on you in fury . . ." Sanctuary. The law, that illusory creator of common community. Calvin Hawke. Sanctuary, again. And throughout it all, the United States: rich, prosperous, myopic, magnificent in aggregate and petty in specifics, unwilling— always, always—to accord mass respect to the mind. To good fortune, to luck, to rugged individualism, to faith in God, to patriotism, to beauty, to spunk or pluck or grit or git, but never to complex intelligence and complex thought. It wasn't sleeplessness that had caused all the rioting; it was thought and its twin consequences, change and challenge.

Was it different in other countries, other cultures? Leisha didn't know. In eighty-three years she'd never once traveled outside the United States for longer than a weekend. Nor particularly wanted to. Surely that was singular, in such a global economy?

"I always loved this country," Leisha said, also aloud, and realized instantly how this disconnected sentiment must sound.

"Leisha, dear, would you like a brandy? Or a cup of tea?" Stella said.

Despite herself, Leisha smiled. "You sounded just like Alice when you said that."

"Well . . ." Stella said.

"Leisha," Drew said, "I think it might be a good idea if you—"

"Leisha Camden!"said the holostage. Stella gasped.

The newsgrid coverage of the White House, the rioting in New York, the satellite shots of Sanctuary, had all disappeared. A young girl with a large, slightly bulging head and great dark eyes stood stiffly on the holostage, in a scientific lab filled with unfamiliar equipment. She wore a thin synthetic shirt, shorts, and simple slippers, and her unruly dark hair was tied back with a red ribbon. Richard, whom Leisha had forgotten was in the room, made a strangled sound.

The girl said, "This is Miranda Serena Sharifi, in Sanctuary. I'm the granddaughter of Jennifer Sharifi and Richard Keller. I'm beaming this broadcast directly to your New Mexico equipment. It's an override on all other Sanctuary communication nets. It's also unauthorized by the Sanctuary Council."

The girl paused, and a slight falter came into the serious young face. So serious—this child looked as if she never smiled. How old was she?

Fourteen? Sixteen? Her voice had a slight accent, as if English were being spoken differently in Sanctuary. More precisely and more formally, both contrary to the way language usually evolved. The differences, too, lent seriousness to her words. Leisha took an involuntary step toward the holostage.

"There are a group of us here, Sleepless but also something more. Genemod construction. We're called Superbrights, and I'm the oldest. There are 28 of us over the age of ten. We're . . . different from the adults, and they have treated us differently. We've taken over Sanctuary, sent the location of all the biological weapons to your president, deactivated the Sanctuary defenses, and stopped the war for independence."

"Oh dear God," Jordan said. *"Children."*

"If you receive this, it means we Superbrights are being held prisoner by my grandmother and the Sanctuary Council, but we don't think that can last long. However, we won't be able to stay here on Sanctuary. We have no real other place to go. I've researched you, Leisha Camden, and I've researched your ward Drew Arlen. The Lucid Dreamer. We Supers are all lucid dreamers. It's become an important component of how we think."

Leisha glanced at Drew. He stared intently at Miranda Sharifi, and at the look in his green eyes, Leisha glanced away.

"I don't know what will happen next, or when," Miranda continued. "Maybe Sanctuary will allow us a shuttle. Maybe your government will send for us, or a corporation you control can do that. Maybe some Superbrights, the younger ones, will stay here. But some of us, soon, will need a place to go away from Sanctuary, since we will have caused the arrest for conspiracy to treason of the entire Sanctuary Council. We need a place with security, a place with reasonable equipment we can modify further, and someone to help us with your legal and economic system. You were a lawyer, Ms. Camden. Can we come to you?"

Miranda paused. Leisha felt her eyes prickle.

"There will be with us, I think although I'm not sure, a few Normals. One will probably be my father, Richard Sharifi. I don't think you can contact me directly to answer this broadcast, although I don't know for sure what your capabilities are."

"Not what *theirs* are," Stella said, sounding dazed. Drew shot her an amused look.

"Thank you," Miranda finished awkwardly. She shifted weight, one foot on top of the other, and suddenly looked even younger. "If . . . if Drew Arlen is with you when you receive this, and if you're willing to let us Superbrights come to you, please ask him to stay. I'd like . . . I'd like to meet him."

Suddenly Miranda smiled, a smile of such cynicism that Leisha was startled. This was no child after all. "You see," Miranda said, "we come to you as beggars. Nothing to offer, nothing to trade. Just need." She disappeared and a sudden three-dimensional graphic appeared on the screen, a complex globe made of strings of words looped and crossed and balanced, each word or phrase an idea that connected to the next, the whole thing color-coded in ways that emphasized the stresses and balances and trade-offs in meaning from concepts that opposed or reinforced or modified each other. The globe lingered, rotating slowly.

"What on earth is *that*?" Stella said.

Leisha got up and walked around the globe slightly faster than it rotated, studying it. Her knees felt shaky. "I think . . . I think it's a philosophical argument."

"Ahhhhhhhhh," Drew said.

Leisha looked at the globe. Her eye snagged on a phrase in green in an outer layer: *a house divided: Lincoln*. Abruptly she sat down on the floor.

Stella took refuge in a flurry of domestic activity. "If there's twenty-eight of them, and if they double up, we can open the west wing and move Richard and Ada to—"

"I won't be here," Richard said quietly.

"But Richard! Your son—" Stella broke off, looking embarrassed.

"That was another life."

"But *Richard*—" Stella's face began to redden. Richard slipped quietly from the room. The only one he looked at directly was Drew, who gazed steadily back.

Leisha saw none of this. She sat on the floor, studying Miranda's string-globe until the broadcast ended and the hologram vanished. Then she looked up at the three left, Stella and Jordan and Drew. Stella took in a sharp breath.

"Leisha . . . your *face* . . ."

"Things change," Leisha said, cross-legged and radiant on the floor. "There are second and third chances. And fourth and fifth."

"Well, of course," Stella said, puzzled. "Leisha, please get up!"

"Things *do* change," Leisha repeated, like a little girl. "Not just changes in degree. Changes in kind. Even for us. After all. After all. After all."

There were thirty-six of them, flown by government plane from Washington; the whole thing had taken much longer than anyone but Leisha, the ex-lawyer, had expected. Twenty-seven "Superbrights": Miri, Nikos, Allen, Terry, Diane, Christy, Jonathan, Mark, Ludie, Joanna, Toshio, Peter, Sara, James, Raoul, Victoria, Anne, Marty, Bill, Audrey, Alex, Miguel, Brian, Rebecca, Cathy, Victor, and Jane. Such familiar names for such unfamiliar people. And with them there were four "Normal" Sleepless children: Joan, Sam, Hako, and Androula. There were five parents, looking for the most part tenser than their children. Among the parents was Ricky Sharifi.

His dark eyes were patient with pain and he moved hesitantly, as if unsure he had a right to walk on the Earth. When Leisha realized why this looked normal to her, she grimaced. Richard, who now looked younger than his son, had looked like that in the months after Jennifer's trial.

Jennifer's first trial. The Sanctuary Council members were all in prison in Washington.

"Is my father here?" Ricky asked Leisha quietly, the first afternoon.

"No. He . . . he left, Ricky."

Ricky nodded, unsurprised. He looked as if he had expected this answer. Perhaps he had.

Miranda Sharifi—"Miri"—took the lead from the first. After the bustle of arrival, the equipment and suitcases and security nets and

Stella's elaborate rooming arrangements, Miri came with her father to Leisha's study. "Thank you for letting us come here, Ms. Camden. We want to work out some form of rent as soon as our assets are unfrozen by your government."

"Call me Leisha. And it's your government, too. But no rent is necessary, Miri. We're glad to have you here."

Miri's dark eyes studied her. They were strange eyes, Leisha thought, not for any physical attributes but because they seemed to see things no one else did. She was a little shocked to realize, despite the admiration she already had for Miri, that the girl's eyes made her uncomfortable. How much did that unswerving gaze see about her? How much did that brain—enhanced, different, *better*—understand of Leisha's private soul?

This must have been how Alice had once felt about Leisha. And Leisha had never known, never realized.

Miri smiled. The smile changed her whole face, opened and lighted it. "Thank you, Leisha. That's very generous. More than that—I think you think of us as your community, and for that we really thank you. Community is an important concept to us. But we'd all prefer to pay you. We're Yagaiists, you know."

"I know," Leisha said, wondering if among the things Miri's better brain could better understand was irony. She was still sixteen years old.

"Is . . . is Drew Arlen still here? Or did he go back on tour?"

"He's still here. He waited for you."

Miri flushed. *Oh,* Leisha thought. *Oh . . .*

Leisha sent for Drew. He looked up at Miri from his powerchair, his handsome face openly interested, and held out his hand.

"Hello, Miranda."

"I'd like to talk to you later about lucid dreaming," Miranda said gracelessly, reddening more. "About the neurochemical effects on the brain. I've done some studies, you might be interested in the results, a chance to look at your art from the scientific side . . ." Leisha recognized the girl's babbling for what it was: a gift. She was offering Drew what she conceived to be the best part of herself, her work.

"Thank you," Drew said gravely. His eyes sparkled. "I'd like that."

Leisha was amazed at herself. She had wondered if she would feel a brief, mild stab of jealousy at Drew's defection from her to Miri—it had been all too obvious how ready he was to defect—but what she did feel was not brief or mild. Nor was it jealousy. Protectiveness flared in her like brush fire. If Drew was just using this extraordinary child to get to Sanctuary, she would flatten him. Completely. Miri deserved better, needed better, *was* better than that—

Astonished at herself, Leisha fell silent.

Miri smiled a second time. Her hand was still in Drew's. "You changed our lives, Mr. Arlen. I'll tell you later."

"Please. And call me Drew."

Leisha saw a dirty ten-year-old with reckless green eyes and appalling manners: *I'm gonna own Sanctuary, me.* She looked again at Miranda, the girl's dark hair falling forward to hide her red face, the misshappen head. The brush fire raged. Miranda withdrew her hand from Drew's.

"I think," Ricky Sharifi said, "that Miri needs to eat again soon. Her metabolism differs from ours. Leisha, we're going to be a great drain on your resources. Let us pay for it. You haven't even seen what Terry and Nikos and Diane will do to your communications equipment."

Ricky also had been watching Miranda and Drew. He looked at Leisha and smiled ruefully. Leisha saw that Ricky, too, was as afraid of his daughter's powers as Leisha had been of Drew's lucid dreaming, and as secretly proud.

"I wish," Leisha said directly to Ricky, "that you had known my sister Alice. She died last year."

He seemed to see as much in this simple statement as she intended. "I wish I had, too."

Miri returned to the question of payment. "And once your—our— government satisfies itself enough to release our assets, we'll all be rich by your standards. In fact, I was going to ask you if you would be interested in doing the legal work to help a number of us set up corporations registered in New Mexico. Most of us have run businesses or done

commercial research, you know, but here we're underage. We're going
to need legal structures to let us continue our businesses as part-time
employees of corporate entities with adults named as CEO's."

"That wasn't ever my field," Leisha said carefully. "But I can suggest someone who could do it. Kevin Baker."

"No. He was the liaison for Sanctuary."

"Was he always honest?" Leisha said.

"Yes, but—"

"He would be for you, too." And willing—Kevin was always willing
to go where the business was.

Miri said, "I'll bring it up with the others." Leisha had already observed her with the other Superbrights, trading glances for which,
Leisha knew, she was missing most of the meaning. Volumes worth of
meaning she would never see. And how much more meaning she would
never see was there in the string-globes they constructed for each
other, or in the string-globes in their alien minds?

The string-globes that reminded her so uncomfortably of the
shapes in Drew's lucid dreaming.

"But even if we use Kevin Baker," Miri continued, "we'll still need a
lawyer. Will you represent us?"

"Thank you, but I can't," Leisha said. She didn't tell Miri why not.
Not just yet. "But I can recommend some good lawyers. Justine Sutter,
for instance. She's the daughter of a very old friend of mine."

"A *Sleeper*?" Miri said.

"She's very good," Leisha said. "And that's what counts, isn't it?"

"Yes," Miri said. And then, "A Sleeper."

Ricky Sharifi said, "That might actually be best. Your lawyers are
going to have to deal with United States property laws, after all. A beggar might know them best."

Leisha said, "If you're going to live here, Ricky, you're going to have
to stop using that word. Like that, anyway."

After a moment Ricky said, "Yes. You're right."

Just like that. Jennifer Sharifi's son, brought up in Sanctuary. And
human beings thought they understood genetic manipulation!

Drew said abruptly to Miri, "Are you going to inherit Sanctuary someday?"

Miranda looked at him for a long time. Leisha couldn't tell—nothing, not a clue—what was in the girl's mind. "Yes," Miri said finally, thought-fully. "Although not for a very long time. Maybe a century. Or more. But someday, yes. I am."

Drew didn't answer. *A century or more,* Leisha thought. A look passed between Drew and Miri, a look Leisha couldn't interpret. She had no idea at all what it meant when Drew finally smiled.

"Good enough," he said.

Miri smiled, too.

26

L eisha sat on her favorite flat rock under the shade of a cottonwood tree. The creek at her feet was completely dry. A quarter
mile downstream a Super moved slowly, face bent forward over
the ground. It must be Joanna; she had become fascinated with fossils
and was constructing a three-dimensional thought string which Leisha
didn't understand about the relation of coprolites to orbitals. It was
poetry, Miri said, adding that none of them built poetry before they began lucid dreaming. That was the phrase she used: "built poetry."

A kangaroo rat burrowed into a mound of dry earth a few feet away.
Leisha watched it whir its short forelegs like a mechanical auger, then
kick away the excavated dirt with long hind legs. The rat turned suddenly and looked at her: round ears and rounder, bulging, lustrous-
black eyes. It had an odd bump on the top of its head: an incipient
tumor, Leisha thought. The little animal returned to its work, incidentally aerating the soil and enriching it with nitrates from its droppings.
Beyond, away from the cottonwood shade, the desert shimmered under heat already fierce in early June.

If she turned around, Leisha knew, she would see a different kind
of shimmer. Forty feet above the compound, air molecules were distorted with a new kind of energy field Terry was experimenting with. It
would, he said, be the next breakthrough in applied physics. Kevin

Baker was in negotiation with Samsung, IBM, and Konig-Rottsler for selective licensing of Terry's patents.

Leisha wriggled out of her boots and socks. This was mildly dangerous; she was beyond the area swept electronically clear of scorpions. But the rock, warm here even in the shade, felt pleasantly gritty under her bare feet. Suddenly she remembered studying her feet the morning of her sixty-seventh birthday. How odd—what a strange thing to remember. The memory actually pleased her; she had only just begun to realize how much, in eighty-three years, even a Sleepless forgot.

The Supers remembered everything. Always.

Leisha was waiting for Miri to explode out of the compound to accuse her. The explosion was already overdue; Miri must have been locked longer than usual in her lab. Or perhaps she was with Drew, home only a few days after his spring tour. If so they would be in his room; Miri's didn't have a bed.

The kangaroo rat disappeared into his mound.

"Leisha!"

Leisha turned. A figure in green shorts was running furiously toward her from the compound, arms and legs pumping. Eight, seven, six, five, four, three—

"Leisha! *Why?*"

The Supers always finished things before you expected them to.

"Because I choose to do it, Miri. Because I want to."

"*Want* to? Defend my grandmother against charges of treason? *You,* Leisha, who wrote the definitive book on Abraham Lincoln?"

Leisha knew this wasn't a non sequitur. She had begun, in the past three months, to learn a little about how the Supers thought. Not to the extent of following an entire complex string shape, woven from associations and reasoning and connections, glinting with shocks from lucid dreaming. And never to the extent of constructing one herself. Nor did Leisha want to construct one. That was not who she was. But she had become able to fill in the skipped links when this girl, more important to her than anyone had been since Alice, spoke to her. At least, Leisha could fill them in if Miri hadn't skipped too many links. This time she hadn't.

"Sit down, Miri. I want to explain to you why I'm Jennifer's counsel. I've been waiting out here for you to ask."

"I'll stand!"

"Sit," Leisha said, and after a moment Miri sat. She pushed the dark hair off her forehead, sweaty after even such a short run, and dropped angrily onto Leisha's rock without even a glance for scorpions.

There were so many earthly things that Miri still didn't know to look for.

Leisha had rehearsed her words carefully. "Miri, your grandmother and I are both part of a specific American generation, the first generation of Sleepless. That generation had certain things in common with the one before, the one that created us. Both generations saw that it's not possible to have both equality, which is just another name for what you call community solidarity, and individual excellence. When individuals are free to become anything at all, some will become geniuses and some will become resentful beggars. Some will benefit themselves and their communities, and others will benefit no one and just loot whatever they can. Equality disappears. You can't have both equality and the freedom to pursue individual excellence.

"So two generations chose inequality. My father chose it for me. Kenzo Yagai chose it for the American economy. A man called Calvin Hawke, whom you don't know about—"

"Yes, I do," Miri said.

Leisha smiled quietly. "Of course you do. Stupid comment. Well, Hawke picked the side of the born-unequal and tried to even up the equation a little, and excellence be damned. Of all of us, only Tony Indivino and your grandmother tried to create a community that put just as much value on its own solidarity—the 'equality' of those who were included as members—as on those members' individual diverse achievements. Jennifer failed, because it can't be done. The more Jennifer failed, the more fanatic she became about trying to do this thing, pushing the blame for all failures onto people who weren't members of the community. Narrowing the definition more and more. Getting farther and farther away from any kind of balance at all. But I suspect you know even more about that than I do."

Leisha waited, but Miri said nothing.

"But even while Jennifer got farther and farther away from her dream of community, that dream itself"—*Tony's dream*—"was admirable. If impossible. It was an idealistic dream of uniting two great human needs, two great human longings. Can't you forgive your grandmother on the basis of that initial dream?"

"No," Miri said, her face rigid, and Leisha remembered again how young she was. The young don't forgive. Had Leisha ever forgiven her own mother?

Miri said, "So that's why you're defending her? Because of what you see as her initial dream?"

"Yes."

Miri stood. The rock had made tiny ridges on the backs of her legs, below her shorts. Her dark eyes bored into Leisha. "In narrowing her definitions of community, my grandmother killed my brother Tony." She walked away.

Leisha, after a moment of shock, scrambled to her feet and ran barefoot after her. "Miri! Wait!"

Miri stopped, obedient, and turned. There were no tears on her face. Leisha sprinted forward, came down on a sharp rock, and hopped painfully. Miri helped her back to the rock where Leisha's boots and socks lay limp in the heat.

"Check them for scorpions before you put them on," Miri ordered, "or they might—why are you smiling?"

"Never mind. I never know what you do or don't know. Miri— would you exclude me from your categories of defensible behavior? Or Drew? Or your father?"

"No!"

"But all of us have changed our minds over the decades about what is acceptable, or right, or even desirable. That's the key, honey. That's why I'm defending your grandmother."

"*What's* the key?" Miri snapped.

"Change. The unpredictable ways events can change people. And Miri, Sleepless live a long time. There's a lot of time for a lot of events"—*time piling up like dust*—"and that means a lot of change. Even Sleepers can change. When Drew came to me, he was a beggar. Now he's made a major contribution to the course of the world by the way he changed you Superbrights' thinking. That's the answer, Miri. You can't call anyone indefensible, ever, because things change. Even your grandmother could change. Maybe *especially* your grandmother. Miri? Do you see what I mean?"

"I'll think about it," Miri growled.

Leisha sighed. Miri's thinking about it would be so complex Leisha might not, if she saw the results in string-edifice hologram, even recognize her own argument.

But when Miri had gone back to the house and Leisha had put her boots and socks back on, she sat on the flat rock looking out over the desert, her arms clasped around her knees.

People change. Beggars can become artists. Productive lawyers can become despairing idlers, sulking like Achilles in his tent, sulking for decades, a world-class sulk—and then repass the bar and become lawyers again. Marine experts can become drifters. Sleep researchers can become failed wives, and then transform themselves back into brilliant researchers. Sleepers may not be able to become Sleepless—or could they? Just because Adam Walcott had failed 40 years ago, just because Susan Melling had said the thing was impossible, did that mean it would always be impossible? Susan had never known about the Superbrights.

Tony, Leisha said silently, *there are no permanent beggars in Spain. Or anywhere else. The beggar you give a dollar to today might change the world tomorrow. Or become father to the man who will. Or grandfather, or great-grandfather. There is no stable ecology of trade, as I thought once, when I was very young. There is no stable anything, much less stagnant anything, given enough time. And no nonproductive anything, either. Beggars are only gene lines temporarily between communities.*

The kangaroo rat came back out of its burrow and sniffed at a primrose. Leisha had a clear view of the growth on its head. It wasn't natural. The fur was a different color, and grew in longer tufts; the growth was too perfectly round; the kangaroo rat tilted it forward to touch the tufts to the primrose and paused. The growth was a sensor of some kind. The animal was genemod—here in this distant place, against all rules and expectations.

Leisha tied her boot laces and stood. She suddenly felt wonderful, like the young girl her body still looked. Full of energy. Full of light.

There was so much to do.

She turned toward the compound and started to run.

Award-winning author NANCY KRESS has won three
Nebula Awards and a Hugo Award (including one each
for *Beggars in Spain*), and has been nominated for many
more. The author of more than twenty novels, including
Crossfire, Probability Space, and *Beggars in Spain,* she lives
in Rochester, New York.

www.sff.net/people/nankress/